The Blighted Fortress

The Allies of Theo, Book 2

David E Dresner

Clink
Street

London | New York

Published by Clink Street Publishing 2019

Copyright © 2019

First edition.

ISBN:
978-1-912850-92-1 - paperback
978-1-912850-93-8 - ebook

*For Nancy, my wife, muse,
and constructive reader
of my tales.*

Prologue

Unknown to the people of Chicago, a very special sanctuary exists in the center of their great city. Unseen and unapproachable, this sanctuary is home to two very ancient beings.

The older is Theo, a god-being who existed before the Big Bang. On Earth Theo chooses to appear as a large, exotic, black cat similar to the Egyptian god Bast. Joining Theo is M, an ancient Egyptian appearing as a young man. M was born before the first pyramid appeared.

Over countless eons Theo has been forced to flee and hide from searching fire creatures. The creatures are demigods born out of the star dust elements following the Big Bang. The fire creatures have pursued Theo to gain his knowledge that predates our universe. Once acquired, the creatures believe they will evolve into gods and rule the universe.

For millenniums Theo and M have searched the world for potential allies to join them in fighting the fire creatures. So far only M's mind has proven capable of accepting the physical and mental restructuring necessary to become an ally of Theo.

At the beginning of the twenty-first century their search was rewarded. They found not just one potential ally, but two. Once discovered, teenagers Glenda and Traveler were brought to the Chicago sanctuary where they learned about Theo, his cosmic pursuers, and their threat to our universe. Once offered, both accepted the challenges to become allies of Theo.

For Traveler and Glenda their Chicago sanctuary became a shared home, but is so much more. The sanctuary is where their individual training and development as future allies takes place.

Sentient books work with them to gradually increase their mental and physical capabilities. These books demand total focus and effort. As hard-pressed students they complain, they compete, they struggle, they persevere, they learn, and they develop.

Chapter 1

Dessert First, Then a Story

Traveler leaned far back in his chair and took a deep breath. He was stuffed. As full as he was, he still had energy left to pull a stealth prank. Stealth was an early skill vested by the books as a form of invisibility. As long as Traveler remained motionless, he was part of the background. To practice his stealth skill he needed to remain absolutely motionless or risk appearing as a fluttering hologram.

Traveler enjoyed practicing his stealth by pranking Glenda, his study buddy. Her startled reactions always amused him and annoyed her, they never got old. One favorite prank was to suddenly appear out of nowhere sitting in his chair and stunning either Glenda or M, or best case both. He wisely avoided pranking Theo.

Sitting and waiting for his victims he realized that his back-leaning chair was a giveaway. He quickly sat forward putting all four legs on the ground. Now he appeared as just an empty table chair waiting for a body to sit down.

Leaning forward now put pressure on his full stomach, his stealth composure was compromised. An involuntary burp of epic proportions rocked the room. Seismic meters shot off their Richter Scales everywhere in Chicago. No way could stealth mask that eruption.

Embarrassed, he instantly looked around to see if the noise had spoiled his stealth trick. A resting Theo was the only audience and was looking at him with what seemed to be a judging grimace. *Cats, even tiger-sized god-cats, don't have facial expressions,* Traveler assured himself.

Moments later Glenda came striding toward him. She stared at his empty chair, "Did you hear the explosion?" she asked with smirk. "I thought they were dynamiting for the subway system." Traveler sadly recognized her "Caught ya, big boy" look. His attempt at stealth humor was foiled and he reappeared in his chair.

"Very witty, princess, I guess a guy has no privacy. The gentleman in me wants to say 'Excuse me', but that would just fall on deaf ears."

"Well, my hearing was just fine until a minute ago. You weren't planning on pulling an eighth-grade prank, were you? So sad your tummy has a mind of its own and calls out. Speaking of tummies, where's M with our dessert? You didn't scare him off, I hope."

Traveler was scrambling to fire back a snappy retort when M appeared carrying a large covered silver casserole dish. "Prepare for the dinner's coup de grâce. I would have been out sooner but I heard a cannon and thought we were under attack." Glenda gave M a high-five grin, while Traveler only managed a weak smile.

First being caught, then being the target of their jokes, stifled his dessert desire. He found himself saying, "Okay, guilty as charged, I was just using the waiting time to practice a skill. You two go ahead, I'm really full and think I'll pass on the dessert."

Glenda and M exchanged looks, they both knew better. Virginia, Traveler's mom, had often wondered whether he had a trash compactor inside his stomach. His dad, the doctor, would smile and nod, "He's a medical miracle."

"Well, I certainly don't want you to force yourself to eat if you're full and can't enjoy it," said M. "I'll just give you a small, tasting-size portion. Glenda, I'll give you the usual 'growing young lady' portion, besides, your coltish figure can easily handle it."

"Pile it on, M. I'll take Traveler's portion since he's too full. I've got plenty of room left, I always pace myself for dessert and it smells delicious."

M ladled out a generous portion first to Glenda then to himself. He gave a petite portion to Traveler. "This is my own version of bread pudding, but it's so much more, it has my special added ingredients. I highly recommend lots of the cream sauce, drown the pudding if you will!"

Glenda immediately dug into her bowl. A look of happiness passed over her face. Looking at Traveler she exclaimed, "This is nobody's mother's bread pudding. It's beyond great! It's dense yet light even with the cream sauce. I'll have seconds as soon as I finish this up."

Traveler knew he was still having fun poked at him, but his ego was refusing to acknowledge the humor. He put a small amount of the cream sauce on his pudding, then took a polite-sized bite. Glenda and M were surreptitiously watching him. They saw the look of delight with his first bite. Neither said anything while Traveler finished the bowl in a second spoonful. "Yes, that is very acceptable M," he acknowledged.

With a now empty bowl Glenda leaned back in her chair, took a deep breath and said, "M, my stomach is a tad smaller than my eyes. I'm not sure I can eat another serving. Traveler, help me out, we don't want M's specialty to go to waste."

Traveler knew Glenda had just thrown him a lay-up pass and he popped out of his funk. Grinning he said, "OK M, I've got no dessert pride, please load me up. Besides my noisemaker stomach will be quiet once I pack it down."

M removed the casserole lid and thick, sweet steam rolled off the pudding. He ladled out three more generous portions. Then he added an extra scoop for Traveler. "A little make up scoop, Traveler. Now let's all enjoy round two."

Dessert time is serious time and it passed without conversation or unwanted air bursts. Finally, they all came up for air at the same time. "M, I have an after-dinner request," said Glenda. "Traveler and I want to hear your own story. All we know is that you became an orphan a very long time ago. Please tell us about your childhood and how you met Theo. Did Theo start your training when you were young like us?"

Chapter 2

M's Story Begins

M leaned back in his chair. He put his hands together behind his head and his eyes took on a distant look. His face then brightened, he smiled to confirm he would enjoy answering Glenda's question.

He had ducked the same question many times, but now felt the two were ready for his personal story. Their escape from the fire creature ambush had affirmed they were ready to join him as part of Theo's team.

"Thanks for asking, Glenda. It's been a long time since I talked to anybody about myself. Being human, more or less, I have the normal urge to respond to people who want to hear my personal tale. Modesty aside, mine is a rather grand tale.

"Being grand, it's a lengthy tale; remember I've been around for a very long time. Perhaps a short time compared to Theo but over-the-top long for anybody else. Like all stories, it has a beginning and, fortunately for me, there is no end in sight."

As M was starting his tale, Theo left the fireplace and padded across the room to sit beside M. The tiger-sized cat never failed to move with dignity and purpose. M instinctively put his hand on Theo's head and began a soft head rub and gentle pulling on the long, pointed ears. A restful purring vibration filled the room. Traveler and Glenda knew something special was coming.

"As both of you now know, for each of us our personal development road began with meeting Theo. He is the constant in each of our universes, our true North Star. By the way, in my case I was much younger than either of you when I met him.

"But before jumping into how I met Theo, I'll start with my own early childhood. My childhood road had many twists in it before it eventually led me to Theo.

"To understand my early life you need to appreciate the world I was born into. This was a world created by the Nile River. Human civilization began on the banks of the mother Nile. Some academics argue that it began on the banks of the Tigris and Euphrates rivers, but I prefer to believe the Nile is mother to all civilization.

"Mine was a time when small semi-permanent villages first began to appear. People were shifting from being hunter-gatherers to early farmers. Farming brought stability to the food supply and that permitted people to stay in one place. It also permitted civilization to arise.

"You have both seen the long mural in the Chicago Museum titled, 'Life on the Early Nile'. It's a realistic picture that came from my own memory. I painted it for the museum a long time ago and am quite proud of the images and mood it projects."

Glenda's face lit up, "Wow, M, you were the artist? You are a man of many talents. Yes, the picture is terrific. Looking at it I can feel the heat of the air. The sly cruising crocodiles gave me shivers." Traveler's head was nodding in agreement. M accepted their compliments with an artist's modest smile and continued his story.

"Egypt at this time was divided into two separate kingdoms. One kingdom was centered on the Upper Nile that flows out of Africa into Egypt while the Lower Nile empties into the Mediterranean Sea.

"While the two kingdoms had separate rulers, the people themselves appeared as cousins. It was natural that they would eventually come together into a single kingdom. The two kingdoms were unified around 3,100 BC by a ruler named 'Narmer', also called 'Menes'.

"Menes is generally recognized as the first pharaoh of a united Egypt. Egypt was now a land empire that ruled the Middle East for thousands of years.

"Menes made his capital on the Lower Nile where the mother of rivers flowed into the Mediterranean Sea. His capital city was called Memphis and this capital name has never been forgotten. We have cities right here in the US, such as Memphis, Tennessee, named after that early Egyptian capital.

"Just as Memphis, Egypt was built beside mother Nile, so too was Memphis, Tennessee built beside the mighty Mississippi. Both rivers are major arteries for civilizations, ancient and modern.

"I was born prior to the unification of the two kingdoms. My best guess is that it was around 3,200 BC to 3,300 BC. Of course, there were no birthday calendars back then."

Both Glenda and Traveler immediately did the math in their heads. They simultaneously said, "That would make you over 5000 years old."

Glenda added, "Really, M, are you pulling our leg? You look to be in your early to mid-twenties. I know you are very old, but 5000 years old? Really?"

M puffed up a bit with her compliment, "Well, in my case, looks are definitely deceiving. It's an advantage of living in Theo's world. Our sanctuary is one that shields us from unwelcome intruders but also offers protection against time destroying our bodies. To the sanctuary's architect I must say, 'Thank you, Theo'." Saying that, M gave Theo several extra firm head rubs and ear tugs. The god-cat's vibrations went up a notch.

Chapter 3

Life on the Nile

"My childhood years were very pleasant, really idyllic. I was born to loving, caring parents. Adding to my joy of daily life were great playmates. We lived outside and were active all day. While the temperature was hot during the day, we were adjusted to it. There was no air conditioning, of course, but cooling breezes helped. Sensibly, all villagers napped in their houses during the hottest part of the day.

"Like today, our parents wanted their children outside. Constant exercise was not only fun but prepared us for the demands of adulthood. As children we had the run of open spaces when not assisting in working chores.

"Every day offered us adventures exploring the banks of the Nile and the surrounding hills. We were young explorers and came to know the secret paths and hidden caves. We also learned how to trap the game that was plentiful. We beamed with pride as we returned home with a rabbit, game bird, or fresh eggs from a discovered nest and received our parents' praise.

"We were a fair-sized, prosperous village with a stable supply of food. The women did the farm planting while the men hunted and fished in reed boats. At harvest time all worked side-by-side in the fields including the children.

"As a prosperous village, we were naturally the occasional target for roaming bands of raiders. They came to steal food as well as to capture women and children as slaves. As you can imagine, defending ourselves was an important task.

"My father was appropriately named Jabari, which means a man known for his bravery; he was in charge of the village defenses. As a young man he had been trained in warfare and village protection while in the service of a regional lord. The lord protected many villages and received tribute for his protection.

"After my father had served his time to the lord, he was sent to our village to organize its defenses. He was an important leader to the villagers and an important asset for our collective well-being.

"My father had a tall, powerful, imposing presence. Upon arriving, he met my mother who was the beauty of our village. Her name, Ebony, was appropriate. Ebony means beautiful both inside and outside.

"Love between them happened quickly. They were each a special person and recognized that same quality in the other. Courtship was swift, the village knew these two belonged together. I arrived a short time later. My arrival was a joy to both my parents and to the village.

"My father created a strong defensive system to protect our village. For early warnings we had numerous large horns surrounding the outskirts of the village. The horns were manned by young men who had the strength of lung to make the horns sound across a wide space. Once alerted, our older men returned from their work places and quickly formed into defensive lines.

"Each man in the village began combat training starting around age ten. My father tested each man for his natural fighting talents. He then organized all fighting men into specialty units. There were units whose men carried heavy, long-shafted spears. In combat, these spears were snapped forward and kept opponents at a distance. A direct hit with one of these heavy spears immediately removed the opponent from combat. The spears also stopped horses from charging into our line. The spearmen were the largest and strongest men, but often a bit older and slower.

"Mixed among the spearmen were sword fighters who carried a one-meter long stabbing sword. These swordsmen were usually the youngest, quickest, and most fearless of the warriors.

"They were nimble of hand and foot and darted between the thrusting spears. They moved quickly to the forward points of the spears to stab at their adversary using the long spear points to protect themselves. They enjoyed looking the enemy in the eye while stabbing at throat or groin. They were masters of taunts to incent an opponent forward onto their sword edge or the spear point. Swordsmen and spearmen formed a coordinated fighting unit.

"The last unit was the archers. They were the elite warriors since they had the most difficult skill to develop. Our archers were selected at an early age to begin their training. I had been identified at age six as a future archer due to my natural skill with a sling. I had an ability to hit a moving target, such as a rabbit, at a distance. Modesty aside, I had very good eye–hand coordination. And still do," M added with a smile.

"So, my early life was filled with daily pleasures, loving parents, good friends to play with, and plenty of food. I lived a young boy's dream."

Chapter 4

Life Changes

"The dream was shattered shortly after I turned seven. I left one morning as dawn was breaking. The great sun god Ra had just emerged from his passage through the dark void. Joining me were my two best friends, Kosey and Lateef."

"What do those names mean, M?" Glenda asked.

"Thank you for that question, Glenda, I appreciate your interest in my early culture. Understand that ancient Egyptians placed great importance on the choice of names. Parents would observe the baby and try to fit a name which either described the infant or could possibly grace it with a future accomplishment.

"In that spirit of naming, Kosey means 'lion'. He was an unusually large baby and very demanding. He tried to rule the house when he was only a few months old. Lateef was quite the opposite in disposition and his name means 'kind and mild'. Both names fit the boys' temperaments and presence.

"To return to my story, my two friends and I were going to explore a newly discovered series of caves that were a long hike from our village. I had eaten breakfast in the pre-dawn darkness, then packed my food and water for the day's adventure. My father was already up planning the day with my mother. He was staying in the village that day to oversee the storage arrangements for the coming harvest.

"They both smiled at my early rising and my mother said, 'He has both your eyes and your energy. He will become a strong leader.' My father said nothing but I saw he was pleased with my mother's comment. Fathers see much of themselves in their young sons and hope for that to be an insight into their future accomplishments.

"I clearly remember that it was a beautiful early morning with cooler temperatures and lovely breezes as we headed out. Many of the men had already left for early fishing. Some of the younger men had stayed back at my father's request to accompany the women to the fields to help with the beginning harvest. When my friends and I left, the village was quiet and serene.

"We were about half an hour out on our hike, walking at a fast pace to avoid the heat of the rising sun, when we heard the first warning calls. We froze in place for a moment then immediately turned and began running back.

"By the time we were close to the village, we saw raiders had already captured a number of our women. I recognized my mother's colorful skirt and knew she was already captured. My heart went from morning joy to sinking despair.

"As I stood transfixed, Kosey and Lateef ran toward their own homes to warn their families. They knew if my mother had been captured, anyone still in the village was in grave danger.

"As women and children were captured they were quickly bound across the backs of small desert horses. These horses were bred for their speed and endurance in the heat of the desert. I knew our village did not have horses that could catch these desert steeds. If the raiders escaped, then the captured would never be recovered.

"I saw that the village elder and several young men had faced the initial raider charge and were now lying on the ground. The younger men lay in their own blood flowing from multiple stab wounds; none of them had weapons beyond simple knives to defend themselves. The raiders had descended so quickly that our men had no time to prepare.

"The elder was the sole armed man. He had been by his home when the raiders came racing in. He had ducked inside and retrieved his sword, then emerged and fought to the death. The elder lay with his head twisted at a sharp angle. His sword lay beside him in the dust. He had done his best to defend against the raiders and one raider lay in front of him. The elder's belly was open and his organs were exposed. The sand around his still-flowing wound was a dark purple. The raiders left him gutted to show the villagers the consequence of resisting.

"I then saw my father with his back against a brick wall being pressed on two sides by swordsmen. My father appeared as a hardened warrior who stood a head taller than his attackers. He had a thick wicker shield over his left arm and his stabbing sword in his right hand. His skill was such that he was keeping the attackers at bay.

"I watched as one of the aggressive young attackers lunged at my father. My father permitted the sword to enter his thick shield where it became stuck. He then twisted the shield, causing the sword to become further embedded in it. Following the twisting motion, he instantly yanked his shield with the embedded sword toward him. The inexperienced attacker instinctively held onto his sword and tripped forward. My father's counterthrust ended his attack and his life. The attacker fell dead at my father's feet.

"My father then advanced a step and the attacking group fell back. My father was greatly outnumbered but his swift kill caused a pause in the attack. I knew that he was trying to buy time by disrupting the raiders long enough for the village men to return from the harvest fields. His tactic was working; he was throwing the raiders off their normal 'hit fast, kill fast, and run fast' tactic.

"I saw one older, long-armed attacker studying my father's moves. He decided he could use his arm length to avoid the shield and stab past it with a feint. He motioned for a second attacker to join him. Once my father's shield was pushed to the side, the two attackers would deliver simultaneous strikes.

"My father understood the feint and double-strike tactic. He waited for the long sword arm to be fully extended outside his shield, then he rotated again. He pushed the man's sword arm far away with his shield, then unexpectedly lunged close to the man. He stabbed up into the man's exposed neck then brought his shield back around. Blood spurted from a surprised face as the tall attacker fell.

"My father immediately closed on the second man who was frozen in place by the attack. Father again rotated his body and used his body's momentum to strike the surviving attacker hard on the side of his head using his shield as a club.

"The inexperienced fighter stood stunned from the blow and instinctively brought his sword hand to his damaged face, it was a natural flinch reflex. My father drove his sword into the man's exposed stomach. He pushed his sword down, then twisted to pull it out. The man's innards burst from their casing.

"By standing still to watch the exchange with the long-armed attacker, the second attacker had sealed his own death. In battle, like in life, to remain stationary is a sure way to remain stationary forever."

"My father now had a look of bloodlust on his face that I had never seen before. He was no longer my gentle father but a true warrior. He was a lion and roared his challenge to the fighters facing him. There were no takers.

"When those accustomed to winning with swift offense find themselves on the defense, the result is typically confusion. Several attackers were trying to work up their courage to attack the lion when a deep voice issued a sharp command. All the attackers immediately stepped away from my father and I saw relief pass over their faces.

"The raider leader had arrived on horseback and was motioning to a group of men with bows. He simply pointed at my father. The archers quickly formed a semicircle about twenty feet away. The third attack was launched. A dozen arrows came at the same time. My father could not use his shield on all sides. The arrows hit him in exposed areas of his lower legs, side, and throat. He was dead before he reached the ground.

"I heard my mother call out to him, and it was the last time I ever heard her voice. That memory still haunts me. The raiders climbed on their horses and left the village as our returning men were forming up to launch their own counterattack.

"Once the raiders were gone the village men were at a loss about what to do. Their leader was dead and they had no horses suitable for pursuit. The returning women began cries of despair for their captured daughters and slain sons. The entire village sank into a state of mourning. There was no leader to guide them out of their confusion and despair."

Chapter 5

Life as an Orphan

"Now at age seven I was both an orphan and still a child. Children only survived by having parents to provide for them and protect them. That's true today, and believe me it was certainly true then. I was fortunate that I had good friends with good-hearted parents. I was moved from family to family so that the cost of my support was shared.

"Working to my advantage was the respect that my father was held in. His heroic stand saved other women from being captured. Those families recognized a debt that they owed him and they repaid the debt by caring for me.

"I also had the advantage that I was selected to be an archer. My skills with the sling were obvious, so I represented a future asset for the entire village once I matured. Sadly, this future value as an archer lost its worth without my father's presence to maintain the fighting units. Without my father's skills and leadership, the village's fighting capabilities gradually eroded away.

"My early advantages of families repaying a debt to my father, and my potential as a future archer lasted for a few years. However, as I grew I became large for my age, I was my father's son. With my larger size came a larger appetite. At age ten I was already taller than many of the men in the village.

"Over time, more raiders picked on us. Our ability to defend against raiders lessened and more of our women were captured.

Women were the glue of our culture as well as the foundation for our farming. Harvest crops became less plentiful. The village was still surviving but the diminishing food supply was now an ever-present threat to the village's survival.

"Hunger erodes the memory of obligations. Our village was in a downward spiral without a bottom in sight.

"I was now viewed as taking the food out of the mouths of family children. I knew that I was on the cusp of becoming resented and that people, including my friends, were pulling away from me. I decided that I would not become a pariah in my own village.

"One morning I thanked my hosting families, said goodbye to my friends, and walked away. I noticed that while they asked me to reconsider, all were secretly relieved at my leaving. I could not blame them."

Chapter 6

Early Life Alone

"Basic to my survival was finding a safe shelter. While on an earlier exploring trip in the surrounding wild hills I had found a small cave built into the side of a steep hillside. It was the perfect shelter. I returned to it and kept a fire in front of the cave in the evening.

"The fire provided protection from nighttime predators. On occasion I head subtle sniffing sounds and fear swept through me. A practical solution was that I had to wake up during the night to add additional fuel, but that was a small price for survival.

"I always feared rain could put out my fire, however, rain was a scarce commodity in the hills of Egypt. On the few nights when it did rain, I built the fire just inside the mouth of the cave. Of course the smoke from the fire made breathing difficult, but I learned to breathe with my mouth close to the dirt floor. I consoled myself that I was still breathing.

"I caught my food using snares. While I had developed skills with my sling, I had been taught by my father the usefulness of a snare. 'Less work and effort are involved to capture dinner than to chase it,' he had explained.

"I became increasingly adept with my snares. I became expert in noting the paths of wildlife, placed my snares accordingly, and caught a wide variety of wildlife. My favorite catches were mountain rabbits but I also learned that cooked snake and scorpion offer acceptable meals when your stomach demands to be fed."

Glenda and Traveler both squirmed at this image of M eating snake and scorpion. M smiled at their facial grimaces and added, "I believe my love of cooking was born while living in my cave."

"My cave was well-positioned for safety and was also close to a good-sized river. The river, like all those in this region, was a tributary to mother Nile. Like the Nile it was also a good provider. I would catch river fish and smoke them so that if my snare was empty I still had a meal. I was always hungry but I lived.

"While I was never formally trained as an archer, I had observed many archers at practice. I constructed a stout bow and practiced a lot. Eventually I developed passable skills as an archer. Armed with my bow, and a natural stealth instinct, I was able to kill larger game such as small deer at a distance. This skill added nicely to my food supply which in turn added to my body's strength.

"As a bowhunter, I learned techniques to stalk prey without their being aware of my presence. I understood how to practice a hunter's stealth including being quiet, avoiding giving signs of motion, and of course, staying downwind.

"I also developed a sixth sense about the environment. I became instinctively aware of dangerous animals who may be stalking me. I was always aware of my place in nature's food chain."

Chapter 7

Fire Creatures Attack

"My hunting skills saved my life. Leaving my cave early one fine morning, my awareness of the environment alerted me that I was possibly being hunted. There was a vibration in the air and ground that I had never experienced. The hunters were, in fact, the fire creatures that we know well. Back then, I had no idea they existed, but I sensed a strange presence.

"I was initially cautious but also curious about the source of the vibration. I carefully tracked toward it. As I moved, I found myself approaching my old village. When I was near the village, I saw my village was under attack.

"The attackers were nothing I had ever seen before. My best description was that they reminded me of small red thunderclouds that were moving close to the ground. They seemed to float without touching the ground. Emerging out of a cloud's mass were arm-like appendages. These arms constantly changed their length and thickness and they shimmered with a reddish hue.

"They were clearly godlike predators, possibly djinn or demon. They hunted down and consumed the people in my village. As they flowed across people, they absorbed them into their central mass. They moved with a purpose that I can best describe as raw hunger. The only similar experience I had observed was watching a crocodile attack a deer by a riverbank. There was no mercy. Once engaged death followed quickly.

"A few brave men attempted to strike the fire beasts with weapons, but nothing made an impact. Men simply disappeared into the beings. I believed I was seeing gods of war at work.

"As alpha predators, the beings seemed to know where each person was hiding and easily found them. As they were discovered, I heard men, women, and children begin to shriek. All of their shouts and screams stopped in mid-cry. These predators were hunting and consuming without mercy. Nobody would be spared. My childhood village was doomed."

Chapter 8

Escape

"Since I was some distance away, I fortunately had a little time to try and save myself. I knew I had to act quickly and find a safe place to hide, but where? I instinctively knew my cave would not be a safe place. My little cave fire would offer no protection against these fire beings. They may well cook me on my own fire.

"While logic failed me, my hunter instincts took over and I knew my only possible escape route was by water. I raced toward my best fishing spot. My fishing river was one of the wide tributaries that flowed into the mighty Nile. When I arrived at my fishing spot, I looked across the wide tributary to a distant island. The island promised the sanctuary I needed if only I could reach it.

"I had often thought of getting to the island to explore, but never had the courage to try. Now my fear of the fire-beings was greater than my fear of the river and I committed to crossing the wide tributary.

"I had no true swimming skills back then. I had never learned how to swim without touching the bottom. My swimming consisted of bobbing up and down by pushing off the floor of the river. I had good intentions to learn proper swimming but today was not the day to start. I needed help to cross and I needed it quickly.

"I looked around and saw my possible water craft, a cut tree close to the river's bank. The branches and trunk were the remains of a tree that I had recently cut down for firewood. Since my cutting tools were simple, I only cut down small trees. This felled tree was about three long steps in length and two spread arms in diameter. Although dead it still retained substantial green branches.

"I grabbed the end of the trunk, hefted it onto my shoulder, and began to drag it toward the river. The tree was heavy but fear gave me great strength. I entered the water then turned my back to the river. Leaning back toward the river I used my body weight to help pull my lifeboat tree forward into the tributary.

"As more of my tree entered the water, the pulling got easier. I was now above my waist in the river. Bracing my feet on the bottom I made a final powerful thrust with my legs and the entire trunk with all its branches was in the water.

"Once in the water, it naturally floated and I found I could move it slowly around. The flowing tributary now replaced my muscle power. I continued to pull it further out from the shore until I was up to my shoulders in the water.

"I then ducked under the tree branches and came up on the opposite side of the floating trunk. I buried myself among the branches and felt somewhat secure. I was hidden from a shore view and my crossing promised to be doable.

"As I began my water escape to the island, I wrapped my left arm around the trunk and grabbed a branch on the back side. Feeling that I was securely attached to my floating camouflage, I began pushing off the bottom while using my free right hand to paddle toward the center of the river.

"Once I had forward momentum, the river took over. My feet quickly lost touch with the bottom and I felt a moment of panic. I knew if I lost hold of my tree raft I would never catch it. I instinctively gripped the branch I was holding even harder.

"This was the ride of my life, no pun intended. Fortunately it was my good luck that the tributary's flow was gentle at this time of year. There had been no rain for several months so the tributary was now a docile body of water moving gently to join mother Nile.

"Additionally, the width of the tributary ensured its movement would be slow but steady. In a rainy season the rush of the swollen tributary would have killed me as surely as the red god creatures.

"While I could not swim, I did have water skills. My strongest skill was mental control, I was not afraid of the water. When I fished in the river with my spear I would walk slowly out to my chest. Then I would put my head fully under water, hold my breath, and look around for my swimming dinner.

"I taught myself to hold my breath for an extended amount of time. I practiced at seeing how long I could stay under. Looking back, I imagine it was easily over two minutes. This practiced style of submerged fishing assured me I was safe as long as I kept my wits about me.

"Now that I was mentally relaxed and with my left arm securely wrapped around the trunk, I put more power into my own body. I scissor-kicked my legs and pulled with my free right arm. My progress toward the island was slow, but that was good. I would appear to an observer on the bank as another floating piece of river debris.

"I remained buried in the branches all the way across. Occasionally I peeked back through the branches. Once I saw several fire creatures moving around the shore and up to the water's edge. They studied the striations left in the earth from my dragged tree. Fortunately, my footprints were covered over by the scraping of the dragged branches.

"I sensed the beings knew there was a missed prey hiding and were searching for it. Fortunately, they did not seem to consider the river a hiding place. Possibly the water interfered with their hunting senses or possibly fire simply avoids water; either way, I was again lucky.

"The crossing was slow and took many hours. The sun god Ra was now descending into the dark void which marks the end of a day. I felt he had been watching me and was rewarding my courage.

"I was beyond exhausted when I finally touched bottom once more. In crossing, I had repeatedly switched arms to paddle and hang on. When I replaced my left hand-grip with my right hand I had to roll onto my back and then pull with the free left hand. With every body-roll I swallowed water and found it going up my nose; I gulped and snorted while keeping my survival sounds as quiet as possible.

"Both arms could barely move when I landed. My legs felt that they would collapse under me without the support of the water. I pushed enough of the tree up onto the shore so that it became an anchor and I could finally rest with my feet on the bottom.

"I continued to fear the fire beings so I stayed in the water hidden within the tree branches until it was fully dark. My other concern, while in the water, was that a river predator, like a sly smiling crocodile, would find me. Ra stayed with me and my luck obviously held.

"When I finally crawled up the river's bank, it was nighttime. The stars were bright but the moon was just a sliver, darkness was my friend. Crawling out I must have resembled an amphibian hundreds of millions of years earlier testing the land.

"I continued to belly crawl until I finally reached the island's tree line. Even then I never stood up for fear of being spotted by the evil demons. I continued to crawl forward until I found a large pine tree. I crawled under the low branches that reached the ground until I reached the thick trunk.

"I found myself suddenly sobbing while hugging the trunk like an old friend. I snuggled against the trunk with less than two feet between my body and the soft fragrant branches above my head. For the first time that day I felt protected. Sleep swept over me as I passed out within the sheltering pine cave.

"Our body has a natural clock and my clock had me sleep deeply through the night and well into the morning. The overhead pine branches shielded me from the sun, so I only awoke when my hunger and body functions required it.

"My early morning wits advised me to crawl out slowly to the edge of the tree line and scout the opposite shoreline. I was naturally scared that the fire-beings may still be searching for a missing victim. I was sure they would cross the water if they knew I was on the island. I lay on my belly for an hour before crawling away into the dense woods.

"At an acceptable distance I finally felt secure enough to stand upright. Once standing I remained still behind a large tree and slowly surveyed the opposite shore. Nothing disturbed the quietude of that forest line as it came toward the river's bank. The demons had apparently abandoned their search, at least from what I could observe.

"The island became my discovered sanctuary and I committed to remaining there indefinitely. I naturally established my home base on the side of the island furthest away from my old fishing shore. This opposite side placed the entire width of the island between me and the fire-demons. I was, to a degree, cautiously accepting that I had escaped.

"Now that my focus could move away from my own immediate safety, I felt a great wave of sadness pass through me as I reflected on the loss of my village friends. Part of me wanted to risk returning to see if there were survivors; however, I instinctively knew none had escaped. If I returned, I would likely become another victim of the creatures. My life would now move forward by staying with the protection offered by my island."

Chapter 9

Island Sanctuary

"My new vocation was being an island explorer. As I explored, I found that the island was in a primal state unbothered by humans. Wild game was both plentiful and trusting, I laid out several snares confident my food supply would quickly grow.

"Fruit was abundant, including ripe berries, and I gathered many large handfuls. I found several fig trees and added figs to my meal supply. As an afterthought, I placed a quantity of the figs in the sun to dry.

"Another dependable source of food came from the river. On this side of the river, I easily caught my meal. The fish had never been hunted and would swim up to me. While I could not risk building a fire to roast the fish, I could eat them raw and found I enjoyed the sweet taste."

M smiled at Traveler's grimace and added, "Today we call this food source 'sashimi' and it is considered a delicacy. I know sashimi sounds much better than 'raw fish,' but 'tomayto' or 'tomahto', it's still the same thing."

Glenda smiled at Traveler and then showed her epicurean sophistication by adding, "We Norwegians love raw salmon, it's a staple for dinner." Traveler shook his head and thought, *Hamburger please for this boy, you two can keep my share of the raw fish.*

M continued, "That afternoon a dinner of raw fish, berries, and figs was the best meal I could remember. Once my hunger was taken care of, I realized how exhausted I was. I found another sheltering pine tree and climbed under. I fell into another deep, dreamless sleep. I slept until the call of morning birds told me Ra had driven his sun chariot from the darkness and it was time for me to rise.

"I felt amazingly refreshed. I ate my remaining food and was anxious to explore. This island was likely to be my home for a long time and I wanted to learn all it offered.

"The island was quite long, possibly two miles. Where I had landed was toward the front of the island. As I moved around, I found that its width increased significantly. There was a lot of land to be explored and I made several base camps as I moved about.

"After a week of exploring I made a major discovery hidden in a sheltering copse of trees and ground growth. At some considerable distant time in the past, man had lived on the island. In the thicket I found the long-abandoned remains of a stone structure. This was my second discovered sanctuary, the first was my island and now my new stone home.

"As I cleared away the vegetation from the base of the structure, I saw there was a solid stone foundation sunk into the ground. Rising from the foundation were four stone walls; they were covered with vines yet they were solid and intact. The stonemasons had done their job very well.

"I measured the size of the structure and found it to be most accommodating. The walls were about twenty-five feet long by fifteen feet wide. The stone walls went up nearly seven feet. At one end was a large fireplace and its size indicated it was intended to both heat the interior as well as being a cooking center.

"One wall had a five-foot opening that was the only entry point, and this entry could be sealed by a door. To accommodate a door there was still a curved stone arch framing the top of the entrance. Standing inside the structure I knew this was to be my permanent home.

"Inside I began to clear away the years of fallen debris. Leaves and tree limbs created a floor clutter that I systematically pulled outside through the opening. As the floor reappeared, I realized it was a work of art. It was built from mosaic tile presenting a variety of colorful patterns. The prior occupants had made their structure as delightful inside as it was secure to the outside.

"As I cleaned, I discovered hidden treasures. These treasures were better than gold or precious stones; they were a wide variety of useful tools. There were saws as well as axes, hammers, chisels, and even a set of planes for smoothing wood surfaces. Mixed among the tools were several sharpening stones.

"Once the interior was cleaned, I set to work using my newfound tools. My first addition was a solid wooden door that I used to seal the opening at night. Once my sanctuary was secure, I began installing a ceiling.

"I built the ceiling rafters from long, thin tree trunks that I placed in a crisscross lattice pattern. Next I needed to determine how to keep my overhead lattice secure to the walls. Luck was with me, or perhaps the stonemasons were with me. I discovered there were stone protrusions jutting out at regular intervals along the top perimeter of the exterior walls.

"I used these jutting stones as anchor points to secure my roof's cross beams. I completed my roof by making a waterproof cover of overlapping reeds from the riverbank.

"With my exterior structure complete I turned my thoughts to what was needed inside. Of course, sleeping on a good bed is essential for everybody's health. I created a permanent bed of thick leaves and soft moss which I placed close to the fireplace. My sanctuary was now a home that offered security and comfortable sleeping.

"I often thought about returning to the mainland but was not sure what life awaited me there. Here I was a king and an absolute ruler. I had adjusted to living alone and found I was comfortable with this state of existence. It's good to be pharaoh even if it's just an island empire."

Chapter 10

An Uninvited Guest

"My kingdom was unexpectedly invaded, and my pharaoh rule short-lived. I awoke one morning to find a very large, panther-like beast camped by my fire. It looked at me as I imagine it would view a tasty meal. Staring at the animal, I was too scared to move or breath. I felt a fear that was greater than my escape from the fire djinn.

"My life seemed to be that of a continuing prey. First, prey to human raiders, then red, fire-god creatures, and now to a huge black, cat-like beast. Time stood still while my heart raced. 'I'm cursed,' went through my mind. First, I lose my family, then my village, now my sanctuary. The gods are angry with me and I don't know why.

"I briefly considered racing for the door and trying to lock the beast inside. That idea died immediately. My door was closed and held securely in place by the crossing bars. 'How did it get in?' I wondered for a second. Then I stared back into its eyes; they were glittering whirlpools promising neither answers nor escape.

"I found myself holding my breath, much as I did when fishing with my head under water. While it felt like hours, in fact it could only have been several minutes. I finally had to exhale and take in a deep breath. I calmed down enough to realize the uninvited guest was not going to eat me, at least not immediately.

"Unsure of what to do, I slowly slid a bowl of morning fruit and fish to him as an offering of goodwill. The food was extended as a peace offering, and more importantly as an alternative to eating me.

"He seemed to acknowledge the bowl more as an offering than a meal. For now he appeared content to rest in front of my fire. I finally accepted my fate, what choice did I have?

"Surprisingly he did not eat me and we coexisted for the next week. I always offered him his meal. Sometimes it was eaten, while most times his interest was elsewhere and fortunately it was not on me. Even when he did eat, I felt he was simply humoring me.

"Like most cats he clearly enjoyed my fire, so I increased its size for his enjoyment. I had known many cats in my village life and I always thought it strange how they sought out a fire at night. Cats and fire seem to go together and I wondered how he would react to the fire beasts. Much later I found out.

"Occasionally he would follow me outside. Once I was bathing in the tributary and he walked down to the bank's edge to observe me. I was in a playful mood and tried to get him into the water. I motioned to him to join me like I would a dog, and he ignored me. Still playful, I hit my palm on the water and sent a splash near him. His stare back suggested I may be starting to look like a large floating mouse. I decided playtime did not fit into his plans.

"As I studied him in the evening, I noted that he had some of the characteristics of the fire beings; he liked my fire and avoided water. I wondered if he was possibly related to the fire beasts, but decided they were at opposite ends of that family tree.

"I gradually accepted that he was not an adversary and I was not prey. To the contrary, I increasingly sensed a protective aura from him. His presence at night felt like I was living with a massive watchdog, or in his case watchcat. I felt he was vigilant even while seeming to doze. As I lay close beside him, I was soothed by his purring vibrations. I never slept better in my life.

"Time passed and we seemed to enjoy a developing relationship. I guess I brought him companionship or possibly amusement while he brought me security. Somehow, I felt I was his adopted pet, and I accepted my place."

Chapter 11

M's Education Begins

"Few of us ever know when something will change our life. The big things frequently slip up on us like ninja. My young boy's life changed on what started out as a typical morning on my island. Again, there was nothing to indicate what was coming into my life.

"I woke up, had my breakfast, and was preparing to explore a part of the island that had an elevated view. As I was preparing to leave, my companion came to the door and blocked it. I was confused and reached past it to open the door.

"The tiger-sized cat placed its jaws around my forearm. When its mouth opened it seemed to offer a bottomless canyon, its gape exceeded that of a river hippo's. Nobody challenges the river hippo or my companion. It was clear I was not leaving.

"'Okay companion, what do you want?' The cat released my arm, walked over to a corner area against a wall, and sat down. It stared at me until I got the message. I followed and sat beside it.

"Then a most remarkable thing happened. The tiger-cat swept its paw across a mosaic tile in a corner. I bent down and found the tile was loose. I slipped fingers under it and lifted it up to discover a hidden storage area.

"Reaching inside I felt a soft leather cylinder. My arm tingled when I touched it and a pleasant sensation flowed through my body. '*Nice*' was my first reaction followed by, '*How did it get here?*' There were no answers I could imagine.

"Upon removing it I realized it was a scroll. My father had described scrolls to me. He said they were instruments that permitted great things to happen. To use them required a form of magical training.

"This secret training permitted the priests to understand the inscribed symbols called hieroglyphs. The knowledge contained in the scrolls was limited to the very top of society. Only priests, pharaohs, and a few privileged businessmen were permitted access to this knowledge.

"Much later I realized that my personal companion's knowledge was far beyond what the priests could ever learn from their library of scrolls. My personal scroll, presented to me by my companion, opened a portal into a universe that I am still learning about to this very day."

Both Glenda and Traveler were captivated by M's story and neither interrupted until Glenda suddenly felt she had to ask, "M, I believe our books are instruments of some science so advanced we can call it magic. Correct?" Traveler was nodding his head in agreement.

M acknowledge her question with a smile, "Yes, what the scrolls give us both in knowledge and power may be best described as magic."

"Naturally, back then I had no understanding of the symbols and what they expressed. My companion understood my study limitations and jump-started my learning abilities. While I held the scroll in two hands, my companion stood in front of me and pressed its head against my forehead. My mind first went empty, then my companion poured into my mind the basic tools to begin my study.

"I remember shaking as this knowledge flowed into me. My human brain was an empty urn that was starting to be filled. I felt myself being lifted outside of my body. I knew I was being changed, but had no sense of how the changes would affect me. I felt I was gaining the necessary power to learn, but about what and to what purpose I had no idea.

"What I knew with a certainty was that my companion was a god. I knew I now lived to serve my god."

Chapter 12

What's in a Name?

"When my companion was finished bestowing my starting knowledge, he sent me a strange request. '*When do gods ask anything?*' I thought. To my great surprise, my companion wanted me to give him a name.

"With great hesitancy I replied, 'You want a name? You are a god, it is not my place to name you.'

"My companion again leaned its head against my head. '*I am alone now and I need a name. The honor of naming is yours.*'

"I thought, '*Naming a god, how can that be my place? I'm a simple, peasant orphan who barely escaped with his life. This is a job for a priest or pharaoh.*' Then I realized the god creature was looking expectantly at me. It was my honor, or my duty, to name it regardless of what I thought.

"With a weak smile I nodded my acceptance, followed by an attempt at a little humor to break my nervousness, 'Okay, but please don't eat me if you don't like my choices.' My cat god simply gave me a look that said, 'Get on with it.'

"I thought, *OK, it's naming time, do your best.* 'Theoretically, I could name you "Mighty One", which I suspect you are. Theoretically, I think "Ruler of the Desert" fits well. Theoretically, I like "Wisest of the Wise" a lot.' As I tried various names, I waited for some reaction of approval. None came.

"In exasperation I finally said, 'Theoretically, there are

countless names that fit you. Theoretically, I can keep creating them, but I'm out of inspiration. Maybe the best name for you is simply "Theoretically" which we can shorten to "Theo".'

"Now cats, regardless of their size, have no ability to smile, but in that moment I'm sure I saw a smile followed by a robust purring vibration. Its head touched mine and I heard in my mind, '*Yes, I have been a theoretically focused being for a very long time. Time beyond your understanding. Time before your universe and this world existed. Time before your concept of time existed. This name fits me. Theo it is, and I approve.*'

"Millenniums later, when Greek was the language in this part of the world, I thought I was prescient. The word for god in Greek is 'theos'. I had truly nailed his name, and he knew it.

"While Theo's head continuing to be pressed against mine a pleasant sensation filled me, '*I approve of my name and will now return the honor by selecting your name. There are several names that could fit you in this region of the world.*'

"'*My initial choice based on your heritage is "Mert".*'

"Now the vibration felt like a chuckle, as if this god being was enjoying a human joke. Again, I thought I saw a smile on the large face. A long fang seemed to briefly appear from a lower lip.

"He continued with, '*Sadly in this land known as Egypt the name Mert means "Lover of Silence" and that will not suit you in the days to come.*'

"'*We will still name you Mert but accept the meaning from a land that will be known as Turkey. In that language Mert means, "brave and trustworthy". Indeed, that is the essence of your spirit. In centuries to come, in distant lands far beyond this desert, you will be called Merlyn, but for now you are Mert. As you wisely chose to shorten my name to Theo so will I shorten yours to "M".*'

"I was beyond pleased. Praise from a god, does it get any better? The meaning of the name Mert as 'brave and trustworthy' would have fit my father and it warmed my inner being. Could Theo have known of my father and his final stand against the raiders? I challenged myself to justify the name both to the god and to my father's memory."

Chapter 13

Training Begins

"My study began that night with my scroll while I slept." M smiled at Glenda and Traveler, "Of course that's no surprise to either of you. Some of your best learning happens while you sleep with your books.

"After dinner exhaustion hit me. While I looked forward to starting my training, I needed to sleep. As I lay down beside Theo and the fire, I felt a paw push the scroll under my head. I discovered how warm and soft it was. It created a perfect cradle for my head. The sleep god Morpheus quickly visited me.

"I awoke the next morning totally refreshed. Lifting my head, I was suddenly concerned. I knew that scrolls were valued objects of magic. They were treated with the greatest of care and honor, and I had used my scroll as a pillow.

"I feared that a god of knowledge, such as the Egyptian god Thoth, would be angry at my pillow arrogance and bring his wrath down on me. Fortunately no angry Thoth appeared. I assumed that my personal god, Theo, would have warned other gods away.

"In the days to come I grew to accept the scroll's thick leather as a soft headrest. Of course, I had no awareness of how the scroll was training my mind while I slept."

M looked intently at Traveler and Glenda and added, "What I initially studied from was a physical scroll while both of you study from a book. Scroll and book are one and the same. The teachers exist inside the scroll, or in your case, the books. They are both sentient and shapeshifters. They take the shape that suits the time and place of their teaching. As the expression goes, 'Don't judge a book or scroll by its cover'."

Chapter 14

Books and Scrolls Rule

"On the first day of my study I carefully opened the scroll to its beginning. The very opening was beyond my understanding. Feeling like the slowest of students I tried looking further down in the hope that I would see something that I could grasp.

"As you both know, I could not go beyond that first section. Since I had no training to read the symbols, I accepted that I was destined to remain simply staring on the open part of the scroll. While staring I found that the symbols began to create a picture story in my mind. The story was beyond strange but I accepted it without question. My whole life was beyond strange now."

Smiling at Glenda, M added, "Unlike Traveler, our resident science student, I never questioned the presented knowledge. In my case ignorance of science was a good thing. I was the perfect empty vessel for the books to begin filling with their absolute truths.

"Over the following days, nights, weeks, and months I discovered that I could indeed advance in my studies. Most of the scroll's stories continued to be total mysteries to me but I felt privileged to hear them. I felt that I was listening to conversations among the gods."

M again smiled at his captive audience. He was pleased that neither had interrupted with questions nor looked sleepy.

"As a student, and unlike both of you, I was totally isolated from my fellow humans. While my god companion was ever present, he was far from offering the social interactions of a human companion. I accepted this social isolation and focused on my studies.

"The good news about being alone was that I had few distractions for my studies. I still had to gather my food supply and on occasion play in the warm waters, but I was increasingly drawn into the scroll's mysteries. I increasingly missed any time away from it.

"As my studies advanced I began to have insights into the meanings of the stories. The stories were puzzles and occasionally I could fit pieces together. When that happened I was elated and Theo seemed to enjoy my happiness. His purring vibrations would kick up a level to let me know that he felt my elation and approved of my advancement.

"Besides Theo and the books, the fire was the other constant presence. The fire now seemed to burn without a replenishment of fuel. During the day it appeared as embers, then as the sun went down and the temperature fell it built itself up. I accepted that strange event as part of my life with Theo. From the earliest time fire was considered a gift of the gods so my god naturally brought it with him.

"Many a cold night I fell asleep snuggled up against Theo in front of the fire. I no longer dreamed of the fire beasts. That memory seemed to belong to another person's life. With Theo beside me I slept without fear. I felt that he also enjoyed my presence as he emitted a soothing, purring vibration."

M broke his tale with a big stretch and a large swallow from his mug. He gave Theo a final head rub and sat forward in his chair. "Well, is that a good story or what?" asked M. Both Traveler and Glenda had been spellbound. Not only was the story great, but M told it in a way that each of them felt they were living the memory with him.

"You are the very best storyteller, M," said Glenda. "And it's a true story of magic. Nobody except Traveler and I would ever believe it." Traveler grinned, nodded, and began clapping. Glenda immediately joined him as M beamed.

"One final question, M?" asked Traveler.

M nodded, "A simple one I hope?"

"Well, my question is simple but only you will know if the answer is simple. My question is, why did Theo pick you out of all of his possible choices?"

M smiled and leaned back in his chair, his hand once again rested on Theo's head. "The answer, as best as I can tell after many millenniums of wondering that same thing, has to do with how the human brain was developing during this time period.

"For hundreds of thousands of years, the physical human brain operated as two separate engines placed side by side inside our skull. These engines are frequently referred to as the dual hemispheres of the brain. While they reside side by side, they perform in many ways as independent thought engines. The traditional view is that the right-side hemisphere controls creative thinking. The left-side hemisphere controls our logical thinking. Over time, the two hemispheres became much more connected; however, for any particular person one side was still dominant.

"The paintings by cavemen in France around 40,000 BC were the product of their right-side brain engine getting to demonstrate its skill. The left-side brain engine showed up later with the development of early mathematics. Geometry and algebra flowed out of the strengths of the left side starting around 3000 BC.

"The early Egyptians had an understanding of dimensional measures and geometric structures when they build the first pyramid in in 2,630 BC for Pharaoh Djoser. Their skills continued to develop and the Great Pyramid of Giza was built in 2,560 BC for Pharaoh Khufu.

"Now to answer your question, I believe Theo selected me because my two sides were somehow perfectly balanced. I naturally used both sides simultaneously and was a freak of nature.

"Theo required this brain balance for the books to advance any human mind. If there was not a perfect balance between the hemispheres, my physical brain would overload and then melt down with the stream of content flowing from the scrolls."

M noticed the not so subtle glances that were passing between Glenda and Traveler, "I'm not a mind reader, however I will answer your unasked question. Yes, you two are also freaks of nature. The books can work with your minds without exploding them. The pacing of your growth is limited to the capacity of your balanced brain to accept incoming content. That's why your early studies were so slow, the books controlled the pace, not you.

"The good news is that the books are improving the balance and the capacity of each of your brains. Since brain and body go hand in glove, as your brains are upgraded so are your body skills enhanced.

"Now on that happy note I am going to retire."

Chapter 15

M's Alert:
A Challenge Is Coming

Breakfast was a distant memory. "Where's lunch, princess?" Traveler asked Glenda.

She glanced up at him with a puzzled look. "Check the time, big boy. It's dinner time."

Traveler looked at his watch, "That's impossible. My stomach is a fine-tuned clock. It never misses a beat or a meal, it never sleeps while I'm on the job."

"Well you better reset that clock. Let's go see how M is coming, I'm starving also."

Before heading to the dining area, they looked at each other, turned, and headed to their respective rooms. Nature calls trump stomach calls.

"I see you have finally come out of your study cave," said M as Traveler returned. "Bet you're starved. I had a nice luncheon platter prepared, but saw you both were in the study groove. Never interrupt a student when they are rolling with their books.

"Since you both missed lunch I whipped up an outstanding replacement dinner. Trust me, you'll like it. As the chef I've tasted it and have sent myself hearty congratulations."

Glenda casually strolled up to the table. "Room for a lady at this place?" she asked smiling.

M welcomed her with a playful bow, then then proceeded to bring out the evening's dish. "This is tonight's dining fare, but trust me it's much better than fair," and he laughed at his own pun.

After a few big bites Glenda said, "You're so right, M, this is far beyond fair. I'd call it scrumptious. What would you call it, big boy?"

Traveler looked up from his plate and grunted. His grunt conveyed what he thought, *It's great, leave me alone, I'm busy.*

When dinner was wrapped up and Glenda and Traveler were standing to leave, M casually said, "Sleep well. I've got a surprise for you tomorrow. Theo and I appreciate how focused you've both been in your studies and importantly how much you've advanced. We have a fitting and necessary challenge for you that will continue your growth."

Glenda and Traveler were instantly at DEFCON One and began bombarding M with questions. "I understand you're curious, but no answers tonight. I'll let you sleep on the possibilities. Treat tonight like Christmas Eve knowing you will open up the big surprise tomorrow morning." Glenda and Traveler grinned like four-year-olds as they headed for their bedrooms.

Chapter 16

Not Your Average Field Trip

Glenda awoke early, she was always up early but this morning she beat the roosters. With some extra time she decided to do a quick wake up shower. She had spent a restless night and felt that even her book was restless. She started with hot water then switched to polar bear freezing. She was wide-eyed as she toweled off.

She saw her day's attire resting on the bed and flinched, it was a sad affair. It appeared like a shoddy version of a wool sack dress. The belt looked like a multipurpose rope. *I can use the rope as a belt, crack it like a whip, or use it to pull a pig around. Lucky me.* On the floor were a pair of plain thick wool socks resting on worn leather boots. They were the perfect footwear to go with the sack dress.

Putting it all on she said to the mirror, "Whatever M has in mind, I'm a girl being dressed for picking turnips somewhere. This outfit falls short for even the most rural barbeque party."

Reconciling to the outfit she thought, *Ok Glenda, quit whining. M's message is loud and clear, it's show time for some real-world action. I just wonder where that world is. Camping out somewhere nasty I bet.*

She bounced out of her room almost bumping into Traveler. She stared at him for a moment then laughed, "A poor man's Indiana Jones I presume? I think our outfits are a hint at what's coming. How did Indie sleep?"

"Pretty bad, Morpheus threw me under the bus last night. Never slept more than an hour at a time. I'd wake up and have to start all over again and I never, ever have a problem sleeping. It may sound weird but I think my book was restless. Lack of sleep bothers me more than this hayseed outfit. By the way you look perfect for a hoedown in the Appalachians."

"Same here on sleep and the outfits," said Glenda. "I think our books know what's coming. They get their vicarious kicks based on our experiences. They probably expect us to bring them something new and exciting. It's the exciting part that worries me."

"Good insight, Glenda. Our books are like nosy neighbors that want to know everything." Pausing Traveler put a serious tone in his voice and said, "But new and exciting was not the message I was getting, it felt more like concern. I think my book was worried for me, and that's a bothersome feeling."

Glenda had two fast reactions to Traveler's comments. The first was instinctive, she liked being called Glenda. Her second response was thoughtful, "That's strange Traveler, I had the same feeling that my book was worried. I guess we'll know shortly what's going on."

The aroma coming off the muffins blended with the smoked bacon and took their minds off worried books and their outfits. They arrived at the table just as M was pulling out his own chair. A basket of browned muffins with crusty tops, a large floral painted bowl of sliced fruits, and a rasher of bacon declared a breakfast feast was waiting.

Theo had left the fire to join them. He was sitting on his haunches looking down at the offerings. His size varied to reflect his mood or his interest in a particular activity. Today he was a very large tiger, possible matching a saber-tooth, not elephant size but well beyond scary big.

His enhanced size told both Glenda and Traveler that something big was in the air. Looking at Theo, then M and Glenda, Traveler quipped, "To quote Sherlock, I think the game is afoot."

Glenda nodded toward Theo and added, "I think his majesty would like a little something, perhaps a buttered muffin? Is it OK to offer him one, M?"

"Of course, just don't limit him to one. He likes to think he has no limits and I'm inclined to agree with him," M said with a chuckle.

Glenda held out a heavily buttered muffin and a long tiger tongue took it into a cavernous mouth. "Seconds?" she asked. The tongue extended and a second muffin disappeared. Apparently satisfied, Theo shifted his body a bit to indicate both "thanks" and also "that's enough."

Following Theo's lead, each of them covered their plates with assorted fruit, bacon, and muffins. Traveler cut a wedge of butter and placed it inside the halved muffin. He paused just long enough for the yellow goodness to melt and then took an alligator-sized bite. A second and then a third bite and his hand was empty. An empty hand at the dining table is a hand looking for mischief.

Traveler's hand made a lightning strike at a choice piece of melon on Glenda's plate. "Your plate looked off-balance. I'm helping you organize your food groups. You can't put fruits that close to bacon."

"Pot calling kettle black. You sound like that dirty kid Pig-Pen from Charlie Brown complaining about plate clutter. I've seen your room and it looks like a war zone. I'm surprised you can find the door to get out." While Traveler was preparing his witty response, Glenda did a cobra strike on his bacon saying, "That adds space to your over piled plate."

M knew today was a critical day for the two young students. His own sleep had been unsettled. He had immersed himself in the kitchen early to balance his mood. His mood continued to improve as he found himself enjoying the breakfast jousting. "Hope I made enough for both of you, there seems to be a run on the food bank today."

Saying that, M felt Theo press against him. He offered a muffin containing thick bacon slices to the open maw beside him and watched it disappear. *I've never seen him like this. It's like he is trying to bond with the two over breakfast. Could he know it's possibly a last shared meal?*

"Yes, I could eat a bit more. My plate has been under attack by food vultures," was the immediate response from Traveler. Glenda nodded in agreement while protecting her own plate with encircling arms.

M rose and came back with a second basket of muffins and another rasher of crisp bacon. With refilled plates they declared a truce on poaching and settled in.

Traveler finally leaned back and gave a low groan, "I'm embarrassed to admit that my reach this morning has exceeded my stomach's grasp. I'm at least two muffins over my legal capacity. Glenda smiled while thinking, *I'm one over, but who's counting?*

M was now also finished, "So how was your sleep last night? I see you are both up early and look ready to go."

Traveler looked at M and said, "I bet you know the books gave us a wake-up kick to get going early this morning, right?" M smiled and nodded.

Glenda added, "I think the operative word right now is 'going'. Based on our caveman attire, the question is 'Go where?'"

Chapter 17

Threats Everywhere

"Direct as usual, Glenda, you have cut to the chase. 'Go where?' is indeed the pertinent question. You two have a most unusual trip in your immediate future. Your attire is a clue that it's an adventure trip and there are serious challenges involved."

"No surprise there," said Traveler. "I bet these challenges are all, shall I say it, potential killers."

"Yes, you are admittedly going on a hazardous trip, but you are the hunters. As you recall there was one fire beast that escaped from the museum. You need to track it down and neutralize it."

Noticing both of their stunned looks, M continued.

"Let's start with the rather obvious question of how to neutralize the creature. Sadly neither Theo nor I have that answer. Nonetheless, we believe you will find the answer when you need to. Don't fear the challenge, accept it and attack it.

"The answer to the second question regarding the 'where' of the journey is more, how shall I say, interesting."

"Forgive me for interrupting, M, but when you use the word 'interesting' a big shiver goes down my spine. Am I right to worry? Were my books worrying last night and keeping me awake?"

M gave her a reassuring smile back, "Glenda, 'worry' is such an underappreciated word. If we did not worry and by extension fear, we would still be living in caves. Worry is a big part of what ultimately makes good things happen. For example, you worried over an upcoming math test so you worked a lot of problems and then you received a good result. Worry leads to effort leading to good results.

"Now permit me to answer the 'where' question. You will be going to a remote part of the Carpathian Mountains. The creature is there and needs to be neutralized."

Interrupting M, a nervous Traveler declared, "Yeah we know, neutralized. Why not leave well enough alone and let it stay in some mountain cave and rot?"

M responded with a sympathetic look and a soft tone of voice, "Of course you have raised a valid question. Sadly, these fire creatures never 'rot away'. Once with us they stay until they decide to leave or are neutralized. When joined by other creatures their power increases exponentially, so we need to neutralize this one while it is isolated."

Accepting M's explanation Traveler continued, "If I recall my sixth-grade geography and my vampire stories, the Carpathian Mountains are in central and eastern Europe and border a large region called Transylvania. The Carpathians were mentioned a number of times in the second *Ghostbusters* movie."

Traveler felt himself relaxing as he was now rolling with his history recall, "The famous Count Dracula lived there in an ancient castle. It's called Bran castle and is a Romanian tourist destination today.

"Dracula was based on a real person whose proper name was Vlad Tepes. His father was Vlad Dracul, which means dragon. Vlad Tepes was, and still is, a hero in the region since he fought numerous invading Turkish armies. He impaled thousands of the sultan's soldiers and allegedly drank their blood.

"These stories led to his becoming known as Vlad the Impaler. The Dracul family name morphed into Dracula and he became the source for the blood-drinking vampire of legend."

Seeing the concerned looks passing across Glenda's face Traveler gave a nervous laugh adding, "Do you think we could recruit the immortal bloodsucker to neutralize the fire beast?"

Glenda was not bothered about vampires, she knew fact from fiction. She simply waited patiently until Traveler had finished with his vampire lore and his gallows humor then she said, "M, exactly what mischief can the creature do in a remote mountain forest? Keeping it isolated seems to me like a solid plan to neutralize it if not kill it."

"Nodding at her rhetorical question M answered, "That would be a sound plan, Glenda, however Theo believes the fire creature intends to gain control over the people of this remote region. Once it controls the people it will use them to build a portal to bring in the full host.

"If it succeeds then the host will locate Theo and absorb him thus gaining his knowledge. With Theo's knowledge the host will become a threat to our entire universe."

Frowning again, Glenda continued, "A threat to the universe? You've got to be kidding. Why use Traveler and me? The Carpathian Mountains are part of Hungary and Romania. Those two countries should be able to destroy any portal or the creature itself.

"This is modern Europe we're talking about with satellite surveillance, drones, airborne troops, and nuclear weapons if need be. The creature will need to stay hidden to survive. No chance it starts building the portal and making itself a target for modern firepower."

"Well, the rub is that it's not Europe as you know it."

Traveler joined Glenda in immediately pushing back, "Not Europe? When did Europe suddenly disappear?"

M understood their justified challenge, there was a lot they had yet to absorb. "The geographic region we frequently call Europe, with countries on a map called Hungary, Romania, Germany, Italy, or France did not yet exist in the time period you two are going. Your trip will be to the mid-fifth century, let say around AD 440 to 450."

Glenda and Traveler sat with stunned expressions. "No way," was all Traveler could finally say.

"That's science fiction stuff," added Glenda. "Time traveling DeLorean cars are Hollywood make believe."

M listened patiently then replied, "Actually, there is a way and the fire creature has already used it. Theo will send you there using physics that's far beyond our current science."

"You are boggling my mind, M, but assuming we can actually get there, why this particular time and place?" asked Glenda.

"Our beast has cleverly chosen a time and place when great social upheaval is occurring. The region had become the eastern boundary of the Roman empire around AD 220. Once Rome had conquered the region it changed the name from Darcia to Romania with Romania being the Latin word meaning 'of Roman origin'. Of course, that name is still with us today for the country we call Romania.

"Over the next several hundred years the conquered region enjoyed what is referred to by historians as 'Pax Romana' meaning the 'peace of Rome'. Business flourished and people felt safe in their homes at night. However, when you are going to the region, Rome is a rapidly collapsing empire. Pax Romana is in the distant past. Rome itself was already sacked in 410 by Alaric, a Germanic leader of the fierce Visigoths. The final fall of Rome is coming shortly by 476.

"Think of this time and place as the Wild West with the cowboys in charge. These cowboys are a mix of indigenous regional warlords and Asiatic invaders from the east called 'the Hun'. The Hun, under their leader Attila, are intent on conquering all of Europe.

"A little knowledge about Attila will help you fit in with the local people. Trust me everyone knows about him, so must you.

"Attila was a brilliant military leader the equal of Caesar and Hannibal. His foes called him 'The Scourge of God', and that pretty much described him. He was a scorched earth, take no prisoners, invader. Transylvania is merely a region he needed to pass through to enter greater Europe."

Listening to M's description of Attila, Traveler shook his head, "I guess having the nickname Scourge of God pretty much says it all."

Glenda nodded, "OK, I get the Attila threat business, but I'm confused. Rome is obviously still around today, and while it has a lot of crumbling columns and scarred statues, this Attila never destroyed it. If he was such a big threat, what happened?"

"There is much we don't know about history. We do know that Attila led his army to the gates of Rome but then retreated. We have no idea why. The 'why' is one of history's great mysteries."

"Why don't you and Theo join us? Theo could easily defeat a single fire creature and put an end to this portal business. Why send us to the Wild West as a pair of lone rangers? Why not bring the serious cavalry?"

"That question, Glenda, strikes to the very heart of this mission. Yes, Theo could easily defeat this single creature, however a far greater confrontation is coming. The two of you must grow much stronger to become the allies that Theo will need for that confrontation.

"The two of you have reached a point in your development where your enhanced skills, developed by the books alone, are not enough. You need adversarial experiences with serious consequences to continue your growth."

Seeing the many disturbed emotions running across their faces, M leaned back and projected a comforting attitude. "Have confidence that both Theo and I fully believe in you. You will meet the challenges as you have successfully met others. Remember, you escaped the fire creature ambush in our alley."

Traveler loved history and he had listened carefully to every word. Looking at M he asked, "I get that these Huns are bad news for the locals, but do we really need to worry about them? Why not stay focused on the fire creature and do our best against him. He's the only true threat to us, right?"

Glenda sent Traveler a sad smile as she answered for M, "Traveler, I think what M is really saying is that it's testing time for us. Despite M's optimistic spin, I believe the unspoken challenge for us is one of survival against lots of threats. The big question is, do we measure up as future allies?" Looking at M she asked, "Are there more threats you can identify to help us survive?"

Again, she cuts to the chase. "Of course Glenda, let me share more about day to day threats in fifth-century Transylvania. These threats come from the indigenous people and the wild beasts. Of course, disease is the greatest threat for the general population but you two having modern vaccinations are fine against that.

"The indigenous people are dangerous due to their superstitions and their survival habits. They survive in part by never trusting strangers. Their knee-jerk reaction to strangers is to assume bad intentions and ask questions later. This is truly a dog-eat-dog world and few people survive past age thirty."

Trying to add some levity M grinned, "But wait there's more! Beyond the fire creature and human dangers there are serious animal threats. In this time period much of Europe is covered by dense first-growth forests and you will need to navigate through these forests.

"The forests are home to stalking carnivores including wolves, huge wild boars, stalking cats the size of Theo, and enormous bears. These predators have no fear of man. Man is just another weak, slow-moving meal to them.

"Attacks can and will come unexpectedly from many different adversaries. Be cautious and plan ahead, but keep yours plans flexible. Remember what the Scottish poet Robert Burns so aptly said, 'The best laid plans of mice and men oft go astray'. Plan yes, but be prepared to change a plan on a moment's notice."

"I've got a big question M, but it's not about our mission," said Glenda. "I don't fully understand the creature's focus on Theo."

"The fire creatures have experienced the unpredictable nature of our universe since their inception. They seek to understand why the universe sometimes behaves like a predictable clock and other times like a roll of the dice. They believe that Theo has the answers to understanding and controlling these unpredictable forces.

"They further believe that by absorbing Theo and gaining his knowledge, they can alter the universe. In a sense they will convert the universe into a very large laboratory for their experimentation."

Glenda and Traveler were shaking their heads in disgust as they visualized the universe being altered at the whim of the creatures. Traveler opined, "To use a fitting phrase from modern psychology, they're psychopaths. They're evil and they're nuts."

Chuckling M said, "Well, I agree their objectives do seem evil from our point of view, however; be careful about judging them too harshly. You may consider their motivations as being not terrible dissimilar to our own."

"How is that?" asked a skeptical Traveler.

"Scientists in many countries are currently conducting experiments to alter life. They actively study *microcondial DNA* and use tools such as *CRISPR-Cas9* to modify our own body's DNA structure at the cellular level.

"At the furthest edge of cellular research, scientists are pursuing the resurrection of extinct animals by inserting their DNA into a living animal. We may see a return of a woolly mammoth born to an elephant. While there is a great deal of philosophical controversy about this resurrection goal, nonetheless the experiments will continue. Future warfare may well be waged based on superior DNA changes.

"So, humans, much like the fire creatures, have an insatiable quest for knowledge. The price we pay to gain that knowledge is often ignored."

Traveler repeated, "There's a big difference. Humans are trying to improve life while the creatures destroy it without regard to consequences. Case closed."

M nodded while thinking, *That's a simplistic distinction, Traveler, but this is not the time for a philosophical discussion.*

Chapter 18

What's in a Name?

Looking at M Glenda asked, "Is there anything else we can do to give ourselves an edge in surviving?"

"There is, Glenda. Now bear with me on this, but giving the fire creature a name will help you to confront it. By naming it you demystify it. It becomes more like a person and less an all-conquering demi-god. I suggest we give it a name right now. Permit me to review names that have been used in the distant past for these creatures.

"The top bad god in Norse mythology was called 'Surtr'. Surtr is described as the ultimate fire monster. Viking legend says he existed forever. According to Viking legend, Surtr fights in the final battle, called Ragnarök, against the Norse gods led by Odin.

"Theo assures me that Ragnarök did happen, he was there. It was a confrontation many thousands of years ago in the far north between Theo and the host. After testing the power of the host, Theo was forced to flee.

"Modern science would explain the legend of Ragnarök as the result of a volcanic eruption in the far north. Combine that eruption with the northern lights and the indigenous ice age people of Scandinavian would naturally view the flashing red sky and trembling earth as a war between gods.

"The next name choices come from the mythology of the Middle East. These names include genie, jinn, demon, and efreet."

Traveler became animated as he said, "I've read about all of them in *Tales of the Arabian Nights*. I don't think we should use the name efreet, the efreet were the fire beings at the top of the supernatural pyramid. Supposedly they stood twelve feet tall and weighed over 2000 pounds and they had powerful magic. I think the efreet could actually have been multiple fire beings who combined themselves for increased power.

"The individual entities, call them jinn, genie, and demon, were likely solo fire creatures but still with great power. All of these creatures are described as having red eyes so that fits into their being a part of the greater host."

M nodded at Traveler's conjecture. "That is my belief also. Now let's do our naming. Glenda, what's your name pick?"

"I'll go with jinn, I like how it sounds.

Traveler nodded in agreement. "I'll go with jinn also. It has a ring to it."

Smiling M declared, "It's unanimous, my choice is jinn. Now when you see one, hopefully at a distance, you'll know what to call it besides an unflattering swear word.

"Now that you are prepared, let's get the adventure show on the road."

Chapter 19

Time Marches Backward

Looking at Glenda Traveler gave a sigh, "I think the talking is over and it's time to 'saddle up, pardner'."

"Back at you, pardner," Glenda said. Then needing some levity to help calm herself, she said, "M, I accept that you're going to show us how we can drive backwards in time. Should I wear cool driving gloves for my DeLorian?"

Traveler chuckled at her joke while inside he was a clenched fist. Mirroring Glenda's humor he added, "Watch out for our time-travel turbulence, Harry Potter, don't fall off your broomstick."

Watching the two put on their game faces and false bravado, M knew they were feeling scared and gave an added reassurance, "Trust me that deciding to send you both back was a difficult decision. Losing either of you would be devastating. Theo and I searched for millennia to finally find you two. You are both as valuable to Theo as I am. Remember we believe in you." M watched their bodies relax slightly and thought, *That seemed to perk them up, at least for a moment.*

"Well that's nice to know," said Traveler trying to joke. "If we go down in flames, we'll create an inconvenient ripple in time for you and Theo."

M shook his head with look that said, "Don't think that way even when joking."

Glenda gave an accepting shrug, and said, "M, it looks like we have our mission laid out so why don't we get on with this adventure."

"I'm ready! Let's saddle up and head for the Wild West right now." Suddenly pausing Traveler asked, "Can I go to the bathroom first?"

M laughed and said, "Of course. It's recommended and necessary. While your travel time will seem short, you will depart and arrive with a churning stomach filled with butterflies. The bathroom is your friend right now and also when you arrive."

Traveled grinned, "M, you sound like my dad before a road trip. Besides calling out 'mache schnell' his other order was 'go to the bathroom, we're not stopping'."

"Your father is clearly a wise, veteran traveler. Now a couple of necessary things while you're in there. Please shower again. Scrub off the sweet smell of soap, deodorant, and hairspray. Scrub hard. Glenda attack that pile of hair, leave no conditioner hiding in there.

"Even the rich back then had a very personal aroma about them. Part of your fitting-in will be looking and smelling like the average person. Your clothes, as you may have noticed, already have a faint aroma of a dusty barnyard added."

Motioning for them to head to their rooms he added, "When you're ready I'll see you both right here. Take your time. Time really does stand still for us in here."

Chapter 20

A Brave Old World

After a scrubbing in the shower and a visit to the necessary, Traveler studied his traveling wear. He looked like a sad Indiana Jones wearing Goodwill rejects. His brown wool trousers were held up by a rope-like belt. The belt had no buckle and had to be knotted to hold up the pants. His shirt served as a coat and was a loose-fitting, heavy, gray smock.

Finally, he looked at the footwear, a pair of broken-in old leather hiking boots with thick soles and heavy woolen socks. The boots slipped onto his feet without laces or buckles. The socks resulted in a firm fit to avoid blistering. Standing up, the resulting footwear was a surprisingly comfortable fit. *Low on style but quite functional, I like that.*

Looking in his mirror and he said "One average peasant coming out to pick turnips, potatoes, roots, or whatever they ate back then."

When he got to the door he had a sudden urge to visit the bathroom again. *M is right about stress and what it does to our bodies.*

He made a final inspection of his room and then went out the door. He thumped on Glenda's door in passing. "Mach schnell, princess." There was no answer. *Probably still showering to lose the perfume, guys can move so much faster.*

When he got to the meeting table, he saw Glenda and M were inspecting a pair of backpacks. *I guess guys are not necessarily faster at everything,* he thought.

Glenda looked up and made a snorting sound. "My man is wearing the very finest in wool this morning. He is a definite fashion statement for today's Dark Age peasant."

Traveler sniffed the air. "I smell something but I can't quite figure it out. Am I back in my high school gym?"

This time Glenda laughed, "I think we're both going to know the answer to that odor question too soon. I'll pretend I don't notice yours if you ignore mine." Traveler grinned back.

"M is walking me through our carry-ons. We're traveling light. Turns out, what we can take is limited to either living things, like us, or prior living things like sandwiches, fruit, and of course, our clothing. No bazookas for us to neutralize threats. Are you up for this, big boy?"

"I'm here and I guess I'm ready to go. Honestly, I feel like we're going to be jumping out of a plane with no parachute."

"I like your skydiving analogy," said M, "it fits this situation. When major challenges are staring you in the face, the best course of action is to just get on with it. During the US Civil War, the Union Admiral David Farragut may have said it best. His fleet was faced with underwater explosive mines. Rather than delay his attack he ordered, 'Damn the torpedoes, full speed ahead'.

"Now please follow me to our launch pad. You will find that rather than jumping out and plummeting down you will feel more like you're jumping sideways or maybe like dice being shaken in a closed container. Think blender."

They proceeded to a far corner of the floor that had an elevated circular lip coming up just below their knees. The lip was an opaque, cream-colored material and was shimmering. The floor inside the circle appeared made from the same material and was also shimmering. The scientist in Traveler thought for a moment, *What kind of material is that? It's a solid for sure but seems to have ripples pulsating inside.*

M handed each of them a woolen bracelet. "Please put this bracelet on your wrist. Either wrist works. The bracelet is your time-traveling instrument but looks like a peasant's arm decoration. Don't lose it. Time travel will be activated when you press your bracelets together so opposite wrists may be appropriate."

Beckoning them forward M instructed, "Trust me this is easy. Just step into the center of that small circle."

As they stepped over the elevated lip, they found themselves toe to toe and nose to nose. An embarrassed Traveler said, "Tight fit, M."

"Actually, it needs to get a tad tighter; your travel bags are joining you at your feet. Each of you needs to hold the other person tightly. Imagine you are at a prom and slow dancing with hand in hand and arms around each other's waist. You need a little dancing music and I think 'Stardust' may create the appropriate mood."

For a brief moment Traveler recalled "Stardust" playing in the bar car while traveling with his mom to Chicago. With the melody in his mind he found himself relaxing with Glenda's presence and hand on his back. Dancing was suddenly becoming quite acceptable.

A grinning Glenda said, "I can lead this dance, big boy, in case you don't know how to slow dance." Traveler now had creeping red in his cheeks. *He looks pretty good wearing embarrassment*, Glenda chuckled to herself.

"Now what?" asked Traveler, ignoring Glenda's gibe. "How do we know we're not going to land underground or in the middle of the ocean?"

"You will land safely. The bracelet is an all-purpose navigation device and is sensitive to placing you in landing areas that are suitable for a living being. Trust the bracelet."

Traveler did not look convinced about his navigation bracelet. M gave him a sympathetic smile and said, "President Reagan used an old Russian proverb while negotiating nuclear disarmament talks with the Russians, 'Trust but verify'. You will shortly find that landing verification is on its way."

Shaking his head Traveler persisted in a very quiet voice, "How do we verify we're even on the same continent as our friendly jinn? We could wander forever in a desert or be wolf food somewhere in Norway."

Listening to him, M understood Traveler's questions were really a way to postpone the scary trip.

Giving both students a reassuring look he said, "Theo knows approximately where the jinn is from its vibration and will place you close enough. However, even Theo has to move cautiously in your landing placement. If he sets you down too close, then the jinn could possibly detect your entry vibration.

"The bracelet will place you close enough to the jinn so that you can approach it without alerting it to your presence, but not too close. You will likely have some forest hiking in store. I believe your boots will be up to that task quite nicely. By the way, these boots have self-generating soles and will never wear out.

"Once you have settled into this time period your own masking abilities will hide your vibration signals from the jinn. The ambush advantage is yours."

Glenda moved her head past Traveler's to look at M. "Will the beast be obvious to see? Is it floating around and visible to everyone?" Traveler was suddenly aware he could barely see M through the auburn red haze.

"Well, there's the rub. Theo has not determined how the beast is presenting itself. It will likely not appear in its natural form. We expect it will appear in a form that permits it to be interacting with humans without disclosing its true self. It could be a cat, dog, or a human, young or old."

"Assuming we figure out where it's hiding, any suggestions on how we neutralize it?"

"That is, of course, the unmarked road for your continued development. Use your combined wits and powers as they fit each situation. You have powers of stealth, strength, leaping, reflex speed, and striking power. Each of these skills is far beyond what the jinn expects from humans. Additionally, your minds are continuing to develop, they are your greatest asset.

"Remember, though, people will react adversarially toward anything they perceive to be out of the ordinary. At all times you need to appear as normal, young adults."

"Final big question, M," said Traveler. "How do we get back?"

"As soon as your bracelets determine that the beast's vibration is silenced you may return by assuming the slow dance position and pressing your bracelets together. Your bracelets will understand the message and return you.

"Any last thoughts or feelings you wish to express?"

Traveler found himself thinking, *A man's last words while sitting in the electric chair. Go away, bad thought.*

Glenda said, "I'd be lying if I didn't say how scared I am. I sure don't feel like a Valkyrie. This may be a brave, new world we're going to, but I feel far from brave."

"A little honesty on my part," said Traveler, "my mind is swirling around Lord Tennyson's poem, 'The Charge of the Light Brigade'. I feel like one of those English horsemen charging the Russian cannon, 'Half a league onward. Into the valley of death rode the six hundred. Theirs but to do and die.'"

M smiled, "The 'Charge' is an apt poem for this occasion. Let me remind you that the poem ends with many of the six hundred returning from their heroic charge. Use your minds as sabers to cut down that creature. You will return victorious, I am sure of it."

Glenda last thought was, *There is a poet hiding in big boy, I would never have thought it. Very cool, Traveler.*

Traveler was scrambling to ask something else when he saw that a towering fifteen-foot-tall Theo was beside M. Theo was now in command. With a final question hanging dead on his lips he heard M say, "Now think of a roller coaster in many dimensions. Hang on tight. Trust the bracelets and trust each other."

The moment they pressed their bracelets together they were sucked into an open elevator shaft. The random dice of the universe began to bounce them together in their space-time container.

Chapter 21

The Time Eagles Have Landed

They landed like two slices of bread stuck together in a peanut butter sandwich. They were clutching each other so closely they could barely breathe. Both had their eyes squeezed shut and their mouths were grimaces. Glenda's hair was wrapped around Traveler's face. Their noses were touching when they opened their eyes and stared at each other.

Every cell in their bodies felt like a dying, space-time echo. "I have to vomit," were the first words out of Traveler's mouth. Glenda nodded in agreement. They each scrambled to find a close by tree for privacy and started the process of adjusting their bodies to the nausea of the Einstein travel.

When they emerged from behind their trees Glenda had a sheepish look and said, "I've never been seasick but I guess this is how it feels."

"Personally," said Traveler, "I feel like Kermit the frog. I must be green, I sure feel green. Just a little detail M failed to prepare us for. I need to sit down and get myself settled."

They sat down facing each other in a cross-legged position. Glenda took a deep breath, "Wow, I feel like a squeezed orange."

"Think I'm a lemon," said Traveler. "I can't decide whether I'm green or yellow. Would you mind if I lie down and take a catnap? I can't imagine moving right now, much less trying to hike. My emotional gas tank is below empty."

"A catnap is exactly what I was thinking. Open your backpack, there's a blanket in there."

Traveler opened his pack found the blanket on top and immediately rolled it into a pillow. He put the pillow under his head, yawned and said, "Nap well, princess, see you in a while."

Glenda had already completed her own pillow-making arrangement and thought, *Nice to be called a princess again. It's good he brought a little normalcy from Chicago to the forest.* "Sleep well, big boy, please don't snore."

Neither knew how long they slept, all their bodies knew was that it was a deep, refreshing sleep. "Are you awake?" Glenda asked in a quiet voice.

"I'm not sure. Are we really in some ancient forest right now or is this a virtual-reality game M is using as part of our training?"

Glenda sat up to study the surrounding forest. "Sadly, this is no training game. Yeah, we're in a forest with lots of very big, very old trees. I could imagine Tarzan swinging by to drop in on us; better yet Robin Hood." To herself she smiled thinking *Either Tarzan or Robin joining us would suit this princess fine right now.*

Traveler was now standing and studying an ancient oak tree. The trunk was nearly as wide as the giant sequoia trees in Yosemite National Park. Looking up he said, "I can't tell if it's getting dark because the sun is going down or if the canopy of limbs stops the sun's rays. What do you think?"

Glenda was also studying the overhead covering. "I think it's a lot darker than when we arrived. I imagine Theo wanted us to get here with enough daylight so we could calm down after that trip. I don't know how long we napped but enough to get most of our equilibrium back."

Glancing up again, Glenda said, "Right now I think it's getting dark. We need to decide where we'll spend the night. Forests at night are not good places to hang out in."

"I agree. It's time to hunker down in a safe place. We need a lot more solid sleep for our bodies and minds to recover. I feel like I'm still running on empty. I suggest we become monkeys and rest up above where we'll be well out of reach of any floor hunters. I don't think wolves climb trees, do they Miss Norway?"

Glenda smiled at the rhetorical question; she knew they were just making conversation to help in adjusting to their new surroundings. "Our Norwegian bears climb trees but not our wolves; however our wolves can jump really high."

"If a bear comes climbing up, I'll give it a kick it won't believe," Traveler said. "That bear will meet a tree demon it won't like, not one little bit." With a thoughtful look he added, "Seriously, we need to climb high enough not to tempt any hungry ground animal, wolf or bear. Let's go tree exploring."

Standing there they looked up and began to survey the surrounding forest for candidate trees offering secure overnight lodging. "So many choices," said Glenda, "trees everywhere."

Traveler laughed, "That's why it's called a forest." Glenda laughed back.

With her head twisting around Glenda said more to herself, "This reminds me of the poem about an ancient mariner lost at sea. He is dying of thirst and laments 'Water, water, everywhere and not a drop to drink'. Unlike that sad mariner, our problem is that we have many tree choices, but are there any acceptable ones? Do you see a winner, big boy?"

"I do, and my pick is right here," and he walked to a massive oak and patted it.

"Works for me but what made you pick it out?"

"Boy scout training. We used to build tree houses and had to find trees with the right limbs to build on. If you look up a-ways, you will notice there are massive limbs that are close together. They are growing out of the trunk almost side by side and appear to be making a natural resting platform. They're easily strong enough to hold a dozen of us."

Glenda studied the limb architecture and finally saw what Traveler was describing, "Well done, Scout Traveler. Now that I see it, you're absolutely right about the natural platform. It's like a nest made for tree people. I don't think I could have spotted it. All I see looking up is a maze of limbs and leaves, they all blur together."

Traveler was enjoying the compliment, he liked being called "Scout Traveler" instead of the slightly pejorative "big boy".

"How do we proceed?" asked Glenda.

"I'll be the first monkey up the tree. I'm no Tarzan but I do have some tree-climbing experience." With that Traveler studied a lower access limb. The limb was about fifteen feet off the ground and very thick. Studying the distance, he made a measured vertical leap and soared above the limb. Slowing he grabbed a nearby limb and hugged the tree for balance. His feet were now resting on the thick lower limb.

"So far, so good. I'm going to climb up to our nest and check it out."

Glenda was impressed as she watched him ascend among the forest of limbs. She laughed to herself thinking, *All boys must have some ape DNA left in them. My classroom certainly had its share of monkeys.*

Traveler returned back down to the lower starting limb. Looking down at Glenda he said, "Found it! A perfect crow's nest, it's even better than what I thought. Toss me up the backpacks and I'll get them up to the nest, then we'll get you up here."

Glenda nodded and tossed the first pack up. Traveler caught it and put it on his back, then called down, "I can take the second one now." Glenda nodded again and threw a perfect strike at his outstretched hand." She mentally patted herself on the back and thought, *Girls can pitch fine, we just need practice.*

Traveler disappeared again into the limb forest. He returned shortly to their starting access limb. "Can I offer a little advice before you start up?"

"Sure, advise away."

"I suggest you attend to your body's natural duties before getting up here."

Glenda felt her cheeks turning a nice red then thought, *Of course he's right, let me get on with it.*

Several minutes later she was again under the tree looking up. "I'm all set. Could you please get out of the way?"

Looking down Traveler cautioned, "Sure I will, but let's err on the side of safety. I'm going to hold onto another limb and grab you on the way up. You are the greater leaper as I recall."

"Sounds good. My equilibrium is still a little iffy from our roller-coaster trip. Ready or not, here I come."

Glenda made a calculated leap but put a bit too much kick in it. She was still going up when Traveler grabbed her arm and pulled her down to rest beside him.

"You don't know your own strength," he said. "By the way, those were two nice 'over the plate', strike pitches with the packs. I see a baseball contract in your future."

Glenda grinned. "No contract if I had clobbered myself on the way up. Thanks for being this pitcher's catcher, I owe you one."

Traveler turned to head up saying, "Watch where I place my feet. Always be secure with a handhold before moving up to the next footrest. I love trees but they can be dangerous."

Glenda said nothing but concentrated on following him up. Then he suddenly disappeared. Out of the darkness above an arm reached down to her and a voice said. "Can a gentleman give a lady a hand?"

Traveler did a Roman grip on Glenda's forearm and she returned the grip. Securely locked together Traveler easily swung her up into the nest.

Chapter 22

Above the Fray

"Wow, Mr Scout, you sure know how to pick em!" Glenda was sitting comfortably on a crisscross of limbs. The limbs created a smooth platform over eight feet across. It extended out from the trunk for over a dozen feet before individual limbs separated on their journeys to find sunlight.

Their platform was a secure nest with sides. There were smaller side limbs coming out from the trunk that created railings that protected against falling out. About four feet above their heads were canopy limbs offering shelter from heavy rains or winds.

The tree nest reminded Traveler of his upper bunk in the train ride to Chicago. *I think boys just know where to find the best places to rest and hide. That's probably how we survived during the ice ages.*

"How high up are we?" asked Glenda.

"Not really sure, probably at least forty feet or maybe fifty feet. No fear of jumping creatures. The trees and overhead limbs cut out most of the view either up or down. I know we are in one very old and very big grandfather of an oak tree. It's amazing how this all started with an acorn, Mother Nature was the original magician. We'll get our bearings tomorrow by climbing to the top for a look-around view."

Glenda nodded and thought *I'll let you lead the way on this tree climbing. Don't think it's my cup of tea. Speaking of tea, I think it's time for a little dinner.* "There are nice sandwiches in our packs and I'm really hungry."

"When you're right, you're right. It's definitely time to chow down." The wit in him added, "Well, technically from here we'll be chowing up." Glenda wrinkled her nose back at him.

"Very funny. Now not to insult you, scout, but M suggested we ration them until we have a replacement food supply." Chuckling, she added, "I think he was talking more to you than me."

"Guilty as charged," Traveler laughed back. "I'll try to control my inner wolf, now let's see what our choices are."

They went into their packs and found layers of food. The top layer was smoked chicken layered on M's heavy black bread. Beside the sandwiches were oranges. "Looks great, my inner wolf is already drooling. The oranges must be here to give us fluid before we find a source of water. And here's a pack of oatmeal cookies, it's a treetop feast! Thank you, M."

They rationed out the meal, one sandwich, one cookie, and one orange. They looked down at the acceptable but limited meal and considered the endless food back in the sanctuary. Traveler thought, *A feast because M made it, but unfortunately a really small feast.*

Watching Traveler study the food, Glenda said, "Eat slowly. Slow chewing makes it seem like more."

Traveler nodded, he knew she was right but his belly was already voting for more. Glenda's belly was sending the same desperate message to her mouth. Both of them ordered their minds to tell their stomachs to shut up. Their bellies accepted this harsh command but knew they would shortly be back in hunger court asking the brain judge to ease up.

Taking a few studied bites and doing his best to chew slowly, Traveler looked at Glenda, "Are you concerned we had a one-way ticket to get here, but not one back? We only return if we defeat the jinn."

"Of course I'm concerned, how could I not be? But when we signed up we knew failure meant we'd be stuck here forever, or worse. Isn't that what you thought?"

Traveler continued to chew his sandwich slowly. "Yeah, I understood that, but did we really have a choice? I think that's why they're called 'suicide missions'. You feel compelled to go even though the odds are really stacked against you."

"Well let's beat the odds. M and Theo believe we will, and I trust them. I also think there's no return ticket because if it unconditionally worked the jinn would be aware of us and know Theo is hunting it. The jinn would simply move to another time and place and everything would start over."

"Bummer," said Traveler. "Your logic, as always, is spot on. This is our 'advance or die' time so I'll stop whining." Glenda gave an encouraging smile back.

Once they were finished eating it was close to pitch dark. They had anticipated the darkness and had their makeshift beds ready. The tree limb platform was warm enough and they used their blankets to keep the chilly night air at bay. For a moment their individual brains suggested that a closer contact would offer more heat, but neither acknowledged this logical move.

As they were drifting into sleep, they heard the night forest waking up. Scampering sounds came from the floor. Battles of wit were taking place between predators and prey. Both had to eat, yet avoid being eaten. Larger predators had to stalk quietly while their empty bellies made them anxious for a meal.

Among the scampering sounds were the heavy treads of large alpha animals. The larger animals could not walk as softly so they used their size to make noises hoping that a prey would panic and bolt. Older prey knew the scare game and would remain motionless while a predator passed within inches, that's how they became older.

Foolish young prey were the ones most likely to bolt and become dinner. Nature knew how to thin the herd while maintaining the balance. Only the fit, either predator or prey, survived.

The last sound that Traveler and Glenda heard was a sad lament from a hungry, lone wolf. No longer able to hunt with the pack, it was on its own. Dinner was increasingly elusive for it; the wolf knew its predator days were numbered.

Chapter 23

A Tree with a View

Morning gradually announced itself. It arrived like a series of blinds being slowly twisted open. The gibbous moon from the night before was reluctant to leave its place in the sky but the sun prevailed as it always did. Sunlight eventually reached the two sleepers and worked its wakeup magic. They stirred at the same time.

Overnight nature's logic had intervened while they slept. It was cold in the forest and their blankets came up short on providing warmth. Their bodies had sensed a nearby heat source and had instinctively moved toward it. Traveler woke up with his eyes closed still fighting the light. He stretched and clonked Glenda on the side, "Ouch," was the response that had him quickly sitting up and moving away.

"That's one way to wake me up, big boy. Thanks for the poke. Now that I'm awake I'm going back down to the surface."

"Yeah, me too," answered a sheepish Traveler.

Their minds had memorized the tree's ladder of limbs. Without thinking they went down the tree quickly. Using their gravity control skill, their descent was fast and efficient, similar to firemen sliding down the firehouse pole. Once on the ground they headed in opposite directions.

When Traveler returned to the base of the tree, he waited a few minutes for Glenda. *Girls are naturally slower*, he muttered to himself and proceeded to climb back to the nest. When he swung into it, he found Glenda sitting there examining breakfast. "How did you do that?" he asked.

"Easy, girls are also natural monkeys. If we couldn't get up trees quick enough there would not have been any girls. No girls, then no boys. End of story. Let's eat."

Their stomachs had their say before the hunger court judge. They had petitioned the judge to add some extra food to the rationed breakfast meal. "An extra cookie would be appropriate," the stomach argued.

"Maybe and maybe not," the wise brain judge said. "Today's travel is going to be hard work and the body will need more fuel later." The stomach sulked, "You're the boss, but feed me something now if you want me to shut up."

The two proceeded to dig into M's breakfast. There was smoked ham, cheese, thick black bread, cookies, and apples. "I'm saving my apple and cookie for later," said Traveler. "Good decision," replied Glenda while thinking, *That apple and cookie have a half-life of maybe an hour.*

They consumed their minimal breakfast but felt surprisingly energized. Their bodies were starting to adjust to reduced intakes.

"Ready to go mountain climbing on a tree?" Traveler asked.

"To misquote Shakespeare, 'Lead on MacDuff'." Traveler gave her a look that said, *Shakespeare right now, really?*

Traveler seized an overhead limb and began a careful ascent. Glenda gave him climbing space while watching his hand and foot placements. She followed him up and never looked down.

As they moved up and gradually out of the enveloping darkness of the tree's thick canopy, stronger light began to appear. Occasional shafts of bright sunlight cut through the canopy and illuminated leaves and limbs. Curious birds were now visible watching the strange intruders moving in their domain.

"Are we there yet? I'm going to get a nose bleed."

Traveler laughed, "Hang on Jane, Tarzan sees what may be an opening."

After another ten minutes of careful climbing, Traveler called back, "Tarzan now standing on the lookout point and the views are amazing. Take your time, Jane, these views are not going anywhere."

Glenda was quickly beside Traveler. There was a natural grouping of top limbs that formed a casual crow's nest. To avoid getting vertigo they leaned against the remaining thin trunk and held onto the surrounding limbs for additional security. They immediately saw that their treetop perch was above the surrounding canopy. They slowly rotated their bodies to get a panoramic 360-degree view.

"Wow!" Glenda exclaimed. "Let me repeat. Wow, what views! Well done, Scout Traveler. You found the tallest, oldest tree in creation. This is so breathtaking, really stunning. I feel I'm looking down on the world when it was just newborn. Everything is so lush and green and natural. It feels like I'm on the movie set of *Jurassic Park*. I can imagine a 130-foot-long titanosaur happily grazing on the leaves below."

"Not to break the wonderment mood, Jane, but I wish all we had to worry about were dinosaurs. The jinn would make short work of even a T-Rex."

Traveler then extended his right arm and pointed, "Look at the river to the east. That river may be offering us a road map about where to head. Villages are usually found along rivers and we need food and water. I bet the water here is fine for drinking, no human chemicals are being added to rivers in this time period."

"You're right, and I believe I see civilization. Follow the river going to the left, that haze is definitely chimney smoke. Where there's smoke there's people."

"Good eyes, Jane, that's definitely a hamlet. There are open fields around it so this hamlet is likely a farming center. I think we've found our starting destination for food, water, and maybe information about Mr Jinn."

Glenda was continuing to stare out past the hamlet then said, "Is that a solid rock mountain a few miles away rising up behind the fields and hamlet? It reminds me of pictures of the Rock of Gibraltar except it's rising up and out of land rather than the Mediterranean Sea."

Traveler looked where Glenda was pointing and squinted hard, "That's no rock mountain, Glenda, that's one humongous fortress. I think I can see battlements running along the top of huge rock walls.

"And that's not morning fog on top of it, that's smoke from lots of huge fireplaces. Look closely, I think part of the river branches away and flows around it. The river must be serving as a water source and a very wide moat."

Glenda nodded as she focused on the smoking rock mountain. "You're right. I've never seen a real castle, or fortress as the case may be, and this one is really a small mountain. It must be gigantic inside."

Traveler was captivated by the fortress, "I think that's a Roman fortress since it's built using stone rather than wood. I bet that's the stronghold that controls this whole region. The Romans must have built it a long time ago to secure this region against local warlords and eastern invaders. It has also stood up to Father Time."

Glenda tapped Traveler on his shoulder, "Turn all the way around, Traveler, what do you see?"

Traveler stared out into the vast wilderness. "Big trees and more big trees. This is an endless forest! It may go all the way west to the Atlantic Ocean."

Nodding Glenda said, "Yes, and thanks to Theo we have been placed fairly close to the edge of the endless forest. If we were a few more miles back into it we'd feel like Lewis and Clark crossing an endless American wilderness. Now that we know where to go, I guess we might as well get started. Are you feeling lucky?"

Traveler winced, "Lucky? Not so much. But yeah, I guess it's hiking time. Let's head for that village and meet some locals." Then laughing, he added, "I think we can skip asking subtle questions with these bumpkin farmers. We'll just ask for directions to their local fire demon. I bet they know a lot."

They started down the tree and took their time descending. They climbed from limb to limb. Their footing was secure but their nerves were not. Both had their minds on the challenge ahead and neither wanted to try a faster descent.

When they finally got back to their sleeping nest, they sat down to settle themselves. "One last little cookie snack before starting?" asked Traveler as he reached into his backpack.

"OK, but save something, you may need it later. I'm going to save my last two cookies and apple, they may be all we have for the rest of the day. Remember food is survival for these village people and I doubt they'll be inclined to share with a couple of strangers."

Half listening to Glenda, Traveler's stomach welcomed the cookie while thinking, *I always get what I want. Brains never get hungry so they don't understand.*

The brain responded, *You'll regret this later, Mr Pig. Act with self-control like the girl and survive.*

As they were ready to descend to the forest floor Traveler quipped, "Do you think we'll ever be out of the woods on this mission?" Glenda shook her head at his weak pun. "Sorry princess, but I'm trying to keep a little humor going, I think humor may serve us as well as food."

"Humor accepted and appreciated." Smiling, Glenda continued, "Seriously, I think we need to make our opening moves very carefully. We certainly don't want to alert the creature we're here and it may have spies. Let's casually approach a local and find out how the village works and who's in charge."

Then she added her own deprecating humor, "Let's ask about their turnip crop this year. We'll say we just fell off our turnip wagon and need directions. A grinning Traveler shook his head. *She can make a joke, good for her.*

Chapter 24

Life in a Field

With the food inhaled they accepted it was time to move ahead. Traveler said, "I think I know the best way out of these woods to the open fields we spotted. Mind if I take the lead?"

"You lead and I'll follow, you are the scout here."

Traveler only heard the "I'll follow" and felt his spirits take a little jump up.

"The good news is the floor is easy to walk on. The overhead canopy is so dense there's not much growing down here."

They descended from their sleeping quarters until they finally reached the soft forest floor. Having their feet back on the ground was reassuring, now they would move horizontally rather than vertically. Resting on the ground they paused for a few minutes to center mind and body. When they were ready they nodded at each other and began their hike toward the village.

They walked for a number of hours constantly weaving around trees and occasional thickets. Time in the forest without a watch was difficult to judge. Just as Glenda was getting ready to ask Traveler if his mental compass was working, they both saw the beginning of the field in front of them. "I see light at the end of this forest tunnel!" exclaimed Glenda.

The surrounding trees were all still huge and dense but they ended abruptly with an open field. One minute they were walking sheltered by the overhead canopy and the next they were squinting into bright sun.

"Looks like the farmers have cleared trees for their crop fields," said Traveler. "Man, the clearing must have been impossibly hard to do. Cutting down these trees would have taken forever, then pulling out the stumps must have challenged even the best oxen team."

Motioning to Glenda he said, "Let's do some easy field walking now. I was getting dizzy circling those monster trees."

As Traveler was stepping into the field, he felt Glenda's hand on his arm. "I think a little caution is in order. Let's stay hidden here and check out the field. We don't want to be spotted suddenly appearing out of the primeval woods. People may view us as advance scouts for some raiding party or as thieves."

Then she added, "Plus we're taller than the locals in this time period. Just our size may identify us as trouble. According to M they are paranoid toward strangers and may automatically view us a threat to their livestock, crops, and lives."

"Good point," agreed Traveler. "You move along the right side and I'll take the left side. Staying within the tree line will give cover while we see if there's anything to avoid. Let's meet back here in about an hour."

Pointing up to the sun, extending his arms then stacking the fists he said, "Watch for the sun to drop down to about two stacked hands from the horizon."

"Nice hand-clock Mr Scout and no battery required." With that they parted and moved through the edge of the woods in opposite directions.

On a regular basis each would stop behind a large tree, pause a minute, and survey the field. Every experienced hunter knows that it's movement that draws the watchful eye of stalking animals and people. When the hunter remains stationary, deer quickly continue their feeding.

Glenda was the first to discover a necessary asset. Using her hand-clock, she was about ready to turn back when she saw a nice-sized stream. The stream followed a manmade channel cut away from the river to water the crops. The wide channel branched periodically as it flowed along. It was a clever form of irrigation requiring little effort on the part of the farmers.

One branch flowed into a manmade depression and filled it to create a small pond. The pond was adjacent to the crop field and close to the woods. It was clearly intended as a water source for the workers. They could drink and seek shade under a nearby tree.

She advanced through the tree line until she was directly across from the pond. There were no people visible and she boldly stepped out and crossed to the pond. Kneeling, she studied the placid water. *No visible sediment, it must quickly fall to the bottom. The top water looks as pure as tap water.* Her inspection satisfied she cupped her hands and began to drink. At first she took controlled, slow sips but quickly they were followed by huge gulps. She realized how thirsty she was, the ham sandwiches had created a strong demand for water.

Finally she was satiated. The restorative feeling was wonderful, *We take water for granted but it is truly the elixir of life. You only miss it when you don't have it. We can go many weeks without food, but water is critical after just a few days.*

Chapter 25

Soldiers Arrive

Traveler was quietly watching the workers as they planted. They were a mix of younger children, men, and women. The adults talked among themselves and appeared to be enjoying their task. Occasional chuckles could be heard interspersed with occasional grunts. The children were given wide latitude to plant, then chase each other. The only reprimands came if they ran into a planted area.

Traveler noted the obvious strength of the men. Their forearms and biceps bulged. They had thick chests and necks. *They could replace the oxen to pull out the stumps if need be*, he chuckled to himself.

The women appeared stout but muscular compared to today's standard of model thinness. As he watched the women working, he realized they had developed muscles to efficiently work beside the men. There were no fat adults or children.

He began to see the division of labor between the children, women, and men. This was a group that seemed to enjoy working beside each other. *Physical labor has its rewards*, he thought. *They have learned how to enjoy hard work without complaining about it. The children see their parents hard at work and will copy them as they grow up.*

He did his hand-clock check and realized that considerable time had passed while watching the workers. He was preparing to return to Glenda when a group of mounted men appeared and rode across the planted field toward the farmers. These men were obviously overseers of some sort and barked commands at the male workers.

The largest rider moved close to a large farmer who was clearly unhappy with the message. Traveler watched a short verbal exchange take place. The protesting farmer was arguing his case with the lead rider. The horseman suddenly bent in the saddle and struck the farmer with a gauntlet fist.

The blow was hard enough that the farmer was instantly felled but soft enough not to disable the man. *Don't damage the assets*, Traveler thought. This time the farmer wisely remained prone and quiet. He carefully avoided any eye contact with the mounted soldier. Direct eye contact is easily interpreted as a challenge.

With their message delivered the riders turned their mounts. To make a point they galloped through the recently planted field. New plantings flew up behind the horses' feet as they galloped away. "Know your place, stay in your place," was a clear message to all field workers.

Traveler observed that the standing men were furious. Several shook their fists. The fist-challenge was offered only when the riders' backs were turned away.

The women were the practical peacemakers. They understood the rules of expected behavior and wanted their men to survive the insults from the soldiers. They were clearly advising caution to the angry men. Live today to plant another day was a common sense approach for farmers in the face of superior hostile forces.

While the female adults reacted with calm subservience to the mounted soldiers, they were direct and commanding with the children. They issued sharp commands to the older children that left no room for questioning.

The youngest children instinctively huddled together trembling, seeking comfort from their playmates. Traveler observed the children were behaving like scared puppies after being given a nip by the mother dog. *Misery seeks company*, he thought.

When Traveler finally met up with Glenda he was in an angry mood. Glenda listened then said, "Relax big boy, we are in the Wild West and the cowboys run things. In case you don't know, the cowboys are the guys on the horses. Horses in this time identify the alpha males. Horses are a significant asset and beyond the common peasant's reach.

"Now to balance your mood, I have good news, follow me." She led him through the fringe of the woods then out to the watering pond. "Drink up. I've already been the official taster and I feel great. This pond water is as clear as a mountain stream."

Traveler was amazed at how much he needed the fresh water. He was equally amazed at how much he drank. When he finally lifted his head he simply said, "So necessary. Well spotted."

Chapter 26

It's a Dog's World

As Glenda studied the buildings ahead, she said, "I believe we're coming in from the backside of this village and that's good, we'll be able to get close without being observed. I think the field workers are still down where you saw them and I haven't seen a single person all morning."

Traveler nodded, "Lead on, this field is your scouted turf, I'll follow you."

Glenda accepted the forward scout role and thought, *Finally, big boy is accepting I'm his peer as a leader.* This reflection gave her spirits a nice lift.

Glenda followed the stream through the field toward the hamlet buildings. The stream was both a boundary to the field and also a source of water to the village. Once they were out of the field, they found the main stream which flowed behind a large wooden building. This was the largest structure they saw as they approached and they assumed it had an important role in the village.

As they were studying the back side of the building, low growls were heard coming from around a corner. They instantly froze in place as moments later a pack of very large, brutish appearing dogs rounded a corner. These dogs would dwarf a German shepherd.

The dogs immediately paused, studied them, and sniffed the air. They remained in place but crouched into attack stances. Their lips were pulled back in snarls displaying long, pointed, front teeth. Deep-throated growls were sent as rumbling warnings to the intruders. Traveler and Glenda were clearly in the pack's territory, and were definitely intruders.

Rising over a head above the pack was the alpha male, it was a giant among huge dogs. Its heavily lidded eyes were narrowed as it assessed them. Thick hackle hairs were raised up from its neck and down the length of its back. Traveler thought, *So that's what having its hackles up means. It means serious business is coming, so beware puny human.*

The alpha's powerful rear legs were bent at an angle for springing forward. The intelligent dark eyes continued to sweeping across both of them. Each was a potential victim being placed into an attack order.

Glenda remained frozen in place, she knew not to move as the alpha's eyes assessed her. Any movement and the alpha could launch an attack. She glanced at Traveler to find he appeared relaxed and actually pleased while he studied the alpha.

"Wow! I believe Fido is an old-world Molossus. He is so cool. Molossus are extinct in our time, but were the original big dogs. Their DNA is still present in English mastiffs, making the mastiffs the largest of modern dogs."

Traveler continued his history lesson on dogs as Glenda remained quiet and motionless. "The Molossus fought with the Roman armies, they probably brought them here when they conquered this region. They were a major weapon for the legions, much like elephants were for Hannibal. Barbarians were scared to death of them.

"This big fellow goes well over 350 pounds, maybe a lot more. Look at his muscle definition; he's the King Kong of dogs."

Glenda found she was still holding her breath and finally exhaled. "Thanks for the history lesson, professor. Personally, I would prefer facing a pack of chihuahuas right now. We could drop kick them over the roof and score field goal points. I'd break my toes kicking this mountain of a dog."

"Well these bad boys are just doing their job. They are trained to protect the building and are likely the only defensive weapon the villagers have. I bet the guys that are in charge around here forbid the farmers to keep weapons. No weapons mean no farmer rebellions."

While Traveler was still talking, Glenda started to relax and move toward him. Her motion triggered the alpha's attack. The dog was smart and knew the man was the greater threat. The alpha sprang at the weak link, the female.

This was a big mistake for the alpha, Glenda was nobody's easy target. While he was in midair Glenda's defensive instincts took over. Rather than turning her back to run, as the alpha expected, she flashed toward him and grabbed him under the chest and his rear legs while he was in midair. In a swift move she lifted the stunned dog above her head, then did a Michael Jordan vertical leap.

Eight feet in the air, she threw the alpha hard into his bunched pack. The alpha hit his pack like a bowling ball hitting the pins for a clean strike. The pack yipped and scattered while Glenda stood over the prone alpha.

Glenda stretch to her full height and stared down into the alpha's eyes and the massive animal began to whimper. He rolled onto his back and presented his throat to the new alpha.

Glenda slowly bent down then talked softly to him. She began to rub his belly then his head. Finally, she gently pulled on his ears. The alpha slowly and gently licked her hand. It was similar to kissing a king's ring hand to acknowledge the leader.

Traveler was enthralled. He heard Glenda whispering, "Good boy" as she welcomed the alpha to her own pack of Traveler and herself. Traveler noticed that she rubbed the head and pulled the ears the same way she did with Theo. *I need her to show me exactly how to do that*, he thought.

Glenda lifted the alpha to his feet and gave him a hug. Traveler watched the Molossus's tail wagging so hard it looked ready to fall off. Finally, she took one of her two remaining cookies and presented it to the massive dog. It gently took the cookie from her fingers, swallowed it in one bite and proceeded to again lick Glenda's hand. The licks were not for lingering tastes, but were licks of fealty. He was Glenda's servant now.

Glenda gave him a final pat followed by a gentle push of dismissal. The alpha raced to rejoin his pack. Traveler noticed that the pack had circled back and had watched the exchange between Glenda and the alpha. "I think you not only own the alpha but all of his pack! Brilliant Glenda, truly brilliant!"

With Traveler's enthusiastic praise Glenda reddened. She tried to pull off a modest, "Aw shucks, wasn't much." Instead she found herself grinning, beaming, and saying, "I was brilliant, wasn't I? I remember an old rock-and-roll song from the sixties, 'Leader of the Pack'." Making the sound of a motorcycle revving she added, "Guess that's me."

Chapter 27

Meet the Neighbors

Looking at the large building Traveler said, "I'm guessing by its size, this is the village inn. I bet it offers more than just shelter, I'm hoping food, lots of food!" Traveler found his mouth began to water with the thought. "Let's go around to front door and see what it offers inside."

They walked around the long side of the building until they found themselves facing a dirt road. The front of the building faced the road and a large wooden door made it clear this was the main entrance.

They paused to study the village, starting with the road. It was something less than a true road yet more than a widened path. "With the Romans gone I bet all these rural roads return to nature," Traveler observed.

Many of the nearby buildings fronted the road. They appeared to be simple farm homes clustered together. Observing the village layout Glenda said, "It's a neighborhood. With my Scandinavian heritage I can tell you our expression of 'being neighborly' comes from combining two old German words meaning 'near' and 'dweller' and that's exactly what a neighbor is."

Traveler acknowledged her history lesson with a smile and nod thinking, *So the princess is a bit of a history buff also.*

As they studied the various structures served by the road, they noticed that at a far end of the village was a large open-faced shed.

The shed was built around and covered a large stone fire pit. Extending into the side of the fire pit was a large bellows. This shed was the workstation for a blacksmith. This village was not large enough to support a permanent smithy so the structure sat unused until a visiting smith arrived.

At the opposite end of the village were stables and these were clearly in daily use. The stables were for protecting the oxen and cattle. The oxen were owned and shared by most of the farming families as was the community bull. Cows were owned by individual families.

At a further distance away from the stables there was a pen built to contain pigs. It was large and the containment fence had a serious, sturdy look to it. The pen's construction declared that the size of its occupants required a structure that could withstand powerful shoves and heavy bodies leaning against it.

While the pen contained the pigs, it failed to contain their smell. Even in these pre-deodorant times, pig smells on a hot day were more than most villagers could tolerate.

Traveler and Glenda had taken in the entirety of this hamlet in a few minutes and proceeded to the entry door. Traveler had a worried look as he stood facing the heavy door. "What's the problem?" asked Glenda.

"I hope M is right that our books have equipped us with the necessary language skill, I don't want to try sign language. Everyone is suspicious of strangers and nothing screams 'outsider' quicker than your language."

"Relax. I trust M and our books. I bet we are the masters of whatever language they use here. If we have a language problem it'll be that we know too many words. These are simple people and unless there is a poet here, which I seriously doubt, their vocabulary may be quite limited."

Then she added, "I understand that the English language has something around 170,000 words, but a working vocabulary of just 3000 words is sufficient to understand most common text sources like newspapers, twitters and blogs."

While he was half listening to Glenda's tutorial on vocabulary facts, he studied the outside of the wooden building. "This place has all the architectural grace of a large wooden box. No Frank Lloyd Wright concepts here, well simplicity maybe."

Standing in front they noted that the only changes in the front of the box were a series of small dormers jutting out from a second floor. There was also a narrow overhanging porch roof that ran across the front of the building. Immediately above the porch roof and below the dormers were a series of open windows protected by thick wooden shutters.

With Glenda watching him Traveler said, "I guess it's time to step up to the plate and confirm we can survive in this place. In this world men always lead, so I'll head in first."

Smiling Glenda answered, "I know it's men first. That's why they call this 'the Dark Ages'." Traveler gave her a grin back. Humor to bolster their confidence.

Traveler stepped to the door and looked down for a door handle. What he saw was a stubby thick iron bar protruding outward. "I guess this is what passes for a doorknob, I'll try it."

He pushed down on the bar and felt the door begin to open. The door itself was heavy oak, clearly it was not just an entry point but also served as serious "lock them out" security. Traveler pushed and the door slowly opened. He stepped inside and Glenda immediately followed him. Once inside she instinctively shut the door. A flashback came as she heard the orphanage staff cry out, "Shut the door kids, we can't heat the outside."

With the door shut the room was instantly dim. Some light filtered in through the slatted windows but large burning candles were necessary for additional illumination. Part of the candle's illumination benefit was lost as they gave off a smoky fume. Their eyes needed time to adjust and Glenda quipped in a whisper, "Definitely the Dark Ages." They remained standing just inside the door doing listening reconnaissance while their eyes dilated. Now with large irises, Traveler grinned at Glenda, "Call me a barn owl."

"Call Hooo what?" she answered back.

As they surveyed the room, they could see it was large and filled with heavy wooden tables accompanied by heavy wooden benches. At the far-left side of the room was an open staircase going up. On the right side was an arched doorway from which cooking smells and sounds emanated. In the center was a stone chimney with a flickering, smoldering fire. The fire now provided more smoke than light or heat.

Traveler made a summary of their surroundings, "Looks like we've found the local tavern. With luck we may have a source of friendly food and shelter, I hope."

"Yes, we can hope," Glenda replied. "The apple and half cookie are ancient history to my stomach."

Traveler was studying the details of the entry door. He wanted to know how to make a fast exit if necessary. "Interesting door handle design," he said, pointing down. "It's an iron bar and acts as an entry and exit key. Note how it rests on an iron fulcrum with holding side rails. When you're outside you push down on it and it lifts this inside bolting bar.

"From the inside it can be pulled out then hung on this nail. Once removed there is no way for someone outside to get in. It's a fast way to have protection when you need it. Someone could batter the door down, but that's a very heavy door. I bet when they pull out the key at closing time they sleep like babies."

Glenda nodded, "Ingenious. Plus, they don't need to pay monthly security company bills or worry about security failures when there's a power outage."

"Don't believe I know you!" called a commanding voice from the open kitchen doorway. A large, slightly portly, gray-haired man stepped in, he had obviously been studying them from the dark hallway.

In the moment he appeared more curious than challenging. "We don't see new faces, particularly young ones. You're very lucky my dogs didn't find you. They can be quite deadly unless I control them."

As he talked, both Glenda and Traveler found they could understand him perfectly. They had the same thought at the same time, *My books are still taking care of me. M is right again!*

"You are correct sir, we're just passing through. We hoped we could earn a meal and a night's lodging."

Traveler paused to show respect before asking, "I assume you are the proprietor and the man in charge of this fine establishment. May I ask your name, sir?"

Chapter 28

Earning Dinner

The innkeeper's eyes remained focused on Traveler. The young man was certainly a tall one and looked like a capable worker. He noticed the young woman kept her mouth shut, a sign of a proper upbringing. He had taught his own daughter to only speak when he signaled permission with a small hand movement. He found similar hand directions worked well on training his dogs.

The innkeeper frowned as he considered Traveler's question. The request could be considered out of line among adult males. Names were given when the adult male decided to voluntarily share it, but not in response to brusque questioning from a young stranger.

The innkeeper noted, however, that the young man spoke like a noble and carried himself with a natural confidence. Nobles of all ages expected answers from the underclass. The keeper decided to accommodate the request, no reason to offend until more was known about the pair.

"Yes, I am the proprietor. With pride I say you may call me 'Hermann'. I am a direct descendant of the great Hermann. Now what are your names?"

Looking at Glenda Traveler said, "My sister answers to 'Glenda' and myself to 'Traveler'." Glenda fought back a major frown, Traveler's phrase of "answers to" made her sound like a dog. Relaxing her face, she thought, *It's not him, it's this time period.*

Innkeeper Hermann now considered their request to work for their lodging. If they had a noble lineage they would simply pay and never request work. At the same time there was something about the pair that said they were not the young traveling peasants their clothing would indicate. *I will err on the side of meeting their request for work and see where that leads.*

"A meal and a room are possible if both of you can give me honest labor until the sun is down. There is still a half day left so you will need to give your best efforts. I'll judge the results and provide food and shelter to match your efforts."

Hermann's response reminded Traveler of his early American history. The first settlers arriving from England landed in Virginia in 1607. Their colony was named Jamestown and the leader was Captain John Smith. The settlers constantly struggled to survive, the lack of food was a recurring threat.

Smith observed that even with survival at stake the gentlemen of the upper class felt work was below their noble birth station. Smith is famously remembered for saying, "He who does not work, neither shall he eat." The gentlemen quickly took up their work responsibilities.

"Sounds fair to us," Traveler answered. "Tell us what you'd like us to do."

The innkeeper reached into a dark corner and brought out a heavy two-headed ax. The ax indicated the likely nature of Traveler's work. Motioning for Traveler to follow him he turned toward Glenda, "You stay here, I'll be back shortly."

Following behind the ax-carrying innkeeper, Traveler noticed a small burlap sack hanging from a peg and slipped it into his back belt. *I can use this,* he thought as he fell into his instinctive routine of planning ahead. They proceeded past the kitchen to a rear exit. Traveler noted this heavy door had the same locking mechanism as the front door. *Security all around*, he thought.

Chapter 29

Trees and Pigs Offer Different Challenges

As they stepped outside Traveler saw a haphazardly stacked pile of cut trees. They were generally twelve to fifteen feet long with trunks that varied from six to nine inches. They still had limbs that were waiting for the ax and he noted the limbs were intertwined.

The innkeeper handed Traveler the ax saying, "That's your work pile. Pull one out, cut off the limbs then cut the trunks into four to six-foot lengths for the fireplace. Try not to hit your leg, blood is a pain to get off wood and bloody wood smells up a room when burning. I'll be out at dusk and determine what you've earned."

Hermann humor. Enough already, thought Traveler.

With that parting gibe the innkeeper went back inside. At the door he turned to observe Traveler. He chuckled to himself. *With a lot of effort, he should earn a nice bowl of oats and maybe a slice of bread and butter.*

Traveler waited until he knew the innkeeper was finished watching him was and back inside. He heard the heavy door as it was pulled shut. Now he turned his attention to the woodpile. He saw the trunks were from hardwood trees. They would generate a lot of heat once the sap was driven out.

As he studied the pile, he knew that cutting was going to be a demanding challenge. Traveler took off his heavy, long-sleeved coat and then his lighter-weight body-shirt. Bare-chested he took the burlap sack from his belt and tore it into long strips.

Looking at his hands he thought, *Not a single callus. Reading books certainly did not toughen my hands and I don't need blisters. Blisters lead to infections.* He proceeded to wrap the burlap strips around his hands to form protective gloves.

Glenda was waiting patiently for Hermann to reappear. When he walked in, he was wearing a wide smirk. Clearly he had enjoyed handing Traveler his job and was ready for Glenda. "Your boyfriend—" he started.

"Brother," Glenda corrected him.

"Either way he's in for a long afternoon. He'll sell his hands for a penny by the end of the day." Glenda did not respond other than with a raised eyebrow indicating her acceptance of their fates.

"I respect ladies, so I'm giving you a chore that the women of the village normally do. You will get up close and personal with the livestock. The pigs are ready to be fed and their slop is in a holding tank in the kitchen.

"You will use two buckets to carry the slop up to the pens at the far end of the buildings. But don't fill the buckets, if filled then they are too heavy, even for a strong man. You will need to make multiple trips. Make as many trips as you can before it's dark."

Glenda listened patiently and said, "Thank you for the advice. I'm a farm girl so I'm stronger than I look."

The keeper looked at her again and thought, *Wait until you lift the buckets, farm girl. Even filled a third of the way they will be more than you can lift.*

"Well my strong farm girl, there is a padded shoulder pole that lets you carry both buckets at once. Again, don't attempt to fill them up too much, I don't want to lose you before you get started. Our biggest women only fill them about a third of the way, and you've seen the size of our women. You should get started now, my little piggies are hungry."

As he turned to leave he added, "One more thing I need to caution you about. The piggies are not really little and they are very excitable and aggressive at feeding time. They will go for the buckets, or you. In and out fast, that's the way to do it. Oh yeah, be sure and lock the pen when you enter. You don't want to try and catch a loose pig."

"Well I'm ready, so lead me to the slop tank." Hermann pointed a finger and Glenda followed him back to the kitchen.

Chapter 30

Transylvanian Trees Meet Paul Bunyan

Outside and tugging on the first tree, Traveler was quickly sweating. His years of high school distance running started the perspiration flowing immediately. He felt his muscles bulge as he grabbed a trunk end and yanked it. The intertwined branches required multiple yanks to separate the trunk from its comrades.

Once he had the tree separated from the pile, he looked at the branches and planned the order of cutting them away. With a plan in mind he braced his legs apart and swung the ax. The largest branch was liberated from the trunk with one blow. He became a limb-removing machine taking one swing to cut off a branch.

Once the trunk was barren of limbs, he studied it for cutting. The trunk was resting on the ground and he knew that the ground would not give him the solid surface he needed to cut down on.

Looking around he spotted his cutting platform. It was a cleanly sawed-off trunk three feet high with roots still buried in the ground. The trunk was at least four feet in diameter and offered a level cutting surface. Possibly it served as an outdoor dining table, but for now it would be a cutting surface.

Traveler dragged his tree to the cutting table and pulled it across so that it was balanced across the trunk's wide diameter. He studied the tree's length and picked the first cutting spot.

Satisfied with his mental mark he lifted the ax and brought it down with a single powerful blow. A six-foot length fell off one end. He pulled the remaining length onto the chopping block and another blow resulted in two more lengths.

Looking at the remaining pile he thought, *One tree down and a lot to go and I feel strong! Let's see how many trees Paul Bunyan can cut before the keeper gets back! I could sure use Babe, Paul's big Blue Ox, to help move these guys while I cut.*

After an hour he looked at the growing pile of neatly cut and stacked logs with pride, *Man's gotta do what a man has to do to eat and I'm a very hungry guy.*

Chapter 31

Should Be Bacon

Glenda looked at the slop holding tank then at the slop buckets. The holding tank was filled with a disgusting mess of accumulated kitchen leftovers, it reminded her of a compost pile for plants but this one mainly had animal remains.

She wanted to hold her nose but refused to give the keeper the satisfaction. Smiling Hermann said, "Use the big ladle to start filling a bucket, fill it about a third of the way but no more. Stir up the slop so you get the good stuff off the bottom. There are lid covers you need to put on after your buckets are ready. We don't want to waste good pig food spilling out as you walk."

For a moment Glenda thought about sticking the keeper's head into the tank but she restrained herself. "OK," was all she said. As he left the kitchen the keeper gave her a head nod to start.

Inwardly he congratulated himself, *What a clever Hermann! I am getting these two to slave for their food. Her brother's hands won't be able to break the bread, I may not even have to feed him.* Then he felt a passing pang of shame, the girl reminded him of his daughter. *Maybe I'll be generous with the girl and include some cheese.*

Glenda waited until Hermann was gone then she studied her task. She took the large ladle and stirred the tank. Can this smell any worse? she thought as she dumped the first ladle into the resting bucket.

Ignoring Hermann's advice, she filled the bucket to the brim then knelt down, held her breath, and sealed it with the cover. She proceeded to load and seal the second bucket. With both buckets filled and sealed, she attached them to the notched carrying pole.

The pole was short and just went across her shoulders. Each bucket hung close to a hand so she could grab a bucket if it began to sway as she walked. She noted with appreciation how the thick padding protected her shoulders.

With the load balanced across her shoulders she left the kitchen. The keeper was waiting in the great room and said in a softer tone of voice, "Follow me slowly. You don't want to hit anything and it's awkward balancing two buckets."

They went out the front onto the rutted center road. Once outside Hermann said in a slightly contrite voice, "I'm sorry for being unreasonable. I never thought you would actually agree to feed the pigs. I never thought you could lift one bucket much less two. I'll make the next trip instead of you." He had no idea both buckets were filled to the top.

Glenda looked at him and gave him a smile, "Really, it's OK, but thank you for your nice words. I'm used to hard work and it's only fair that my brother and I earn our keep."

As they walked toward the pen the keeper continued, "There's a little more to tell you. The pigs are dangerous due to their size but there is a boar in there and he's much nastier, he even bothers me. I usually just heave the slop toward the trough and let them eat off the dirt."

"I appreciate the warning. I'll take care and be sure to stay safe. You can go back inside and get dinner going. I bet you'll have other hungry travelers tonight and it's a chance to make money for the inn."

"Thank you, young lady, and now you've shamed me. I will give you and your brother a fine dinner tonight and a solid breakfast in the morning."

"Oh," Glenda said, "since you are being generous there is some good news for you. I believe I can spare you a second feeding trip. The buckets are full and that should be plenty even for hungry pigs."

The keeper made an involuntary flinch. "You actually filled the buckets? That's not really possible, could you put them on the ground for a moment."

Glenda did a weightlifter's squat and placed the load on the ground and held the carry pole up in the air. Hermann bent down, put the carry pole across his shoulders, gave a small grunt, and went to stand. He remained fixed to the ground. He gave a larger grunt which turned into a groan. He then placed the carry pole back and stepped away.

"Please show me how you lifted that." Glenda stepped in, squatted again, and stood with the pole across her shoulders.

She gave him her sweetest smile. "My father calls me a freak of nature as he does my brother. We grew up doing heavy lifting on the farm. We would challenge each other to see who could lift the most bales of hay. My brother would usually win but not by much. Of course I'm a faster runner, so it all evens out.

"Now I'm going to be really hungry so I'll leave you to take care of the kitchen." The keeper was staring at her and could only nod his head.

Glenda watched the keeper going back toward the inn and then she headed toward the pen. When she got to the pen, she put the buckets down and took inventory of the situation. The trough was about eight feet away and was too far to hit with an accurate throw. Even worse, it was surrounded by a pack of hyperexcited, snorting pigs. She ignored their narrow black eyes watching her.

She looked for, and then spotted, the boar. It was lurking in a corner watching her with its beady red eyes. For a moment she thought of the fire creature and chuckled to herself, *Yes, there are definite similarities. Too bad we can't make bacon out of the jinn.*

She focused on the animal in greater detail. This boar was at the upper end of hams-on-the-hoof. A full-grown boar could easily weight well over 200 pounds and this was trophy-sized.

Boars are easy angered, fearless, and highly intelligent. Glenda knew how fast they could move despite their size.

Long tusks jutted from its lower jowls with thick saliva dripping down from a long tongue. It had evil intentions written in its stare and stance. It did not fear a human and was now crouching in attack mode.

While pondering whether to just throw the slop in, she heard a whimper beside her. The alpha Molossus was there with his pack. She reached for his head and gave a big rub followed by a gentle ear pull. The pack approached and she rewarded them with rubs and pulls.

A crazy idea came to her, *I'm not going to let a big male pig intimidate me. Let's see how tough Mr Boar is with uninvited company joining him.* She placed the pole with the two buckets across her shoulder, unlatched the door and went inside.

The instant she was inside the boar made its move. It saw an easy prey and an open gate to freedom. It barreled through a group of large squealing sows and charged her. As fast as the large boar moved, the alpha Molossus was larger and faster. The Molossus hit the boar from the side knocking it down. The pack immediately followed and began circling the fallen boar. The sows and small pigs ran to a far corner making submissive grunting noises.

The alpha had its mouth open by the boar's throat. Huge canines were exposed. A low vibration came from the Mosossus's throat. Accepting defeat, the boar wet itself.

Glenda slowly walked to the trough and emptied both buckets. She ignored the boar and the huddled pigs. She walked to the open gate, stepped out, and gave a low whistle. The alpha snapped its jaws shut and slowly walked out maintaining the deep throat rumble. Once all of the pack was outside, Glenda securely locked the gate.

As she turned, she found the keeper was standing a short distance away. His eyes were wide and he seemed frozen in place. He started to talk and the words caught in his throat. He cleared his throat and finally said, "I've never seen anything like that. How did you do that? Trajan answers to nobody but me."

Glenda smiled, "Dogs just love me." Patting the alpha's head she added, "I met Trajan earlier and removed a splinter buried in his paw. He is a grateful friend now."

The keeper was fascinated by the girl. He was not sure he believed her story about a splinter in the dog's foot. It reminded him of the ancient story about a runaway slave named Androcles and a lion. According to the tale, the slave removed a thorn and won the lion's gratitude.

The keeper's face was wrinkled in concentration, *Is she copying that old tale? Maybe she borrowed the story to cover up something else. I wonder what the "something else" could possibly be? She deserves close watching, there's something strange about her.* With a final head-clearing shake he pondered, *Is she a goddess masquerading as a farm girl to study us?*

"Well, have I earned my supper?' Glenda asked as they returned.

"More than that, you will be treated as my privileged guest and enjoy the best this poor innkeeper can offer."

Grinning to herself Glenda answered back, "Thank you Hermann, that is so generous. I would ask you to extend the same courtesy to my brother. He is strong of back but not always strong in self-control. Let's check up on him."

When they entered the inn, the keeper immediately headed to the rear exit. "Let's see if your brother is still standing or has gotten lost in the pile of trees. Just pulling them apart for cutting is a challenge for our farm boys."

Glenda followed him with a hidden smile. *Let's see how big boy did.*

Chapter 32

Stunned Again

The keeper removed the locking bar, opened the rear door, then hesitated. He stood to the side and made a slight bow for Glenda to go out first. "You are a true gentleman, sir." The keeper's face developed a warm glow as he watched the tall girl step out. *Goddess or girl, she is a marvel,* he thought.

Glenda and the keeper both saw a sweaty, bare-chested Traveler sitting on a massive stump. There was still a huge pile of branches and the keeper thought, *Hardworking sister and lazy brother. I understand he needs her as his keeper. He would starve without her.*

Traveler gave them a welcoming wave, a big grin, and flexed his arm muscles. *Show off,* went through Glenda's mind.

Hermann looked at Traveler and was annoyed that he was relaxed sitting on the picnic stump. *Let's see how he likes watching his sister eat while he begs for her scraps.* As he was opening his mouth to deliver a harsh reprimand, Traveler pointed a finger to the side of the building. The keeper turned, looked, and his mouth opened and closed. Once again words got stuck coming out.

An astonished Hermann was looking at a full cord of neatly piled logs by the side of the inn. The logs were all cut to the requested lengths and were totally bare of branches; they were ready for the fireplace. Looking back again at the large brush pile the keeper realized that the trunks were gone and only branches remained. "Not possible," finally came out of the keeper's mouth.

"Well it was demanding work. I'm tired and very hungry. I assume you're pleased and there will be a hearty dinner and comfortable rooms for my sister and I."

"You will eat like nobility tonight and tomorrow. I don't know how you did that, but the name Hercules comes to my mind." The keeper paused and with a serious look asked, "You're not a god, are you?"

Before Traveler could answer Glenda laughed, "He's sure no god," and she laughed again. Traveler found he was annoyed over the laughing dismissal of his Herculean wood cutting.

"Well neither is sis here a goddess. Did she do anything to earn her supper or just sit around wiping tables?"

Hermann had a serious look when he said, "She did something remarkable. She carried two full buckets of slop at one time across her shoulders up to the pens. That load would have been beyond our biggest farm boys.

"Then she went inside the pen and emptied the slop directly into the trough. The bully boar charged her and Trajan, the alpha of the pack, knocked the boar onto his back while the pack circled the fallen beast. Afterwards Trajan licked her hand. Believe me nobody wants Trajan around their hand. It was all amazing."

Glenda beamed as the keeper continued to praise her. *Enough already,* went through Traveler's mind. *So, she fed pigs and petted a dog, big deal.*

Hermann was now in his most accommodating innkeeper role as he said, "Let me show you the sleeping room, it's the best one in the inn. The duke stayed in it one night when he visited to review one of Trajan's litters."

"Wait a minute, Hermann," Glenda said, "we need two rooms."

Hermann was surprised at the young woman's reaction. *She must be a noble with her own room.* Scrambling he said, "I'm sorry Glenda, but that is not possible. I'm expecting a group of the duke's guards to show up shortly. They will arrive hungry, tired, and likely in foul moods. They will need to be doubled and tripled up in the rooms. They would cause all of us a great deal of trouble if you had separate rooms."

As an afterthought he hastily added, "And that was not what I offered. I offered food and a room, definitely not two rooms."

As a final conciliatory point he added, "The duke is a huge man, larger than the two of you together and he spent a comfortable night spread out on the bed. Now if you would, please follow me and I'll show you the room. I believe you will find the quarters are very acceptable."

Traveler and Glenda followed Hermann up a wide set of heavy wooden steps to the second floor. He led them to the last room at the end of the hallway. Opening the door, he pointed with pride to the large bed and dormer window.

"We just changed the bedding for the fall season and it's not yet been slept in. The window is open but you may want to close it, it gets quite cold at night.

"Also note that the door has a security bar for untroubled sleep. The duke's men occasionally have a wandering hand and items end up missing." Pausing he added, "Of course, nobody would ever accuse these guards of stealing, not unless they wanted a beating."

"I understand what you mean," said Traveler. "I believe I have seen these guards in action with the local farmers. Not a nice group, sitting on their horses and showing off their gloved iron hands and swords." Hermann nodded without saying a word.

After the keeper left the two looked at each other and started to laugh at the clean bed comment. "Now I understand the tradition of spring and fall housecleaning," said Traveler. "Death to bedbugs twice a year."

Glenda moved to a chair in the far corner by the window. She took deep breaths by the open window, then declared, "We really stink. I smell like pig pen, slop, and sweat. And you're no rose either. I can't separate our respective sweat smells but the pig smells are definitely all me."

Traveler grinned back, "When you're right, you're right. Let's find out our bathing options." As an afterthought he added, "Let's leave the window open for now."

Chapter 33

Polar Bear Bathing

Glenda found Hermann in the kitchen moving heavy pots and deep pans around in a massive fireplace. When she questioned him about the bathing options, he gave her an embarrassed look. "Even though we are in a remote area we are still civilized. We adhere to the Roman custom of bathing and do it twice a year. We empty the slop tank and fill it with hot water and it serves as our inn's bathing tub. Of course we cannot do that now since it's full of piggy food. We'll empty it in a week or two. Sorry about today."

Yeah, I'd sure want to bathe in the slop tank, thought Glenda with a shiver. *I'd kill for my sanctuary shower right now.* Realizing Hermann was embarrassed Glenda casually asked, "Is there any place for bathing? We are both past our own semi-annual bath and don't want to soil your fresh bed linens."

The keeper's face took on a look of concentration, he wanted to accommodate the request if possible and also keep the bedding clean. Inspiration hit and his face lit up, "You could go to the stream beyond the wood pile. There are several wading pools that the kids play in during the summer. Of course the water is a bit cold since it flows down from the mountains."

Glenda rapidly nodded her head, "That will work, we love cold. Do you have any soap and clean blankets?"

The keeper immediately smiled back, "Indeed we have both. We make our own soap right here and sell it to the farmers.

It takes the grease off the most crusted pots and pans and is great on cleaning clothing." With that he opened a cabinet and handed her a pail of white looking putty. "I'll be back in a minute."

Glenda sniffed the putty as she took the pail, *It's unscented lye soap. This stuff has been around since the time of the Babylonians, and that's nearly 5000 years ago. It will sure clean us.* As an afterthought she mused, *Must keep out of the eyes.*

The keeper returned with two large blankets and two small hand towels. "I warmed the big ones by the fire. Wrap quickly when you get out and it will feel like your own dear mother is holding you."

Traveler had joined them and caught the bathing options. "I'll carry the soap pail and you carry the toasty blankets. They'll keep you warm on the way there. It's already getting dark so we need to hustle, fortunately I know where the path to the stream is."

As they got to the rear exit the keeper appeared with a burning torch secured to a sharpened pole and handed the torch to Traveler. "Not much light from this torch but enough to see your way. Have fun and don't fight with any wolves."

Outside Glenda said, "Country innkeeper humor, I love it."

Traveler led the way going slowly enough so that they both had the benefit of the torchlight. Upon arriving Traveler anchored their torch in the ground then pointed to the right, "I looked at this stream earlier. I know there's a nice spot for washing to your right. There's a flat rock about two feet under water and the stream moves slowly right there. Be careful moving away from the rock since the bottom deepens pretty fast."

"There's a spot to my left with a sandy bottom. It brings the water up to my chest in a couple of steps. If you prefer a faster immersion you can take that side."

Glenda looked and spotted the sitting rock resting under the slow-moving steam. "I'll take dibs on the right side and thanks for the heads up on the bottom. Here's your warm blanket and a nice pail of lye soap."

Traveler scooped out a large handful of the soapy putty and put it on a small flat rock beside his entry place. He handed Glenda back the soap pail saying, "I'll leave the torch in the middle. It's dim enough for privacy but still gives some light for what's around us."

As Traveler was turning around Glenda quickly stripped off her clothes. She dumped them on the rocks beside the soap saying, "Make sure you wash your clothes, and wash your hair, everything stinks. Don't let the soap stay on your skin too long and absolutely keep it out of your eyes." With that she entered the water and shrieked.

Traveler knew how cold the water was. He turned partially around to grin at a now seated Glenda, "Did I mention it was a bit chilly? Is the Nordic princess loving it?"

"Get in and you'll see how much I'm loving it. I've been in Norwegian polar bear club swims, and this is colder. It's the Antarctic on a cold day."

Traveler was preparing a quip about how soft the modern Norwegian ice princess was when he entered. Of course he was quickly much further into the water than Glenda. *Oh, man! This water temperature must be fifty degrees colder than it was this afternoon.* His immediate instinct was to get out.

He heard Glenda laughing and splashing like crazy. "Throw water on yourself and move around. Moving helps you adjust faster." Traveler gritted his teeth, partially to stop them chattering and partially to get his nerve up. "I am in, and no, I won't warm up I'll just stay numb."

Then he did the ultimate big boy move and waded out nearly chest high then ducked completely under. He came up blowing out water and laughing. He returned to the edge of the shore like a crocodile testing the land, took a handful of the soap and smeared it across his body. He put it into his hair, under his arms, and everywhere. He repeated the scrubbing several times before heading back up to his chest.

He could vaguely see Glenda rubbing the putty on herself then on her hair. She had moved off the rock and had joined the faster moving water at a deeper spot.

Even though they were some distance apart, Traveler did the natural boy thing and hit the water with the palm of his hand. A perfect spike of water hit Glenda's face just as she was bringing her head out of the stream.

A grinning Traveler said, "Just following the lady's orders to be active and move around. I'm keeping my arms active right now." Before he could add more witticisms a bolt of water struck him in the face.

Mutual retaliations followed immediately. Traveler ducked down to avoid the returning strikes but found Glenda had his submersions and returns well-timed. After a few minutes Traveler called out, "Truce, please."

"OK, but only because I need to wash my clothes."

Both of them retrieved their clothes and began serious scrubbing. "Three times a charm," Glenda called over.

Traveler thought twice was plenty but then realized she was right. *Women definitely had a better sense of smell.*

When Traveler looked up, he saw Glenda was already standing and wrapped in the blanket. He noticed she was staring hard across the stream at some noise. *Wolves? Probably polar bears,* he thought.

He was out of the water quicker than a leaping salmon. He was wrapped in his blanket faster than anything could move except a freezing boy. Both squeezed their clothes hard to take out the water.

Traveler said, "Do you want to use the torch and lead the way back. It's about burned out so there's not much light."

"No, you lead and I'll be right behind. I'll take the soap pail so you can manage your clothes and hold the torch. We just need to hustle."

Hustle they did. In a few minutes they were at the rear exit to the inn. Traveler confirmed that the door was open and held the now sputtering torch for Glenda to see the steps. She was up the steps in a small leap and inside, "First to the kitchen," she said, "we can dry our clothes out by the fire."

Once inside the warm kitchen they felt the heat wrap around their bodies. There was a rack for drying and they spaced out their clothes to minimize the drying time.

As they were leaving the kitchen the keeper entered. He grinned at them, "You two keep amazing me. I thought you would be frozen and float out to sea. I'll bring your clothes up when they're dry. They'll be fine in half an hour. I'll rotate them as needed.

"As I mentioned, we have a full inn tonight. A group of the duke's men have already arrived. They eat and drink a lot and are noisy but they pay well. I'll warn you they can be rough when drunk and I've set you up at the furthest table. I suggest you eat quickly then retire to your room. Remember to bolt the door."

Both acknowledged the advice and thanked him for managing the clothes drying. "We'll wait for you to knock." Grinning, Traveler then added, "Follow the Tony Orlando and Dawn song and knock three times."

Hermann frowned, "Don't know that song. You can teach me tomorrow."

Chapter 34

Recovery

Once in their room Traveler said, "Imagine the money we could make by introducing songs they've never heard?"

Glenda laughed, "Yeah, we'll need a lot of money to defend ourselves against the EPA for water pollution with that soap. I bet we killed all the fish downstream."

Traveler lit several of the small candles placed on a central table. He then shut the window and collapsed into the chair. He began to softly chuckle, "It was kind of an adventure, but man, that water was cold. I think I left parts of me back there, I'm afraid to count my toes."

Glenda was sitting in the bed with another blanket wrapped around her. "I know I'm going to stop shivering I just don't know if it's today, tomorrow, or next week. My teeth sound like they're sending Morse code to my brain."

"Change of subject but what do you think of Hermann? He is quite proud of his name in case you haven't noticed."

"I think under his rough exterior he is a decent guy, certainly much better than the mounted soldiers I saw."

Traveler continued, "It's understandable why he wears his name with pride, it's the name of a famous German tribal leader."

Glenda settled back thinking, *Here comes another history lesson. Lucky me.*

"It was AD 4 and Rome was at the peak of its power. It had conquered all of Gaul, what we call France today, and decided it was time to conquer the vast territory we call Germany.

"Before launching the invasion, Rome had planned ahead. They had a time-proven method of creating future allies among conquered tribesmen. The young sons of tribal leaders were brought to Rome to be Romanized and young Hermann was selected.

"Hermann was given a Roman name, Arminius, and was raised with Roman values and military training. Over time the Romans believed he was now loyal to Rome and he was sent back to help with the conquest of the Germanic tribes.

"The invasion of Germany was launched by General Tiberius. He invaded with a massive force of thirteen legions and auxiliary support, about 100,000 men. The invasion force was initially successful in defeating a number of Germanic tribes and the conquered territory was renamed 'Germania'.

"Tiberius moved on and an experienced administrator named Varus was placed in charge of managing Germania. Arminius was a trusted advisor to Varus. Unknown to Varus, Arminius remained loyal to his Germanic roots, he was still Hermann.

"Hermann lured the occupying Roman army deep into the forest then ambushed it. He crushed Varus and his 30,000-man army. This stunning victory, referred to as 'The Battle of the Teutoburg Forest' is considered the greatest Roman defeat. The battle changed Western history and made Hermann a German hero. That's why our innkeeper is so proud of his name."

With Hermann's name fully discussed they fell into silence which quickly led to a pre-dinner nap. Both were in a deep slumber, Traveler in his chair and Glenda in bed, when there was a robust knock on the door. Traveler's head snapped up. He cleared his mind and called out, "Yeah."

"Hermann here with nice warm clothes, I'll set them beside the door. I suggest getting into them before they get borrowed."

Traveler glanced at sleeping Glenda and muttered, "Relax princess, I'll bring them in."

He carefully unbolted the door and stuck his head out. The long hallway was partially lit by flickering candles. Looking down he saw their clothes, surprisingly they were folded. He brought them inside and bolted the door.

He placed part of the pile beside Glenda, who was making stirring noises. "These are yours. I'd put them on while they are toasty warm."

He proceeded to his end of the room, turned his back and quickly got dressed. "Take your time, I'll go down and secure our table."

Once he was gone Glenda stretched out in the bed, it was soft and comforting. She felt like a kitten wrapped up in a snuggly blanket. Then she realized she should bolt the door. Once out of bed, the room's chill gave her an unwanted wakeup call. She bolted the door then quickly dressed.

Before putting on her boots she lay back in bed again. *I wonder if I could order room service? Fat chance.* She lay there while gathering herself and thinking of the day's events. *I guess Hermann is a decent enough guy. I wonder if he's a decent cook. I'm sure he's no M in the kitchen, but right now I could eat warmed over roadkill.*

Chapter 35

Dinner Guests

Traveler came down the stairs to the sound of large men making large noises. He reached the bottom step and slowly entered the dining room. There was now light coming from wall sconce torches as well as from a blazing fire. He noticed with some satisfaction that several of his cut logs were providing light and heat.

Looking casually around he saw the room had tables filled with military men wearing assorted leather jerkins and junior officers with light chain mail armor. He recognized several of the men from the group that had disciplined the field farmers. *A nasty bunch*, he thought.

At that moment the keeper came out from behind the bar with each hand holding multiple large mugs. He casually approached Traveler and quietly said, "I gave you two that corner table. It's as out of the way as I could find. I suggest you eat, spare the conversation, and retire behind a bolted door. They appear to be in an even fouler mood than usual."

Traveler nodded, "My dinner plan exactly."

As Traveler slowly walked to the table, he felt eyes tracking him. The eyes only stopped watching him when Hermann began placing ale mugs in front of them. Traveler knew these men would load up on ale and food then look for entertainment. He was sure that he and Glenda needed to be gone before it was show time.

While sitting he kept his head down in a submissive stance. He used his peripheral vision to study the men while avoiding any eye contact. He felt like it was another night at the Chicago museum but with nasty guards present rather than fire creatures. *Keep a low profile and try to remain innocuous.*

The keeper placed a large plate of bread and cheese on Traveler's table with two mugs of a potable drink. Looking at the drinking mugs the keeper beamed, "It's my house blend of aged cider and ale, you'll get a double kick. It's a bit sweet but it grows on you." Placing a tankard of water on the table he added, "Feel free to add water to slow down the kick."

Traveler tore off a piece of the thick black bread and thought, *This crust could replace my shoe soles if necessary.* He took a tentative bite of the soft inside bread, then a larger bite of the cheese. He washed the food down with the mug offering. A smile lit his face, *Well, this is surprisingly good. M needs the recipe.* With that he began to tear off more of the bread.

As the food and ale were doing their job Traveler suddenly noticed the room had gotten quiet. He lifted his head to see Glenda approaching the table. She had entered the room with her usual striding bounce and a mop of drying red hair reflected the light from the wall sconces. Traveler saw the many sets of eyes tracking her movement. *Deer in the hunter's rifle scope,* flashed through his mind.

When she reached the table Traveler whispered, "Not the best time to make an entrance, princess! Sit down and lower your head, quickly."

Glenda slid into the other chair and took a subservient position. "Start to eat and avoid looking around. The good news is the bread, cheese, and drink are surprisingly good."

Fortunately for the two young diners, the seated guards were distracted by the keeper bringing in heaping plates of meat. Large hands immediately grabbed hot chunks of the offering. The room filled with the sounds of open mouths tearing and chewing. Grease flowed down forearms from gripping hands onto the table tops.

"Feeding time at the zoo," Glenda said with a low chuckle.

Traveler's spider-senses were tingling hard. "Princess, I suggest you focus on eating. Let's get out of here ASAP. There's only one zookeeper and the lions are free to roam."

Glenda looked slightly annoyed. "I'm chewing as fast as I can. Besides I'm really hungry and I need this time to relax."

Traveler knew better than to debate and he also knew the more they talked the less eating got done. Gradually, the room returned to a normal level of chewing, slurping, belching, and other undesirable sounds.

Glenda had consumed several helpings of the bread and cheese when she took a long drink of the ale. Her eyes immediately began to water and she snorted a bit out her nose. Traveler naturally started to laugh.

Embarrassed she answered, "Thanks for the head's-up bozo, I almost choked and that would have made a scene."

Traveler tried to look repentant but the grin failed to leave. "Sorry," was all he could mutter without laughing again.

Chapter 36

A Peace Offering

A shadow suddenly fell across their table quickly followed by a smell of dried sweat and bad breath. "I'm known as Throbb and I believe the lady needs a choice piece of the pork." A very large hand lowered a hunk of dripping pork hanging from a long dagger onto Glenda's plate.

Glenda and Traveler looked up at the mailed man standing over Glenda. Traveler immediately recognized him as the lead rider who had intimidated the farmers and then rode through the plantings. Traveler had a flashback to the first time he ate with M on the train. *I don't think this meal is going to be as enjoyable as M's hidden wine and dessert.*

Glenda kept her head down as she responded, "Thank you, sir, but I'm already stuffed. One more bite and I'll explode."

The man pulled a chair over beside Glenda and handed her another mug of ale. "What you need, farm girl, is a bit more of the keeper's famous ale but not watered down. A tall girl like you can hold a lot. Besides it's not polite to refuse an offering of pork. Farm girls rarely get to eat it so don't insult me."

Traveler now looked around the room. It was suddenly showtime. The entertainment was at his table and the soldiers were in a mood to watch the big man's moves. Traveler realized that after Glenda, he was also on the entertainment menu. Rather than waiting for the mailed leader to continue, Traveler took the initiative.

Traveler reached across the table and put his hand on the mailed arm. "Sir Throbb, please excuse my sister. She is very timid and she talks in a very soft voice. I can barely hear her myself so you likely did not hear her whisper 'No, thank you'. Sadly, she is unable to eat most meats, particularly pork, but she appreciates your generous offer."

The keeper was standing in the doorway again holding multiple pitchers of his ale as he watched the emerging drama. Part of him felt like a coward for not intervening but his survival instincts overrode his emotions. He decided to return to the kitchen and ignore the lad's coming beating.

As Hermann was retreating he heard large fists pounding tables and loud voices calling back at him, "Innkeeper! Ale! More Ale!" The keeper thought, *Ale is essential for these louts to enjoy the coming spectacle.*

The oversized man was now staring across at Traveler. He was acting like Traveler had just appeared and was of no consequence. "Puppy, remove that hand or lose it. Be thankful I do not choose to look closely at you right now. You had best remain unseen and unheard."

Returning to Glenda, he pointed to his seated comrades lifting mugs of ale and laughing, "You need a grown man to protect you against those drunken oafs. Fortunately for you, I'm here as that protector. Of course my protection comes with a small cost. Let's start with a short dance to create a friendship." With that he started to rise while lifting Glenda from her seat. He lifted her with ease.

Overlooked, Traveler was now standing beside the man. He kicked the rising man's legs out and the unsuspecting man fell heavily back into the chair. The sound of iron chain mail rang out and the room was deadly quiet. Traveler's aggressive move was totally unexpected.

A voice ringing with embarrassment and rage shouted, "A sneaky ambush you little coward while my back was turned! You do not belong in this room with warriors. I brand you a coward and pass judgement on you."

By now the man had fully risen and pushed his chair away. He was massive and stood like a great tree swaying slightly in a heavy wind. The wind was generated by a combination of ale and the jolt of falling back into the chair.

As he was rising the man had quietly slipped his left hand into his gauntlet. Once erect he immediately threw a mailed fist at Traveler. This blow had very bad intentions, it would have felled a lion. If it landed on a chest it would have broken ribs and sternum.

Traveler's reflexes anticipated the blow and he moved just enough that the iron fist slipped past his chest. Red-faced, slightly off-balance, and totally embarrassed, the man looked down to his sword. The sword would give greater reach to his thrusts.

As he was pulling the sword from its sheath, Hermann now moved to the table and asserted himself. Nobody was more surprised at his intervention than the keeper himself.

"Enough now, Throbb! You know this inn is a secure haven for travelers. These two are my guests and earned their meal. There can be no harsh beatings here on orders of the duke. Do you care to challenge the duke as well as the lad?"

Before Throbb could reply to the keeper's intrusion, Hermann added, "The mage is also quite fond of staying here. He appreciates the good food and the quiet atmosphere. Do you also want to incur the mage's anger?"

The mailed Throbb blinked at the warnings regarding the duke and the mage. He lost his assertive attitude for a moment and seemed to physically shrink. Then he reasserted himself and swelled up like a bullfrog calling into the night.

"Fair enough innkeeper. While there will be no beating here, I am entitled to compensation for the insults. What do you suggest?"

The keeper had no reply when Traveler answered, "May I offer you compensation in the form of a man-to-man challenge right here at our table or yours?"

Throbb shifted from the keeper to face Traveler, "You have a wagging tongue, puppy. What's your challenge, to see who can duck the quickest and talk the most?" This retort brought loud guffaws from the seated soldiers. The bullfrog swelled further with the encouragement coming from his crew.

"Actually I was thinking more of a test of arms. I don't mean arms in the sense of swords but just plain arms. My arm against your arm."

A disbelieving smile came across Throbb's face, "You mean to arm-wrestle me, puppy?"

"Indeed, that's my offer of compensation. While my sister talks in a very soft voice, I acknowledge my mouth can sometimes place me in difficult situations. As an alternative to the arm contest would my sincerest apology in front of all be sufficient compensation?"

Throbb looked more closely to appraise Traveler. Tall he was and fast but hardly a heavyset build. The arm test was solely about muscle power and Throbb had a lifetime of building his muscle power. He planned on wrenching the puppy's arm so hard he would snap the shoulder then smash the puppy's hand as he drove it into the tabletop. He would have two rewards, a broken puppy and the dance with the sister.

"Puppy, we'll do the test of arms. The apology is just another use of your mouth but if your arm is as strong as your mouth you should do well." Again a round of laughter came from the soldiers. They had seen Throbb defeat many an opponent in arm wrestling and knew he would destroy this arrogant farm boy.

A sly grin crossed Throbb's face. His wit was now on display as he added, "Do you want to use this table to save your strength from walking to another?"

Traveler ignored the suggestion and accompanying soldier hoots. He turned and walked to a center table near the front entrance. The table hosted a group of seated soldiers and Traveler tapped one older soldier on the back, "Mind if I use your chair, sir?"

The veteran was stunned at the boy's insolence. *He's crazy but I'll have a great view of everything.* He slowly rose, smiled at Traveler and pointed to the empty chair. "Claim it while you can still talk, boy."

As Throbb was gathering himself for a stately walk to the table Glenda stood up beside him. Throbb realized the farm girl was quite tall and was now looking him straight in the eye. She suddenly did not seem timid at all. She smiled faintly and whispered, "Looks can be deceiving Throbb, I suggest you accept his apology. You will be considered as a man of honor for not attacking a younger, less-experienced man."

Throbb paused, the girl seemed relaxed and that was offsetting. Then he thought, *She's acting bold to throw me off my game. She has no idea of the men I have put down in battle as well as the wrestling table.*

He smiled back, "I would accept his apology if you accept my invitation for a good night's dancing." Then he added, "You don't smell like a farm girl, more like nobility and I like noble women."

Continuing to look him in the eye as she replied, "Bad decision, sir, and tonight is definitely not a dance night, so lead on MacThrobb." The innkeeper heard the weird Mac phrase attached to Throbb's name and wondered what it meant. *Possibly it's a term of respect*, he thought. *But she is certainly not inclined to compliment Throbb. Very strange.*

As Throbb moved toward the seated Traveler, Hermann touched his arm. Throbb paused to note the innkeeper had a strange look on his face. "Throbb, neither of these youths are what they seem. I know you are a man easily roused, sometimes over small unintended slights, but I also know you as a man of courage and battlefield honor. I have seen you do notable good deeds for friends.

"I strongly advise you to accept his apology. The boy is much stronger than he appears and the girl has a mysterious way about her. Leave him and the girl alone."

Throbb recognized this was the second warning in less than a minute, but pride overruled the warnings. He chose to believe the keeper was simply trying to protect his guests. *Maybe they are visiting relatives and he has an obligation to protect them.* His hesitation was gone as he strode to the table.

The chair across from Traveler was now vacant as another soldier rose to make a place for Throbb. A confident Throbb sat down.

The two standing veterans were beside each other holding their mugs. They congratulated themselves with smiles as they looked down at the seated contestants; they had secured the best seats in the house.

As they studied the young man more closely, they suddenly thought the boy seemed a bit older than he had appeared back at his own table, he was also taller and broader. *Not that it matters,* they thought. *In this contest speed and slyness don't matter, only power does, and Throbb has great power.*

The seated soldiers were laughing and drinking. Life was giving them an unexpected night of entertainment. Normally they would be betting among themselves on a contest of strength but there was no bet to be had here, the outcome was a certainty. They banged the tables hard again for the keeper to bring fresh pitchers.

Throbb was removing his layers of upper-body protection. He wanted to have unencumbered movement for his upper body as well as to display his massive arms. His forearm was larger than most men's upper arms. His upper arm was the size of a grown man's leg.

Once Throbb was fully on display everyone became silent as they compared the two combatants. Several of the older soldiers began to feel sad for the boy. They understood how Throbb would permanently destroy the boy's upper body and his right arm and hand. "He'll never plow again," one older veteran whispered to his table.

"Let's make this a little more interesting," said Throbb. "Small daggers please," and he pointed at the two seated soldiers beside him and Traveler. These were young men but they immediately understood the request. Grinning they took out their hand daggers and placed them on the table in front of Throbb and Traveler.

Eying the daggers he said, "I suggest we have a dagger's edge held in place at the spot where each wrist would hit the table. This just adds a little more risk to losing. Nobody wants a dagger slicing into their wrist, do they puppy? Of course you may slap the table with your left arm and the contest will immediately end but don't delay the slap too long."

Traveler was watching Throbb play to the audience. Throbb looked like a larger version of Big Bob the football player. Traveler recalled his magic act in high school using Big Bob as his unknowing shill. Both Throbb and Bob were supremely confident in their physical skills. Neither saw the train coming straight at them.

Traveler nodded his acceptance. "If you're sure you want to go that way. It seems you're making a very big deal out of a simple slip of the lip on my part. In any case let's get this parade going, I'm tired and want to get to bed."

"Hospital bed," a standing soldier offered to the crowd. More hoots and drunken laughs followed.

"Is the right hand acceptable, puppy?"

Traveler nodded, "Fine with me if that's your weapon of choice."

They put their right hands together with arms vertical to the table. One of the standing soldiers used a piece of rope to bind their hands together. Now neither could break the other's grip.

"Call it, keeper," directed Throbb.

Hermann stood at the end of the table and surveyed both combatants. He assured himself neither had a starting advantage. We have a fair contest, at least to start," said the keeper, eliciting a round of hoots and claps from the guards.

"I will count down from four to one then I'll say 'Push'." Looking at Throbb he added, "Remember you must remain seated, no using body weight for an advantage."

The keeper then did the countdown. When he said "Push", Throbb's arm muscles bulged even further. Veins stood out from his shoulder down to his hand. His massive hand enclosed Traveler's and appeared to be trying to crush the youth's grip.

The watching soldiers had seen this act numerous times. They knew Throbb would permit his opponent a moment of hope. The opponent's arm would remain vertical for a few moments. Throbb always held back to savor the moment. He was the cat controlling the mouse and play time came first.

The arms remained vertical longer than the cat normally permitted. The soldiers smiled at each other thinking this was a new wrinkle in Throbb's act. To the surprise of all, except Glenda and possibly the keeper, their arms continued to stay vertical.

Throbb was no longer playing with the mouse. He found he was pushing against a stone wall and the wall did not move. At the same time, the wall did not seem to be pushing back at him. Throbb's strongest grip felt like he was simply shaking the young man's hand. This was something he had never experienced.

After half a minute Throbb took a deep breath then blew it out in a sudden exhale. The wall was now moving slightly away from him. Taking a quick second large breath, he again exhaled in an explosive grunt and the boy's arm began a slow decline toward the dagger.

Confidence had returned and he stared at the boy's arm as it was slowly approaching the sharp edge of the dagger. One final burst and the boy's energy would be exhausted and he would see the dagger biting into the boy's wrist.

He expected the boy's left hand to hit the table at any moment. Maybe he would ease up and maybe not. *The young only develop by receiving harsh setbacks from their betters*, he thought.

The soldiers were now leaning forward while holding their breath. They saw the mouse's inevitable end was close. A few felt pity for the young man as the dagger was ready to slice into his wrist.

Throbb took a final deep breath to end the contest but made a mistake. Just as he was ready to make the final strong, exhale push, he looked into the boy's eyes. What he saw stopped his exhale. The boy was studying him similar to how Throbb had done against an opposing enemy on many battlefields. *I'm being set up for an ambush*, flashed through his mind.

The boy's eyes told him he had indeed walked into a trap and the trap was now sprung. He felt the stone wall return and the boy's forearm move away from the dagger's edge. The wall pushed him to a vertical position and stopped. He suddenly wanted to accept the boy's apology. He wanted to apologize to the girl. He wanted his mother.

The boy's arm began a forward push. There was no strain on the boy's face. His breathing was controlled but his eyes bored into Throbb's. The soldiers were stunned. They were watching the impossible happen and it seemed to be happening in slow motion.

Traveler now had Throbb's forearm touching the dagger's edge. He stared into Throbb's eyes and saw pure fear. He pushed down enough to start a trickle of blood flowing from the wrist.

The soldier holding the dagger suddenly removed it. Throbb was his leader and he would not permit his leader to be crucified through his wrist. Traveler then pushed the hand flat against the table. "Yield?" was all he said. Throbb nodded.

The keeper felt conflicting emotions running through the room. The soldiers were looking for direction from their leader Throbb. This was Throbb's defeat but it was also theirs. Armies and soldiers are not created to make moral judgements during a battle, they are trained to support their leaders regardless of the circumstances.

Throbb was now standing with a slow trickle of blood oozing from his wrist. Traveler had also risen and was calmly looking at Throbb waiting for his next possible challenge.

Throbb had regained his composure and his challenge followed. He studied Traveler for a moment then declared, "He is not a man, he is a demon. No man could so easily defeat me in such a manner. I looked into his eyes and I saw the demon inside him laughing at me and each of us.

"Keeper, there are no rules that protect a demon in your inn. This thing needs to be burned immediately." Throbb saw that his men were nodding their heads in agreement. Whether the young man was simply strong enough to beat Throbb or was a demon they had an explanation they could accept. Their leader's honor as well as their unit's honor needed to be salvaged. They all nodded in agreement with Throbb's verdict, this was a demon.

The soldiers were now standing with hands on sword hilts and daggers when a cold wind blew in from the open door.

Glenda had quietly slipped to the door, removed the blocking bar and opened it.

She smiled at the standing soldiers, "This room needs a little cooling off before emotions take over. Throbb, I warned you my brother is much stronger than he appears and he's younger than you. He's no demon, he simply beat you. Act like a noble warrior, and accept the outcome to a fair contest."

As Glenda was challenging the group, Trajan the alpha male and his pack had quietly entered the open door. The inside heat and Glenda's presence had called out to them. Trajan pressed against Glenda who gave a few tugs to his ears.

Once inside the pack sensed the tension. They could smell the anger and fear coming off the soldiers. Their hackles all rose. Their instincts were to follow the pack leader who was clearly siding with the girl.

Throbb studied the potential new adversaries. The room with heavy tables did not give his men room to fight efficiently and these were warrior dogs trained to attack and to kill. "Keeper, I have known you a long time. You are usually a sensible man. These two demons have fogged your mind. Be sure you do not join them in a demon's fire pit."

Bolstered by his own voice Throbb continued, "We cannot spend the night in a place that protects demons and wild dogs. Keeper, the duke and the mage will find this story not to your liking. I suggest you rid the inn of these two before I return."

With that admonition Throbb went through the open door. As he passed the alpha male, he saw its shackles were fully raised and he felt a low vibration coming from the beast. His nearest hand automatically rose to avoid brushing the dog's head and dripping jaws.

As he passed the tense animal, he remembered that the alpha was the favorite of the duke. The duke used the alpha as his stud dog with his best females. If Throbb somehow managed to damage the alpha, the duke would have Throbb's head on a pole outside the inn.

Chapter 37

Bedtime Reflections

Once the soldiers were gone, the keeper came over to the door, shut it, removed the iron key, and placed the heavy locking bar in place. He turned to Glenda and Traveler with a sad smile. "He will carry his story to the duke and likely the mage. He will exaggerate and claim he was defeated by demons.

"The duke knows him as a bully and liar but also as a brave and capable leader in a battle. Who knows if his story will be accepted, however Throbb's men will certainly support him.

"The duke does not believe in demons but the mage is reputedly a strange sort. The mage is a mystic so he may accept the demon story. It's also to the mage's advantage to keep us common folk believing in evil demons. Part of our taxes are justified to support the mage and his acolytes."

Suddenly laughing, Hermann added, "And his spells work! Nobody has seen a demon in these parts." Glenda and Traveler laughed along with the keeper.

"At the end of the day, regardless of what he personally believes, the duke will probably accept his demon story to show support for Throbb and his men." Pointing at Traveler he said, "I expect they will return in a few days with more men and a charge to kill you by whatever means they can use. Sword or bow, the outcome will be the same."

He turned to Glenda and said, "You will be found guilty of something simply by association with your brother. Given your physical beauty and sharp mind, it's likely the duke or mage will bring you to the castle to instruct you in acceptable behavior. You can imagine the instructions."

"For this evening the best thing each of you can do is to sleep. We'll have time tomorrow morning to discuss the best escape plan." Traveler and Glenda nodded in agreement.

Once upstairs they bolted the door, removed their shoes, and collapsed on the bed. There was illumination coming through the louvered window and their eyes adjusted to the soft lighting. Glenda said, "Well, I guess this inn is no sanctuary for us. Do you think this duke person will harm the keeper?"

Traveler was on his back staring at the overhead beams and lost in his thoughts. "I think Hermann will be OK. His inn is protected for whatever reasons. Maybe it's a reward for his past services. Maybe the Hermann name is still respected enough to give leeway against harsh judgements."

"I hope so. I find I like Hermann, he's a gruff guy but underneath a good man. To change the subject, what was it like arm wrestling that huge guy?"

Traveler laughed, "The toughest part was his breath. Every time he did a big exhale it was a wind of roadkill, raw onions, and rancid food in my face. They never brush their teeth, so add that into the mix.

"The physical part was easy. He never knew what he was facing. What he saw was just an inexperienced young farm guy and he's put farmers in their place many times. What he could not see was the power of the books.

"I think he did have a revelation when he looked me in the eyes. He expected to see desperation coming before his final push and instead he saw something else. He certainly saw more than just my irises.

"While I was toying with him, I had a flashback to a magic act I put on in a high school assembly before our Thanksgiving break. I was Mr Magic back then with a cape, hat, and wand.

"On stage I challenged the biggest kid in school to join me and lift a weight. His name was Big Bob and he looked like a young version of tonight's Throbb. Bob was a football player with huge arms and a bigger ego. As soon as I invited Bob to the stage to lift a barbell, he raced up to show off his arms and strength.

"Like Throbb, Bob never had a chance. I rigged the barbell so it could not move until I did some magical hocus pocus. Of course I actually used science to control the barbell."

Glenda was enjoying the story and the parallel to Throbb's humiliation and said, "Please continue Mr Magic, what science did you use on Big Bob?"

"In a word, electromagnetism. The science teacher helped me rig a powerful electromagnet right under the barbell. I could turn the magnet on and off with my wand. It was really cool when Bob could not lift the weight until I did the magic wand movement. Unlike Throbb, Big Bob was a good loser. When he finally lifted the barbell, the school wildly applauded him like he had scored a touchdown, foot stomping and clapping shook the auditorium."

Traveler glanced over at Glenda saw she now had the pillow pressed against her ears and was breathing deeply. The rhythm of her breathing reminded him of the train's wheels as they rolled over the steel tracks on the way to Chicago, he was asleep in moments.

Chapter 38

A Cold Wakeup Call

Glenda woke to a freezing room. Traveler was curled up on his side with a   pillow over his head, he reminded her of a hibernating bear. She was facing the opposite way and realized they were unintentionally sharing a reversed hug of sorts. Pressed together their heat was shared and had helped them survive a night in the igloo.

She sat up, stretched, then put her boots on. *Iceberg shoes, feels like Norway in the winter.* Once up she grabbed the blanket and whipped it down. "Rise and shine, cowboy. We need to ride out of Dodge before Throbb and the duke's gunslingers come looking."

Traveler gave an annoyed grunt, then relented and sat up. Glenda watched as he put on his boots. "Cold, cold, cold," he exclaimed.

"In Norway we kept our shoes warm overnight by the hearth. Putting them on warmed the rest of our bodies once out of bed. It was a great way to get moving. I'm going down by the fire and warm up. See you there."

When he got to the kitchen Hermann gave a welcoming smile and said, "By the way, we offer the best not only in food but privacy visits. It's a heated space with running water. We followed the Roman designs to maintain civilization out here. The only thing missing is their heated baths, but that's not possible. Way too expensive for this simple innkeeper to build."

Then the keeper's face lit up with a crafty look passing over it, "Unless I had a man with unusual strength to build the containment pit."

Traveler gave him a sad smile. "Yeah, I would love to help out, but you-know-who is coming. Nothing good will happen to you if we're still here."

The keeper nodded. "I understand. And thinking about the bath I realize cleaning the water after filthy soldiers would be a fulltime job."

Glenda returned and handed Traveler a bolting key, "Works just like the rooms and doors, assured privacy. Enough said on that subject." Traveler made a speedy exit down the hallway to prepare for the long day ahead.

The keeper had set up a table with a generous serving of foods. There were the usual warm breads and cheeses. Joining them were a slab of rich yellow butter and a jar of honey. Ale mugs were on the table filled with creamy milk.

Just as they were seated and beginning to eat, the keeper brought out a platter of cooked eggs. The eggs were partially scrambled, partially poached and partially sunny-side. Despite their confused shapes they were delicious.

Joining the eggs were slices of ham. Looking at the ham Glenda laughed and said, "After meeting Mister Boar yesterday I have no concern for how my pork is served, it's welcome in all forms from bacon to chops."

The keeper joined them while Traveler and Glenda ate. "You'll want to head out after you're finished. Throbb will reach the duke's fortress tomorrow and spin his tales of demons and other lies. You will be described as an eight-foot giant with hands like shovels. He will never admit being bested by a youth and his men will nod at his tales."

The keeper chuckled, "I warned him about your hidden strength, but he can only accept what his pride permits. He deserved your humbling, I have seen him at work tormenting the local farmers, and on those days he belongs in my pen with the other pigs."

"The duke, to his credit, is a fair man and knows Throbb; however, he is also a practical man. He needs to support his soldiers and their unit leaders, including Throbb. The best outcome for you is to be long gone. I'm sure the duke will have Throbb on a short leash to return to duty after a quick visit to my inn."

Traveler looked up from his empty plate. "We may have a problem, Hermann. We were sent to talk with the duke. We need to know how to get there without running into Throbb and his men."

The keeper shook his head, "That's a meeting that's unlikely to happen. Even if you avoid Throbb, you will find a well-guarded gate into the duke's fortress. No stranger gets in without permission and nobody talks to the duke directly.

"To meet the duke you must first meet with his mage and make your case. The mage then determines whether the requests are worthy of the duke's time. Few, if any, are granted an audience. The mage passes harsh judgement on those attempting to bypass him and meet with the duke in private.

"Be warned that the few who have met the mage have all returned in a confused state of mind. He has great powers over those he meets with, it seems impossible to keep secrets from him."

Glenda looked at the keeper and frowned, "What do the people say who have seen this mage? Is he old or young, tall or short, and how has he gotten into this position of power? Where did he come from, is he a relative of the duke's? Has he always been the duke's gatekeeper?"

The keeper looked at Glenda and gave a shake of his head. "Definitely older and stooped of back. He was an important advisor in the court for many years. He grew up here and was trained by his father, the prior mage. He was well-liked and respected. His job was only to advise, nothing more."

"Sounds like he was a good guy, what happened to change that?" asked Traveler.

Hermann leaned back in his chair. "If you are determined to meet with the mage there is a rather long story you should hear.

I have heard it many times from visitors to the inn and they all tell basically the same tale. Do you wish to hear it?"

Traveler and Glenda nodded. Glenda added, "Hermann, this story may be critical to our success, we'll make time. And spare no details. The devil is often in the details."

Hermann smiled at her reference to the devil then said, "As you request. There should be enough time for the tale and for you to leave well ahead of Throbb." Chuckling he added, "Besides, Throbb always insists on a large meal and lots of ale when he arrives, followed by a long nap. Now here's the story.

"The mage's role changed when the duke's lands were threatened by an invading army of Huns from the East. They were sweeping through the mountain passes and valleys on their way to invade the rich western cities. Under their leader, Attila, they were an unstoppable force. Their army destroyed all opposition that faced them.

"Some mountain lords tried to negotiate a treaty but without success. It is said that the Hun leader laughed at them saying, 'Why bargain when all is ours? You have nothing we cannot take.'

"Our duke assumed there could be no negotiation and prepared to defend our land."

Chapter 39

Best Laid Plans of Mice, Men, and Dukes

"The duke's strategy was to take the initiative and launch a surprise ambush attack. His attack would be centered around the final mountain pass. The pass's narrowness gave him a strong advantage facing the much larger army. The duke patterned his strategy from the Spartans confronting the invading Persians at the entry pass of Thermopylae. A small group of Spartans was able to hold off the massive Persian army."

Glenda nodded, "So, that is how the duke stopped Attila."

"Sadly no, he did not. This is what I've heard from soldiers who were there.

"The duke planned to arrive at the pass with his army a week in advance of the Hun's earliest arrival. He would prepare the battlefield, both on the steep cliffs and in the open field. Sadly, the plan never got put into action. We later came to appreciate the skill and brilliance of the Hun armies and their leader Attila.

"I am told that when the duke arrived at the open field he was stunned. He found the Hun army facing him. The Hun had already come through the bottleneck of the pass. There was no element of surprise. We were encircled and vastly outnumbered.

"Somehow, facing certain defeat, the duke was able to meet with the Hun leader. How he secured the meeting is a mystery. He was alone with Attila except for the mage. How and why the mage was there is another mystery. After some time passed, the duke and the mage emerged from the tent. The next morning the Hun army had disappeared and we all survived. That ends the story."

"Well we'll sort that story out when we meet these two," said Traveler.

"Perhaps you will meet the duke but probably not. Rumors coming out of fortress claim the duke is not just ill, he is a changed man. He is a recluse staying in his personal quarters in the fortress.

"The mage now oversees all activities and appears to make all decisions. Even when the duke attends occasional dinners in the great hall, he speaks little. When he does, his voice is soft and hesitant. Our men who have known him in battle fear he has suffered a head trauma or possibly was poisoned by this Attila, others whisper the mage is at fault. No one knows the truth.

"Now the sun is rising and you need to choose your course of travel."

Chapter 40

Leaving Dodge

"There are two routes to reach the fortress. One route is easy. Just stay on the narrow road in front of the inn. Follow it and it leads directly to the fortress in several days of brisk walking. Of course, that is the same route that Throbb will be on. You could stay on it until you hear him coming, then hide in the woods until he passes.

"The second route is along the river which also flows directly to the fortress. That route is slower but keeps you from running into Throbb. You can follow the animal trails that are along the river and these well-worn trails should offer acceptable passage.

"Regardless of the route taken, Throbb will likely have the master-of-hounds with him and of course the tracking hounds. Dogs need a starting scent, and I saw Throbb pocket Traveler's table napkin when he left. Using the napkin scent the hound chase will be on. These tracking hounds are amazing at following a scent. It is impossible to elude them once they are on your trail."

Great, Traveler thought, *show good table manners and what do you get? A pack of hunting dogs after you.*

With his travel advice over, the keeper handed each of them a cloth bag filled with various foods. The bags were cinched with a rope which served as an over-the-shoulder carrying strap. Glenda gave the keeper a hug, and Traveler offered a warm handshake. They put the bags over their shoulders and stepped outside.

Chapter 41

River or Road?

Once outside Glenda said, "We really need to know what went on in that Attila meeting. I think there are big clues for us regarding the dangers ahead. If we're lucky we may find tips about how to possibly neutralize the jinn."

Traveler agreed, "I have no idea how the duke managed to escape, maybe he bargained by selling out his fellow lords. I do have a strong reaction to this mage. He doesn't sound like the sharpest blade in the world of mages. I bet he was just a loyal dog following his master, then he got very lucky and survived. The duke is probably ill from all the stress, possibly poisoned, and so this mage falls into the power position.

"Anyway, let's save that mystery for later. Right now we need to survive a pursuing Throbb and whatever hound pack he's bringing with him. It's a shame we can't turn Trajan's pack loose on those hounds."

"Well we can't, so let's start down the road right now. We need to get some distance from the inn then we'll figure out the best route," said Glenda.

"Agreed, and it's better for Hermann if he doesn't see what we decide to do. In his case, the less he knows the better off he'll be when Throbb shows up.'

As they were finding their walking pace, they discovered it was a warm fall morning. Birds announced themselves and a soft breeze promised to cool their hike. The cooling breeze also delivered fall pollen and Glenda gave a big sneeze. Traveler started to laugh when his own nose itched followed by a sneeze explosion.

After Traveler's sneeze Glenda laughed, "Stealth is defeated by pollen! I bet even the Garden of Eden had it. God's little joke to keep humans in their place." She then wiped her nose while Traveler answered with another big sneeze.

"OK Sneezy, do Tarzan and Jane use the road to move faster or go slower beside the freezing river?"

Traveler pondered his answer, "To paraphrase old Paul Revere, 'One is by land, and two is by river' and Sneezy votes for land. We have the forest as cover on both sides of the road. We can leap up into trees if need be."

"Road trip it is then," answered Glenda, "and a fine morning for hiking it is."

The calmness of the day wrapped around them, the village and Hermann quickly disappeared. The road continued ahead as a wide dirt trail. It was more than a path but less than a true road. The width of the road varied as it converged and diverged depending on the surrounding trees and rocks. Still the road was serviceable for horses pulling wagons as long as they could move to the side when necessary.

"I wonder how this road fares in the rain, it has to be one very long mud puddle," said Traveler. "Probably the result of minimum maintenance. I'll bet it's only here so the duke can collect taxes and food from the locals."

Now that the morning meal had settled, they fell into a natural striding rhythm. Each of them thought about the huge road investment made by Rome to connect and civilize large parts of Europe.

Suddenly Glenda exclaimed, "Watch out! I just stepped in a small pothole filled with mud and never saw it. We can't afford to twist an ankle and then try to run from Throbb and his hounds." Traveler nodded and began to look more carefully at the road's surface.

As they walked in silence, they observed the massive trees on both sides of the road housing a multitude of birds. "This must be nesting season, there are a lot of birds carrying twigs somewhere," observed Glenda.

Traveler nodded, "As a boy scout, I was a birdwatcher back in Charlottesville. There are more types here than I've ever seen. I don't think some of these birds even exist anymore. Speaking of birds. Since you're Norwegian I bet you don't know that the American passenger pigeon died off in the early 1900s.

"They had flocks in the millions but were hunted to extinction for food and sport, just like the great buffalo herds. The last pigeon was a female named Martha after George Washington's wife. Martha passed in 1914 and never laid a fertile egg. Civilization and people are killing off lots of animals and birds and that's sad and wrong."

Glenda now had the history bit in her own mouth, "Since we're discussing nature, you know birds and buffalo but I know ice. Did you know that the Ice Age ended in Scandinavia around 11,000 BC? In Norway we grow up with ice and snow. We are a country of ragged mountains and fiords all created as the glaciers cut through our land then melted. The melted ice created the most clear and beautiful lakes."

In the middle of their conversation Traveler suddenly smacked his arm, "Ouch! That fly was the size of a sparrow, and hungry. We need hats to swat these monsters away."

Glenda walked to the side of the road and snapped several small branches off a leafy tree. "Use this as a swatter. Pretend you're a cow or horse and just keep the swatter tail going non-stop." Traveler took his swatter and immediately began creating a protective force field around himself.

After walking and swatting for some time he found he was a bit bored. He suddenly swatted Glenda's hair, "Big fly ready to nest in your locks. I probably saved your life."

Boys and swat toys, dangerous combination when bored, she thought. "I really appreciate that. I'll keep a keen lookout for you also, trust me."

Continuing on the dirt road they noticed a sharp narrowing ahead, "Looks like the road maintenance money ran out up ahead. Maybe they changed work crews and somebody got lazy or maybe the flies drove them off."

"Likely all three," Glenda said.

"I'm hot, thirsty, and frankly getting tired," said Traveler.

"Well, I couldn't have said it any better. Let's head for the sound of a running stream, fill up on water, and cool off."

Chapter 42

Off the Beaten Path

"Lucky us," said Traveler. "This narrow part of the road has a path starting behind the big stump and heads toward the river. I bet the road guys created this access trail to water their horses and oxen." The two headed into the dense woods following the trail.

What was once a cleared path was rapidly becoming part of the forest. Fresh saplings had rooted in the open space and were climbing for light. Existing trees had their lower branches spreading to capture the open space and discourage the sapling growth.

As they walked single file Traveler cautioned, "Better keep a safe distance behind me. Some of these branches are whips when I push through them. This path is going to be ancient history in a couple more years."

Glenda gave a grunting "OK" as she followed, pushing aside challenging undergrowth. The branches seemed to resent Glenda's second pushing away and she heard them snap back with a crack. "I think the woods are mad that we're moving them out of their sunlight territory. Light is scarce down here and nobody gives up their share of sun without fighting back."

Traveler turned to acknowledge her comment and found a thorn bush was scraping across his arm. "Ouch! New growth with an attitude."

Leaning down he picked up several recently dead limbs and handed one back to Glenda. "Use this to push stuff away before using your body."

"Thank you, good idea." Glenda thought to herself, *So obvious, why didn't I think of that. The forest is dumbing me down.* Just then a nasty green fly took a bite of her clearing arm. Traveler heard her loud "ouch" followed by an unladylike word.

Going was slow and after half an hour of pushing brambles out of the way, Traveler announced, "Break time."

"That's the second good idea you've had in an hour. The forest is making you smarter while it's dumbing me down."

"Nothing smart going on here. I need to rest; my arms are ready to fall off. I feel like Stanley looking for Livingstone."

"Stanley who?"

"You don't know about Stanley finding Livingstone?"

"I guess the answer is 'no' and I don't think I ever did. I bet you're going to educate me."

Traveler grinned, "Well it's a true story, and a great one. One of the most famous people in England in the mid-1800s was a missionary explorer named–"

"Wait, let me guess, he's Livingstone. Am I right?"

"Give the little lady a stuffed panda bear. Yes, you are correct. May I continue?"

"I can't wait. Keep educating me, please."

"Well at this time explorers were just beginning to explore and survey the dense African interior. One of their goals was to find the source of the mighty Nile River. Did you know the Nile is the longest river in the world? It's over 4000 miles long. To appreciate that distance, the mighty Mississippi is only a bit over 2000 miles. The Nile is twice as long."

"Wow."

"That sarcasm just lost you the sweet panda bear. Anyway, Livingstone was charged with locating the source of the Nile somewhere in the heart of Africa. Over time his progress reports slowed then stopped. All England felt they had lost one of their great explorers and a great man. So, a second man–"

"Don't tell me, I'm betting its Stanley, right?"

"The little lady is correct, but an answer with attitude again loses the panda. I suggest you consider your limited entertainment choices right now. Listen, learn, and enjoy the tale.

"To continue, both men become exhausted in the unforgiving jungles. They wandered separately for years. They each encountered a host of dangers including debilitating diseases, poisonous snakes, hungry jungle cats, and river crocodiles.

"Indigenous tribes were another great threat. When Livingstone finally stumbled upon a major village, he had to witness Arab slave traders shooting the villagers for sport.

"Their survival challenges were simply remarkable but I'll cut to the end. Livingstone is past exhaustion. His bearers have long since deserted him. He has had little to eat and is a walking skeleton. He has found refuge inside a native hut and is preparing to meet his maker when he hears a commotion outside. He rises up with great difficulty, and hobbles forward to see what's happening.

"What he sees is a white man walking toward him. Of course, it's Stanley. These two men have come together in the middle of an unexplored continent. It is a miracle of faith or endurance, or luck. Probably all three.

"When Stanley first greets him, he utters one of the most famous lines in English history, 'Dr Livingstone, I presume?'

"The quote is famous as an example of understating a great achievement. It's also considered an exaggerating caricature phrase of British pluck standing against all odds."

Glenda found she had actually gotten caught up in the tale. She had to admit Traveler was a good storyteller. "That's a cool story. I'd like to hear more of their adventures when we get out of our jungle. Right now, though, I need to get to the crocodile-free river, have a nice long drink, and cool off."

Traveler hefted his walking stick and opened the path again. "Normally, as a gentleman I would say 'ladies first' but in this case I think a gentleman should beat the path first, unless of course the modern woman wants equal rights on fighting the forest."

"This modern woman appreciates the gentleman. Consider me Livingstone. You keep showing these nasty brambles who's the Stanley here."

Another hour of slow walking had them ready for another stop when they heard the inviting sound of a flowing stream. When they got to the bank Glenda gave Traveler a small curtsy. "Well done Stanley, you have found our hidden Nile."

They quickly removed their boots, then waded to a long flat rock formation jutting out from the edge of the bank. Worn down from centuries of past floods, it presented an inviting surface. Once seated they rejoiced in the soothing caresses of the cool water as it flowed across their toes and ankles.

Glenda bent down, cupped her hands and took a handful to drink. She studied it for a moment, nodded her head, and drank. She immediately repeated the move, "Trust me, it's safe and so good. Better than any store-bought, brand-name water."

Traveler nodded and was quickly filling his cupped hands. After numerous deep drinks he let several handfuls trickle across his head and down his shirt. As the cool water trickled down his back, he felt his overheated body temperature dropping and a relaxed smile crossed over his face.

Glenda immediately followed his lead, "Boy, the simple things in life you don't think about until they're missing."

They sat for a while in silence letting the strain of the long hiking hours flow out of their bodies and into the river. As their energy returned Glenda looked up at the sky, "I believe we may want to spend the night here. It's secure with the river as a buffer, besides I'm hungry and tired."

Traveler nodded, "You're right again. Let's find our sleeping nook and then eat. I'll patrol to the left and you try the right side. Maybe the road workers left some shelter."

They put their boots back, grabbed their walking sticks, and went on their separate shelter searches. Within a short period, Glenda heard Traveler call out, "Found it!"

Chapter 43

Cave People

Glenda hustled toward the sound of his voice. "Look at this," Traveler said and pointed at a nearby opening into a rock formation. The opening was three feet high and well above the riverbank.

Glenda studied the opening then said, "I'm not Alice in Wonderland. I am definitely not going down that rabbit hole."

"It's not a hole, it's an opening to a small rock cave. I looked into it already, so please just stick your head in and appreciate the security."

Glenda bent down and cautiously stuck her head through the opening. Traveler was correct. The opening led to a small cave. The center of the cave's rock ceiling was slightly above their heads, they could almost stand up once inside.

The cave's rock sides curved down to join a soft dirt floor. "It's like an igloo," she exclaimed. "You found us a perfect place! Well done, Stanley. You have earned the coveted cave finder award."

Traveler grinned, "Good scouting never fails you, let's get our packs inside. I'm going to forage for leaves and anything soft to upgrade the floor into a mattress. I know from years of camping you want your bed to be as soft as possible. If you sleep all night on the ground, you'll wake up feeling like you're a hundred years old."

Glenda nodded, "I'll get our bags inside, then I'm going to build a fireplace in front. I still get chills remembering how cold our room got last night. If we can throw heat back into the cave, I think the inside rocks will retain some of it."

"Excellent thinking, you would be a great addition to my scout troop. Now let me go on mattress patrol."

Traveler moved away from the river and walked looking down at the forest floor. His search was quickly rewarded when he discovered a supply of large, broad leaves and thick forest moss. The surrounding forest floor was mattress central.

Taking off his outer coat garment he began peeling wide strips of the moss using a sharp-edged cutting stone. As he worked he put the folded strips into his coat. Once the coat was loaded, he returned to the cave.

When he got back, he saw a series of rounded river rocks had been placed in a semicircle about five feet in front of the cave opening. In front of the rocks was a dug-out indentation in the ground, clearly intended as a fire pit. In front of the rounded rocks and leaning vertically against them were higher flat rocks. These were the rocks that would reflect the fire's heat into the cave. *Clever*, he thought.

He then stepped to the cave entrance. He pushed his coat into the cave, then crawled in behind it. He proceeded to stack the thick moss in one corner and the leaf pile in another corner. As he came out, Glenda appeared with an armful of kindling. "This place is like kindling central. There is so much dry wood. I'll get bigger stuff after I have a kindling base. How's your mattress search going?"

"Piece of cake, I found the mattress king's inventory, just need to make another couple of trips."

"You may want to speed it up, it's already dusk. The sun goes down really fast in this forest. Take my coat and you can make one trip." Taking her coat, he looked up, indeed it was already dusk.

He put a spring in his step and was quickly back at the mattress warehouse. After fifteen minutes of kneeling and cutting he had two coats filled with moss for their ground cover.

Standing up he saw it was now beyond dusk, it was almost pitch black. *Great, now I can get lost looking for a dark cave.*

Naturally he headed to the river to get his bearings. *Sound still works even when the eyes don't*, he thought. He began to slowly walk along the river bank but found it was difficult to judge distance in the dark.

Then he saw a torch coming his way and called out, "Hey, can you help a lost Traveler, pun intended?"

"Yeah, I figured it would turn dark on you. Need a hand with one of those coats?"

"I'm OK, that torch is my return beacon. My scout training doesn't help much in the dark woods. I was close to yelling or crying, not sure which would come first. I have no pride when alone inside a dark forest."

Glenda chuckled back at him.

They were quickly back at the cave opening. Glenda took one coat and handed Traveler the torch while saying, "Give me a minute to spread this. I'll call out for the second load."

Traveler stood holding the torch up and noticed a large gathering of kindling was inside the stone circle. *We're ready to heat the cave*, he thought. He then noticed a stack of small diameter logs resting beside the fireplace. *Fuel for later. Bet I draw the short straw for going out later and adding logs, and that's fair, she built all this.*

His thoughts were broken with, "OK, hand me the last coat." Traveler put the wrapped coat in front and saw a hand grab it and take it inside.

"Want me to start the fire now?"

"The torch is yours to command, fire it up Stanley."

Torching the kindling he watched as it quickly grew into a small blaze. *Guess she does have fire skills*, he thought. As he watched the fire, he felt a message of warmth, caring, and protection emanating out. *I understand why early man felt they were in the presence of a gift from the gods. Thank you, Prometheus.*

Traveler gazed at the kindling fire as it slowly built a nest of red-hot coals. He then began placing the larger logs across the bed of coals. He crosshatched the layers ensuring that air could easily reach all parts of the fire. *Air is to a fire as water is to a person. Both are essential for survival.*

Just before he came into the cave, he added two large logs to the top of the stack. *Here's our all-night comfort and protection. I bet it will still be on duty early in the morning. I'll toss a few logs on it when I wake up.* "I'm coming in, ready or not."

Once inside Traveler saw that the sleeping mats were well laid out. Glenda had first laid down a thick layer of leaves several inches deep. On top of the leaves she triple-layered the moss sod. The effect was a soft elevated platform that was a good eight inches off the dirt floor.

"Great job! Not just the floor covering but setting up the fire. Placing those flat rocks vertically for reflection was a stroke of genius. I can feel the heat being reflected in already and also some light. We can dine without biting off a finger." Glenda smiled as she accepted the well-deserved compliment.

They reached into their travel sacks and took out a generous portion for dinner. They began to eat their offerings from Hermann. Traveler tore into his chicken sandwich. He consumed the entire sandwich too quickly. He fought a burp as he considered how the sound would echo in the small cave. *Must remain a gentleman*, he chuckled to himself.

When he came up for air after a second sandwich he said, "You know it's only around five but it feels like it's ten at night. Once the sun is down, time seems to move in a different pace. The daily sun cycle sure controls us without our thinking about it."

"Well in Norway we do think about it… a lot. Our winters are six months long and our day time is described as a long twilight without a bright sun. Trust me, to stay sane and survive the twilight of winter we needed to adjust to that. The fun about our twilight winter is that the northern lights are visible during the long daytime hours."

"Well this southern boy only knows that right now it's pitch-black outside and he's dead tired. The good news is he's literally snug as a bug in a cave rug. See you in the morning."

Traveler folded his jacket into a pillow, put his blanket across himself and pulled the top up to cover his head. Resting on his back he realized how soft the bedding was. He was ready to compliment Glenda again, but Morpheus whispered, *Save that thought*, and he did.

Chapter 44

Run from the Hounds

Traveler woke first. Sitting up he looked outside at the fire and saw a few embers but no flames. He noticed he could see the rocks so he knew a soft lit dawn had arrived. He glanced over at Glenda and saw a mummy totally wrapped in her blanket. *OK Traveler. First up gets to see if the fire can be resurrected.* He pulled on his boots and headed outside.

Once outside, he stretched and then flinched. A sustained shiver passed through him. It was at least thirty degrees colder than in the cave. He appreciated that Glenda was spot on with her reflecting fire rocks. The reflected fire had warmed the interior rock sides of the cave and had kept the freezing night at bay.

He placed some kindling on the embers and a few minutes later a small fire was alive in the pit. He added more kindling, then put several smaller logs on top. In a few minutes there was a roaring fire again radiating heat into the cave. *I need my coat but I'll sit here until the princess wakes. Might as well let her get all the rest she can, we've got a long day's hike.*

Sitting by the fire Traveler found his body was quickly adjusting to the chilly morning. *Might as well move around,* he thought. Picking up his walking stick he decided to backtrack toward the road. As he walked he found the undergrowth and brambles still resisted his best efforts. After less than a ten-minute effort to clear the path, he gave up. *Breakfast first then hiking.*

As he turned to go back, something in the morning air was different, something was annoying the birds. The birds were declaring their morning joy but adding a warning call.

He suddenly realized what he was hearing. Coming through the dense forest at a distance were the muffled baying sounds of hounds. They were not close but not far either. Their calls seemed to be getting slightly louder and more excited as he listened.

Traveler's adrenaline kicked in as he knew they were being tracked. He headed back to the cave at a trot. He held his walking stick in front at the vertical and used it as a shield to move the thick briars and branches out of the way. When he got to the site, he saw Glenda was already outside with their packs.

She immediately noticed his expression, "What's going on?"

"Hounds followed by men. That dolt Throbb is on our trail, we'll have to eat later. Right now we need to lose the hounds. I'll smother our fire using the rocks but we need to move fast."

When the fire was buried, Glenda handed Traveler his carry sack then slid her own sack across her back. "Should we go upstream or downstream?"

"Definitely down, that's heading toward the fortress. But first let's give the hounds a little morning confusion. I'll take lead, watch and copy." Glenda prepared to mirror his moves; she knew Traveler the scout was going to lay down a false trail for the pursuing hounds.

Traveler's first running leap was more than twenty-five feet and Glenda copied it. They landed on the edge of the opposite river bank. Their footprints were barely visible. They would appear as two runners trying to stay in the water to hide their scent.

They were just warming up. The baying hound sounds were generating a lot of adrenaline to fuel their jumping.

A second leap upstream followed. The second running leap carried them over thirty feet. "A new Olympic record," announced a pleased Traveler. They made a number of additional rapid jumps, always scuffing the bank's water line edge.

"Now let's jump in the water far enough from shore to fully cover our tracks. We need to be at least halfway up on our boots. The moving water will quickly wash the underwater prints away."

The two jumped into the center of the stream and stood together in the moving cold water. Facing Glenda Traveler said, "I'll follow you, Glenda. You're better at this leap-frogging than me. We'll make smaller jumps going downstream. Stop after each jump and be sure your footing is on solid ground. We'll stay in the river until we're well past the cave, then we'll get back on the trail.

"I'll stay far enough behind you to avoid crashing into you. The footing is going to be tricky but we need to move as fast as possible." Smiling at Glenda, Traveler gave her a thumbs up and said, "Leap away, frog leader."

"I'm on this," Glenda said as she cautiously jumped forward to land ten feet further downstream. She paused to judge the surface under her feet. "It feels like packed sand, we can make longer jumps. I'm pushing off now." Her next jump forward was a solid fifteen feet. She paused again, then said, "All's good on the bottom. Let's keep the leaping show moving as fast as we can."

An observer to this jumping spectacle would see two very large salmon leaping rapidly from flat waters to flat waters. Fortunately for the two salmon, the banks were clear of hungry bears waiting for their meals to come within paw reach.

They continued their salmon leapfrogging for a demanding thirty minutes, then Glenda stopped. "Traveler I'm exhausted. Do you think we've come far enough to get back on land?"

"I do. Our cave is far behind. Jump onto the river bank then jump to the edge of the forest. When you're out of the way I'll join you."

Glenda nodded, took a steadying breath followed by a final strong leap. She was on secure grassland bordering the river. She forced a final leap to reach the edge of the forest. Traveler was quickly beside her.

"My thighs are exhausted," said Glenda.

"Mine are beyond exhausted; they feel like overstretched rubber bands. Worse than any cross-country race. I could barely breathe and follow you the last ten minutes. I feel like I'm running up those museum steps again wearing lead shoes." They began to laugh as they recalled their early footrace to the top floor of the Chicago museum.

Traveler added, "Permit me to lead now. I seriously need to go slower to recover my leg muscles and breathing."

"Please feel free," was all Glenda could answer.

They moved at a steady pace while recovering. After half an hour Traveler said, "We need to refuel. He pointed to a spot ahead saying, "There's a nice grassy spot on that little rise ahead, let's collapse there."

"Looks perfect for a riverside picnic or a collapse," said Glenda.

As soon as they arrived, Glenda immediately sat down as did Traveler. She took out a sandwich and piece of cheese. "Too bad we can't enjoy the tranquility. This forest and river are stunning examples of nature's best before seven billion humans put their footprints all over the planet."

Then Glenda suddenly changed gears from reflecting on the beauty of nature to the pursuing threat. "Do you think we fooled those hounds?"

Traveler was eating a leg of Hermann's chicken with a wedge of cheese. "I'm sure we could fool Throbb and his crew, but hounds are another story. To start, they're smarter than Throbb. I think we must assume the hounds will pick up our trail."

"What do we do then?"

"We need to totally lose the hounds, one hundred percent. We need to force Throbb to return. As long as the hounds have a trail to follow, Throbb and his gang will keep after us so we need to kill our trail."

"I definitely agree," said Glenda. "We've got some time to change tactics right now. Instead of continuing on the ground, let's go vertical."

"OK Jane. Swing up and show Tarzan where we rest."

Chapter 45

Up Another Tree

Glenda studied the surrounding trees, then pointed, "I like this huge old tree by the river. I see a nice thick limb with our names on it, follow me."

Glenda positioned herself under the massive limb then did her Michael Jordan leap. She was on the limb looking down and grinning at Traveler. "Time to rise above the barking crowd, Tarzan."

Traveler picked his launch site and pushed off. He was passing Glenda when she reached out and grabbed his coat, "Slow down, you're not trying for a moon shot."

Traveler grinned back. "Thanks. OK now that we're here, what next?"

"First, we go higher, I want to see everything around and below us but be hidden enough where we aren't easily spotted. We should also move closer to the trunk to take advantage of the thick limbs to rest on. We can lean back and maybe even get a snooze in. When the hounds arrive we'll go into stealth mode and they'll never see us."

After ascending they saw the perfect crow's nest. Traveler leaned back against several large limbs saying, "Scoot over by me, there's a nice spot here perfect for balancing and resting."

Glenda slid across the large base limb and settled beside Traveler. "This would be a perfect place to bird-watch and river watch. I bet there are lots of animals that will show up to drink; we've got our own private zoo right here. Wake me up when there's some action going on." She shut her eyes and fell into a restful catnap doze.

Traveler found that he was too wired to sleep. He sat upright listening for the sounds of approaching hounds. His eyes focused on both sides of the river bank. The air remained undisturbed and the river remained a quiet, slow-moving haven for frogs and fish.

The serenity of the forest gradually relaxed him. The sun was bright and warmed the canopy above. The coldness of the night was gone. Mother Nature's fall blanket produced a perfect temperature for dozing and Traveler soon joined Glenda in a deepening slumber. Their bodies gradually slanted to the common side until they were comfortably leaning against each other.

Time passed as slowly as the river flowed. Faint calls came on a breeze. They ignored the calls until the sounds got louder and more excited. The hounds were approaching and sensed they had found their prey.

Traveler and Glenda jerked awake and straightened up at the same time. Traveler looked down at the approaching pack, "Guess we're going to the dogs," he said with a grin. Glenda gave him a "You've got to be kidding" look.

They jointly inspected the lead dog, it was a beast. Not nearly as large as Trajan but a definite cousin. The beast looked up at the sitting prey, tried a few leaps combined with snapping jaws, then settled for peeing on the tree. "Well he's marked us for sure," said Traveler.

The rest of the pack had now caught up. Several of the lighter dogs tried their luck at jumping up, but of course none came close. Several of the leaping dogs crashed into their mates when they fell back producing a lot of snarling and snapping.

The pack leader immediately stopped the nastiness from escalating. A couple of deep growls and the young members of the pack sat down and refocused upward.

"I think it's time to mess with them," said Glenda, "let's go stealth."

"In a minute, let's first annoy these guys like they've annoyed us."

Traveler called down, "Here doggie, doggie, big but stupid doggies," while throwing insults he waved his hands. All eyes were on him. Drool was marking the anger of the pack. The dogs understood they were being taunted. Their jaws quivered and their bodies shook.

Glenda had to laugh, "OK, Tarzan, let's stealth them on a fast two count, one, two, stealth."

The pack froze. They saw the two people simply disappear. There was instant confusion as they studied the empty space above them. Next the pack circled the tree looking up at nearby trees. The pack leader stayed in place looking up.

After fifteen minutes the pack sat with the leader looking up. "That's too weird," whispered Traveler, "don't they see we're gone?"

"Rats. Of course they smell us, big boy. They are master hunters and use all of their senses."

"Now what?" asked Traveler.

"Give me a minute, I'm thinking. I don't think we can fool them by jumping to other trees. When we move our stealth is broken, plus they follow our scent. Even if we could cross the river they will swim after us and we'll be stuck in another tree just on the other side."

"Bummer of a situation. I feel like a prison-break convict with the hounds after me."

Glenda sat quietly and Traveler quit talking. He recognized her concentration face.

"Ah, ha. I have something we can try," she said. "Remember M said we could tap into the jinn's mind, but not to because it could twist our own brains?" Traveler nodded.

"I think we can try and enter the minds below. Their brains are stupid simple compared with the jinn. I don't think we will mess ourselves up and maybe we can mess them up. Want to try?"

"Why not, how do we proceed?"

"I'm not sure exactly. Let's relax and concentrate on the big guy below. Let your mind try and read his brain. If we can read his mind then I think we can write on it, alter it so to speak."

They looked down at the big head staring up at them. The hound sensed they were there even though it could not see them. The pack leader had a lot of hunting experience when prey "went to ground" and seemed to disappear. The leader had learned to trust his instincts and wait out the prey.

Glenda relaxed and let her mind go into its study mode. Her mind joined with the book and became part of their symbiotic relationship. Then she was suddenly at the base of the tree and looking up. She was in the hound's mind and aware of its upwards focus following their scent.

She explored the mind now as she would an interactive video game. She found she could retrieve memories of similar hunts and she understood how the hound followed its instincts.

Animal instincts involve far more than applying logic trails from past experiences. Their hunting decisions combine all five senses to go along with past experiences. They can use their senses to augment past memories.

She next prodded the mind to see if she could influence it. She sent a smell memory trail to a close by tree. She saw the large hound cock its head, then move toward the falsely scented tree. The leader was now studying the overhead limbs on the new tree. Smiling to herself she thought, *I own you, big doggie, you are my puppy to train.*

She looked over at Traveler to tell him what to do but saw Traveler had three young dogs chasing their own tails. *He's brain connected to them.* Next she watched as all three begin to roll on the ground. She was now quietly laughing and whispered, "Very funny. I see you have mastered 'Tail Chasing 101'."

"And you have mastered 'Dogs Looking at Empty Spaces', reminds me of some of my high school classmates during math class. Keep it up and give him one very sore neck."

Traveler laughed as he watched the tail-chasing dogs and the staring dog, "It's payback time for this pack. They will be sorry they made us leave our nice cave and do a forced march." As an afterthought he asked, "Do you think we could control Throbb?"

"Not sure," answered Glenda. "Maybe together we could, but I don't think we should try. Human minds are far more complex than Fido below. Worse case we accidentally end up creating weird memories of demons that he will take back to the duke and mage."

"Agreed," said Traveler. "If we try to plant false memories and fail, that will reinforce we're demons. The last thing we want is for the creature to get a heads-up there are other supernatural beings around. We need to stay low profile and just try to discredit Throbb."

Glenda continued, "A good approach right now is to throw down a false trail for the hounds and Throbb will follow them. The more time he spends chasing a ghost trail then returns empty-handed, the dumber he'll look."

"Agreed," said Traveler, "and I have an idea about a false trail."

"Enlighten me," said Glenda.

"First, let's remove our scent memory coming from this tree, that will calm the pack down. Let them relax a bit. When we're ready, we'll give them a new scent memory that says we crossed the river right here. They'll swim across and then wander on the wrong side looking for our scent. We can even give them a memory scent on the other side that they'll follow."

"We'll wait until Throbb shows up, then trigger the new scent memories. The hounds will rush off and Throbb will be right behind them. We'll just wait here in the box seats and enjoy watching the show."

"Brilliant! We can even implant a visual memory of us sitting in a distant tree. Let them howl and circle an empty tree while Throbb loses confidence in his tracking hounds and heads back."

Chapter 46

Mutual Support

An hour passed. The forest was now a sauna at ground level. The heat was beginning to rise off the ground and the hounds were repeatedly going to the river to drink. Once back they lay on their sides with open mouths cooling their bodies and conserving their energy. They were in no mood to begin another random chase, it seemed pointless since the scent of the prey had disappeared. They waited patiently for their master, Karl, to arrive. The master would know what to do.

Finally the sound of approaching men and horses disturbed the quiet air. Traveler spotted Throbb coming first, he was leading his horse on foot. Both man and horse looked tired and grumpy.

Following Throbb were his men leading their horses on foot. The dense undergrowth had forced them to dismount and save their horses for better ground. All of the soldiers had long ago stripped off their heavy, padded jackets and placed them across the saddles.

Throbb spotted his resting hound pack and a look of frustration and anger passed over his face. He turned to the master of hounds and growled, "Karl, your dogs are useless. They've led us through an unforgiving forest, now they decide to rest. How do you answer for them, hound master?"

Karl ignored Throbb's temper outburst. He had experienced it many times before. When Throbb was angry he stopped thinking and needed to be calmed down much like a petulant child throwing a temper tantrum.

The hound master studied his pack. He knew they were relaxed and that meant they had lost the scent trail. He also knew the pack would be very tired from racing through the undergrowth in the heat. "They know it's time to rest and wait for us to catch up. They are a smart pack." The implication was that the hounds were smarter than Throbb.

Karl then circled the large tree they were resting under. His eyes suddenly noticed the area his leader had peed on. *He marked this tree for a reason*, the master thought. He looked up into the tree not expecting to see anything. If there was anybody hiding in the thick foliage the hounds would be barking their heads off.

Karl saw Throbb was now beginning to think again, he was studying the opposite shore. "Is it possible those two crossed here and your hounds decided to wait for us before crossing?"

"A distinct possibility. Let me suggest we cross over but let's rest the men and horses now before we go over."

Throbb nodded, he also needed to rest his large body and wanted to think about excuses if he returned empty-handed. "If we fail to capture those two, I think you know I will blame your hounds, and by association you."

"Of course I know that. I also know you will need to present the failure to the mage. I don't envy you that task regardless of how you try to pass on blame. The duke would be more forgiving but the mage seems to have little sympathy regarding failure. He is a changed man and very difficult to read."

Throbb was now thinking about the possibilities. He realized he would benefit with the hound master as an ally. Better the two of them describing their efforts as a team than doing it by himself and becoming the sole target of the mage's anger.

"I was overly brusque, Karl. You know me too well, you understand the heat and walking through this underbrush have me on a short temper. Your hounds are the very best trackers, and were trained by the best master of hounds. I will make both of those points with the mage. We will focus on our joint effort, and failure can be blamed on the demons."

The hound master knew he was being solicited as an ally. He also knew it was in his best interest to have Throbb supporting him. At the end of the day Throbb would still be the one held responsible. Trained hounds and a hound master were valuable assets for the duke. Throbb was a replaceable unit leader.

He gave Throbb a sympathetic nod. "Thank you, Throbb. Rest assured I will equally support your strong leadership efforts."

The two had now agreed upon their reporting strategy and settled into a relaxed atmosphere of goodwill.

Chapter 47

The Hound Master's Tale

While relaxing, Karl took a long sip of water and leaned toward a resting Throbb. "In the event we do not capture the two runners, and return empty-handed, let me share tales of our mage. These stories have come to me from my fellow masters of hounds and I believe them. We are a fraternity of sorts and share information and advice among ourselves."

Throbb moved from his resting spot and sat across from the master. "Tell me the tales you've heard from your hound master brothers, Karl. The more we share, the better our story can be presented to the mage." Throbb knew all soldiers enjoyed gossip but this sounded like more substance than just gossip.

"It's an unpleasant story, Throbb. Unpleasant because of the invading Hun and their threat to all of us, but also unpleasant because of the superstition it created among our own soldiers. Like all campfire stories told by soldiers, there is much exaggeration added to make it a better tale. Experienced listeners know to cut these stories in half. As a unit leader you know this of course."

Throbb nodded his understanding. He knew he had told his own tales with embellishments to hold his listener's interest. Naturally his tales included exaggerations about his own exploits.

"The true unpleasantness comes from the barbarian leader. You have heard his name, Attila, and how he destroys all armies that face him. He never takes prisoners. He has never backed down nor been defeated."

Throbb felt a shiver pass through him at the name Attila. Of course he knew of him. The barbarian was called the "Scourge of God", and soldiers across the world dreaded facing him.

"The stories I have heard from my fellow hound masters claim to have come from our scouts who had gotten close to the Hun camp. They overheard the Hun guards talking and this is their tale.

"According to the guards' story they claim to have seen a red demon emerge out of the mage, kill the captains and guards inside the tent and then return into the mage's body. Attila was said to stand very still during this killing time and seemed to be dreaming."

Karl smiled at his captive audience, "Relax Throbb, of course I don't believe the Hun guards' stories about a red demon. They are campfire stories told to entertain.

"What I believe likely happened was the mage used his dining hall magic tricks to impress this Hun leader and convinced him to leave us alone. Mine is a much more logical explanation than a red demon. You can relax now."

Chapter 48

The Snipe Hunt Starts

Thinking out loud Throbb said, "Karl, I'm not sure I needed that story right now but I understand your explanation, it makes a lot more sense. If the mage can convince a warrior like Attila of his magic, then he will likely go along with our story of demons. To deny our demon story would be to undermine his own claims of mystical powers. I think we can end this chase now and declare the two as demons who have fled before us."

Before the hound master could respond, bedlam started among the hounds. The pack of hounds suddenly stood up together howling and ran to the river. Two young hounds were already in the shallow water at the river's edge. They were eager to cross while the older hounds waited for permission.

Karl grinned at Throbb, "The wind has shifted direction and they have discovered a fresh scent, it's coming across the river. "I believe our two demons are in human bodies and waiting to be caught. We may come out of this as heroes. Let's release the pack and take up the chase."

With the hounds yelping Throbb had regained his confidence. The two youths were out there and he would capture them. Throbb commanded, "Karl, release them!"

The master gave the approving signal and the pack threw itself into the river. They were rested now and eager to pursue the scent. Even in crossing their calling-out bays rose to the heavens as their legs thrust rapidly through the slow-moving water.

Taking his lead from the released hounds, one soldier had already mounted his horse and led it into the river then called back, "Throbb, this is a shallow passage spot, we can easily ride across." Throbb nodded approval.

The men cheered and quickly mounted and followed. As they crossed, the cooling waters refreshed both horse and rider. The hunt was back on.

Watching the mounted soldiers riding across the river following the hounds, Traveler grinned, "That in boy scouting tradition is what we refer to as a 'snipe hunt'."

Glenda had a puzzled look on her face, "What's a snipe hunt?"

"There are no actual snipes but the young scouts don't know that. They will stand in the woods holding open bags to catch the snipe that we older boys are supposedly beating toward them. Of course we are already back in our tents laughing."

Glenda's returning chuckle was halfhearted, "We have sent them on a well-deserved snipe hunt, but there is a much bigger game here. What did you think of the Hun guards' story about the mage?"

"It sounds like a story made up to explain Attila's change of direction. If anything weird really happened in the tent, I think Karl's explanation is very plausible. The mage is most likely a strong hypnotist as well as a sleight of hand magician.

"Between us there is no unsolvable situation. Consider yourself Nancy Drew and I'm Sherlock Holmes. Once we get to the fortress, we'll study the duke and this mage as well as any other weird-acting person. The jinn can run but it can't hide. Besides there's no reason for it to hide, it doesn't know we're after it."

Glenda shook her head, "Brave words, Sherlock, but I'm not so much worried about it hiding from us as how we'll hide from it. There is no cavalry here to protect us. We need to go very slowly and use our wits. The worst thing for us is that the jinn becomes aware we're here."

"Agreed, 'caution' is the word of the day. However, for right now, we have an opportunity to move fast while Throbb is on his snipe hunt. Let's get back on the road where we can move double time."

Chapter 49

Where's Our Path?

With speed as their immediate goal, they dropped down to the forest floor and began searching for an animal trail back to the road. Once again, moving through the dense forest was slow, exhausting work. On the forest floor the temperature had jumped another ten degrees. Both were quickly sweating from the heat and the effort.

"I know we got to the river in about two hours", said Traveler, "but we were on a path then. This is just ridiculous, Stanley had to be nuts to do this for years."

"He was not nuts, just motivated and focused like we need to be. Look around and not just at your feet, there may be another trail." Another hour of slow progress and Glenda said, "I need a rest," and she sat down on the forest floor. Traveler semi-collapsed beside her.

The two lay there quietly recovering their energy. Neither spoke, that took too much effort. Sitting there they heard twigs snap at the same time. They both looked slowly around to see a full-grown red buck deer with a large rack of antlers. The buck was moving through the woods apparently following a nearly invisible path toward the river. They waited until it had disappeared into the protective trees.

"I do believe we have found our easier way out," said Traveler. "Did you see the size of those antlers? He needs a path wide enough to keep his head from being yanked around."

They stood up and worked their way toward the spot the buck came from. Once there they realized there was indeed a hidden path. The path led toward the road and they put their heads down and followed it. Being larger, Traveler led the way. Glenda was quite happy about following him as he moved branches away with his walking stick.

"I think we are approaching dusk again. Maybe we need to call it a day," said Glenda.

"It's a day!" laughed Traveler. "Time for the army to camp down."

Chapter 50

Nighttime Resting Retreats

"I miss our cave," said Glenda. "Plus, I think it's going to rain. I smell rain in the air."

"Yeah, I feel it coming also. I think our best bet is pick a dense tree, go up then huddle against its trunk. We're in for a long miserable night."

"Well you're Mr Tree-Picker so go pick our shelter, I'll follow your lead."

Traveler studied the surrounding forest. *Too many choices*, he thought. Then he spotted the grandfather of all trees. It was a giant among giants, maybe the great grandfather of the forest. It was majestic with a diameter well over twenty feet. As Traveler studied it, he suddenly saw what might be their sanctuary for the night.

Above the lower limbs there appeared to be an opening carved into the massive trunk. "Let me explore grandfather for a minute," and he leaped to the lowest limb.

Looking up Glenda was puzzled, *What does Tarzan see that I don't?*

Her answer came quickly from the dense overhead foliage, "You won't believe this. Come on up, bring your sack with you and toss mine up." Hesitating a moment, he added, "You'll like what I found."

Moments later Glenda was beside Traveler and studying the natural opening that was carved into the massive trunk.

"Lightning hit here and took out a big piece of the tree. It literally burned out this space. We have a tree cave.

"Based on the layers of scarred sealing rings, I'd guess lightning struck maybe fifty years ago. This tree was so large it absorbed the strike. Most trees receiving a major strike split apart. Grandfather was way too large and strong to split. Bark never regrew but the internal sap and fiber formed a perfect protective seal."

"I'm very impressed with Grandfather but I'm really impressed that you found this tree cave. You have a genuine talent for finding safe lodging, first the land cave now the tree cave. To repeat, I'm impressed."

Traveler was ready to modestly agree about his lodge-finding skills when an enormous clap of thunder put an explanation point right behind Glenda's praise. "Uh-oh, here comes our rain," she said.

The forest canopy became an instant kettle drum with Mother Nature beating out a Gene Krupa pulsating rhythm. The rain hit in sheets with a determination to reach the floor far below. Traveler and Glenda instinctively moved inside as far as they could.

"Wow, I'm able to be completely inside," said Glenda as she put her back against the back wall. "We can lay down in here."

"Well I could fit completely if we lay in a more diagonal position. Right now my feet will stick out, but that's OK I guess. Wet feet never killed anyone."

"Let's keep your feet dry, Mr Cave Finder. We can sleep on a diagonal and we can make a little more room by placing our boots together on either side of the opening."

Traveler was running the possible resting layouts in his head when his stomach took over. "Let's eat first, then arrange the sleeping quarters." Glenda nodded as she was already opening her bag.

They reached into their sacks and removed wrapped slices of sausage, cheese, and the heavy dark bread. "Save something for tomorrow," advised Glenda, "it may be a while before we can resupply."

Traveler felt a moment of annoyance at her advice, *Like I don't know how to pace myself.* He opened his sack and saw his remaining supply was smaller than he had thought. *I don't remember eating three chicken sandwiches. I swear I only ate two.*

Glenda watched him and saw he was surprised about his diminished store. For a moment "I warned you," started to come out. Instead she bit her tongue then took out a large chicken sandwich. She ripped it in half and handed the larger half to Traveler. Before he could protest, she said, "The fact is you're a lot bigger, so no argument please."

Traveler gave her a sheepish smile, "I'll be a gracious accepter, but know I will even the debt scales. This elephant never forgets a good deed. Thank you."

"You evened any debt scale just by finding this retreat. Now please eat that before I reclaim it."

They ate in silence then folded their blankets into sleeping bags. The blankets were large enough that they double-folded the bottom layer and kept a single layer to go over their tops. Boots were place by Glenda's side since Traveler had the longer legs.

Once they stretched out, they squirmed around to find the best shared diagonals. Once Traveler's feet were inside they quit squirming and were asleep in minutes.

Chapter 51

New Day, Old Woods

"My back is broken," said Glenda. "The blanket was not last night's bed of thick leaves and moss. I don't think I can move."

"Well whatever you do," grinned Traveler, "don't think about today's walk."

"Nice reminder, thanks a lot."

"Once you're down I'll throw down our sacks. Call out when you're there."

Glenda moved on her knees to the opening, held onto the side to stand up, and then grunted, "It's worse than I thought. Every vertebra is mad at me." She worked her way out onto the access limb, looked down and said, "Here goes nothing. I hope gravity is still my friend."

Gravity still loved her and she came down in a controlled descent, she was Mary Poppins sans umbrella. Looking up she called, "The eagle has landed in one piece but I feel like there are lots of me held together with Krazy Glue. Throw down our sacks."

Traveler responded and both sacks cleared the bottom limbs. Moments later Traveler joined her, "You'll feel better once we get walking."

"Sure," was her only response.

They began to follow the path again. In daylight the path was easier to see than it was at dusk the evening before. Also helping were various animals' tracks. The path had been well traveled during the night. Various footprints affirmed it was forest freeway. As they walked Traveler found himself looking at the various tracks. "Lots of deer, rabbit, and I believe a wolf or two," he periodically announced as he showed off his animal lore. Then he went suddenly silent.

Glenda glanced over at him, "See any T-Rex prints, boy scout?"

Traveler did not respond to the gentle gibe. *That's unlike him,* she thought. "You're awfully quiet, anything bothering you?"

"I'm not sure. I don't want to bother you, it's probably nothing."

"That's great, just leave me hanging with 'probably nothing'."

"OK, What I saw back there were bear tracks. They were so large I wasn't sure they were bear, but there's no elephant in this part of the world."

"That's no big deal. Bears need to drink and catch fish, and this is the wildlife highway road to the river. Right?"

"Yes, it is. The problem is that the tracks were coming away from the river."

Glenda shivered for a second. "Not the best news to start the morning, but it's likely gone off in some other direction. I'm sure we're OK. Right?"

Traveler made a noncommittal grunting sound. "Speak up, big boy. Elucidate me on bears and tell me why I should worry, I know you're dying to."

"Dying is not the word I would choose, but OK since you asked. The bear is a natural hunter with great senses of hearing and smell. It's also at the top of wildlife intelligence. It's clever, unpredictable, and frankly a killing machine. Prehistoric bears grew very, very large. A modern grizzly would definitely avoid a meeting. Think of a 4000-pound hound with long knife-sharp claws tracking you with dinner on its mind.

"Even worse is that at least you can hear the hounds coming. The bear on the other hand is pure stealth. Oh yeah, and it's extra ferocious in the fall since it needs to build up body fat for hibernation."

"Well I'm sorry I asked. Seriously, any thought about how we can avoid Mr Bear if he is stalking us?"

"Not really. Our best escape is to jump up into a tree. At the same time, he's a natural climber, but at least that saves us for a while."

With Traveler's treetop escape plan now firmly in her mind, Glenda walked with an eye upward as well as on the path in front. With the bear lecture she had forgotten her aches from sleeping on the hard floor the night before. She was on full alert. She was well aware she was expending a lot of nervous energy. As they continued to walk Glenda felt her fear gradually recede. *You can only hold your breath so long,* she thought.

The path suddenly opened up to offer both sunshine as well as a grassy resting spot. "Let's take a break and have breakfast," suggested Traveler. Glenda saw he looked relaxed and that put her into a similar mood.

Chapter 52

Bear Days

They sat in the center of the dell, lay on their backs and stretched. Glenda looked up at the clear blue sky, "I never knew how good soft ground could feel. It's like a five-star mattress. And I can't believe how good Mr Sun feels after being trapped in that underground forest. Mother Nature is a good mother."

They finally sat up cross-legged and pulled out their late breakfast fare. "I think we must be less than an hour to the road," said Traveler. "Once we're on it we'll put good distance between us and Throbb."

"Speaking of Throbb," Traveler said grinning, "I wonder how he and his crew survived the storm last night? Bet they are just miserable right now. They must have slept on the cold wet ground while we had a warm tree cave. Even with the hard floor, our tree house was the winner in that sleeping contest." With that self-congratulating comment, Traveler bit off a wedge of the sausage.

Glenda was chewing pieces off the hard cheese. She had a witty comment about Throbb smelling like a wet dog. As she cleared her throat to speak, her mouth froze open. A brown mountain was rising off the forest floor, it was well over Traveler's standing height then it went up another story.

Traveler stopped eating the moment he saw Glenda's eyes widen and fear cross her face. He turned his head and also froze. The brown mountain was now a bear giant towering over twelve feet.

It was a mass of thick fur with paws larger than a catcher's mitt. Out of these mitts extended butcher knife claws. Its mouth opened to form a volcano. Rather than lava the opening spewed out saliva. Similar to lava the spittle was thick and hot. No longer a stealth hunter it declared its presence with a mind-numbing roar.

"Don't move," was all Traveler could mutter.

"I can't breathe," whispered Glenda. "There's no escape tree around us, this is really bad."

The bear had finished its assessment, no threat here just tasty early morning food. As it dropped to the ground Traveler threw his sandwich at it. "Throw your cheese."

Glenda's trance broke and she threw the remaining chunk at the bear's head. The scent of the cheese had the monster swing a few feet away to capture the morsel. "Don't run. We need to try and change its mind about us as food. Go stealth then try to change its scent memory."

Glenda immediately became one with their grassy sitting area. Once she was blended into the grass, she felt some of her control return. She forced her mind into its newly developed skill to change animal memories.

Traveler was staring at the beast with a distant look in his eyes, he had also entered his mental control state.

The beast had found the cheese and the sandwich. A long, thick, black and pink tongue brought both edibles into the cavernous maw. There was no chewing, the food simply went down the gullet tunnel. With the food consumed the tongue licked the fur around the mouth for any remaining treat. Then its head came up looking for the two larger meals.

A look of bear confusion crossed its muzzle, the two humans were gone. It narrowed its eyes, then sniffed the air for a scent. Like the hounds the bear had a terrific sense of smell.

"Let's give it a scent of a honey, high up in that tree behind it. Make it climb up to the top."

Glenda understood. Her mind called up a memory from a National Geographic TV show. The show presented the life of bees and their honey lodes. This lode was built into limbs at the top of a tall tree. The show's narrator explained that bees knew all about honey predators and placed their golden treasure in difficult-to-reach places. Her memory included the bees buzzing in and out.

The bear turned and sniffed in a new direction. It was visibly excited. The anger at the missed meals was overcome with the image of its honey meal. Once it headed for the faux honey tree, Traveler and Glenda slowly stood, picked up their sacks, and eased back onto the path.

"That had to be the father of bears. He could eat a grizzly and still be hungry."

Glenda put her finger to her lips signaling to be quiet and whispered, "We're OK for the moment. That guy has one thought right now and it's honey not us, let's not change its mind. Hopefully we'll be long gone and long forgotten before it finds there is no honey tree."

With a young man's bravado Traveler declared, "Stupid bear ruined my breakfast. Lucky for him he missed my Sunday punch." Traveler proceeded to throw shadowboxing jabs while Glenda smiled to herself. *Sure, big boy. Sometimes you get the bear but sometimes the bear gets you. Let's call it a draw and avoid a rematch.*

The late morning turned into early midday. Occasionally they found small pools of water from the night before but most of the rain had sunk into the forest floor. They drank what they could find. It was not nearly enough.

Chapter 53

Some Days the Bear...

Traveler and Glenda emerged from the forest path at last. Their woolen shirt coats were soaked as well as their faces and hair. "I feel like a drowned rat," complained Glenda. "The humidity must be two hundred percent. Where's our cool river when we need it?"

Traveler shook his head like a wet dog and moisture flew off. "Hate to tell you but you're also having a skein hair day, I pity you trying to comb out that mess, and no conditioner either. Bummer for you."

Glenda appreciated Traveler's use of an obscure word and laughed saying, "Please, enough with skeining me. It's bad enough we smell like wet dogs, no reason to rub it in."

Traveler sniffed the air, "Yep, wet dog. The scent that keeps on coming."

Glenda's mind switched from conversation to studying their immediate surroundings. "Call me cautious or call me still scared, but I'd feel better resting in a nice shady tree." Spotting a large tree beside the road she elevated herself to a thick limb hanging out over the road. Traveler rose to join her. They moved along the limb and settled down against the thick tree trunk.

"I think we're about out of food thanks to the uninvited guest, but let's take in what we have left," said Glenda. She opened her sack, retrieved a piece of the remaining sausage, broke it in half, and offered half to Traveler. He reciprocated with his untouched chunk of the hard cheese.

"I've got two apples left," observed Traveler.

"Likewise. We better save one for this evening."

For the first time that day they relaxed. They ate their small meal then discovered they were drowsy. "It's nap time for this girl. I see a nice secure nesting area above us, feel free to join."

Traveler followed her up and saw that Glenda had indeed spotted a solid resting place in their tree. Surrounding limbs intertwined to offer an inviting nest. *She's boy scout material, no question. I've taught her well.*

Midday naps can be foolers. Usually an hour does the job for kindergartners or adults. In this case the combination of exertion, stress, and heat required a longer recovery. They were both in a deep sleep when they were awakened by the sound of dogs, horses, and cursing men.

"Stealth," whispered Glenda.

Coming down the road was a bedraggled band of searchers and tired hounds. They were strung out in a staggered line and moved slowly. Throbb was in the lead while Karl, the master of hounds, brought up the rear.

Karl played rear guard to be sure that no dog decided to collapse in the weeds beside the road. He was responsible for every hound, they were each a valuable asset of the duke. Beyond being assets, they were Karl's friends. Each hound was an individual to him, he knew their strengths and weaknesses having raised them from birth.

As he rode slowly along looking down at the hounds, he planned how he would feed and comfort them when they were back. They deserved rewards for the difficulties endured. He was not at all concerned about Throbb or the soldiers; they could take care of themselves.

Karl's head suddenly jerked out of its daydream. There was great shouting at the front. He heard a man scream and a horse's shrill call of fear. His own horse was suddenly agitated and twisting away from the front. He regained control and stood up in the stirrups. His hounds were now a war pack making their deep, challenging growls.

In an instant Karl saw the conflict ahead. While standing in the stirrups he saw a massive brown mountain in motion. The mountain had swept two soldiers off their horses and was smashing the fallen riders and mounts. His hounds ran forward like courageous soldiers to the rescue. Karl knew this charge would lead to the early death of his hounds. This brown mountain would destroy every arriving dog with ease.

He saw an enormous tooth-filled mouth open and close on a soldier's arm holding a sword. When the brown head lifted the arm was gone, so was the man.

Traveler and Glenda stared at the battle below. The bear had received multiple wounds but appeared unfazed. Froth flowed from the bear's jaws and its claws dripped with blood and shreds of horse flesh.

Two soldiers lay unmoving while Throbb and the remained three mounted soldiers fought to control their horses. Each man knew if he was tossed from his horse his fate would be sealed. The bear was a killing machine and the odds were in its favor.

Karl took all this in at a glance. He had seen wild bear and boar attacks and he knew they were formidable, deadly opponents. The best way to hunt them was with archers and spearmen. This unit had neither. The hound master had to make a quick decision, save the men or his pack.

While standing he gave the long whistle that told each hound to focus immediately on him. Their training overcame their instincts and they turned to look at their master. He signaled the two largest and oldest hounds to sit. They sat but were quivering, eager to move back into the fray.

Still holding the pack's attention, the master gave the younger hounds a circling motion with his raised arm and grunted a loud command. The pack understood, and several of the young hounds leapt upward snapping at the bear. This attack briefly caused the bear to abandon its own attack on the horsemen.

The remaining pack circled the bear and with a signal from the master two hounds leaped onto the bear's back. The two clinging hounds proceeded to chew and claw at the bear's back. The thick fur made their chewing annoying but it could not do serious damage.

The back-clinging hounds suddenly found themselves hanging on like rodeo riders on a bucking bull. Similar to a bull's twisting motion the bear made several sharp reversing body-turns. The two hounds hit the ground hard.

Before either could jump away, the bear was upon one as quick as a cat. The hound was bitten in half. While the bear bent down to kill the second fallen hound, two more hounds were on its back. This new attack distracted the bear enough that the second felled hound was up and limped away, it lived to fight another day.

One zealous young hound leaped directly onto the bear's stomach and sank teeth into the softer belly. The bear instantly wrapped arms around the invader and squeezed. The hound was lifeless in a moment.

Throbb had regained his years of soldier discipline. His fighting blood raged. His fallen soldiers were more than simply men in his command, they were comrades of many shared battle campaigns. They had defended each other in battle at risk to their own lives.

Throbb jumped off his horse and approached the brown mountain of fury. Throbb was filled with the fearless battle lust that Vikings called "going berserk". While the bear was furious, Throbb was berserk.

Without hesitation Throbb came at the bear from the side and drove his long sword up and into the beast's neck. The blade emerged on the other side. He motioned to a soldier for another blade. The man leaped off his horse and handed the blade to Throbb. At this moment Karl released the remaining two hounds. These were the largest and most experienced. They were instantly attached to the bear's belly.

The bear had its paws on the sword buried in its neck. The neck pain was so great the beast was not aware of the razor teeth tearing into its belly. When it finally dropped a massive paw to crush the two hounds, Throbb brought the heavy battle sword down from above his head.

Throbb had a lifetime of fighting. All of the power of his body was behind the blow. The sword tore into the bear's descending arm and sliced it off at the elbow.

The bear reeled, then collapsed to bleed out on the road. The hounds continued to maul at the now open belly flesh and Karl permitted them their time of victory.

Glenda and Traveler sat stunned at the battle. They had seen a lot of action movies but this was beyond a filmmaker's capability. The sounds and the smells had stunned their senses. The bravery of man, beast, and hound was forever etched into their memories.

"I wonder what the books will think of this." said Traveler in a whisper to Glenda. She could only shake her head. The experience was still holding her in its powerful grasp.

They watched the scene below as the ritual of taking victory trophies took place. Each soldier was permitted a foot or paw as their proof of valor. The beast was subsequently dressed out with Throbb receiving the intact skin with the massive head. The hound master received the remaining paw.

The dressing took several hours and the soldiers were quiet as they reflected on the battle and their fallen comrades. It was time to return home and the two killed soldiers were put across a remaining mount. The felled hounds were placed across the back of Karl's horse.

Chapter 54

Deep Thoughts

The sun was descending and promised a few more hours before darkness. Traveler and Glenda watched the depleted unit of horsemen and hounds as it proceeded forward. "When do we start to follow?" asked Traveler.

"Call me superstitious," Glenda answered, "but I would wait until tomorrow. This is a strange day and I think we need to let it finish itself. Nothing has ever come close to watching that battle in real life, not movies or video games. My senses were overwhelmed with the sight, sound, and smell of the battle. This confirms what M said, we need real experiences to bring reality to our book studies."

"I agree one hundred percent. As a guy with a lot of gaming experience in virtual reality, this is far more intense than those computer-generated adrenaline rushes."

Glenda was leaning back as she said, "Another night in the forest, I hope it's the last one. While I love Mother Nature, I need so many things right now like a bath, food, and rest. I've had all the 'real' experiences I can take. I'd like to be sleeping in a real bed, shopping tomorrow with Virginia, then dining at her French restaurant. I miss pulling Theo's ears and hearing him making his vibration sounds."

Traveler nodded, "Let's end this day right now and hope Morpheus gives us pleasant dreams."

They decided to stay in their tree. It had proven to offer acceptable sleeping space and offered good views of the road in both directions. They ate their final apples right down to the core. Each of them got ready to pitch the core then thought better and ate them. "Seeds are good roughage," reflected Glenda.

"Yeah, I bet bark is too, but I draw the line with seeds."

As they were relaxing and preparing to sleep Traveler asked, "Before we pass out, I've got a question, well a couple. What did you find when you went into Mr Bear's mind?"

"Strange you should ask. I've been thinking about that now. What I found was that the bear's mind was more complex than the hounds. The hounds run hard on all five senses as did the bear but the bear had an added sense, call it thinking."

Traveler was listening carefully, "Go on."

"The hounds are smart, but they have little ability to use guile or subtlety. As trackers they announce their presence with their constant braying. The bear is a planner and uses his own form of stealth. The bear gets surprise on his side. He wants to win with one quick attack before his foe can form an action plan. He likes an ambush.

"We only escaped his charge because we had food in our hands that we instinctively threw at him. In many other ways he outfoxed us."

"I agree. When I first entered the bear's mind it was like one of those Russian Matryoshka dolls. I sensed wheels within wheels. It was a more challenging place for me to navigate than with the hounds. I knew what I wanted to do, but had to shift through more layers of its mind to find the connections necessary to change its thinking."

Glenda nodded adding, "The good news is that we are upgrading our new mind-altering skill through experience. Our books have implanted the ability but we needed to actually apply it to make it real. Each new experience forces us to deal with greater brain system complexity."

"I can compare it to my video gaming. Managing an animal mind in real-time is an over-the-top challenge. Playing DOTA is simple compared to what we just did. Fail at DOTA and you restart. Fail here and it's really 'end of player'."

Glenda was listening then said, "When the bear came at us, we were fortunate to have food handy. I'm not sure how we would have fared if we had to face an attack without the benefit of some distraction."

"Agreed," said Traveler. "We should always be secure before using our evolving mind skills. I also think there is something more going on with this mind-control business. When I was inside the bear's mind, I felt another presence; it had to be you. My thoughts seemed powered up by your presence. I was still me with my own identity, but with enhanced powers, rather like having a supercharger put on my racing car."

Nodding Glenda said, "I felt the same thing. I think somehow our minds come together once we are inside another mind. We became a single more powerful mind yet remained ourselves."

"The math guy in me says that our combined power is following an exponential curve. The more we exercise our combined minds the greater the power becomes." Traveler grinned adding, "Want me to draw you an exponential curve?"

"You can do that drawing in the dirt whenever you want. Feel free to go down right now and I'll look at your work tomorrow. As for me, sleep is where I'm heading." She gave Traveler a wink and a quiet, "Good night Mr Math." They slept like babies.

Chapter 55

Meeting the Locals

The sun woke them up earlier than when they were in the dense forest. A streak of light worked its way up the road from the east. It hit both of them in the face and announced a new day was starting. "Rise and shine, I guess. Well at least we can rise, shining takes too much effort." Glenda nodded her acceptance of Traveler's truism.

They drifted down to the ground, confirmed their sacks were totally empty of food and headed west down the road. After a while Traveler said, "Was it just a coincidence that the bear was close to us the second time? Was he continuing to stalk us?"

"I've thought about that and, 'No'. I think the crafty beast just picked up the smell of our sacks. Maybe it didn't remember smelling us personally, but our packs would be a dinner bell calling out to him. He happened upon Throbb and the hounds by accident while following our food-scent trail."

"I think you're right. That's one dinner bell he should not have listened to."

As they walked along Traveler noted the road was gradually widening. "I think we're approaching civilization by the looks of our road. There are fewer potholes and it's now wide enough for two wagons to pass. Should we stay on it or start the parallel walk in the woods?"

"It's a new day and I believe it will be a positive day. Let's stay the course right now. Besides, I don't think there will be any 'wanted' posters out on us yet. Throbb won't have had time yet to tell his tale. He's probably working hard on how best to present his demon story."

They continued walking for a while then Traveler said, "You know, I'm reluctant to say it, but looking back now, Throbb showed me a side of himself that I never would have guessed existed. He was really brave and put himself on the line for his men. Few ever do that and those that do are called 'heroes'.

"Generals create great battle strategies, but when the battle horns blow the individual soldiers needs to think and act under great pressure and Throbb did that. He out-thought the bear by getting to its blind side then making the neck blow. It took bravery for sure, but also required thinking under great stress. None of the other soldiers could get their minds out of the horror of the bear, but Throbb did."

"Well I'll grant his self-sacrificing courage but he's never going to get on my dance card. Enough of Throbb, I think I hear people noises in the distance."

"You're right; now that I've stopped talking, I hear them. Let's detour back to river."

Glenda nodded and they moved off the road into the forest. Once they were off the road, they quickly noticed the forest was thinned out. They saw stumps from cut trees bordering the road and wagon tracks.

Glenda noted, "Looks like civilization is making its mark so there's got to be food. I bet the local farm kids are sent here for berries, nuts, and roots and maybe some fishing."

"Let's move a little further toward the river for cover, I think people are likely a big pain in this neck of the woods." Glenda grimaced at Traveler's bad pun and he grinned back. "You want killer humor you go to a New York or LA comedy club."

They only had to move a short distance to once again find a dense forest surrounded them. Their forward progress slowed as they again had to weave through and around the dense foliage.

After a while they heard the sound of the river again and Glenda reflected, "Settlements were always placed close to water sources and we are likely approaching hamlets. We need to approach with caution."

Moving slowly forward, Glenda suddenly held up a hand and pointed, "Do you see that? There is a major berry patch to our left that's hidden inside a thorny thicket. It'll be a pain to get to but we can fill our sacks. With luck maybe we can barter the berries for real food when we hit a village."

"Good eyesight, princess, permit me to blaze a way into the berry patch."

Smiling back Glenda said, "Blaze away Stanley, and Livingston will follow."

Using his heavy walking stick Traveler proceeded to smash a path through the thicket's brambles. When they reached the patch, they found it was even larger than it had appeared from a distance. The berries were red, ripe and not yet discovered by birds, animals, or humans. Glenda took a small bite of a large berry, smiled and declared, "We've hit the mother lode of berries."

Traveler immediately joined her, "Delicious! A cross between a raspberry and a strawberry, I've never had a berry like this. This is a hybrid Mother Nature formed all on her own, I wonder what happened to it."

"People and civilization," said Glenda. "We have destroyed a lot of nature as we expanded our fields for crops. Farmers always assume there is an endless supply of natural foods as they clear the land. Once cleared, they too often discover they have destroyed a lot of nature's best offerings."

They stopped talking and began serious picking. They moved their carry sacks around to rest against their stomachs and began filling the empty bags. The filling ritual started with three berries for their bag and one for their stomach. As they ate more of the sweet berries they began to put more into their sacks. After an hour of picking they had filled both sacks and bellies.

Traveler announced, "I'm really thirsty from those berries and I've got a little sugar buzz. Love them, but I need fresh water. Let's get drinks then follow the river to the town."

"I'm right behind you Stanley, lead the way."

Following a clear game trail, they were quickly at the river and located a small pool of clear water set back from the flowing river. At their first drink they realized how thirsty they were and began slow, steady drinking. Finally Glenda said, "My stomach overfloweth with berry soup."

Traveler agreed, "My sugar buzz has calmed down so I'm good to go."

Moving back to the river's bank they found it offered easy passage. In half an hour of brisk walking they heard the various noises of people at work and play.

"OK, let's meet the locals," said Traveler. "They'll be startled so act casual."

How else does he think I'll act? Maybe throw stones or do handstands? Silly boy.

Fortunately, the first group they came upon were young children playing beside the river. They were building sand castles and jumping into the shallows. A few of the older children were in the river up to their waists, ducking under the water then emerging like seals shaking their hair and blowing water at each other.

"Looks like some things never change," said Traveler. "These kids could be playing beside the Rivanna River in Charlottesville. I guess they won't be tubing down the river though, since inner tubes won't be invented for another 1500 years."

Glenda nodded as she focused on kids enjoying the river. It offered fun and needed cooling to the still hot day. *I was a playful kid not that long ago. What happened? I guess M, Theo, and Traveler happened. All things considered, that's still a pretty good tradeoff, and I'm still young and playful.*

They did not try and hide their presence but walked casually toward the children. When they were spotted silence dampened the outbursts of laughter. The older children immediately came out of the river to stand with their younger siblings. They formed a protective shield wall while they assessed the potential threat presented by two strangers.

Glenda instinctively set the mood of "No problem here." She gave the older boys her most endearing smile. "Can you direct us to your village? We got lost picking berries and need to find food and maybe shelter for the night."

The tallest boy stood for a moment staring at Glenda. Her height, beauty, and composure held him fixed in place. Even in peasant clothes she was intimidating. He stuttered a reply before composing himself.

Traveler enjoyed the boy's discomfort as he reflected on his own identical reaction to the Nordic princess when she came striding toward him at their first meeting. *In this meeting she is giving off her most charming, warm look, while with me it was all icicles.*

The boy cautiously approached her but was intimidated by her height and the even taller young man beside her. The man looked friendly but exuded power. The boy knew he had no chance against him if the man decided to best him. The boy's confidence built slightly when he saw they carried no weapons beyond walking sticks.

Glenda reached into her sack and held out several large berries for the boy. His eyes lit up, without hesitation he took them and immediately pushed them into his mouth. Red juice flowed out and down his chin and he smiled.

Swallowing he answered, "These are very good, thank you. Please follow me."

As an afterthought he added, "My father and older brothers are close by." This was a veiled message that protective adult men were nearby so the two strangers should behave.

The boy proceeded to walk them away from the river on a well-cleared path. In minutes they saw the older men, and the children immediately ran toward them. One father looked up at the incoming pack, clapped his hands in a playful gesture, and then saw Traveler and Glenda. His face became fixed and he motioned his large sons to join him.

Chapter 56

Berries for Barter

This time Traveler took charge. It was a man's world and he was clearly the leader to the farmers, not the red-haired girl. "It's a glorious day for berry picking, but a dumb day for getting little lost! My sister and I got mixed up in the forest but fortunately found the river and now you."

The three men relaxed as they sensed no threat. They saw both Traveler and Glenda were still young adults and they also noted the lack of weapons. They accepted how these two could easily get lost in a strange forest.

"May we look at the berries?" asked the oldest brother. He approached Traveler and motioned to his sack.

"Take a look," said Traveler, "have some." As the brother opened the sack Traveler noted his hands. They were large and callused with thick fingers. *These guys don't need to go to the health club to work out. They have muscles that have long since disappeared from our soft bodies.*

The son removed one large berry and handed it to his father. The household pecking order was clear. The father bit it in half, smiled, and put the other half in his mouth. He simply nodded his head.

"We thought we could possibly barter these berries for dinner and shelter. We're going to the fortress in the morning."

The father's mind was sorting out what to do. Being cautious toward any stranger, his instincts were to reject the offer. He also considered the message that they were headed to the fortress. He certainly did not want to offend the lords of the castle, particularly the duke's advisor, referred to as the "mage".

He found it interesting that these two were choosing to go to the fortress when few went unless summoned. At one time the duke was a welcoming host to all, now he was indisposed and his mage advisor was the sole contact. Few wanted any visit with his advisor.

Fear of offending the nobles of the castle ultimately prevailed and he accepted their offer. His fear was tempered by the two large sacks of outstanding berries.

"Yes, we can accommodate you, follow me. My wife will be pleased with the berries and company." Smiling he added, "I see pies in our near future." At the mention of pies, the three brothers and the younger children immediately had smiles cross their faces. Traveler and Glenda were now being labeled "good guys" by the father.

Chapter 57

Dinner Tales

Following the large farmers and young children on the path, Glenda and Traveler saw it was a relatively short path that quickly led to well-maintained common fields. Around the commons were set cottages of varying size. Livestock barns and storage structures were at one end of the field and separated from the homes. This village was a larger version of Hermann's village.

The farmer led them to a large, two-level cottage set among similar but smaller homes. This cottage's size declared the owners were of some importance and prosperity. The farmer opened the door and called out, "Martha, visitors with gifts."

A pleasant appearing woman was immediately at the door. She sized up Traveler and Glenda then smiled. "Welcome, young travelers."

Traveler extended the bags. "Please take these small gifts. I'm called Traveler and my sister is Glenda. We want to thank you and your husband for your hospitality to weary travelers."

Smiling back at both young people Martha replied, "I believe I see berry pies for this evening's meal. I bet Arthur has already tried a berry but I better double-check". She sampled a berry, nodded and said, "Excellent! The fire is just right for baking. Let me get going on baking and dinner. Would you like to start with fresh milk?"

The two travelers rapidly nodded in acceptance and quickly had mugs of a cream-heavy milk in their hands. These farmers needed calories not diet pills. Plaque on arteries was a distant problem. Glenda took a deep sip and grinned at Martha, "Wonderful! This is saving my life."

The woman smiled back as she studied Glenda, "You're a very tall young lady and you need more meat on your bones. I'll take care of you over dinner. Now would the two of you like to wash before dinner? You must be dirty after a long day's walk on our dusty road."

"You're saving my life a second time," exclaimed Glenda.

The woman returned in a minute with several large wool towels and a jar of the same white soap as the keeper had offered. Pointing to one of the older sons she said, "Lars, show them the washtub then leave." Pausing a moment, she added, "Don't try peeking at this young lady."

Lars, the oldest boy from the creek turned a bright red while his brothers and father laughed. Traveler joined the group laugh as he noted that Glenda was developing red in her cheeks.

"Follow me please, the washtub is outside," said Lars in a formal sounding voice. His voice had recently deepened and he had to practice controlling it. Occasionally it reverted to a squeak much to the laughter of his family.

Glenda and Traveler followed Lars outside to a fence surrounding a large outdoor fire pit. Heat was rising off the pit toward a large clay pot which was elevated several feet above the pit. Steam was coming off the pot's water as heat escaped to meet the cooling night air.

Resting on the ground adjacent to the bubbling pot was a large wooden tub. Steps led up to the top of the tub for easy entry. Looking down at the offered bath Glenda noted it was filled with clear water that looked cool at best. She saw there was no steam coming off the surface, *Great, another polar bear soaking.*

With obvious pride Lars explained, "We have the best soaking tub in the village. Our grandfather copied it from

Roman design. To heat the water, pull this lever and hot water will pour down the clay pipe from the container on top of the fire."

Glenda nodded, *OK this may be a genuine soaking tub.* Her gaze shifted to the fence with a skeptical look. Watching her Traveler said, "It's not there for privacy, it's to keep out small animals." With a smirk he added, "Watch out for bears and farm boys."

Unfazed she smiled, "I have had my quota of bear today, you can keep my share when it shows up. Keep the farm boys also."

Traveler looked at Lars, "Lars, let's head back. Glenda, leave the soap here for me."

Watching the two head back to the house Glenda stuck a hand into the tub. The water was still surprisingly temperate. *The sun is doing some good*, she thought. She opened the sluice lever and watched steaming water flow down. There was a large wooden paddle leaning against the fence and she used it to mix the water.

After several more intakes of the hot water she stripped down and stepped into the deep tub. The water was perfect for bathing. She immediately ducked under the water, came up, and began to vigorously wash. She soaped her hair, stood up and lathered her body then submerged herself again.

She chose not to linger since Traveler was waiting. She also had endured enough heat during the day so that the idea of a long hot soak was less appealing. She dried herself off and put her clothes back on, wishing she could have washed them, but she still felt clean and refreshed.

Upon entering the house she motioned to Traveler that his tub awaited. "That was fast, princess, thank you," and he was out the door. Glenda noted Lars had no interest in helping Traveler find the tub.

The farmer and his wife exchanged looks at the word "princess". The farmer mentally congratulated himself on a good decision. These two may be royalty simply traveling as commoners to size up the mood of the duke's people. The farmer knew that with the ascension of the duke's advisor, the mage, there was increasing oversight of the common folk by soldiers. The soldiers seemed to act more as spies than protectors.

When Traveler returned dinner was ready. They ate in two shifts. First the mother and father joined Traveler and Glenda. The best choices were for the heads of the family and guests. The older brothers understood this protocol and accepted it with good humor.

After the first round of eating was completed the second round became conversation. The farmer tried to put a casual spin on his words and their tone when he asked, "What brings you to the fortress?"

"Dogs," replied Traveler, "specifically a new litter that Hermann the innkeeper's alpha male Trajan has sired. Trajan is easily the largest dog I have ever encountered. His pups will be exceptional. We have been sent to bargain for one, possibly a female for breeding. The duke is aware, of course, of these recent Trajan additions and may decide to claim them all. We'll find out our chances to buy one when we meet him."

Glenda added, "These pups are already huge. You could put a saddle on them," and she laughed. Both the farmer and his wife accepted the stated mission. They knew Karl the duke's keeper bred champion dogs for fighting and protection. The litters were famous across regional boundaries. The duke maintained cordial relations with his peers by presenting pups as presents.

They also looked at Glenda, trying to remain casual. Once washed her hair was a cascading flow of colors. Her naturally beautiful face had a perfect frame to bring out its fine features.

The parents saw their sons were fascinated by the tall girl. "She is a princess, boys, don't begin to think about her," they would later tell their sons. "She may be a future bride for the duke." *But hopefully not his advisor*, they thought but never said the words out loud.

"Now comes the pie," said the mother as she rose up. She had put one pie to cool on the table and now cut it into four portions. A single portion filled their bowls. Eating was serious business and pies were unexpected treats. The mother and father settled into their shares and Traveler and Glenda followed suit. Despite the portion size all bowls were scooped clean in a matter of minutes.

Traveler stretched, suppressed a burp, only to hear the farmer shake the room with his own release. The mother followed suit as they grinned at each other. Glenda stopped a grimace from appearing.

"Thank you for a wonderful dinner!" said Traveler, with supporting thanks from Glenda. "But I'm beat. We may leave very early tomorrow so we need our sleep now. May we retire?"

The farmer stood up and the mother said, "Follow Helmuth. We have cleared out the older boys' bedroom. The covers are clean. The room is at the end of the hall, so it's quiet."

Traveler nodded and spoke to the displaced sons, "Thank you, gentlemen, for generously giving up your room. My sister and I are in your debt." The sons grinned and gave a small bow to Traveler and deeper bows to Glenda. The older sons had watched their parents and understood these two travelers were special.

Once they arrived at their room the farmer opened the door. There were candles lit beside each bed. "Sleep well. Pleasant dreams and think well of us." Traveler and Glenda knew the last statement was a request that they tell the duke about the hospitality that had been extended to them.

Once they heard the footsteps recede Traveler said, "We need to get out of Dodge before the sun is up. These farmers are early risers and we need to be gone before they ask more questions."

"Agreed, big boy, just don't fuss when I wake you up."

Chapter 58

The Castle Road

True to her warning, Glenda woke before the night owls had settled down and before the roosters crowed. It was dark but her internal clock said it was time to put a few early miles on their boots. She gave Traveler a soft shake and was amused as he grabbed his pillow. "Rise and shine, big boy, can't sleep the morning away."

"I just lay down, Morpheus was spinning a great tale when you broke it."

"That's a very sad ending to your tale. You can get the rest of his tale tonight. Let's move out, and please carry your boots, Mr Stealth."

They walked on tiptoes past the other rooms. Once downstairs they sat by the tired fire and pulled on their boots. Their sacks were on the table and they realized their carrying sacks were resupplied. "What a great family," said Glenda as she put the sack's belt over her shoulder.

They found the door had a simple latch and they were outside in a moment. Traveler quietly shut the door and they were back on the path leading to the castle road. Traveler started to talk and Glenda gave him the universal signal to be quiet with a finger on her lips and whispered, "Don't talk for a while. There are sleeping dogs, let's be sure they remain quiet." Traveler immediately nodded.

After ten minutes Glenda said, "It's OK now. Those sleeping dogs will lie there until the roosters blow their bugles. Can you see OK to walk?"

Traveler grunted, "Not easily. These potholes are a minefield, and I'm sleepwalking. Let's go slowly until the sun shows up." Traveler used his walking stick and tapped the road in front.

Glenda decided to follow a few steps behind him. *This is the blind leading the blind,* she thought. *Who would figure it's this pitch black even on the road?* "Who stole the moon?" Glenda asked.

"I'm blaming the trees," answered Traveler. "They are live growing skyscrapers. They're so crazy tall that sunlight is a fugitive trying to break out of tree jail."

Half an hour passed before the first light beam escaped the tree jail and came hustling up the road. Where one escaping beam came, many comrades quickly followed. Now the trees were lit up and the morning sun claimed the day.

The day was glorious. The temperature had warmed up enough that walking was a delight. They found a comfortable walking pace and became pilgrims heading to their meeting with fate.

The road began a soft incline, then made a turn onto a steeper rise. In the distance was the mighty stone structure they had first observed from the treetop crow's nest. Some would call it a castle, but "fortress" was a better description. Details were lost in the covering morning fog.

As they got closer and the fog burned off, battlements and turrets appeared across the top perimeter. The dark stone walls climbed from the ground and rose over fifty feet. Given their height Traveler knew the walls were extremely thick to support the wall's weight. *They might be forty feet thick at their base*, he thought. This was a fortress which could withstand the strongest attacks.

As a further defense the wide river curved around the fortress. The moat was more than a wide, water-filled trench, it was a significant river flowing with power.

The road advanced to meet a wide bridge that crossed the river. Once across the river the road continued toward a large entrance cut into the base of the fortress. The entry was a deep tunnel of stone with an iron gate securing the front. The gate was closed, announcing that the fortress was not currently accepting visitors.

Traveler shook his head in admiration. "Wow! This place looks like it's built to withstand any attack. Look at how high the walls go. I bet there is a road on top of the walls; they can move small armies quickly to defend against any point of attack."

"I see a mountain of rocks that must have taken an army to carry and place," said Glenda. "I wonder how long it took to build and who were they afraid of."

"It's Roman built. This place must be the final outpost to secure the Roman Empire against invaders from the east."

Traveler was again a history horse with the bit in his mouth and he charged into the subject. "The Romans were the masters of stone fortresses. Most indigenous people built defensive structures from wood. Their wooden walls were only about fifteen feet high and vulnerable to ladders and fire. The Romans built to last.

"A thousand years later stone castles returned after the Normans conquered England. Although they were the conquerors, they were under frequent attacks by the defeated Saxons. To maintain control, they built stone castles and smaller stone towers called keeps."

"So how did you learn all this castle stuff?" asked Glenda.

"I was fascinated with stories of knights and their time period. I grew up reading about Ivanhoe, Robin Hood, and the struggles of the Saxons to survive under Norman rule."

Glenda gave Traveler a sweet look then said, "That's really interesting but enough history about castles. Let's stop and eat. My tank is on empty. I suggest we picnic by the river, it's close, and I'm thirsty."

The river was indeed close and there were wide walking trails leading down to it. This was a rest area obviously used by merchants and other travelers. Visitors could relax and dine in an area that enjoyed the protective shadow of the nearby fortress. This morning there were no merchants evident since the castle was closed for visitors. They had the run of the area.

Once by the riverbank they drank their fill, then settled down on the soft grassy moss of the bank. They opened sacks for their breakfast. Both were ravenous after their early morning hike. They ate in silence until Glenda said, "How do you think we should get inside? I don't think we can just walk through the gate when it's open. There may already be stories about us. Who knows what Throbb has said. We need to be careful."

"Agreed. You keeping eating, I'm done so I'll take a closer look for entry points. Maybe the river will give us another way to sneak in. I sort of remember from the crow's nest seeing a tributary that appeared to go into the fortress. My eyesight may be wrong but moving water seemed to head in or out, hard to tell at that distance. I'll check it out and be back fairly shortly."

"Good idea. Scout ahead and let's hope you spot another way in." To herself she thought, *He eats faster than a starving lion. I wonder how he was at his family's dinner table.* Glenda took her own time to enjoy her fare and had just finished when Traveler returned.

"I think I have good news. As I followed the river on the left side, I noticed there was a lot of land between the river and the fortress. I continued until I saw another road coming to the castle. I imagine there are a number of villages out there serving the castle.

"While our present road leads directly to gate in front of us, this second road crosses a wide stone bridge then it curves around to the same entry gate in front of us.

"Now here comes the good news part. I continued past the bridge and saw a small tributary branching from the river toward the fortress. It appears to actually flow into the fortress. It's our likely entry point and definitely worth a closer look.

"We're probably going to end up in the river so I think we need to hide our carry bags. Don't want them around our backs when we're swimming." Grinning he added, "We'll go when you're ready princess, but please don't let me rush your morning breakfast."

Biting her tongue Glenda only said, "Excellent scouting! I'm ready to roll now, but maybe you should have another drink and sandwich. Don't worry about slowing us down, we need our energy and that fortress sure isn't going anywhere."

With Glenda's prompt Traveler suddenly realized that indeed he was thirsty and hungry again. With a sheepish look he said, "Thanks for the suggestion and yeah, scouting uses up a lot of energy."

As Traveler dug into his food store Glenda took her own advice and joined him saying, "Better we fill up now, who knows when the next time will come." With that they settled back on the grassy bank and let the sun warm them up while they finished enjoying Martha's offerings.

Once they were ready Traveler took their carry bags into a nearby clump of thick brush and hid them from sight. Refreshed and without their back sacks, they began following the river as it wound past the dominating stone fortress. Both of them were overwhelmed by its sheer size. It was an engineering marvel much as the great pyramids of ancient Egypt.

As they walked they saw what Traveler had found earlier. The river flowed under a large stone bridge. The bridge was another work of experienced engineers. It was wide and sat well above the river on stone abutments. Its wide arch spoke of Roman aesthetics, "Blend beauty with function" was the Roman statement for lasting structures. This statement is still found today throughout the great city of Rome.

"Maybe we need to take a lower profile," said Glenda. "We're close to the fortress, anybody on the top wall could wonder who we are and why we're here. The bridge looks like a good place to drop out of sight."

"Good thinking," said Traveler. "You're the leader now but please take us down the bank slowly, it looks slippery. We don't need to act out the CCR song about rollin' on the river." Glenda nodded and smiled back.

They descended with caution to the river, then quickly moved under the bridge. Once inside they saw the bridge's width offered significant cover from the road and the fortress.

Resting below the bridge's surface they suddenly heard the tattoo cloppings of approaching horses. Once the horses were on the bridge their hoofbeats echoed loudly in the space below. Could they have been spotted going down to the river? Instinctively they scrambled upward to bury themselves in the darkness of the space where the bridge met its ground support.

The horses continued then silence returned. Traveler shook his head, "Hoofbeats are lots louder down here than above, my ears are ringing. I understand why bridge trolls are annoyed all the time."

Glenda smiled back at his troll quip while her own ears were ringing, and she thought, *Next time put fingers in your ears, Glenda.*

They cautiously approached the far side of the bridge to look downstream. They studied the tributary leading into the fortress and considered their options. "I see what you mean. That tributary definitely flows into the castle; that may be our stealth way in." Then she added, "Good scouting Hawkeye, you must have some American Indian blood in you."

Traveler accepted the compliment with a shrug, "It's a gift. I can find stuff in my room at home that seems impossibly hidden to my parents, it drives them nuts."

Glenda continued to study the flowing river. "Bear with me on this, but I think we can hitch a ride on one of the trees floating down the river. When we are close to where the river branches into the fortress, we can leave our ride and swim to the entrance.

"Many of these floaters have leafy limbs offering good camouflage. We'll be copycats and follow how M escaped the jinn to get to his island. We'll stay close to the trunk and just let the current carry us to where the tributary goes in. Do you feel like a tree ride and a little swim, Mr Scout?"

"I'm a frog and love the water. You pick our ride."

They both studied the debris as it floated by. Suddenly they pointed at the same time to a tree that was approaching the bridge. "There's our Uber tree taxi," whispered Glenda.

Stepping into the river they began to dog paddle forward to catch the tree as it entered the bridge. Once positioned in the river they paddled in place watching the tree as it came toward them.

Glenda was closest to the approaching tree and would be the first passenger on board. Suddenly she had a panic attack. The approaching tree appeared as a great green locomotive and she was standing in the center of the tracks. The locomotive appeared intent on running over her.

Traveler saw what was happening and called out, "It's a slow-moving freight train and you're a hobo hitching a free ride. Relax, grab a limb, and swing aboard."

Traveler's voice broke her hesitation; she was back on her game. Surging forward she grabbed a limb and became a passenger on the green, freight train express. Traveler paused a moment to see all was well then hitched his own ride further down the trunk.

Staying as passengers was harder than it appeared. Both had grabbed onto limbs and pulled themselves closer but immediately found underwater limbs were catching their leggings and boots. Traveler watched as Glenda was starting to fight the ensnaring limbs, "Relax, princess, you're doing great. Hold onto that limb and just float along, we don't go very far."

He added some boy humor with, "Keep your head as low to the water as you can to hide that mop of red hair." Glenda wasn't worried about being spotted while under the bridge but she did need to keep the mop from getting tangled in the tree limbs. She used one hand to stuff it into the back of the sack dress while holding onto the limb with the other. *I need another arm,* she thought.

Before they cleared the bridge Traveler called, "You're the lead scout now, so tell me when we need to jump ship and head into the tributary."

Once out from under the bridge they kept their faces close to the water, both had to arch their necks to breathe. Occasionally the trunk twisted in the moving water and they were dunked under. They came up coughing and snorting water from nose and mouth.

Lifting her head up, Glenda saw the small mouth of the tributary approaching and said over her shoulder, "It's almost time to cut and swim. Let go when I say 'Now'. Traveler nodded and waited for her signal.

A minute later he heard "Now" and shoved away from the trunk. He dogpaddled in place until the tree's caboose passed him and he saw Glenda paddling hard. He began to paddle toward the center of the river and was surprised at the effort required to move sideways in the current.

With his head so close to the river's surface, he was approaching the branching point before he spotted it. He saw where tributary entered the fortress but realized he was in danger of passing it by. He forgot dogpaddling, put his head down, and began his strongest crawl stroke.

He picked his landing spot on the tributary's bank and doubled his effort. Swimming at an angle to the river added the river's force behind him. His mind stayed focused on the intersection path. Physics and the strength of his stroke paid off. Suddenly he was in the eddy part of the tributary.

He turned to look for Glenda and saw her struggling. Since she was on the leading part of the trunk, she was now further down river and was at risk of missing the entry point.

Traveler took a deep breath and swam hard toward her. He caught her waist-belt and gave a hard scissors kick. His kick was powerful and moved her slightly toward the last part of the entry bank. "I'll pull on your belt and scissor kick. Keep your face close to the water, side stroke and kick as hard as you can. I'll navigate."

Neither could talk, that only wasted precious energy and air, each grabbed large lungfuls of air when needed. With their heads almost in the water, three arms pulled and four legs kicked. Pull, kick, pull, kick. They had a steady rhythm that advanced them despite the river's flow.

Then they were suddenly out of the current and their kicks shot them forward to touch the embankment. Looking at their landing point Traveler noted they had just made the cutoff by a few feet.

They continued to gasp for air while resting against the side of the bank. Finally they were recovered and floated comfortably with small leg kicks. Looking at Traveler with respect Glenda said, "You're the real river Uber, I was heading for big trouble. I misjudged the drift in the river. I don't know what's downstream and I don't want to know."

"You did really well. Your leg kicks are what did the trick." For a moment Traveler was ready to add a comment about always helping a river rat, but wisely bit his tongue. The best line he could muster was, "Bad hair day all around, worse for some than others." Glenda gave him a sweet smile, then rubbed the top of his head. For a moment Traveler felt a Theo purr coming out of him.

Fully recovered, they studied the tributary's access into the fortress. They saw the entrance was through a dark tunnel that protruded out from the side of the fortress. The tunnel was twenty feet wide with an overhanging stone roof that was less than two feet off the water. No saboteurs could slip into the fortress on low-lying craft.

Chapter 59

Down and Out

Traveler pushed off to enter the tunnel, "Wait here while I scout." Glenda watched him disappear, then heard his voice echo inside the tunnel, "There's a serious 'No Trespassing' iron gate here. Let me give this puzzle more thought." He was hanging onto the iron bars of the gate when Glenda joined him.

"What do you see ahead, Hawkeye?" she asked.

"I see what looks like a small interior lake. This is clearly one water source for the fortress."

"Can we get past the blocking gate?"

"Not sure but maybe. I'll pretend I'm one of the Bajau water people. Let's see how far down this grate goes." He took a deep breath and became vertical in the water. Glenda watched his feet follow his head down.

Traveler hung onto an iron rail and pulled himself down hand over hand. It was pitch black and not even a Bajau could see. As he went lower, he felt the water pressing against his ears and chest. He kept his mind steady and fought against the natural claustrophobia. He did not permit himself to consider time passing.

His left hand was moving down for another hold when it discovered there was no bar to grip. He had the presence of mind to use his right hand to run over the bottom of the adjoining bar. He swept his left hand back and forth without hitting a bar. Using his two-handed grip, he pulled his body down further and felt a muddy bottom.

Rolling onto his back, he used both hands to bury his backside in the mud, then pushed his body under the bars. Once his feet could push against the bars, he knew he was on the other side. He scissor-kicked upward. Cupping his hands, he pulled downward on the water while he kicked. It was like doing water chin-ups combined with powerful leg kicks. Going up was much faster than going down.

His head emerged followed by half his body as he shot out of the water. Fortunately there was no tunnel ceiling above him. His lungs pulled in huge gasps of air. He pulled in three more giant breaths, then began to stabilize his breathing.

Once in control he looked through the bars. Glenda was wide-eyed and staring at him. There were no witty jokes. Both of them were aware he had survived when another outcome was equally possible.

"Can I do it?" Glenda quietly asked him.

Traveler thought about simply assuring her, then thought again. "Honestly, it's challenging. I'll help you and we'll do this together.

"First you need to grab onto a single bar and pull down on it. It's pitch black but don't let that bother you, your handhold will always confirm where you are. Keep going until you get to the bottom. You'll know it since the bar ends and there is soft mud under you.

"Turn yourself to face up while holding onto the bars. Use both hands to push your back and butt into the mud, then push yourself through. Make sure you're completely through with your legs against the bars. Once free your body will do the rest. Big leg kicks and arm pulls. Keep your hands cupped so you have more force when pulling down on the water."

Glenda had an "I'm not sure at all" look on her face. She looked intimidated. It was just her against the water and book magic could not help her. Traveler knew a moment of truth was coming, they both needed to be on the inside.

It was time to problem solve. When he set his logical mind free, a possible solution came to him. He remembered a buddy-air trick he had read about in SEAL training. "I can help you, but we need to work together. There is a technique to share oxygen."

Glenda's eyes were wide and she was starting to shiver from the cold water. Traveler saw they only had one chance at this. "Please tell me what to do." Traveler never considered how unusual this statement was.

He felt her fear and fought against becoming equally scared. He forced his face and voice to appear matter-of-fact. This was just another exercise and they could manage it. His outward confidence helped Glenda to focus on what she had to do. To reassure herself she thought, *This is easier than facing the jinn in the alley. Of course we can do this.*

"Here's how a buddy system for sharing air works. Part way down when you feel you really need another breath, you signal me and I will blow my air into your lungs."

"Sounds like a sneaky underwater kiss, big boy."

Traveler grinned, "That's one way to describe it, but believe me all you'll notice is the air.

"I'll keep my hand on your belt and I'll help pull you down faster. Between us we'll make you sink faster than by yourself. When you want the air, squeeze anything like my hand, my arm, even my nose. Any squeeze works then we'll do the breath exchange. We'll both be upside down so use the bar as your frame of reference.

"Now let's take a practice dive. Invert yourself so you're upside down and I'll have my hand on your belt pressing down."

Traveler again saw how nervous Glenda was. Grinning he said, "Try not to break your nose when pushing your face between the bars for my air, it's one of your best features." Glenda could only give a scared, sad smile back. She knew gallows humor when she heard it.

Glenda took several slow, deep breaths, then nodded and flipped upside down. She went down far enough until her feet were well under the surface and she felt his hand on her belt gently pressing down. *Moment of truth*, she thought as she reached over and squeezed his hand.

They made an awkward joining of lips after Glenda first exhaled through her nose. She immediately felt Traveler's air coming to her. She felt her lungs accept the new air and knew she had partially replenished her supply. She then reversed her vertical direction and returned to the surface.

"Did it work OK?" asked Traveler.

"It did, we have a plan. One request though."

"Sure, what is it?"

"Do you have any breath mints?"

The two began to laugh and Traveler said, "When you're ready let's get this diving show underway." They both calmed their breathing, then repeatedly took deep breaths. Glenda reversed her direction and pointed down with Traveler following her lead.

The trip down was a journey into blackness for Glenda. She paced herself with a hand-over-hand descent. She felt Traveler pushing down on her belt. She did not think about a saving breath. If Traveler could make it, so could she. She remembered she was an accomplished distance runner in Norwegian mountains. Her lungs were as capable as any person's could be.

She was progressing down as planned and felt in control when suddenly, somewhere on a new handhold, she had an overpowering urge to take in a breath. It came from nowhere. An intake breath would be her undoing. She froze.

Traveler knew what was happening. He held her head from behind and pressed it between the bars then pressed his lips against hers. She exhaled by instinct through her nose then took a gulping intake of air through her mouth. Her body stabilized and Traveler gave her belt a final powerful downward thrust. He immediately reversed direction and surged toward the surface. His own empty lungs burned and he fought the overwhelming need to breathe.

Emerging from the water he gasped and gasped as his heart was beating hundreds of times a minute. This was body stress well beyond his solo dive. He felt his lungs, heart, and mind were just beginning to stabilize when a body shot past him.

Glenda was an orca whale at Sea Garden as she burst from the depths. She seemed to hang for a moment at the top of her ascent, then she came down smacking the surface and immediately bobbing up again. She pulled desperate breaths in and out before finally settling into the lake. A joyous Traveler bit his tongue to keep from announcing, "Thar she blows!"

Now Glenda was all bright grins and smiles. "Well, let's never do that again! I can't believe we pulled it off. I never could have survived without your breath of life."

Traveler was calmly treading water beside her. "You were terrific. You kept your cool all the way. Something you don't know but in school my jock buddies and I would practice holding our breath, we were your basic high school idiots. It's an acquired skill and I was a record holder. I knew I was good for two minutes so I had a big leg up on you."

"Maybe so, but you were the cavalry and arrived just in time. When I felt the mud I was just about gone. Pausing she suddenly laughed, "It was so weird but as I passed under the bars pressed into the mud, all I could think of was how dirty I'd be. Female pride is right up there on the smart scale with boys holding their breath."

Chapter 60

A Hidden Place

As their eyes had now dilated to the dim interior, they began to observe their surroundings. They were at one end of a small lake. On the right side they saw a stone landing with a staircase. Docked beside the landing was a small crossing craft. On the left side was another landing that appeared to lead to an interior space. "Let's go left," said Glenda. "The staircase goes up to the castle and I need to rest and gather my wits, I'm sure I lost a lot of brain neurons down there."

The two swam forward toward a set of stone steps on the left landing. When they reached the steps, Traveler climbed up and offered his hand. As she accepted it she thought, *Always the gentleman, and right now I've got zero female pride. I really need to rest.*

She grabbed Traveler's hand and was quickly beside him on the landing.

They saw an arched entryway leading somewhere and proceeded to it. Before going through they stopped and listened. The air was as still as the lake's surface. They cautiously stepped through the arch and into a good-sized room. The room was a combination kitchen, dining room, and all-purpose space. Defining the kitchen was a massive stone fireplace with burned-out embers. Various sized pots hung from iron hooks that could be swung over the fire. Other pots hung down on the sides of the chimney.

The dining table was built from heavy, thick, wooden planks and the chairs were built to match. The impression was a setting for very large, heavy men who had no use for fancy eating or cooking arrangements.

The curved ceiling rose up almost eighteen feet. It had inlaid tile with hunting scenes and battle scenes. Hanging down from the center was an iron chandelier. The chandelier had two connected concentric circles that each held large thick candles. The candles were lit.

Given the size of the candles it appeared they would they could burn for at least a week. Each candle rested inside a vertical cylinder to catch wax as it melted.

The candlelight gave the room a welcoming glow. As the light reflected off the tile ceiling, it made the various scenes appear to have movement. As Glenda and Traveler looked more closely at the detailed scenes, they saw goat-footed Pan chasing woodland nymphs. In the center were giants looking down with swords, spears, and hammers at the ready. "That ceiling fresco is an amazing work of both Greek and Roman art," said Traveler.

Glenda was studying the rest of the room and saw another arched doorway. "I think this is a safe complex for the fortress. It's a fortress hidden within a fortress. That's why it has cooking and lighting set ups. I bet it was a secret hiding place for the nobility and their families if the fortress fell. Let's check out the rest of this place."

They proceeded out of the dining room into a short hallway. There was a door to the left and they slowly eased it open. Inside was a large pantry with a full inventory of hanging meats, barrels of apples, and covered storage pots filled with various roots and potatoes. Stacked against a wall were wooden casks of ale, wine, and cider. The contents were identified with simple pictographs. In a far corner was a tarp covering sacks of flour and ground cornmeal.

"The lion eats tonight," quipped Traveler.

"I'd say there's enough to feed a pride of lions for a month."

They shut the pantry door and went to the door at the end of the hall. Standing outside they heard the pleasing sound of rushing water. They opened the door to find a cascading stream of water falling down from an overhanging rock ledge. The water was flowing into a grated opening in the floor.

Behind the waterfall and tucked into the rock was a wooden bench. On the bench were long-handled scrub brushes and a large jar of the ubiquitous soap. Later they would be pleased to discover this odorless soap was a big step up from the lye soap used to scrub pans.

"Well this sure seems familiar," said Traveler. "Let's test how cold it is."

He stuck his hand into the falling stream and pronounced, "Better than our freezing river, but not nearly as hot as I like."

Glenda was studying the sides of the interior water cave and said, "There's an iron lever on each side of the bench. See what happens if you can pull one down."

Traveler extended a hand through the opening, stretched out and used his fingers to move the lever down. Instantly a new flow of water came down a rock channel to join the existing stream. This water was steaming as it joined the original cooler flow. Traveler cautiously reached into the waterfall, grinned and said, "Our ship has come in. Those Romans knew how to build heated showers."

Glenda immediately said, "Dibs! Finally, I can bathe properly. I so need a hot shower."

Traveler saw stacks of heavy, wool blankets on top of a stone pedestal. He picked one up and began to open it. It seemed the stack only contained two blankets. He immediately laughed, "I think this will handle your drying needs. This is either for an elephant or a boy scout troop's tent. It should be enough to dry you three times over."

Finally they saw the nearby indoor plumbing throne. The throne was oversized and Traveler decided to skip his funny comments. He doubted Glenda would appreciate middle school humor right now.

They shut the bathroom door and walked to the last door. Again they opened it slowly and peeked inside. This was a bedroom with a bed of epic proportions. Above the bed a vaulted ceiling displayed the same inlaid tile mosaics. Any person lying in bed could construct various story lines by linking various scenes together.

"Wow!" exclaimed Glenda. "This must be the bed for the whole family. It's got to be every bit of twelve feet square. We can safely say families were large back then. There's plenty of room for husband, wife, and a dozen kids. These blankets would cover a small circus, they're even bigger than the shower towels."

While Glenda was studying the bed, Traveler was looking up at the overhead scenes. As he studied them he felt movement happening among the mosaic scenes. He was becoming dizzy. He remembered his dad telling him how doctors looking intently at slides had to lift their eyes away periodically to retain their balance as well as their focus. His own eyes returned to the bed and then Glenda.

"OK, I guess that's the tour. You have dibs on the bathroom so go first and take your time. There are lots of great foods in the pantry I'll see what I can scrape together for dinner."

Glenda nodded as she was already moving toward the sound of the running water. "This girl is shower-bound. I'll leave the water hot so you can move right in."

Traveler answered, "While you get shower-hot, I'll make us a cold meal. I don't want anybody to know we were here. The cold fireplace should signal all's well if anyone shows up, and I can't imagine who would."

Traveler headed to the pantry and selected samplings of ham, yellow-red roots, and cider. Finally, he sliced an apple into sections and sprinkled sugar on it. He took a piece of the thick ham and proceeded to test it. *Outstanding! We have a feast.*

After setting out their meal he studied the fireplace. *Since nobody's coming, why not heat this place up? Everything will be burned down when we leave, so why suffer dampness tonight?* With that conclusion he removed the few ashes into a large iron bucket, stacked fresh wood, and shortly was rewarded with a blazing fire. *Princess will love this. Just like a dinner in one of her Chicago taverns.*

With the dinner preparation completed he went back to the dock. He walked to the end and found another skiff moored to a vertical pillar. *Now we have an easy way to reach that staircase, no more freezing swims for us.* He then looked a second time at the skiff and noticed how high the gunnels were above the water. *High sides so they can carry heavy loads without water coming on board. Very smart these old-timers were.*

When he entered the dining room he stopped and started to laugh. Glenda was standing by the fire with a circus tent wrapped around her. "Where's the rest of the circus? I think the elephant is missing its overcoat."

Looking at Traveler she sweetly answered, "Well, the clowns have already arrived and I see they have done a super job with the fire and the dinner. Well done, ringmaster."

Smiling she lifted her arms, "This is the world's biggest bathrobe. I think it's built as an all-purpose covering. It's a multiple-wraparound robe for freezing nights. I had to pull it up from the floor over three feet before belting it. Even the arms had to be rolled up so much I look like Popeye."

Traveler was laughing. "Correction princess, you are Olive Oyl and I'm Popeye. Right now this sailor man needs his water. Lots of hot water. Did you leave any for me?"

"Judge for yourself, but I recommend sticking a hand in first. I backed off the hot water intake but trust me there is more than you need." Wrinkling her nose she added, "And you certainly need a lot, don't spare the soap. By the way I think it's close to real soap. No perfume in it but much milder than the Babylonian pot cleaner we've been using."

When Traveler got to the bathing room, he stuck his hand in and instantly confirmed Glenda was correct, it was not quite scalding but too hot for immediate entry. He dialed back the hot intake, found just the right amount of acceptable hotness and was quickly under the falling water.

This is just like my bathroom in the Sanctuary. Only difference is, I need to move levers instead of saying what I want. I'm just going to sit here a while and let the hot water do its job. This is just heaven.

After an extended soak he realized he was close to falling asleep. He took one of the large scrub brushes, and proceeded to work on his entire body. *Never do one scrubbing when two are better.*

When he did his first scrubbing, he confirmed Glenda's take on the soap. He soaped his hair and vigorously rubbed it in. This soap made his scalp tingle but in a good way. The cascading water carried some soap down into his eye and he yelped but not the scream associated with the pot-cleaner soap.

Rinsing and rubbing at the same time he wondered, *What is this stuff made of? It's not my mother's baby shampoo but I can live with it.* Finally he dialed back the hot water and got out just as he felt the temperature falling. *I don't need a polar bear wake-up. Right now it's time to eat, then sleep.*

He lifted the remaining heavy bathrobe and found it fit him no better than Glenda. Even though he was taller than Glenda his added height made no difference. It took him five minutes to fold until he had manageable heights off the floor and up his arms.

Entering the dining room, he saw the small feast laid out on the table. Glenda had added cheese, a dark bread, and honey to his setting. "How did you find this other stuff? I looked."

"Life in an orphanage with hungry kids, you learn where to look."

They settled down to the pleasant task at hand. Food and drink went in and bellies applauded. Glenda noted that Traveler was taking it in at a more relaxed pace. *Maybe he wolfs it down when he's under stress, a male survival trait.*

Glenda finally looked up from her empty plate and said, "I think it's nighttime, and for a change I'm collapsing in a real bed."

Traveler nodded, "Me too."

They got to the bedroom and Glenda chose the far side. Traveler waited until she was settled, jumped in, then said, "We need to leave the door open. If there's a visitor, we need to be ready." Another thought came to him as he found himself drifting off, "Be careful looking up at the ceiling scenes, they're hypnotic, I swear they move." His warning was already too late for Glenda.

With that final comment, Travel pulled his blanket over his head and was with Morpheus in seconds.

Chapter 61

Into the Fortress

They awoke with the energy that only comes from long, deep, uninterrupted sleep. Glenda took her dry clothes and went into the bathroom. A short time later she reappeared dressed as a village peasant. Traveler followed suit. Coming back he saw Glenda had placed a breakfast fare out. Despite the intake the night before, they discovered they were again starving.

With rested bodies and happy stomachs, they were eager to explore. "I found another skiff at the end of the dock. We can row across."

They walked down the dock. Traveler held the boat steady while Glenda climbed in and then he joined her. Glenda was studying the high gunnels. "Do all rowboats have sides this high?"

"Not usually. I think the boat probably carries a lot of heavy supplies across. There must be a ton of food stored in the pantry. If the survivors need to hide out, they'll need a lot of food."

"Makes sense."

"You want to sit at the back center to balance and direct us. You can look ahead and see the torch at the base of the staircase. Since my back is to the landing use your hands to direct me."

"Aye, aye, captain. You row and I'll direct, sounds like a good division of labor to me."

Traveler gripped the oars that were resting beside the oar guides. Lifting the oars into the water, he pushed away using the dock side oar. He then pulled on the dock oar while keeping the left oar steady in the water. The small boat pivoted, then he pulled both oars at once.

Glenda used the bow of the boat as her pointer. Using both hands she gave directions for their crossing. The lake was small but still of sufficient size that Traveler settled into a rowing rhythm. His boy scout training came back, he turned the oars parallel to the water as he pushed them forward, then rotated them ninety degrees for the returning power stroke back to his chest.

Glenda watched him closely, "You've done this before. Skimming the oars forward on the surface looks tricky."

Traveler grunted and said, "It's called 'feathering the oars' and just takes practice. If you accidentally dig into the water going forward, the oars jump out of your hand and the boat will spin around. Not really hard, but practice builds muscle memory, rather like riding a bike."

After several more minutes of rowing Glenda said, "Better slow down now and check the distance. A couple of hard pulls and we'll be on top of the landing with a missing bow."

Traveler stopped rowing and looked over his shoulder. "Good call. Watch this."

He made a final hard pull, then dropped the left oar as a pivot point and the boat turned parallel to the landing. Their forward momentum had the boat rest against the dock. "Hop out and keep the boat steady."

Glenda semi-leaped out and caught the skiff's rope when Traveler threw it to her. Traveler took a big step out and was beside her. "Let's tie this at the end of the dock and keep it hidden."

Chapter 62

Inside the Walls

With their craft secure they walked to the ascending stone staircase. Sconce torches provided enough light to guide them up. Passing by them Traveler said, "The caretaker must replenish these torches when bringing down fresh supplies. Let's hope we don't meet him on the way."

The incline case was six feet wide with the risers going up over a foot. As they began to walk up, they quickly found the riser height was difficult on their thigh muscles and their balance.

Grunting Glenda said, "Is this me being leg-weary from all the walking and swimming, or are we climbing up a mountain?"

Traveler nodded, "These riser heights are crazy. Who climbs up staircases like this? Goats would have to jump from stair to stair. This is very bad architecture for most people. Children and the elderly would struggle and likely fall. In our time OSHA and its lawyers would sue the designers for creating a health hazard. This is an accident just waiting to happen, let's be sure we're not the accident."

They continued to climb in silence. Each step required a push off with the lower leg then tension on the elevated leg. Their breath was quickly coming in short intakes. "I feel like I'm sprinting up the museum staircase," said Glenda, "but this is definitely harder." Traveler just grunted to save his breath.

Finally they reached the upper landing. The landing was a simple platform that jutted out from the facing wall. There were no protective handrails.

"One way they could thin the soldier herd would be races up and down, that would sure determine who was in fighting trim. The Marines would love this gauntlet climb as a fitness test."

"All right Mr Marine, let's get inside. I think it may be nighttime and we can start scouting this place before the halls are filled. We need to find places we can hide in while we figure out our game plan."

Traveler was standing in front of the door and saw the massive sliding iron bolt used to block entry. Glenda looked the door up then down, "More security locks," she said and pointed. On the top and bottom were thick vertical iron rods that could be sunk into the stone. The locking bars were all in a free state and the door appeared ready for an outward shove.

"Our hiding place is an 800-year-old safe room," said Traveler, as he slowly pressed against the massive door. Despite its size the door cracked open with ease.

Traveler cautiously stuck his head into the corridor. It was pitch black. "I can't see anything."

Glenda stepped past him, torch in hand she waited for Traveler to step beside her. They looked in both directions and saw only impenetrable darkness beyond the limited light cast by the torch. In a whispered voice she said, "Do you feel lucky going right or left?"

Traveler whispered back, "I'm a contrarian; people instinctively go right so let's try lucky left."

They advanced slowly. The torch only illuminated the walkway about ten feet ahead. They had seen far too many Indiana Jones and mummy movies to rush forward. "This feels like we're inside a great pyramid. I hope arrows don't shoot out of the sides," Traveler said.

"I think we can be optimistic and speak up. It looks like we're in a hidden passageway built for either escape or spying. These walls are thick stone and nobody can hear us. Somewhere there will be places to exit or peep holes to view the other side. Watch the right-side wall for cut-in places."

As they walked they began to relax. They were in a passage that was likely long forgotten. Their torch burned steadily indicating there was sufficient oxygen but no air movement. Ventilation was apparently adequate but the source was not obvious.

"I wonder who maintains the pantry in our safe place?" Traveler reflected out loud as they advanced.

"Probably some old servant who knows the castle and is trusted by the duke," said Glenda. "After all, if the hideout is well-known, then it's no longer a hideout."

"Makes sense. Do you see anything ahead yet?"

Glenda was ready to answer "No" when she stopped and put her hand on the wall about five feet off the floor. "Here's something. It feels like a wooden shutter set into the stone."

Traveler began to study the shutter, "I think it slides to the side, I'll give it a try. Easy does it," and he slowly slid the thick wood along its holding tracks. An observation opening appeared in the stone.

The viewing slot was cut through the stone and widened toward the exit point. The narrowness of the opening limited the width of the viewshed. Looking out was similar to using a telescope. Unlike a telescope that can be moved to capture a wider view, the stone was not moveable. Score one for the telescope.

Glenda pressed her face into the opening, "Wow, wait till you see this." They took turns looking into the open slot. The thick stone opening guided the eye into a great hall.

The hall was set up to easily host hundreds of attendees. Heavily planked tables were surrounded on both sides by heavy benches. Elevated at the front was a dais. Centered on the dais was a massive carved table with carved chairs.

The elevated seating declared who the rulers were. As those seated below enjoyed their wine and ale, they were constantly reminded of who their superiors were. The superiors were those looking down on them.

Looking straight out Traveler saw the high ceiling was supported by heavy stone pillars. There were scenes carved into the stone columns. The carved pillars reminded him for a moment of the glyphs on the portal in the Chicago museum. He shivered and pushed the memory away.

Connecting the walls to the support columns were wide horizontal wooden beams. Looking at the crossbeams he noted their unusual width. *A good four feet, I wonder why so wide?*

Glenda looked through the opening and studied the beams, "These seem overly wide to just provide support to the pillars. Wait, I see there's an enclosed platform built around the top of the column where the beam meets. It reminds me of a crow's nest on old sailing ships."

Chapter 63

A Shooting Gallery

Traveler focused a second time, "You're right, I didn't notice it at first glance. The crow's nest is decorated to appear like a part of the aesthetics of the column, but I don't think that's its real purpose. I think it's a shooting platform for archers. I have no idea how archers could get to it, though. It would take thirty-foot ladders to get them up there."

"Take a look at this," Glenda said as she knelt down to the base of the wall. "There's another shutter down here."

The lower shutter was three feet high and the width of a big man's shoulders. She slid the shutter open and saw the crossbeam was right there ready to carry a man to the crow's nest. "They get to the crow's nest on the wide beam, no ladders required."

"How clever," said Traveler. "This place was built to ambush the occupants on the floor level. The crow's nest is a protected place for archers and reminds me of a shooting gallery."

Glenda lifted the torch higher and walked forward a short distance then announced, "We're at the end of this tunnel, solid wall here. Let's backtrack and see if there are more openings we missed. Let's shut this access opening up tight, we don't want the torch light to betray us."

Traveler nodded and quickly sealed up the bottom opening. Before sealing the upper shutter, Glenda took a final look out, "I can just see the end of another column to our right. It looks about twenty-five feet away. Let's pace off the distance and see what's there."

They counted eight strides and then studied the wall. They immediately found a window slot and a lower access door and carefully opened both. Again, the lower exit tied into a crosswalk to a column. Traveler looked out the upper shutter and concluded, "Looks like the shooting gallery comes every twenty-five feet. There is a covered field of fire so there's no place to hide below. Death from above for your enemy. Sweet."

They continued to backtrack and located the other hidden openings. At each opening they took in the sights. "Notice how the surround stone is black," said Glenda. "If you were looking up all you would see is black support walls. The openings are not visible since the open slots are all black. The only way these windows and exits could be spotted is if a torch created visible light."

At the eighth and final opening they agreed on the hall's size. "This hall is around 200 feet long and I'd guess it's a good eighty feet wide, almost a small soccer field," reflected Traveler.

Chapter 64

Stables and Haylofts

"We've returned to the door that leads back to the hidden safe room. Let's see where this right-hand way takes us," said Traveler.

They continued forward, carefully watching for covered window slots or lower exit doors but nothing appeared. After ten minutes Glenda softly called out, "I see what looks like an escape door ahead. It looks small and is only about three feet off the ground."

When they reached it, Traveler squatted down and declared, "You're right, good catch."

Traveler noted a heavy sealing bar across the stone. Bending down, he slid the bar to the side to free the door. Studying the stone more closely he announced, "There's an iron ring built into the center of the stone, I'll give it a push." He gripped the ring and pushed forward, nothing moved. "OK, if 'push' doesn't work let's try 'pull'."

Pull worked and the heavy stone moved slowly but easily into the passageway. Looking down Traveler saw there were iron runners grooved into the hallway floor. "That explains why it's easy to move," he said to the standing Glenda. He then proceeded to poke his head and shoulders into the narrow access opening.

"What do you see?"

Traveler's answer was muffled by a sneeze. "Straw, and more straw."

He began to crawl forward on his stomach using his elbows. Finally his feet disappeared. *The straw monster got him*, Glenda chuckled to herself.

A voice whispered back, "Come on in, the straw's fine."

Glenda entered the access tunnel and emerged to a clearing of old straw. Standing up in the center was a grinning Traveler. "Welcome to sneeze city."

The straw came up to their chests and Traveler proceeded to clear a narrow path out. Once free of the mounded straw they were standing on heavy wood planking. Mounds of straw were everywhere. It was a graveyard of straw from past hay harvests. Hay was the food for horses and sheep while the residual straw was likely used as floor and ground coverings.

Glenda surveyed their loft and noted how the straw was organized into large piles. There were pitchforks frequently sticking out of the mounds. "This is obviously where the old straw gets stored. They probably bring it down in the rainy season to soak up mud. I bet nobody comes up here unless forced to."

Traveler looked at her and started to laugh, "You've collected your own share of straw, be careful barn swallows and owls don't try and nest in your hair."

Glenda immediately put her hands into her hair. "Oh great. I'm the scarecrow in Oz, with straw sticking out of me everywhere." She proceeded to shake her head and finger-comb her hair. Every time she combed more straw fell out.

Traveler just wiped his hair and the straw was mostly gone. "Just another advantage guys have." Glenda ignored him.

Traveler walked to the edge of the storage platform, dropped to his knees and carefully looked down. Immediately below was the main storage loft for the feeding hay. The hayloft extended fifty feet beyond the upper straw platform and ran over a hundred feet in both directions.

Below the hayloft were long columns of stabled horses and Traveler noted the efficient design. Hay and horse were close together for easy feeding.

Traveler saw there were frequent ladders to access the hay platform but few for the straw loft. He looked for access to their present loft and only saw one distant ladder built into a wall. "This place rarely gets visitors, I think we have a secure base of operations."

Glenda joined him and looked down into piles of stacked hay, "I don't see anybody down there, let's jump down and explore. We can leap back up if we need to."

Looking down, Glenda was suddenly a little girl again. She did not need to use her Mary Poppins gravity skills, she just leaped down into an inviting pile of hay. Again a head of hay-hair became a potential bird's nest. *Rats, forgot about this.* Running fingers through her thick hair she repeated to herself, *Double rats. The price of fun.*

Traveler picked an open spot below and landed softly, sans hay. He sent the princess an annoying grin. She read his lips, "Look before you leap." She stuck out her tongue.

They proceeded to the edge of the large hay storage loft and could hear multiple voices below. They worked themselves to an end of the platform that was away from the voices. Slowly peering over the edge, they viewed a massive stable.

The stable had hundreds of occupied stalls. Each stall had a watering trough and a holding basket for hay. The stalls were arranged in long columns broken by wide aisles. Each column ended in front of a large door. If all doors were open, hundreds of horses could trot out in minutes. Later they discovered the enormous central courtyard for released horses.

Glenda and Traveler watched as a small army of stable workers attended to the needs of the large warhorses. Each horse had its hooves picked clean daily to remove embedded stones or piercing objects. Their faces were wiped down as well as their bodies. The horses generally enjoyed the attention and soft nickering echoed through the massive building.

After watching the activity Glenda whispered, "Let's go back. There's more of the walkway to explore."

Chapter 65

Ground Zero

They moved back until they were close to the overhead straw loft. With a single leap up, they landed back on the higher storage platform. "You go in first, I'll pull the straw after me to seal the opening and cover our tracks." Glenda gave an appreciative smile and ducked into the opening.

Traveler studied the return path. He then positioned large mounds of straw on each side of the path. To return he did a backward crawl while pulling straw down to cover the path. Once inside the passage he started to slide the vertical locking bar down then stopped.

"We better not lock it, we may need to get in here coming from the other side. I think our path is well-covered with straw and the opening has a mound in front. Nobody should ever know this stone opening exists."

"Good thinking-ahead. You're right, we may need to come back here from the other side and don't want to be locked out."

The torch continued to light their way as Glenda proceeded ahead. Suddenly she gave a startled gasp, "Watch out, there are stairs here! Easy to miss in this gloom."

"Good catch partner, I might have easily fallen without that heads-up."

Holding the torch up higher she slowly descended while Traveler remained several steps behind, he didn't want to pressure Glenda as she descended.

Traveler knew from his middle school days how dangerous it was going down school steps for recess or lunch with a thundering herd on your back. He had seen nasty falls from the herd pressuring the lead students to descend faster. *Thoughtless school lemmings*, he thought.

The stairs continued downward, and the riser distance was the same as the long staircase from their safe house. As they descended they had to control each downward step and they quickly noticed their thigh muscles were getting exhausted.

Traveler found an additional problem while descending was vertigo. Distance runners know it's easier to remain balanced going up versus going down. After a few minutes of descending Traveler said, "Let's stop and gather ourselves. My legs need a rest and my head is starting to spin a bit."

"Thank you. I feel the same way. I thought it was just me."

After pausing a few minutes they continued to descend. Just as Traveler was ready to suggest another stop Glenda announced, "We're here. I'm not sure where 'here' is, but I think we're at ground zero. The stairs end and there's a small landing area with a very big door."

They studied the door. It went up ten feet before arching higher. "Built for giraffes," quipped Traveler, "I wonder where it goes." An easy answer appeared when they noted the heavy locking bar had been pushed to the side. The door was not locked from this side.

Traveler pushed against the door. Nothing. Then he pushed much harder. There was still no movement. *The door must be locked from the other side.* As he studied the door Glenda pointed to a lever cleverly built into the wall. Traveler looked over, grinned and said, "Since brute force doesn't work, pull the lever down and let's see what happens."

Glenda gripped the lever with two hands and slowly brought it down until it stopped. Then they heard soft clicking sounds from the other side. "Good eyes and good reasoning, Glenda, I think you've unlocked it! I don't hear any sirens going off, so let's see where this door leads us. I've got no idea what's on the other side so 'caution' is still the word of the day."

"Like all our days," Glenda responded.

Traveler placed his ear firmly against the door. He held his breath and listened. After several minutes he nodded. "Cross your fingers, the coast is clear… I think."

Traveler pressed against the door and this time it moved slowly forward. He could tell by the effort of his pushing that this door was massive. As the door slowly moved, he continued to press it forward. Once the door was open enough to exit, light came in. He peeked out, "Good news, we can see. You can leave the torch here for our return."

Once Traveler stepped into the room Glenda came right behind him. As she stepped out, she paused to look at the width of the door. It was a foot deep made of solid heavy oak. As she inspected the wood, she saw round holes cut into the door's width and had an epiphany.

She motioned for Traveler to step back. She pointed to the holes, "This door is built to be sealed from both sides. We need to find the sealing device similar to the side we just came from. It's good to get in here but we need to be able get out quickly."

Traveler nodded in agreement. "You're right. We need a two-way street not a dead-end alley. We've already had our share of dangerous alleys."

They knew the opening and closing devices had to be near each other, just separated by the thick wall. Knowing where the lever was located for their entry, they looked for a similar mechanism on the other side.

A large wall sconce next to the door held an unlit torch. Just like in the movies they found there was a hidden latch. When the latch was released the torch became a lever that opened the door. "Very clever," Glenda said, "there is a spring to bring the torch back to its resting position once you are on the other side and return the lever to its vertical position."

"I'm very impressed," said Traveler. "Coordinated locking and unlocking levers. How clever were those Roman engineers!

Rome ruled as much by brain as by brawn."

Nodding Glenda added, "When brawn fails and your life is on the line and you need a fast, undetected escape to your safe house, place your bets on 'brains' to stay alive."

Chapter 66

Stored Weapons

As they began to survey the room, they immediately saw it was an armory. Glenda had a worried look and asked, "Do you think we're going to get caught? Will somebody come in looking for a sword or spear and instead find us?"

Traveler shook his head, "I doubt it. Armories are not generally open to the guards, much less servants. Rulers kept a tight control over weapons. No weapons equals no rebellion."

They began to explore the large room. The ceiling went up at least fifteen feet. There were bundles of iron-tipped lances over ten feet long. Traveler pointed at them, "Punching death. This spear did double duty in protecting the man holding it. The spear could deliver death at a distance to a swordsman and it discouraged a charging horse. Warhorses are smart and prefer not to run into a long iron point."

They continued to walk along a long wall. Stacked against the wall up to the ceiling were hundreds of barrels. Several barrels on the floor were open and they observed hundreds of arrows inside a single barrel. Taking an arrow out Traveler commented, "All archers know that arrows must not only have straight shafts but must also have well-placed feathers for accurate flight. The feathers are called the arrow's fletching. These containers are designed to protect both shaft and importantly the fletching feathers."

"Why so many arrows?" asked Glenda, "There must be thousands in these barrels."

"More like tens of thousands," answered Traveler. "A skilled longbow archer could release five to six aimed arrows a minute.

With a hundred archers that's a minimum of 500 arrows a minute. You can do the math as more archers are used.

"What's amazing is how accurate the longbowmen were in hitting moving targets at a long distance. I've seen YouTube demonstrations of modern archers doing rapid firing and hitting moving objects, it's unbelievable.

"Modern experts believe the old archers were much better than our modern ones. The earlier archers started their serious training around age nine. Their back and arm muscles became enormously strong to pull the long bows."

As they walked around, they studied the massed fighting armament including swords of varying length and weight. Traveler continued his dissertation on ancient fighting equipment and its use, "Having the right sword in combat was essential. Certain swords were built to cut through shields while others were used for fighting at various distances.

"A Roman sword, called a gladius, was only two feet long. Basically, the Romans fought up-close and personal. Their swords were intended for fast strikes at the neck and groin. The experienced sword fighter's adage is, 'There are old sword fighters and there are bold sword fighters, but there are no old, bold sword fighters.'"

Traveler realized he had lost his audience and said, "Want me to continue?"

"I'm good, but thank you,' Glenda answered. "My Viking ancestors had a simpler approach. Just hit the other guy with whatever is handy and keep hitting until the victory ale gets served either in the longhouse or in Valhalla."

"Yeah, that's a good summary for your distant cousins, and it worked. Of course the Vikings created a technological breakthrough with their ship designs. They were first in their class in terms of moving men quickly into places other boats could never reach and they could cross oceans. They had a lot of brains not just big berserker muscles."

"Thank you for that 'brain' description for my Viking ancestors instead of 'berserker'. We never seem to live that berserker word down."

Chapter 67

Into the Fortress Heart

With the hidden armory door sealed behind them, they worked their way to the main hallway door. Again Traveler cracked it open slowly. He held his breath hoping there would be no telltale squeaking. The door opened softly and Traveler peeked out.

He came back inside and reported, "We're in luck. This hallway takes us almost immediately outside into a huge courtyard. The armory is right at the entrance to the stable and the courtyard. That makes sense, since soldiers and mounted men can grab their weapons and be battle-ready in a short time."

Glenda nodded, "Let's walk right out and act like we're on a mission. People never question workers who seem to be carrying out some important task, just look busy."

With that truism she slipped into the hallway and strode confidently toward the courtyard. As she walked she tossed her hair to complete the look of a busy, disheveled worker. She was a young woman on a mission. Traveler followed her lead and they proceeded to walk across the expansive courtyard.

Their immediate destination was clear. An enormous fountain was in a corner of the courtyard close to the stable doors. It was obviously the watering source for the horses. The fountain was both functional and decorative. In the center was a thick column rising over fifteen feet with water cascading down from the top opening.

As the water fell it flowed into a series of catch basins. Each basin contained outlet pipes around the circumference. The pipes distributed the catch basin's inventory into a larger basin resting below it. The final catch basin was elevated four feet off the ground level with a diameter over fifty feet across. It reminded both of them of the fountain in their Chicago sanctuary.

Studying the water flow Traveler said, "They are not only distributing water efficiently, they are aerating it in the sunshine as a purification step. We aerate water today for the same reason. Well done again, Roman engineers!"

Glenda was thinking about how quickly all the horses could be watered. She did the necessary mental math to find the approximate answer. Recalling that circumference is pi times the diameter she announced, "It's a circle with a circumference almost 160 feet. They can water a lot of horses at the same time. If each horse needs three feet of standing space, they can pack at least fifty horses around the basin. Even with hundreds of thirsty horses they can all drink in a short period of time."

Traveler was impressed by Glenda's fast math and her insight into the military value of fast watering. He gave her an appreciative look and said, "Strong insight, Glenda. You could have been a Roman engineer and you're right about this watering efficiency. It looks like another example of Roman planning and engineering. No wonder they were the bosses for over 600 years."

Glenda accepted Traveler's praise with a modest nod but inside she was delighted by his recognition of her fast analysis, *And that's how we Vikings used our brains!*

Needing to show there was purpose to their presence, they noticed stacks of buckets with leather carrying-straps. Acting like it was a routine task they each took two buckets, filled them with water and went into the open stable doors. Upon entering an older man pointed to an aisle and said, "About time."

They nodded and began filling the stall buckets. Nobody except the horses paid them any attention. The horses immediately began drinking and Glenda said, "It gets hot in here so these big guys must need a lot of water."

"I can relate to that," said Traveler as he moved from stall to stall. Their buckets only filled four stalls so they were quickly in motion back to the outside basin.

Chapter 68

Fitting In

After half an hour of watering a voice whispered to them, "Slow down, you're making us look bad." Traveler focused on the sturdy young man around his own age who was trying to apply the brakes to their efforts. His first instinct was to tell the boy to mind his own business, then he reconsidered. He did not want to draw attention to himself by starting an argument.

He recalled his dad telling how, when he had worked in a factory in the summer doing piecework, the older workers had slowed him down. "We do this all year and need to pace ourselves. You're just here for the summer. We don't need a kid raising the hourly quota that we're paid against."

Traveler acknowledged the comment, "You're right. Sorry. It's just one of those feel-good days and I lost track of what I was doing. I appreciate that the steady tortoise wins a lot of races."

The boy looked relieved. Traveler was much taller with broad shoulders and projected a "don't mess with me" look. The boy was smiling now and added, "You're new here but believe me it gets hot by midday. Save your strength for later."

"You're right about being new here. My sister and I worked on a farm several days away and came here for better food and frankly for safety."

Traveler continued, "We hear there are Hun invaders from the east and the farmers are scared. They all have families and feel they must stay with their homes and livestock even when they know they should run. You know farmers; nobody ever says they are adventurous. They take root and that's where they stay regardless of the threat."

The boy was nodding his head, he came from a farm family. He appreciated that the bigger boy was a farmer and was sharing a bit about himself as well a bit of philosophy. This sharing convinced the smaller boy that this new stable worker could become a friend. He subtly glanced at the nearby sister. He let his imagination dance for a moment with the idea that maybe she could become his friend also.

"More work and less talk," a strong voice projected across several aisles. Traveler and the boy gave each other knowing smiles. There is nothing like a shared rebuke to create immediate buddies.

Once outside Glenda asked, "What was that all about?"

Traveler laughed, "Making friends to influence people. We want to be invisible workers and the quicker we fit in, the easier it will be to figure out where our foe is. We can't start asking direct questions until we're part of a working clan, stable serfs in our case."

Glenda nodded, "Good thinking. For a minute I thought you were going to rough him up. I know he said something that annoyed you."

"You're right, he did annoy me at first, but I got through that quickly and his advice was sound. We're already best friends. Plus, we have an ace in the hole, you certainly caught his eye. I'll be his best bud and the bonus for him is a chance to mingle with the princess."

"Great, I'm the princess of stable boys. Whatever happened to being prom queen?" Traveler laughed back.

They proceeded to water the horses for several more hours, then the boy reappeared. "I'm getting lunch, would you like to join me? My name is Robert."

"Absolutely Robert, lead the way. By the way, I'm Traveler and my sister is Glenda."

Chapter 69

If You Can't Stand the Heat

As they followed the young man their noses quickly identified their destination. The aroma of baking bread spread from the open kitchen doors into the courtyard. By the time they got there, hunger replaced any anxiety. The three walked in together as friends sharing a lunch break.

Overpowering the smells of cooking was the jump in temperature. Upon entering they felt the heat strike their faces but Robert seemed oblivious. Working in a hot stable had conditioned him against the kitchen's heat. On the other hand, Glenda and Traveler had to adjust to the mini-inferno.

Glenda and Traveler took in the kitchen's operation and saw it was a highly efficient food factory. It was in a constant state of activity. The fortress housed over 500 resident staff and soldiers. This small army ate in nonstop shifts. "M would love to watch this," said Glenda. "It's impressive beyond any restaurant I've ever seen."

The words "food factory" did not begin to describe the room's frenzied activity. A dozen cooks with a score of assistants were moving small mountains of flour, meats, barrels of vegetables, and barrels of wine.

Along one wall large fireplaces were spaced in a line. They were generating heat which challenged the cooks to prepare food without cooking themselves. Master cooks stepped in to confirm quality while apprentice cooks had to bear the heat. As the old adage went, "If you can't stand the heat stay out of the kitchen," and many would-be cooks were weeded out on that reality.

The young man motioned for Glenda and Traveler to follow him. He led them to a large open serving area. Rows of tables were stacked with the freshly prepared offerings. "Lunch is usually a hearty soup, bread, cheeses, fruits, and watered ale. Dinner adds meats and stronger ale. Just take a plate and help yourself."

Following Robert's lead, they piled their plates and joined him along a long table. The table was flanked on each side by equally long benches. They had just taken their seats when three more stable workers joined them.

Robert greeted the arrivals then asked Traveler to introduce himself and his sister. Traveler responded in a casual, matter-of-fact way that implied he had been part of many work settings. The new arrivals studied Traveler to assess him as worker. They assessed Glenda but for different reasons.

The workers responded to Traveler's self-introduction by briefly grunting their names, then they began shoveling in food. Watered ale washed down full mouths and frequently dripped down on hands. Hands were immediately dried off on their trousers.

Glenda looked at the accumulated areas of wiped food on clothing and thought, *You can read their last ten meals. It's like reading the age of a tree from its rings. "Ring around the collar" in this time period is replaced by "ring around the trouser". Do they ever wash their clothes?*

Chapter 70

How Did You Find Us?

With the first round of food consumed, conversation started. Naturally Traveler and Glenda were the focus for direct questions. A large man who projected a level of authority had joined the table and he started the questioning. Looking directly at Traveler he bluntly asked, "What brings you here? I didn't know we were adding to staff."

Traveler immediately knew that his earlier casual answers would not satisfy this man. *Be direct back at him,* Traveler thought. "Fear brought us. However, we are strong workers with farming skills and felt we could earn our keep here. We can work with all animals including horses and pigs. Also, my sister has a gift with dogs. We heard that Karl, the master of hounds, may need an experienced trainer so she will try to meet him.

Robert now interjected himself by saying, "They are very strong workers." Giving the leader an insider's look he added, "I actually had to suggest they slow down the pace."

The man nodded in agreement with Robert's comment, "Good advice. When you carry water and feed from dawn to dusk, proper teamwork and pacing is critical."

Listening Traveler thought, *Now I understand who he is. He's the stable foreman and his job requires setting the standards for the stable workers. He can't overwork them or he has a mutiny. He can't underwork and under deliver or he's fired.*

The foreman was now relaxed. He had an understanding look on his face and his tone of voice had softened as he asked, "Tell us more about your fear, what has scared you enough to bring you here?"

"In a word, Huns." Traveler and Glenda both saw the mention of Huns had frozen their tablemates.

"Continue," was all the foreman said.

"My sister and I lived in a remote village, named Nadrag, deep in the Carpathian Mountains. Destruction struck our bucolic lives when the Hun appeared in the spring. Our sister villages to our east were destroyed but we never received warnings.

"My sister and I had been gathering berries on a far slope when we felt a vibration in the earth under our feet. The ensuing sounds of despair froze us in our place. We immediately lay flat so we were not visible against the sky. We saw our entire village destroyed in minutes."

Then Traveler took a deep breath, shook his head, and continued, "When nighttime came we carried our lunch and the picked berries and began walking west along paths that served sheep and goats but not a mounted army. By the time dawn arrived we had distanced ourselves from the Hun both in mileage and in terrain.

"When we were satisfied that the Hun had passed by, we stopped and began to work at small remote farms for our food and shelter. Most of the farmers welcomed our muscles and livestock skills. From farm to farm we always moved forward and eventually found ourselves here in this mighty fortress."

Traveler grinned wryly, "Since horses can't climb high walls, I believe we have found our safe harbor."

The foreman had quit eating and was listening carefully to Traveler's tale. "Tell me the route you took to reach us. There is a well-traveled road that leads directly to our front gate. Is that what you followed?"

Traveler suspected this was a trick question. The man was possibly probing whether they had crossed paths with Throbb and his men.

"We avoided established roads. If you saw the speed with which the Hun move you would know there is no time to hide. We walked through the forest when traveling and met no one. We had been lucky once in escaping the Hun and were scared of our luck turning. We sacrificed speed to gain safety."

The foreman was totally relaxed and was looking at them with respect. "You are lucky and smart. Lucky to escape the first Hun attack and smart to avoid them by moving through the thick forest. As to losing your parents and village, simply accept that is the world we live in. Few of us die peacefully in our beds after a long life."

Glenda looked at Traveler and they had the same thought, *Don't look for sympathy here, there are no consoling counselors. Young people must accept their fates and move on with their lives as best they can.*

Chapter 71

We Met the Hun

Glenda watched as the foreman resumed eating. When she saw him pause with his ale, she thought he was now relaxed and had accepted Traveler's explanation.

Glenda looked around the table before asking, "Have the Hun threatened in this region?"

All those sitting at the table immediately looked to the foreman for the answer. He was the leader among this group and was expected to speak first. There was a recognized pecking order for talking and many a young stable hand had received cuffs for speaking out of turn.

Traveler saw the immediate deference given the leader. He compared this deference to how many of his schoolmates felt free to speak out of turn in a classroom. Their undisciplined behavior was frequently described by teachers as, "What's in their head is in their mouth." *Times have changed a lot*, he thought.

The man finished chewing his food and swallowed before answering, "Sadly, we have more than simply seen the Hun, we have faced them on a battlefield."

Glenda sent a sympathetic look then asked, "How did you escape them?"

"How indeed? That is the unanswered question.

"Our duke received word of their coming and chose to fight

them. All men were conscripted into the army. I was a made a unit leader and drafted to lead the stable men.

"It was considered an honor to be chosen as a leader, but that's an honor best avoided. When facing any enemy, the unit leaders had to lead from the front. Surviving the initial contact was a challenge that few survived."

Traveler repeated Glenda's question asking, "How did you stop the Hun? I thought they were invincible?"

The foreman sighed and shook his head. "We never stopped them in battle. Our hoped-for success was all predicated on being positioned to surprise the Hun when they arrived, instead they surprised us.

"We greatly underestimated the speed with which the Hun horde moves. When we arrived at the battlefield, we faced a great mounted army waiting for us. The Hun had secured the pass and were spread out in their classic flanking position.

"What happened next is a mystery, perhaps a gift from the gods. The duke sent an envoy requesting a meeting with the Hun leader called Attila. We all knew the Hun leader never negotiated so we were stunned when a meeting was accepted. The only terms set for the meeting by the Hun leader was that the duke must advance on foot at a rapid pace holding his flag up high.

"As the duke proceeded forward we saw that his advisor, we call him our mage, was trotting beside him. This was equally unexpected. We assumed the mage had chosen to die with his longtime lord.

"We all watched and held our breath. We expected to see the Hun guards emerge with both heads fastened to long spears. After some time passed, the tent reopened. The duke emerged first followed closely by the mage. Last came the Hun leader.

"The duke and mage walked toward us and never looked back at the Hun camp. When they entered our defensive line of wagons the duke had a strange look on his face, 'They will leave now,' was his only statement.

"As we looked up the hill, we saw the Hun horde was indeed mobilizing and was leaving. Silence hung across our army then a cheer arose that shook our wagons. Men began to stomp the ground with boots and spear butts. Swords clapped against shields. Calls of 'Duke!' 'Duke!' 'Duke!' carried to the retreating Hun riders.

"Some of the Hun rear riders turned to face us and lifted their bows and shook them. Their message was clear, 'be quiet or die'. We went immediately silent; victories are best celebrated when they are fully secured."

Glenda and Traveler exchanged knowing looks. The foreman's tale agreed with Hermann's story. Something unbelievable had happened at the meeting.

Chapter 72

Shovel and Push

The man rose from the table. "Enough lunch tales. The horses are thirsty and stalls need to be mucked out. I trust all of you will expend as much effort with those chores as you have eating and listening."

Traveler and Glenda waited until their tablemates hurried back. They fell in step with their new friend and returned to the land of horse stalls.

The afternoon sun had raised the stable temperature and the oppressive heat was only surpassed by the smell of stalls that needed mucking out. The stable crew worked in teams to load large wheelbarrows with the horse leavings. "Want to shovel or push the barrow?" asked Traveler.

"Neither of course," said Glenda with a forced smile, "but I guess I'll shovel."

"Don't overload the barrow, thank you. Remember we've been told slow and steady is the best pace. Last thing we want is for it to tip over."

At the end of the pushing route Traveler studied the dumping ground, *So this is how you spell "organic". They're recycling all-natural stuff and producing all-natural fertilizer. They may die from a lot of causes but not from chemical additives.*

Once they had completed their turn at the stall mucking, they switched to becoming water carriers. Naturally Glenda had already adopted favorites among the horses. The horse that gave her a sweet nuzzle earned a bigger supply and a pull on its ears. *If a dog is man's best friend, I think horses are a girl's best friend*, thought Traveler.

Joining them was a sweating Robert. "It's about bell time," he said just before a deep sound resonated from the courtyard. The horses ignored it but Traveler and Glenda jumped. Their friend laughed, "Thought I'd warn you it's loud, but I guess I was a little slow. Anyway, that bell means we are free to enjoy our own time now."

Chapter 73

The Mage

"If you can put up with me a little more, I can lead you to dinner."

"Lead on, MacDuff," said a grinning Traveler.

The young man had a puzzled expression. "I'm Robert, not Macduff."

"Sorry Robert, it's an expression said with intended good humor. Consider it a compliment of sorts."

Robert beamed, stable workers rarely received compliments from any source. Work orders and criticisms were the daily bill of fare for the laboring class. The war horses may appreciate their efforts, but even they seemed to regard the stable workers with condescending looks. Being taller, the horses literally looked down on their servants much as elevated, dining nobility looked down at the feasting attendees.

When the three friends reached the dining area, they immediately heaped food onto their plates. Dinner was similar to lunch but with meats added. Sausages, chicken, and cuts of beef were offered. Each worker took samples of everything. A darker ale was poured from large pitchers into mugs held out by large hands.

After the initial intakes, all at the table took a slow breath then sat back on the bench. Robert had a mug of ale which he drank quickly, while Glenda and Traveler had taken cider to avoid any missteps over alcohol.

"There do not appear to be nearly as many here as there were for lunch," observed Traveler.

Robert nodded then explained, "You are perceptive, my friend. Tonight there is a ceremony in the great hall. Many of the older staff are attending to the tables. While serving the lords and warriors they can watch the events. Naturally the servers don't want to miss the happenings so they are incented to move fast delivering food and ale. The system works well for both sides at the feast."

"Could we sneak in and watch from a dark corner?" asked Glenda.

"Absolutely not. You would assuredly be caught and then whipped. Likely they would whip you as entertainment for the attendees and as a message to the servers.

"As for me I'm going to simply go to my sleeping place and rest up. Tomorrow the attendees will be in foul moods lamenting all the ale they consumed this evening. Tonight is fun for them while the morrow will be a hardship for us."

Once Robert was out of hearing distance, they immediately faced each other. "Of course we're going to join the show," said Glenda. "Stealth gives us the best seats in the house. While the show is happening, we can look for the jinn. I also want to see this duke and his mage. This is going to be a big discovery night for us."

Traveler was nodding in agreement when Glenda said, "We need to get there early and secure our observation places."

"You're right, we need to secure the high ground before the crowd comes in. I'm thinking of the crow's nest that is close to the dais, we'll see and hear everything. That work for you?"

"That's my thinking also. Even though it's early I think we should head over and settle in."

When they entered the stable again, they each carried water and feed buckets in the event they were questioned, however their return was unchallenged. Inside, the stable was quiet and tranquil. The heat of the day had been blown out by evening breezes passing through the open doors. The horses were relaxed after their feeding and watering and seemed to appreciate the mucked stalls and fresh air.

Walking to the end of the stable they looked around to confirm they were alone. Rather than leaping up they remained cautious and climbed the ladder to the first loft. Once on the hay loft they moved back to disappear from ground view, then leaped to the second loft.

They landed in piles of stacked straw and Glenda immediately sneezed.

Traveler discovered the long day of stress had taken a toll and he needed playtime. He fell into a high mound of soft straw and rolled. He threw handfuls of the straw into the air and blew gusts into it causing clouds to float toward Glenda.

Glenda instantly grabbed huge handfuls of straw and proceeded to bury Traveler. He accepted the cover and disappeared.

Glenda laughed as she saw him crawling through mounds of straw tunneling along like a groundhog. His head popped up in the center of a mound as he said, "Forget what you're thinking, princess! This is definitely not 'whack-a-mole' time." Laughing, he submerged himself.

A short minute later he popped up with a pile of straw resting on his head. It had the appearance of a dunce hat and Glenda started laughing. "I've found our perfect hiding place, princess. We're safe as long as you don't sneeze. By the way you've got a lot of straw in your hair. You're a Vogue model for scarecrow girls."

Laughing back she quipped, "Right now you remind me of the Scarecrow trying to find a brain, let me know when you succeed."

"Touché, princess. The good news is that my Scarecrow brain has woken up. It's telling me we need to mache schnell to our crow's nest."

As they wiggled backward to enter the passageway Traveler again swept straw to obscuring their path. Once inside they stood up and combed straw out of their hair. After repeated hand combings Glenda felt satisfied, "Don't want straw drifting down from our observation roost."

Taking her cue Traveler made several more pass-throughs and declared, "We have conquered the straw threat, let's head to our crow's nest and settle in."

Walking beside each other Glenda suddenly covered her mouth to stifle the sound of an impending sneeze. "Relax, princess, and let it rip out. These stone walls are absolutely soundproof. Get it out now before we're camped in our nest."

Glenda gave a sheepish smile in return. She pulled out a small handcloth from the stables and proceeded to do the nose honors. Traveler was ready to joke about not blowing bugles inside tunnels but thought better. It was time to get serious. Time to get to their hiding place in the great hall.

Chapter 74

The Jinn Reflects

Seated in the duke's private quarters, the jinn studied the seated giant with satisfaction. Over the weeks following their return to the fortress, the jinn had increased his hold over the human leader. The jinn was confident the giant had no awareness beyond what he permitted.

For reasons not yet clear to the jinn, its control of the duke was not as complete as it was with other humans. However, his increased control permitted him to direct the giant at a greater distance.

With time available before the evening's feast, the jinn began a review of its past decisions. The jinn was a highly evolved decision-maker. This review was not to gloat over past successes but to confirm there was nothing further to be learned from their outcomes.

The jinn naturally started its review with its initial decision. This decision was simply how to survive. It had just arrived through a portal resting in a building the humans called a museum. As it was exploring the large room that housed the portal, it was set upon by a young human male. It had quickly determined the aggressive male was no threat and it prepared to absorb the human for information.

Suddenly a great threat arrived in the form of an ancient dark god. To survive the dark god, the jinn had instantly projected itself to a distant time period. The jinn knew that "out of sight, out of mind" would not save him from the god, but it only needed enough time to build the portal so the greater host could arrive.

The location was picked as it offered the necessary materials to construct the portal. The quarry stones used to build the fortress contained the electrical properties required for the portal.

The jinn recalled that its second decision was made in a more controlled, analytic manner. It had to decide which of the two confronting armies to take control of. The chosen army would provide the required workforce to construct the portal.

A quick assessment concluded that the duke's encircled army was more easily controlled. The jinn's final decision was how to eliminate the Hun army as a threat against the selected army. The jinn saw the answer was to gain control of both leaders and imprint them with his orders.

To gain control of the leaders' minds, the jinn initially needed to make physical contact. The first leader to be controlled was the giant referred to as the duke. To gain physical contact with this duke, the jinn would first enter a body that could easily approach him.

The jinn recalled the details of its search for a suitable host. It moved through the surrounded army in the form of a small cloud of early morning fog. If a soldier took time to notice the moving fog, he would simply see a lingering, reddish, night-mist reflecting the light from a rising sun.

As the jinn cloud passed through the camp it identified several candidate bodies, but none felt right. As it approached the command tent the correct choice was identified. The choice appeared as a burly guard standing in front of the duke's tent. The jinn cloud flowed unnoticed into the unsuspecting guard.

The guard's only awareness of the jinn's entry into his body was a paralyzing shock running up his spine. The guard's face registered a moment of surprise and confusion. An observer would have noted how the eyes suddenly dilated and the legs stiffened. For a moment the mouth seemed ready to utter a sound, but nothing escaped the lips.

Once inside the guard's body the jinn instantly flowed along the electrical conduits of the nervous system call the spine. The spine offered an electrical superhighway to control all parts of the body, and the jinn took immediate control. All senses and muscles now obeyed the jinn's wishes. The first command it issued was to maintain the body's standing position to remain unnoticed.

While controlling the guard's body stance, the jinn traveled upwards to the brain stem. This small structure rests on top of the spine. It is the oldest part of the human brain and is charged with operating the routine but critical body needs, such as breathing and heartbeats.

Flowing up and past the brain stem, the jinn assessed the higher brain functions and found the guard's brain was typical of the species. It was physically divided into two similar but separate parts. One part controlled logic skills such as mathematics, while the other part controlled abstract competencies such as art and music.

The jinn immediately understood how this physical separation limited the brain's potential to develop further. This two-sided structure acted like a mental flywheel with humans going to their dominant side for a wide variety of actions and decisions. The result was an unbalanced thinking machine.

With the analysis completed the jinn rewired the guard's cognitive abilities and slaved them to its wishes.

The guard's cognitive brain had a fleeting final moment of self-awareness, then it fell into an endless nightmare trapped in a black void without sensory awareness. The cognitive mind screamed and screamed into the void. The jinn considered the screams as background static without purpose and ignored them. The screams were not even a small distraction to the jinn.

For a moment the jinn reflected on humans being the planet's dominant life form. The jinn's determination of dominancy was the rule of the universe: "Who is the eater and who gets eaten?" While humans ate a wide variety of animals, the jinn could consume humans with ease.

Once inside the guard's mind, the jinn identified each sub-leader in the tent. These lesser leaders were called captains and were slaved by training to obey their leader, the duke. True to expectations, this uber-leader was by far the largest among those in the command tent. The jinn mused about size being a critical component of human leadership and how this bias limited planning and outcomes.

The jinn's control and assessments were over in less than a second. Wearing the guard as an external suit, it entered the tent to join a small group of captains and guards. The guards knew him and simply nodded at his presence.

The jinn observed that the duke was receiving a stream of news from breathless scouts. These scouts conveyed their information using a mixture of breathless words along with excited hand gestures. The jinn found the undisciplined flow of information highly inefficient. The efficient acquisition of factual data was its own lifeblood. Sorting out facts from emotional expressions slowed its data intake.

Unlike the jinn, the duke accepted the muddled information with an inward and outward calm. He understood the scouts were running on emotional highs generated from fear. The duke was superior to the jinn in separating fact from fearful conjecture.

Chapter 75

Jinn Meets Mage

After the scouts had finished their reports, the jinn observed that the duke was now focused on discussions with his captains. Using this moment, the jinn slowly approached the duke. As it neared the large man the jinn noted a much older man in a robe standing next to the duke. From the guard's memory it knew this man was called their mage, and was an advisor of many years.

The jinn also knew the mage was well known and respected by the soldiers due to his past advice. This advice was frequently described as being prescient or involving magic. Both explanations were acceptable to seasoned combat veterans who simply said, "Listen to the mage." As the creature studied this mage it was clear that he had no true power.

The discussions were now over and the duke was being outfitted for the coming battle. Young men, called squires, were suddenly surrounding their leader to begin the placement of battle armor. The jinn was forced to stand back.

First on was a doubly thick coat of tough leather, this was the last line of defense. Over the leather was placed his iron chain mailed hauberk. The hauberk offered a flexible iron dress and reached below the duke's knees. The outer wall of protection from the thick iron skin would deflect the strongest bow shot. The duke would stand as an iron giant on the battlefield inflicting woe on any who approached his long reach.

The mage followed the duke's lead and put on his ceremonial robe. The robe was a Roman red with gold threads woven through the fabric. Standing in the sunlight the robe cast a glittering glow that suggested a magical shield surrounded the mage.

The jinn observed the other guards and captains as they watched the dressing ceremony. Their faces declared their acceptance of the coming battle, and the inevitable outcome. One veteran captain announced their collective thoughts, "My lord, we will fight with valor beside you. Our families will tell tales for many years of our bravery at this place."

The duke smiled for the first time, "Well said, captain."

Chapter 76

Mage and Duke Meet
Attila the Hun

With the duke fitted for battle the jinn walked confidently to him. Standing beside the duke, the jinn prepared to enter his body. Transfers of control were always instantaneous upon contact. The jinn felt the transfer begin, then it unexpectedly stopped. *This level of resistance was not possible.*

The jinn paused to consider whether the iron contained in the layers of protective armor was impeding its entry. The jinn had secured partial control but had not fully entered the duke's body. Its control was effective but only at close quarters. The jinn made an immediate decision to revisit the duke later and establish absolute control.

Now it shifted from leaning against the duke to leaning against the adjacent mage. This transfer was immediate with complete control established over the mage's body.

The mage's eyes lost their normal twinkle and took on the dead look of a shark's eye. The mage's head made a few small jerks as his mind fought the takeover, then it became still. The battle for the neuro-network was over. The mage was in lost in the dark void. Perhaps he heard the echo of screams from the guard beside him, perhaps he only heard his own screams.

Simultaneous with the transfer from the guard into the mage, the guard's nervous system shut down. The brain stem stopped its efforts and the guard collapsed. The duke, startled by the falling body, instinctively moved away. Guards immediately surrounded their fallen comrade, then looked to the mage for medical help.

The jinn understood that as the mage he was the medical advisor and immediately knelt down by the fallen guard. He made a pretense of studying the guard before declaring, "Sadly our friend and comrade has passed from this life. His passing appears due to the stress we are all under. I know he is in a better place now. His spirit will be with us as we confront the invaders."

The mental haze was lifted for a moment as the duke said, "Place these coins on his eyes." The guards saw a hand holding two gold coins and thought how generous the duke was. Then they realized that none of them, living or dead, would have any use for gold by the end of the day.

Chapter 77

Mage Sends a Message

The mage turned to the duke and said, "Sire, may I suggest this is a time to make a final effort to escape the barbarian's trap. Although we are surrounded, there is still a possible move on the chessboard, we are not yet checkmated."

The duke could barely nod his head as he replied, "Continue your recommendation."

"I suggest you request a formal parley. This Attila is considered to have a keen mind. I suggest we try to test his mind with a parley."

The duke hesitated as he replied, "He does not negotiate. I only see checkmate on the battle board."

The jinn knew it could force the duke to follow his parley suggestion; however, he needed the attending captains to believe their duke was still the leader.

While the jinn was impatient with the fog-brained man's resistance to his words, he knew the listening captains were his true audience. They were desperate for any possible escape plan and they wanted to hear the mage out.

The mage continued, "Attila may decide it is in his best interest to negotiate. He is aware of your reputation for battle and the valor of your men. He has never faced an opponent of your stature and he knows a serious loss of men will result. This Hun's pride will want to avoid calling for reinforcements after a draining battle. Asking for reinforcements would be viewed by other Hun leaders as a call for their help.

"Finally, this parley request will boost morale among our soldiers. They will appreciate that you are willing to place your own pride behind their lives."

The duke understood the mage's advice was, in fact, a hidden command and he replied, "You are wise, my mage, and have proven right many times in the past. I will request a parley."

The mage watched relief pass over the captains' faces. The duke was following the proven adage, "Listen to the mage." As the mage, the jinn was quickly increasing his influence over these important humans. They would follow his future instructions without question.

The jinn permitted the duke to select the contact person. Even in a fog the duke knew the likely fate of the messenger and chose the oldest and least capable in battle. "Josef, the honor of carrying our flag and message to the Hun leader is yours. May God speed and protect you."

"An excellent choice, my liege. Please permit me to draft a formal parley request." The mage walked to the table covered with maps, extracted a blank parchment and prepared a short, written message which he handed to the duke for approval.

The duke made a cursory look at the document then slid it into a leather cylinder. Finally he pressed his seal across the lid's opening and gave it to Josef. Accepting the cylinder, Josef looked briefly at each man in the tent. Each gave him a simple nod of both respect and farewell. None expected to see Josef again.

Unexpectedly, the duke asked, "What did you write?"

The jinn was surprised at a question. This large human should not have the capacity for questioning him. The jinn reaffirmed that it needed to increase its control once the Hun threat was removed.

The jinn realized the captains were listening for his answer. "It is as you read it, sire. A parley request, but written in his own language. This Attila may find it intriguing coming in his own script, his curiosity may give us the parley." The duke was already lost in his mind fog. The question that had come to him when the fog had been eased to select Josef was already forgotten.

Bowing slightly to the duke the mage said, "My lord, let us go outside and watch Josef's fate from a lookout tower."

The two men walked to the barricade line, then climbed the recently constructed tower. The duke had no memory of what the purpose of this tower was. He had no idea of why he was climbing up.

As they ascended the mage noted there were multiple landings offering firing platforms for archers. As they passed each landing the mage acknowledged the standing archers. Once on the highest platform they joined six resting archers.

To lessen the somber mood of the archers the mage said to them, "You have the advantage of being stationary, as well as being protected by walls up to your waists. Shoot down on them with all your skill."

The archers considered the mage's insight and acknowledged his suggestion with faint smiles. They knew their elevated position would not last long. The Hun horsemen would quickly tie ropes to their tower and pull it over. The archers would soon be lying on the ground and easy targets for Hun arrows.

The mage raised his robed hand and pointed out Josef as he approached the Hun camp. Josef held the parley flag high in the air. This initial contact was the telling moment. The Hun guards would follow Attila's orders. They would either cut Josef down or permit him to approach. Both sides watched with interest the fate of this lone rider as it mirrored their own.

The group standing on this high tower had the best view. They were the first to see a Hun guard step forward and motion for Josef to approach slowly. The guard immediately took the reins assuming control of Josef's horse while another guard seized the parley flag. The flag was the first of many spoils of war. The surrounding guards expected Josef's head would be the second trophy.

The guard holding the reins motioned for Josef to dismount, kneel, and extend the leather cylinder upward. Josef quickly obeyed.

A powerful warrior emerged from the largest tent and strode toward Josef. The surrounding horsemen quickly backed their mounts to clear a wide path. This was Attila himself.

Attila reached Josef and barely glanced down at him. Josef wisely kept his head bowed and his eyes lowered. Attila took the leather cylinder, broke the seal and removed the parchment from the inside.

Josef noticed that when Attila first grasped the cylinder the Hun leader's body seemed to stiffen. Glancing cautiously upward Josef saw Attila's hand had a subtle tremble in it. *Strange*, thought Josef.

Attila looked at the message, then lifted his head to stare across the field at the tower holding the duke and the mage. He read the message a second time. Twice he shook his head as if chasing bothersome flies away.

He then acknowledged the parley request with a few short sentences. He spoke in Latin to the kneeling Josef, "I accept the parley but with conditions." Continuing in Latin he gave the conditions. The conditions were clear, there was no diplomatic subtlety in his words.

Josef was stunned at the barbarian's use of Latin. Apparently, Attila had an education beyond horses and battles. With his head still bowed Josef confirmed Attila's return message.

When the Hun leader turned and went back into his tent, the guard holding the reins motioned for Josef to mount. As he rose in the stirrup, he felt his legs and hands trembling. He was barely able to mount without falling. The stress he had controlled was now beginning to take its toll.

Once mounted, he moved past the Hun horsemen at a walking pace. He felt the Huns' eyes boring into his back, they had expected his head as a second trophy and were clearly confused and disappointed.

Both the Hun guards and the duke's army were captivated by this exchange. The Hun had never seen their leader accept or honor any message to parley. Both sides had expected to see Josef pulled down, then made sport of. The duke's army felt a tremor of hope. Could the mage have worked his magic?

Chapter 78

Attila Responds

The mage quickly descended from the tower and waited for the slower duke to join him. The two proceeded back to the duke's tent where they met up with the returning Josef. Josef dismounted, waiting for the duke to question him. Instead the mage engaged him, "I assume you have a message, other than we will all die?"

A still shaking Josef answered, "Indeed, my mage. Their leader seemed both puzzled and intrigued by your message, he read it several times. Your message led him to focus on our camp and tower.

"Fortunately for me he seemed oblivious to my presence until he spoke to me. I was shocked that he spoke in Latin. The man is more than he appears."

The creature was annoyed at Josef's failure to simply deliver the Hun leader's message, "We are all pleased you survived, now give us the message!"

"He has agreed to the parley, however, there is a condition attached." Josef was now visibly trembling, he was uncomfortable passing the message.

Annoyed at the continued delay the mage commanded, "Speak up man! Deliver the message."

Josef quietly answered, "While he accepts a parley, the message is an insult. His condition is an insult."

The duke felt the fog lift slightly as the mage was now intently staring at Josef. Whatever his mage had written had created a miracle. The duke began to ask again about the message but found questions could not come out of his throat.

"What is this condition?"

"Sir, perhaps it would be best shared without an audience," Josef stammered.

The mage's eyes briefly flared then he quietly said, "Tell us right now."

"He will accept our unconditional surrender but expects an immediate, visible display of the duke's fealty to him."

"Continue. How will this test of fealty be demonstrated?" Josef realized the mage was looking at him with cold, hard, flickering red eyes. He felt like a confused dog being reprimanded by its master.

"The duke must run hard without armor or weapon across the field to Attila's camp. He must run holding his personal flag high in his left hand. Upon reaching the camp he must kneel and wait for Attila to accept his flag."

"Did this barbarian demand our lord come alone, or can he be accompanied by his advisor?" asked the mage.

"Sir, he did not say. I was not in a position to ask him questions, I was a simple messenger. Any question from me could have been considered an insult and the last thing I wanted to do was cause an insult to alter the parley."

The mage nodded and Josef noted the eyes had lost their red flicker, "Wise of you, messenger, I understand why our lord chose you."

The mage turned to the duke and said, "Sire, with your permission I will accompany you. I have knowledge of the barbarian's language and customs and will be an asset. In any case, your fate is my fate and I always choose to stand by your side. Should we enter your tent and inform the captains of the next step?" The duke simply nodded.

Inside the tent the captains had been listening and were speculating on the parley role the mage was taking. The captains greatly respected the mage's commitment to enter the lion's den with his lord. They knew they were all bound for the lion's den, but possibly their mage could once again outmaneuver a stronger opponent. The captains softly clapped their fists together to applaud the mage's bravery.

Chapter 79

Into the Lion's Den

The squires prepared the duke for the run. He was rid of the armor and stood wearing only the protective leather coat. Even dressed in only the coat, he projected a massive size and power.

The mage gave another suggestion, "Sire, I suggest we sit and build our energy back up. Stress drains energy and you must project confidence and power when you engage this Attila. We should also drink much water. Water, more than wine, is the true friend of physical and mental power." Again the captains nodded their heads at the mage's wise advice.

The duke nodded and immediately chairs and filled cups were brought. Once seated both men lifted their cups and drained them. Looking at the duke the mage said, "My final advice is to drink another cup. This Attila will likely keep us waiting in the hot sun to study how we control our bodies. If he finds you wanting in any way, he will end the parley with our heads on a pike."

The cups were quickly refilled and drained a second time. Prepared as best they could, the two proceeded toward the tower and the barricade of overturned wagons. Looking across the field they saw a long line of mounted Hun horsemen elevated in their stirrups. Clearly these were senior officers having the best view of the giant running like a scared field rabbit. They would enjoy the giant's run, his likely trips on overturned clumps and pot holes and possible collapse. The morning promised great entertainment.

The duke's subdued army watched the relaxed Hun horsemen. They were clearly enjoying the morning's entertainment. They passed leather bags of the mild alcoholic drink kumis among themselves, toasted their past bravery, and made bets. After their assumed battle victory, they would consume large amounts of arkhi, a much stronger drink.

The duke was now standing outside his defensive barricade. He raised his personal battle flag high in the air, then he appeared to shake it. Several Hun captains read this as an insult and a challenge. A look from Attila stopped their desire to charge forward.

Attila watched as the two men began their long field run. He had become a battle master by maintaining control of his emotions and he demanded the same control from his captains. He had seen many younger warriors rush forward to attack, become outflanked and isolated, then cut down.

Attila watched the massive warrior running across the wide field. The man was a true giant, broad-shouldered and heavily muscled. *Big, strong, and quick to slow. We easily cut these men down in battle*, he thought.

He studied the giant's running feet. He knew from many battles that foot movement was the first to show failing strength. In watching his own men in boxing matches he was less impressed by arm muscles than by footwork. Footwork speed permitted many a smaller man to defeat a larger brute.

He also studied the man's breathing as he was exerting himself. Most soldiers who are running toward an enemy start with a sprint, then necessarily slow as they lose their breath. This man's size permitted Attila, even at a distance, to watch his chest movement. Chest movement signaled his need for faster breaths.

The giant was now halfway across the field and maintaining a runner's hard pace. There was no weakness appearing on either his foot speed or his breathing. The older, smaller man had fallen behind, but surprisingly not as far as the bettors had wagered. Attila appreciated that this older man was well conditioned to maintain his own measured pace.

Attila listened as his captains changed their bets to cover early losses. He also noted the leather bags of kumis were no longer being passed. All his captains were now quiet and focused on the runner giant.

The unwanted thought came to his mind, *Perhaps I should not have made this running challenge. It is not good karma for my warriors to gain respect for a foe.* He put that thought behind him as he found himself drawn into the excitement of watching the runners continue their strong pace. The giant continued to carry his size without effort and the older man was able to move quickly forward despite his advanced age.

The race ended with the giant standing in front of the line of Hun horsemen. The horsemen saw that while sweat flowed across his face and down his hands, his breathing was steady as were his staring eyes.

This giant was a warrior ready for battle. The run had simply elevated his fighting spirit. Those who had earlier been eager to engage him now had second thoughts, *Let the young warriors prove themselves against him while I watch.*

Upon arrival the duke immediately recognized the Hun leader sitting on a large black stallion. Their eyes met and a slight nod of Attila's head confirmed he was the Hun general. The duke gave a returning nod. The duke walked slowly toward the mounted warrior, knelt and held up his flag.

As the mage trotted pass the mounted warriors, the warriors who had placed bets on when and where the old man would collapse studied him more closely. The old man appeared composed after his exertion.

A few warriors studied his face and suddenly found themselves looking into flickering red eyes that seemed to be taking their measure. No warrior held eye contact. No warrior challenged the old man as he followed the two leaders toward the parley tent.

The jinn knew, of course, they had met the conditions for the parley as Attila slid off his horse and motioned for the duke to rise and follow him. Had Attila not honored the meeting, the jinn would have instituted Plan 3. Attila and the surrounding Hun would not have liked Plan B.

The jinn had the mage walk closely behind the duke as both entered the parley tent. Continued control of the duke was essential.

Once inside the jinn prepared for the next step in eliminating the Hun threat.

Chapter 80

A Strange Parley

The duke's height required him to stoop down as he followed the Hun leader into the large tent. The tent was constructed from thick woven hides. The tent sides were supported by carved wooden support poles. The elevated interior was supported by similar but larger wooden beams.

Hanging above the entry door was a pagan symbol of Hun battle intentions. Multiple skulls were bound on a chain of horse hair. The symbol proclaimed to their foe, "As you enter expect to die." The entry sign did not suggest fruitful parley outcomes.

The interior was a strong contrast to the threatening entry symbol, it was culturally magnificent. While the Hun leader moved each day on horseback, he enjoyed a high level of comfort once their camp was established. The floor was covered with thick piles of oriental rugs. Each rug was a work of art and presented a tale of heroes, faraway cities, and mystical creatures.

Any one of the rugs would require four or five skilled workers over a year to construct. The craftsmen built the rugs by tying together a plethora of small knots of varying colors. These rugs had such a high density of knots that their pictures jumped out in great detail. The greater the density of the knots the greater was the rug's value. As art, they rivaled the finest Roman floor mosaics.

Asian gods were well represented, confirming the Huns indeed had a strong cultural belief in supernatural beings. The

Hun's central god was a god of the open skies. The sky god was based on the Hun's daily lives spent on vast open plains with an endless sky above. Lightning and thunder alerted the mortals below of the sky god's mood.

Attila walked to a throne that rested on an elevated platform. He ascended several steps and sat down. The platform's elevation had been constructed so that while seated he would look down at his taller opponent. He never accepted an opponent being at eye level, a level line of sight implied they were equal in power to him.

Even with the added elevation Attila found the duke was looking back at close to eye level. The giant was easily more than two heads taller than the tallest warrior he had ever met. Attila unconsciously arched his body upward for additional height. His servants would pay a price for this error. He ignored the old man standing well below him beside the giant as being of no consequence.

Standing on each side of the platform were pairs of archers and swordsmen. The archers stood a short distance away and had arrows notched. They could release in an eye's blink. The guards were closer to the standing giant with drawn swords ready for a fast strike. The pairs were experienced teams and each member of the team was deadly in his craft.

Attila made a hand motion to one of his captains, who immediately hit the standing duke hard on the back of his knees with a thick spear. While he was not struck himself, the mage understood the message of the strike. "Sire, you are being told to kneel at once. Your height offends this Hun leader."

The duke was unfazed by the leg strike but immediately accepted the command from his mage. He assumed a kneeling position. In other circumstances, with a clear mind, he would have turned on the striking captain, lifted him above his head and broken him across a knee. The archers and swordsmen would have followed shortly.

Beyond humbling the giant, Attila knew from past experiences that this kneeling position ensured the giant would be slower to rise and attack. His archers and swordsmen would strike the giant down long before he was upright.

As the duke knelt down Attila made a hand motion indicating the old man would be permitted to stand. Age was respected among the Hun and Attila was impressed with the old man's endurance in the run. It was also good psychology to permit the servant to stand while the leader was forced to kneel. The servant looking down became superior to the master.

While kneeling, the duke stared ahead at the throne which was now at his eye level. The throne was carved from an exotic black wood and featured sculpted demons protecting the chair's occupant. Little did the seated Hun leader realize that a true demon was hiding in the old man standing in front of him.

Attila made a second hand-motion and a captain approached the kneeling duke. This captain was an experienced interrogator. He would inflict increasing levels of pain so that the Hun leader could study a kneeling opponent's reaction.

The captain had proven himself many times in his ability to intimidate and interrogate captured foes. He had mastered the art of physically humbling a foe before Attila's questioning began. The other captains enjoyed watching him as he broke the strongest man down to a whimpering child.

Facing the kneeling duke, he lifted a flexible switch in his right hand. He made it snap through the air with a whistling sound, then delivered a stinging stroke across the duke's lower face and lips. Lips are very sensitive. The duke remained motionless.

Attila had agreed to the parley to gain critical information. He had instructed the captain to make the application of pain a slow and humbling process. Attila knew from many experiences that to advance torture too quickly led many captives to say whatever they thought the leader wanted to hear. That information was useless.

This duke was an important source of information regarding the treasure lands and their guarding armies to the west. These western lands held numerous wealthy cities, the greatest of which was Rome. While his advance scouts had assured him that the once mighty Roman empire was a shadow of its former self, Attila knew he needed to advance his horde swiftly. Food, water, and information were the keys to victory.

The captain watched his first strike hit the giant's face and saw there was no anticipatory flinch. Every person instinctively flinches when a known blow is coming. The captain was annoyed and embarrassed that his blow was ignored.

He held the switch in front of kneeling man and moved the end across both cheeks. This time the captain made a much louder snapping sound with the switch. Maybe this giant needed to really hear what was coming. This would be a stronger blow across the sensitive middle face and nose. The blow should break the nose.

When it was delivered there was still no resulting flinch. *This man must have a face made from stone*, the captain thought. *But even stone breaks with a strong enough blow.*

Attila watched as he expected a third and even stronger blow to quickly follow. This third blow would be higher up and across the eyes. Nobody can ignore a blow across eyes, all people automatically close their eyelids and jerk their heads. This third strike would tell Attila much about this duke.

While retaining control of the mage, the jinn used its cloud form to approach each warrior. It easily passed through each warrior, read their minds, and then controlled them. They were easily controlled and they now stood expressionless. Their cognitive skills were gone and their bodies were only containers for their organs.

The jinn read the interrogating captain's mind last. It provided a history of similar encounters. The jinn felt no emotion in considering the sad fate of prior victims. It did not judge the captain, it simply observed and understood. What it found was that human leaders frequently sought knowledge using a wide variety of pain techniques. Before returning to the mage, the jinn wiped the captain's mind clean as he stood motionless, poised to strike.

Attila ignored the nearby mage. His focus was on his captain and the kneeling giant. He saw the captain's switch was poised but was not delivering the expected third strike. Annoyed he barked a command, "Strike now, captain, before I strike you!"

His words had no effect. Angered he immediately leapt down to the carpeted floor and proceeded to another captain. "Replace our inquisitor, you know the steps." This captain simply stared at his lord without recognition. Attila slammed a fist into the warrior's chest, then stood stunned as the warrior collapsed.

He moved to other captains and saw the same blank looks on their faces. Attila was instantly on high battle alert. Could his captains and guards have been poisoned? Was he personally in danger, and how could that be?

Before he shouted for help, he returned to the kneeling duke and studied him. The duke looked back at him much as a milk cow looks at the person milking it. For a moment he considered taking the switch and applying it, then he considered the size of this man and the absence of guards.

When his eyes left the kneeling giant, he became aware of the old man beside him. The man was studying him and Attila's frustration and anger bloomed into a rage. Attila knew he was at risk to lose his control and he never lost control.

The old man's impudence to approach him and then study him demanded immediate punishment. There was no risk in applying the switch to this old man. He lifted his arm to strike, then found himself lost in the flickering red eyes that stared back.

Attila fought to maintain control of his anger and his confusion. He had studied many adversaries both at a distance and as captives. He could read the obvious and the hidden. On the surface this was simply an old man, an advisor to the kneeling lord. His clothing consisted of robes similar to Roman nobility, not the garb of battle warriors.

The second reading was the insightful one. The robed man projected an easy confidence in front of a feared conqueror. He reminded Attila of the mystical shamans from his own homeland. Shamans were valued for their power to foresee future outcomes as well as to advise on best courses of action.

They were thought to have a link to the gods and could petition the gods for advice and help. These shamans treated warrior kings as their equals. When shamans spoke, rulers listened.

Attila instinctively knew that the true leader in this parley was not the kneeling giant but this old man. The eyes looking back at him had dancing red flames in the center. Then the man spoke his name "Attila", but in his mind. Attila was mesmerized.

While Attila was frozen in place the man spoke again in his mind. A single command formed in Attila's mind. The command was to cease his army's battle plan. The Hun army would retreat. No person, soldier or farmer, would be touched. No grain or livestock would be taken. Once past the duke's lands, the Hun leader could proceed westward on routes of his choosing.

Finished with Attila, the mage spoke aloud to the kneeling duke, "Rise up. This invader understands he will bypass our lands. We will return to our camp and celebrate the outcome of this parley."

As he walked to the tent opening, the mage turned to Attila and gave a final vocal command in Latin, "You will begin your retreat immediately. The day is young and your horses are rested. By evening you will be beyond this region. Seek your plunder on a different route."

Once the mage and giant were out of his tent, Attila regained control of his mind. He began to shake. He took a series of slow, deep breaths to calm his body and his mind. He accepted that he had been in the presence of a god.

Fortunately, this god was permitting him to continue his advance west with only the loss of a few captains and guards. Attila felt relief. This was a generous god. Attila's invasion luck was still with him.

Chapter 81

The Jinn Looks Back

The jinn was pleased that his review of past events confirmed the correctness of each decision. Further, each action had provided great insights into the human body and mind. Humans were easily understood and controlled. They offered no threat to the jinn.

The jinn was mildly concerned over the lingering blockage to fully control the giant but it would sort that out in good time. The jinn loved to solve puzzles.

For now the jinn was content with its total mastery of the mage. It had carefully integrated itself into every aspect of the mage's mind and body. Integration had taken more time and effort than anticipated but now its control was perfect. It had even, with considerable practice, learned how to make facial muscles form a smile. It knew human leaders had to smile on occasion.

Following the encounter with Attila, the jinn used the mage to take control of the army and the workforce. The captains saw the duke was an ill man and had delegated much power to the mage. The captains initially accepted this shift of authority with ease. The mage was wise and had saved the entire army from the Hun. The mage had also saved their own lives.

With an obedient workforce the jinn had commenced construction of the portal. Progress was made but it was slow progress. The portal was a highly complex structure for humans to work on. Workers tried to learn but they now feared the mage. The mage was constantly dismissing, in some cases eliminating, inefficient workers. Fear clouded learning which slowed their efforts. Humans were slow students scared of making mistakes.

Tonight's feast was the jinn's attempt to regain goodwill and motivate the leaders. If this failed the jinn would consider a Plan B approach to the portal's construction. Tonight's attendees would not like Plan B.

Just as it had completed its review, the dinner bells rang out. It was time for them to join the feast. The mage motioned for the duke to follow him as he stood and headed to the great hall. The duke rose slowly and the two moved in unison toward the great hall.

Once at the hall the jinn stood off to the side and waited for the slow-moving giant to be the first to take his place. The jinn continued to demonstrate outward respect to this leader. Having a puppet leader enabled the jinn to place unpopular decisions back on the duke. The jinn had mastered the blame game. It was developing human political skills.

Chapter 82

The Jinn Is Studied

Well before the arrival of the first diners to the great hall, Glenda and Traveler were on their way. They knew their route and were soon at the low exit door that led onto the selected crossbeam. Traveler eased the shutter to the side and slowly looked out. He saw serving people busy preparing for the feast. While they were generally looking down, he knew body motion was what attracted curious eyes.

Whispering to Glenda he said, "You know stealth requires that our bodies must remain motionless, we can't use stealth until we're inside the crow's nest."

Glenda accepted the comment with a nervous smile, "I know, and you are the master of stealth, lead the way."

Traveler continued, "We need to be snakes staying close to the center of the beam and slowly wiggle our way across. If you sense we're spotted, freeze in place."

Traveler gave Glenda his encouraging smile, "This is as good a time as any to move out. It's a piece of cake compared to our deep dive. Let me get about ten feet ahead so we don't get backed up at the crow's nest."

His parting gibe was, "Don't get a splinter in your nose, it's already had a tough day sneezing."

"Lead away, big boy, and let's hope your oversized head doesn't draw attention."

With the brief repartee exchange over, they transformed into lizards moving on the log. Several times one or the other had to stop and slowly remove a splinter that was snagged on the wool clothing. Finally, Traveler reached the observation nest and wriggled inside. Once inside he moved around to allow Glenda to wriggle in beside him. They immediately went into stealth mode.

Breaking stealth slightly, they moved their legs into crisscrossing positions with their backs against the wide stone pillar. "Not exactly a comfortable position," whispered Traveler and Glenda smiled back.

"Our consolation prize," whispered Glenda, "is that we definitely have the best seats in the house. We have a wide view of the room and most of the tables. The dais is right in front and that's where the important people will sit. We'll see and hear everything that happens there."

With their whispered exchanges over they settled into a stealth meditation mode. Their minds went back to their Chicago sanctuary with its safety, great food, books, and their study alcoves. Both remembered sitting under their cascading waterfalls with sweet soaps and lotions. They thought fondly of being rested, clean, well fed, and only struggling with the demands of their books.

Those memories seemed a lifetime ago. Their current proximity to each other, absent deodorants, and wearing stable work clothes brought the present situation up-close and personal. Their meditation was broken by a roar similar to that heard in a zoo at feeding time.

The roar was coming from hundreds of men entering through the massive doors. Their sound was a cacophony of shouting, boasting, challenging, and laughing. Chairs resisted being pulled across a rough stone floor with loud screeches. Tables groaned as massive arms descended to rest on them. Later they would groan again as massive drunken heads descended on them.

With the influx of the large number of soldiers the air changed both its direction and its odor. Glenda poked Traveler, breaking stealth for a moment to show her holding her nose and Traveler grinned back.

Simultaneous with the men sitting down, dozens of servants entered with large jars of ale for the soldiers. On the dais servants were pouring wine into the steins. Wine was for the nobility, it was far too expensive to waste on the average soldier.

Many a nobleman had quipped "Ale is for the louts to get drunk on, while wine is for the educated to discuss philosophy and politics." Other nobles quietly reflected that alcohol in any form quickly levels the playing field between the louts and philosophers.

In the midst of cascading sounds, heads suddenly snapped up. The great hall was instantly quiet. A massive man entered the dais and walked slowly to the dining table. Most people would simply call him a true giant. NBA players would quickly agree.

The man was suited in heavy leather with a chain hauberk that climbed up a thick neck and fell below his knees. His massive shoulders pushed the top of the armored shirt straight out from his neck. Thick dark blond hair fell outside the mail's neck protection and landed on the squared shoulders. The duke, lord of all he surveyed, had arrived.

That suit must weigh a ton, thought Traveler, respecting the giant's strength.

That suit should keep his body odor contained, thought Glenda.

Then a second man quietly emerged. While the duke presented a physically commanding presence, this man projected the calm confidence of a behind-the-scenes puppet-master. A red cape fell across narrow shoulders and was cinched at his chest. An aged face looked across the seated warriors. The mage had joined the duke at the elevated head table.

As the mage rotated his head to scan the seated men, Glenda stared down at him, then grasped Traveler's arm. Hard. Pressing her lips against his ear she whispered, "His eyes!" They simultaneously wrapped themselves in their deepest stealth covering.

Chapter 83

The Jinn Assesses His Workers

Looking out at the packed great room, the mage's eyes swept across every warrior and occasionally paused. There had been a moment when a vibrational warning had come to him. It was a vibration not expected from this herd of human men. He instinctively poised himself to attack, defend, or retreat. Then the moment passed as quickly as it had arisen, there was no threat here. He was the only threat.

The seated warriors who had been relaxed in the presence of their duke felt a primal fear pass through them when the mage appeared. The mage had somehow changed. His prior persona reflected an easy competency mixed with caring and a hint of humor. Now his face showed no emotion. His eyes seemed to contain a flickering flame that that mirrored the dais's blazing hearth with its ascending sparks. No warrior chose to look into those eyes.

As he paused to study the assembly, the mage observed their individual and collective fear. He knew fear was a survival instinct built into their cellular development over many eons. Their instinctive fear came from an unconscious awareness they were being studied by a great predator. Every goat knows when the tiger is approaching well before it hears the soft tread of heavy paws.

The jinn inside the body of the mage calmly assessed the human herd as his assets. Brute strength, animal cunning, and pack obedience, but little else. These human resources were limited in their cognitive capabilities; however, under his continuing firm oversight they would complete construction of the portal.

Once completed the portal would provide the gateway for the host to enter and end his isolation. The full host would find the dark god, absorb it, and end this too-long pursuit.

The soldiers slowly relaxed as mugs of ale brought a needed calm to their nerves. As feasting and drinking progressed the jinn found itself concerned over the time being wasted as these humans gorged on food and alcohol. He recognized their feasting cycle. The more they drank the more they ate, and the more they ate the more alcohol they would consume.

The jinn knew that alcohol in any form greatly disrupted human behavior. Even worse, their ability to fully function the next day was impaired. The creature decided that when they began work the next day on the portal he would abolish alcohol. *They are not intelligent enough to drink and work. Drink goes.*

Chapter 84

Observing the Creature from Above

Traveler and Glenda studied the mage, as the mage in turn studied the feasting warriors. They watched his face which had an expression similar to a teacher looking with disapproval at a class. "How best to manage you?" was the unspoken message coming from the mage.

They also watched his eyes. One moment they were calm and the next moment they held dancing red flames. They knew with a certainty this was the sought-after jinn, the fire creature from the museum. Now they understood the stories from Hermann and the stable foreman about the Hun army retreat and the rise of the mage. The jinn was in control of the fortress.

Glenda again squeezed Traveler's arm and finger pointed toward the seated duke. Both of them were struck by the rigidity of his face and his body. This was not the normal, animated duke they had heard about. In past feasts he would raise his large drinking horn to toast a selected warrior to accompanying cheers from the seated warriors.

In prior feasts the toasted warrior would typically try to stand and bow to his lord first, then to his comrades. Frequently a saluting warrior only made it halfway up from his seat before swan diving onto the table. This drunken fellowship would generate another round of cheers from the men.

This feast now had a different tone. It was quiet and subdued. The tone could be described as bordering on sad, similar to the mixed emotions generated by alcohol at a funeral wake. Warriors quietly drank as much as they could hold, but tried to remain inconspicuous.

These warriors reminded Traveler of a group of middle school boys brought to the principal's office on discipline charges. These school boys expected a serious lecture and possibly a suspension. These seated warriors felt the duke was no longer the principal in charge. There was a new principal and it was the mage. You did not want to visit him, his idea of a suspension chilled your bones.

While the feasting continued, Glenda and Traveler noticed the mage had stood up and was leaning over the duke to whisper in his ear. The duke now rose and pointed to a seated warrior below to join him and the mage.

The warrior slowly rose with obvious trepidation. He was struggling to clear his head before a visit to the dais. Traveler and Glenda immediately recognized the reluctant warrior, it was Throbb.

Throbb approached the steps to the elevated dais knowing all eyes were on him. Any misstep and he would be tomorrow's joke. His first challenge was ascending the four steps to reach the top of the dais. There was silence as the seated warriors watched him slowly place each leg and foot to ensure he did not tumble backwards.

The short walk and climb up seemed to refresh him. Once at the top he approached the duke and mage with a steady-enough walk. Standing in front of the duke, he bowed his head. Once again the size of the duke stood out. Throbb was a very large warrior himself but appeared as a child beside the giant.

Both Traveler and Glenda immediately sensed this was not the confident, assertive Throbb they knew from the inn, nor the fearless warrior challenging the huge bear. This was a scared Throbb doing his best to hide his fear. They saw that while Throbb looked to the duke he never glanced at the mage. It was the mage he feared.

Again the mage whispered in the duke's ear. The duke placed a large hand on Throbb as if he knew the trembling warrior needed assurances. "We understand you had a set of experiences over the last several weeks and we would like you to tell us about them. We have heard about a young man who bested you in table wrestling. I find that hard to believe, you are a proven battle warrior with arm strength that few would seek to challenge."

Throbb visibly straightened and appeared to gain back some of his composure. However it was a two-edged compliment. One edge was high praise regarding his arm power. Mitigating the praise was the rumor that he was bested by a farm boy.

The audience was fully entranced. Many of them had contested Throbb at a wrestling table to live with a sore shoulder for weeks after. Noisy drinking was now stilled as each seated warrior listened to Throbb's response. Instead of Throbb answering, the mage whispered to the duke and the duke answered his own question.

"Now the story claims," said the duke, "that you and Karl, my master of hounds, pursued these two youths across dense woods to no avail. After several days of pursuit, the only creature discovered was a giant bear. I understand this was the father of bears and stood higher than a seated warrior on horseback. This bear attacked your men and the hounds. It was a killing animal without fear.

"I was told by our master of hounds that you alone went on the attack against the beast. Your courage was remarkable. I have witnessed you as a true warrior in battle. In most battles we fight with our brothers on each side. In this battle it was only you against the beast. I once had to defend myself against such an animal and never have I had a more dangerous fight. I survived and you survived, so I salute you!"

With this praise the hall's tension was broken, loud cheering and table thumping rocked the hall. This was the duke they all knew. Ale mugs were raised and pointed at Throbb and the duke. Somehow the mugs never quite pointed at the mage.

Throbb was now the man of the hour. He began to envision the rewards that may come from the duke. Possibly he would receive a farm or an inn and be able to retire from this warrior's life. Throbb believed that each warrior had a fixed number of successful battles he could survive. His instincts told him he had reached that limit.

As the duke told the story, Glenda and Traveler considered their own part in all of it. The duke had made an accurate telling of certain events but had omitted others. Glenda and Traveler realized that the "other" details were the real reason Throbb was on the stage.

The mage now rose and moved to stand beside Throbb. The mage made a curt bow to Throbb and attempted a smile as he stared into Throbb's eyes. The smile was twisted and the eye contact petrified the warrior. Throbb shivered and felt his knees weaken. He had to clench his lower body regions to avoid humiliating himself.

Maintaining his warped smile the mage said, "We are all impressed with how you brought this giant bear down. Now let's hear more details about the two youths. Given the events we all heard about from our lord," and the mage nodded toward the duke, "they seem to be something beyond simple farm youth. Given your personal encounters with them, would you agree?"

Throbb's mind was a kaleidoscope of swirling thoughts and emotions. Part of him was trying to recall the events while part of him was still engaged with controlling his body's nether region. Fear was an overwhelming force. He looked to the duke for support but found the duke was looking away from both him and the mage. The duke appeared as a man whose mind is elsewhere.

Gaining his voice Throbb answered, "I am a simple warrior so my knowledge of things beyond normal is limited. I was naturally stunned when this youth bested me in wresting. He was tall and had solid shoulders but lacked the fullness of battle muscles. I remember looking him in the eye while our arms were contesting and saw a confidence rarely seen in any of my opponents either at wrestling or on the battlefield. I should have scared him yet he seemed above fear."

Throbb found that once he began to talk his mind and body settled down a bit. Now he began to accept the attention focused on him in front of his comrades. He again began to think ahead to his acclaim at the dinner tables. He would retell these stories many times and add subtle details.

The details would present him facing a young man who was far from normal. He would strongly hint the man was a possible deity. Throbb, the giant bear killer and wrestler of gods, that was a story of Throbb the hero, not Throbb the vanquished.

The mage seemed to accept this explanation with a slight nod, "Did you see or hear of other feats of strength?"

Now relaxed, Throbb recalled the tales he heard from the innkeeper. "Indeed. The innkeeper offered overnight room and board if the boy would chop into firewood some portion of a large log pile. The keeper shared with me that the pile was easily several days of chopping for an experienced woodcutter; however, the boy did it all in an afternoon. The keeper said the boy must have gotten help, but he added that he never saw any help. It was unexplainable to the keeper."

Again the mage nodded in encouragement and Throbb suddenly produced another tale. "Before we began our arm contest one of my men, well into his cups, was a bit frisky toward the boy's sister. She was dressed in simple clothes, however she was a beauty. Long russet hair on top of a very tall body with striking green eyes. A Viking may have called her a Valkyrie."

Glenda had a sweet smile on her face and nodded as she gave Traveler's arm a strong squeeze. Traveler gave her a simple "get over it" look back.

All the seated warriors were captivated by this image of one of their own being forward with a Valkyrie. They loved where this tale could go and were holding their breath for Throbb to continue. Many took deep draughts of ale sending their imaginations on fantasy trips fueled by the ale. *What next?* they silently pondered while waiting for Throbb to continue.

Throbb saw he had the full attention of the warriors and he continued, "The boy was obviously going to challenge my man's behavior when a great beast intervened. The innkeeper raises a fighting breed called Molossus. The Romans used them in battle and they are terrifying. The keeper breeds them to guard all sides of the inn. They obey only his commands.

"This beast, named Trajan after the great Roman Caesar, was the alpha of the keeper's pack and outweighed me. It had fangs that were as long and thick as my thumb. When it appeared in front of the girl, we all thought it was going to attack her. Maybe she appeared vulnerable or gave off an odor that stirred it.

"Then she placed a hand on its head and we realized it was protecting her. It stood braced beside her and swept its eyes across each of my men to look for a threat. Trust me, there no challenge made toward the beast. The girl's brother then sat down for our arm contest and that ended the focus on the girl."

As Throbb was speaking the creature was frustrated. The usable information was limited. All the creature could determine was that the young man was strong, but many farm men have power beyond their appearance. Big muscles don't always mean superior power. The woodcutting story sounded like a keeper's tall tale to amuse his guests. The young woman had likely been the object of Throbb's own pursuit not some nameless soldier. The girl had probably fed the beast and it was simply protecting her as its food source.

The jinn was annoyed, this man Throbb was more a storyteller than a credible witness. What the jinn needed was hard information, such as what did the two actually look like. The jinn decided to enter the man's mind and recover all relevant information including the visual images. Naturally this intrusion would destroy the cognitive mind, but that was not a concern to the jinn, gathering accurate data was the only thing that mattered.

As a beaming Throbb was standing, his hoped-for retirement arrived, but not as he had wished. The watching audience saw he suddenly had an expression cross his face similar to those caused by a killing spear or sword thrust.

In a moment his life as a human was over as the creature extracted all of Throbb's thoughts and memories. The creature would later sift through the recovered data to determine if there was any possible threat to itself.

The creature did not bother to reinstate Throbb's nervous system, he was as disposable as a tissue. Without a sound, Throbb, the giant bear killer, collapsed to the floor. He was dead before his body was at rest.

The audience sat stunned in their seats. There was no sound or movement. Then the mage knelt down, put his hand on Throbb's neck and pronounced, "He has passed on. The stress of reliving these dangerous events has taken its toll. This feast should end now but each of you will remember and respect the experiences that warrior Throbb told us tonight. Tomorrow we will give him a proper burial."

The creature had no emotional reaction to Throbb's death nor the need to provide a proper burial. It only offered what it knew these warriors expected. The duke continued to gaze out at the far walls, then prompted by the mage he added, "Farewell, my faithful Throbb."

Chapter 85

Cleanup Time

Traveler and Glenda watched the warriors slowly stand and silently leave the great hall. This was not the typical ending to a feasting night. The alcohol's effect had quickly worn off following Throbb's death. Death in any circumstance is sobering and Throbb's unexpected collapse generated a natural drug in each warrior that sobered mind and body.

Heads were bowed and there was no gibing between friends. There was an uneasiness that wrapped around the departing warriors like a fog. The evening's dinner and drink were sour in their stomachs, they were anxious to leave.

Leaving together one older warrior whispered to his friend, "My father is a farmer. He has many fields and occasionally a field goes bad. Crops fail to develop and simply return to the earth. Dad calls it a 'blighted field' and claims it needs to be abandoned. Our fortress feels blighted to me. I know we can't tell the duke to abandon it, but my dad would say it is blighted and nothing good will live here."

His friend nodded, "Your father may be a wise man but I strongly caution you to never mention your thoughts to anyone. There is a change here that started when we returned from confronting the barbarian horde. Maybe the barbarian's god cursed our duke and fortress as punishment for resisting the Hun's army."

Glenda and Traveler remained in stealth mode as four husky men struggled to carry Throbb's body across the dais, down the stairs, then out the great room doors. They heard them panting as they passed under their beam on the way out. Throbb was a big man and they thought about how easily he was killed by the creature.

They remained hidden in place while dozens of servants removed the table settings as well as the various items that had landed on the floor. Finally they swept the tables clear of the remaining meats, bread, cheeses, and spilled ale. The swept-up remains would feed a small village for many days.

Finally, they heard the main doors close with a solid thump. Traveler was preparing to stand when Glenda squeezed his arm and nodded toward the dais, Traveler instantly froze. Moving out from the side of the dais was a robed leg followed by the body.

The mage had made a fast appearance back and was surveying the empty hall. His eyes were red flames scanning for hidden intruders. The creature had sensed something early in the evening and was now seeking out the source of the vibration.

Traveler knew what to do, *look away immediately*. He squeezed Glenda's hand and tightly shut his eyes. Glenda felt her stealth cover slipping as her heart was racing. Then she recalled Traveler's advice when he had been surrounded by the creatures in the museum. "Shut your eyes and focus on your book. The book will strengthen your stealth skill."

Glenda had her eyes so tightly closed her eyelids quivered. Suddenly her book came to her mind and she felt herself calming. Time passed then she felt her arm being squeezed again. She forced herself to look out slowly through squinting eyes. The dais was clear and Traveler was wearing a weak smile. She hesitantly smiled back as she took controlled breaths and felt her body relax.

For a moment she understood why ostriches would seek safety by burying their heads in a hole. When danger is out of sight, we can easily deceive ourselves that it has passed us by. She knew the mage was always a danger even when not in sight.

Traveler whispered, "Let's crawl back slowly. I think it's gone but let's be prepared to freeze and go stealth if we need to."

Last in and first out, accountants call that LIFO for tax purposes, she thought. *I'm no accountant but sure am happy to be first out.* Traveler followed and stayed focused on her shoes. It was easier for his mind to keep stealth ready when it did not need to focus to the beam. *Not quite tightrope walking, but close,* he thought.

While crawling back Traveler's mind shifted from the scene on the dais to the necessary slow return. The mage's body clearly contained the jinn and the jinn was a crafty foe, it could still be lurking out of sight.

He focused on managing the return crawl when his hand hit stone. He realized he had reached the entry point and crawled quickly inside to find Glenda standing up. He stood then slid the shutter back into place. He took a deep breath, then said, "Wow, that was intense."

Glenda nodded, "Intense and informative. Now we know what we are dealing with. The jinn creature is inside the mage and has complete control. It clearly has no concern for human life. I guess that's no surprise but seeing it in action is scary."

Traveler said, "It's worse, much worse. I think it has control over the duke. Did you see how passive he was during the entire evening? He knew Throbb as a man but showed no emotion when he was killed. Besides the duke, I wonder how many other zombies the jinn controls."

"Just one more zombie is one too many." Then she added, "I have to say that I felt sad for Throbb, he did not deserve that ending."

"He did not!" agreed Traveler. "We saw brave Throbb at his bear-fighting best and that is how we should remember him."

Walking quickly down the passageway carrying their torch Glenda added, "Let's get back to our safe house asap. I'm out of gas, hungry, and need to collect myself. Stress and stealth take a lot out of me."

"Ditto with that," said Traveler as he hustled to keep up with Glenda's fast pace. They walked briskly since they knew the return route; going somewhere new always takes a lot longer than returning. The torch was beginning to burn down and throw off smoke as they reached the entry to the armory's wall tunnel and Glenda quickly quenched it. If smoke got into the armory room it would raise unwanted questions.

Easing the armory's access door from the passage open, Traveler cautiously looked inside. "The coast is clear, let's move."

The two moved quickly through the armory then into the hallway. Generally, the hallway traffic was servants coming from or going to the great room. Since it was nighttime the servants were all in bed, but a few guards were awake maintaining a quiet post-feast presence.

As they passed a candlelit room, they heard guards discussing the evening's events. They were sitting at a long bench with a soft fire warming and lighting the room. Ale mugs were held tightly in hands as they spoke in quiet voices.

A few of the younger guards began speculating about Throbb's death. They commented on the closeness of the mage. They noted that the mage showed no reaction to the large man falling beside him. They questioned whether Throbb's sudden collapse and death surprised the mage, and if not, why not.

These talks were cut short by an older guard. He gave each of the talking guards a stern look then said, "Lads, consider the wisdom of the Romans. The Romans had a saying, 'In vino veritas'." The young men reacted with puzzled faces, they did not understand the words.

The older guard replied, "It's Latin, the language of the Romans. It declares that, 'In wine, truth'. While the Roman nobles drank wine and we soldiers drink ale, the effect is the same. Judgement is lost. Too much ale or wine and speaking truth can lead to a swift sword to the throat.

"Watch what you say and who you talk about. Tongues and heads have been removed for less. There is no forgiveness in the mage." Castigated, the younger men accepted this admonition and focused on their ale steins. No further speculation about the evening's events were offered.

Listening to the conversation Traveler and Glenda nodded at each other. These simple soldiers understood that while the fortress was impregnable to an outside enemy, it was now a dangerous place inside. A blighted fortress.

Chapter 86

Olaff's Sanctuary

Glenda and Traveler moved quickly along the deserted hallway to the door leading down to their safe house. They opened the lock, stepped inside, and again locked the massive door. Once inside they breathed a deep sigh of relief. Glenda said, "Tonight was a dangerous discovery. If not for our stealth skill we would be captured and absorbed by the jinn. It would absorb our minds as easily as it did poor Throbb."

"So true. Stealth and our books saved the day this time, but if we are discovered and caught, we're history. Theo is not going to be the arriving cavalry saving us this time."

They proceeded slowly down the long staircase. The stairs were lit by flickering wall torches. Dark shadows danced on the edges of each deep step, making the descent dangerous. As Traveler chose a slower descent pace, he chanted, "Go fast and risk a stumble, followed by a killer tumble." Glenda was mildly surprised at the simple ditty, *Oh my gosh, poet boy appears.*

At the bottom they went to their moored boat and were preparing to board when Glenda wavered. "What's up, princess?"

"Too much adrenaline, big boy, I need to burn it off." With that she dove into the dark pool. Coming up she began a controlled mix of a crawl stroke, sidestroke, and backstroke. Grinning back at Traveler she called, "It's probably too cold for you. You should take the boat. For a Nordic girl it's a summer swim."

Traveler nodded and called back, "I'll help you climb out on the other side. Take your time," then he did a strong push-off dive to gain crossing momentum.

The race was naturally on. Both fell into strong crawl strokes and rotated their heads every third stroke for air. Neither looked at the other's progress as they were each committed to being first. Less than ten minutes later two hands slapped hard against the rock pier. "Victory!" shouted Traveler as he looked around.

"Catch your breath then I'll help you out," replied a standing Glenda.

Traveler looked up in astonishment. He started to claim her head start was unfair, then he laughed. "You must be part Norwegian salmon; you definitely swim like a fish. You deserve a fitting prize." His hand slapped the water sideways and a long stream of water shot out hitting Glenda across her shoulders but missing her head.

"Poor sport, big boy. If you need a pull up just shout when you have your breath back. See you inside."

Traveler pulled himself under then gave a mighty dolphin kick and shot out of the water. Landing on his stomach he flinched, *Very cold stone, must get inside.* He quickly followed the light coming from the entrance to the great room. Once inside he moved to the roaring fire to stand beside Glenda. "Well done, Ms Norway."

Glenda nodded back but likely her nod was just her body shaking. The water was not cold, it was freezing. Traveler was ready for a smart comment until he found himself shaking. "Our stress-relief swim has me close to hypothermia, maybe I'm already there."

Glenda nodded, "That's exactly how I feel right now. Hypothermia is a fancy word for crazy shivering from the cold. We get a lot of it in Norway when we get wet. I know the cure and I'm hitting that hot shower right now. I suggest you strip down, wrap yourself in one of these big blankets and huddle close to the fire." With that she fast walked through the archway.

Sitting by the fire and still shivering Traveler thought, *As always, ladies first. I'll camp here and count shivers and fire flames until you get back. Don't worry about poor Traveler, just take your good old time enjoying the hot water.*

Glenda entered the shower room and pulled the lever down for a hotter mix. Testing the water with her hand she was satisfied. Once under the cascading water she felt her body adjust to the welcoming heat. Of course the fire had briefly helped to warm up her body, but one side was always facing away. Now the hot water flowed over all of her body, offering a much better warming source than the fire.

After adjusting the lever downward several more times she sat on the large wooden bench. The bench was elevated to a height that her feet never touched the stone floor. For a moment she wondered if taller Traveler could sit and touch the floor, then she promptly dismissed the thought and reached for the soap.

After several soap scrubbing of hair and body she sat still and reflected on the day. She wondered how she and Traveler could ever defeat the jinn hiding inside the mage. Her mind considered a range of possibilities but nothing worked. Feeling herself getting tired again she thought, *Forget it. Traveler and I will figure it out together, but not tonight. I'm hungry and exhausted.*

Wrapping herself in a fresh thick woolen cloth she again created a Roman toga of sorts. She cinched the toga's waist with a hemp rope and headed back to the fire.

Her face lit up as she approached the table. There was a roasted ham, cheese, apples, and thick bread. A cup of brown honey promised a sweet topping for the bread. Mugs of clear water offered wholesome libation. Traveler had been busy in the pantry and the results were wonderful.

"Kudos to Traveler! M would appreciate our feast, simple yet elegant. It is exactly what this girl needs. Thank you, many times over. Now go get your shower, I'll wait."

Traveler felt some of the chill vanishing with the praise. If he were a dog his tail would be wagging and not from the shivering. "I live to serve," was the cleverest reply he could come up with. "I'll hit the shower and scrub well so you don't need to sit at the far end." Glenda smiled back then pointed toward the shower.

Once in the shower Traveler felt the stress of the day gradually fall away. He recalled a famous quote from his English class attributed to William Congreve, an English playwright and wit from his 1697 poem, "Music has charms to soothe a savage breast." *I'd modify that,* thought Traveler, *to "Cascading hot water soothes the freezing soul." I don't think people back then truly understood the benefits of a long, hot soak. Actually, the Romans did. Score another civilization point for them.*

Traveler felt his shoulders slump and his body relax. He had to jerk upright to fight falling asleep. As he found himself again drifting off, he instinctively put a foot down and found once again the floor was too far below. Adrenaline shot through him as he caught himself and he was jerked fully awake. *Whoever built this bench was an idiot,* he thought.

Now awake he soaped and scrubbed hard. The scrubbing massaged the skin. With the cascading hot water, the shivering disappeared. Relaxed, he continued with a scrubbing to ensure dirt and sweat left along with the shivering.

Finally he felt ready to join the princess for an evening meal. Taking the hanging cloth off the post he wrapped himself several times for modesty but also to retain the shower's heat. The hemp rope served as an effective belt and he felt like a new man and a very hungry man.

He walked quickly back to the table and was pleased to see Glenda had created a hanging rack by the fire. As he put his clothes on the rack he said, "I don't know about you, but right now these clothes are not deserving of our cleanness."

Glenda smiled and nodded. "Yeah, but in this world of no washing machines or dryers, it's the burden we live with. Right now let's get our priorities straight and dig into the feast you've set out."

Once seated the conversation stopped. Both focused on the dishes in front of them. The only sound was the tearing of thick bread and muffled chewing. The speed of their intake seemed to declare the table would be shortly cleared. *Eat fast*, they thought, and they did.

At last Traveler looked up and said sheepishly, "All this eating has me sleepy."

Nodding Glenda stood up, "Yeah, big meals and hot showers do that, not to mention exploring inside castle walls and hiding from an evil jinn. The food was a lifesaver and so is sleep, I'm off to slumber land."

As they headed toward the sleeping room, they noted the table was still covered with the remains of the feast. Traveler paused to consider cleaning up when Glenda said, "Relax, Traveler. You prepared so I'll put everything away when I wake up." With that they continued toward the sleeping area.

Coming through the twelve-foot-high arched door they stared again at the elevated platform rising four feet off the stone floor. Traveler observed, "I feel like one of the tiny Lilliputians in *Gulliver's Travels*. Looks like a bed for a really big NBA center like Shaq or Yao Ming. Or maybe that duke, he looked at least their size, probably a lot more. Viewing at a distance makes sizes confusing."

"Well, this bed would be an even better fit for Robert Wadlow."

Traveler wrinkled his nose, "Who's that?"

"If you want to feel really tiny let me tell you about Robert. Born in Alton, Illinois he was the tallest man ever medically confirmed. He was an honest eight feet and eleven inches tall and weighted almost 500 pounds. He had an arm span of nine and a half feet. His hand was over a foot long from his wrist to his fingertip."

"Wow! How do you know that?"

"Living in Norway there are a lot of big people. As the sons and daughters of Vikings we are fascinated by them. We studied them in with our Viking history classes. The Viking blood is still with us. You probably know Hafþór Björnsson as 'The Mountain' from *Game of Thrones*. Watch the TV show *World's Strongest Man* sometime and you'll be amazed by his size and strength.

"Here's the sad ending to Robert Wadlow. He was a good natured giant but died at age twenty-two. He had a brace designed for a foot problem, but it was not put on properly. The brace caused an ankle blister which got infected and he died."

Traveler looked at Glenda with renewed respect. *A girl who knows about Vikings and giants, now that's usually boy stuff. Very impressive.*

"Ladies first," Glenda said as she dove onto the platform and rolled a couple of times across to the far edge.

"Bet I'm asleep before you, princess."

Glenda's retort was a fake snore. Morpheus visited both and their bodies and minds went into an immediate deep hibernation sleep. Two bears in bed, and the bear bed was appropriately inside a stone cave.

Chapter 87

A New Ally

Without sunlight to wake them, their bodies remained in a deep sleep. Time passed without any awareness for either sleeper. Eventually Traveler felt the gentle call of his lower body, the call was quickly turning into a shout. He accepted the inevitable, stretched several times, and took deep breaths. He felt great. He would visit the throne room, put on his dried clothing, then clean up last night's feast. The princess could extend her beauty rest and he would plan the day.

As he sat up he noticed that most of the dining room candles must have gone out, the doorway was dark with just faint shadows of light coming in. Fortunately, his eyes were already dilated. As his eyes took in the room's dimness, the doorway shimmered and moved into the room.

Without thinking he was instantly on alert. He extended his left leg and poked Glenda. She muttered an unladylike sound and tried to kick him back. "Glenda, wake up right now! We have company."

Glenda went from a deep sleep to instant alert. She turned to the doorway and immediately saw the huge darkness entering the room. The darkness stood six feet away from the platform and was studying the two recent sleepers.

"Did he send you?" demanded a voice coming from a cavernous chest and out a thick neck. The words were deep and reverberated as they hung in the stone ceiling then faded into the stone walls.

For a moment Traveler was a smart aleck high school boy with a ready response of, "Who he?" Good judgement mixed with fear prevailed and he answered, "No, sir. We thought this was a little used storage place. We are simple workers in the stables and thought this was a place to sleep before returning to stable work. We were going to head back up the stairs after a quick breakfast."

"I think not. Your clothes are at the foot of the bed. Get dressed and join me in the dining room."

As the figure turned and passed into the doorway the room was darkened again. *That Wadlow giant never died, he's here with us right now. This guy makes our biggest NBA guys look short and puny.*

Turning to get his clothes, Traveler saw Glenda was already dressed and coming around the foot of the platform. "Speed it up, modest boy, I don't want to entertain a giant by myself."

Traveler pulled on his dried clothes and noted that they felt like wearing cardboard. Stiff from the drying and cold, they resisted a leg coming down a pant-leg and an arm going into a sleeve. Socks felt like wooden shoes. He knew how poor Wadlow must have felt with the bad brace. Then his mind jumped, *How did she dress so quickly?*

Dressed, he moved cautiously into the dining room and saw Glenda holding court with the seated giant. *Beauty does have a way with the savage beast,* thought Traveler. *I think it's a good thing she got out first. Even giants don't club ladies, I hope.*

Glenda appeared relaxed, as was the giant. As Traveler entered the room she smiled saying, "Traveler, let me introduce you to the man in charge. This is the famous Olaff."

Traveler's first impression was a flashback to an exhibit he had visited that depicted early man. That exhibit was titled "Homo Sapiens" and Traveler thought this guy would be labeled "Homo Gigantus". The second, third, and fourth impressions were power, size, and danger. The man radiated power that went beyond physical strength, this man would be an unbeatable adversary.

Size started with his head covered in long, thick, matted, dark blond hair. His eyes were a blazing blue that reminded Traveler of a welder's arc cutting through steel. His face was a balance between modern man and Neanderthal. The forehead was large, the chin jutted out. Overall the head belonged on Mount Rushmore.

While Traveler was making his assessments, the seated giant was reciprocating. Glenda had obviously passed muster with the giant and now Traveler was under the giant's microscope.

A look of studied curiosity and interest passed over the Mount Rushmore face followed by the hint of a smile. Olaff's assessment verdict followed, "You can shake my hand, lad. Step up and show me your man grip."

Traveler knew this handshake request was more than a friendly greeting. It was not a threatening request but rather a way to take his measure. Traveler knew that men in this time period read a lot into the simple act of handshaking. The handshake confirmed there was no hidden weapon as well as innate strength. Aligned with the shake was the eye contact. Men of equal stature expected direct open looks.

Traveler cautiously extended his hand and watched the giant's hand engulf it. He was drawn to the man's eyes and found himself staring deeply into them. The eyes conveyed a message of interest and nothing more.

Now Traveler felt the pressure of a hydraulic press squeezing down. For a moment he hesitated to squeeze back, then he knew he had to meet the shake challenge. *I'm more than your lad. I think you may be another Throbb showing off for the young princess, but I hope not.*

Glenda watched with an amused look as both men gradually increased the pressure. *Boys showing off. Go Traveler!* she silently cheered.

There was no noticeable strain of effort on either face. Both seemed determined to find the other's "quit point" without doing serious injury. Both were staring hard into the other's eyes.

Traveler was the first to blink. As he increased his squeeze to his maximum effort, he realized the giant was holding back.

Maybe a lot. Traveler's maximum squeeze would crush the strongest man's grip but it had no effect on the giant.

How much additional power the giant had did not seem like a question to pursue. The fact that the giant was controlling his power meant he was not trying to humble and dominate Traveler, nor impress Glenda.

Traveler accepted the giant as being something far more than just appearance. He was a man of restraint. Restraint implied a solid character. This revelation came to him in an instant and he was both relieved and pleased as he thought, *We may have found our home-grown ally.*

"I yield to the mightier man, Sir Olaff."

Glenda sent Traveler a look that said, "Sometimes you're smarter than I give you credit for."

Olaff was now openly staring at Traveler. "I don't know who you are lad, but you are far more than meets the eye. No man has ever stood up to the hand strength I gave you, nor has any ever shown me the power of your arm."

Traveler sensed a bond had been created and he decided to build on this. Relaxed, he said, "I agree, sir, that you can tell a lot about a man from his grip. My dad always told me to look a man directly in the eye and give a firm grip."

Olaff nodded, "Solid fatherly advice. Now what hidden skills does the lass have to offer? Or, being a fair maiden, does she rely solely on you for her protection?"

Glenda's instincts took over her reply. She saw that a bond now existed between Traveler and the giant. Traveler was accepting the giant into their small club. She wanted to be a bona fide member of the club and needed to pass the power muster with the giant in her own way.

Glenda looked first at a grinning Traveler, then at the massive warrior. She shook her head at each of them, smiling back. "Decide for yourself, Olaff, what protection I need from men including the young one beside me." Traveler was amused as he waited to see what Glenda was going to demonstrate.

Sitting in her chair she focused her mind to employ her mastery of gravity. While her gravity control only operated over short distances, that was enough. She slowly rose off the floor. She continued her ascent while Olaff's mouth fell open. Resting close to the ceiling she asked, "How's that?"

Neither Olaff nor Traveler had a response. "Now watch this, gentlemen," and she blinked out of sight.

Olaff was staring up where the floating girl and chair had been a moment before. He shook his head and muttered, "Not another mage in the fortress. This is a sad day, we already have one mage too many."

Looking at Traveler he said, "So I guess you are her servant or squire. She picked you for brute force while she provides the higher-level magic talent."

Traveler frowned as he heard a chuckle coming from above his head. "I'm not her servant or squire, I have rather impressive skills of my own." With that he also ascended from the floor until he was near the ceiling. Looking down at the resting giant he blinked out.

Olaff remained motionless in his chair. A series of expressions flashed across his broad face. Confusion was followed by concern followed by fear and finally alertness. He was deciding between a fight or flight response.

He spoke in a low growling voice as his neck was strained from looking straight up and searching the high ceiling. "Are you two with the mage? Has he sent you to find my retreat?"

Rather than answer, Glenda and Traveler appeared back in their chairs, then both slowly descended to the floor.

Once settled, Traveler saw that Olaff was gripping a giant war hammer in his right hand. The hammer's massive head, flat on both ends, rested on the floor. The thick stock of the hammer was covered in glyphs that seemed to flow from the stock onto the giant's hand and arm.

Suddenly Traveler had a flashback. He was in his bedroom selecting his travel book for the Chicago train adventure. He recalled pulling the old leather book from the back of the shelf, then studying its back cover. He remembered being unsettled because the cover presented a different scene than what he remembered as a child.

The original cover had presented a standing giant with a peaceful face holding a long staff. He recalled how the pictured glyphs on the staff seemed to move and flow from staff to arm. Staring at the book many years later, he saw the original smiling giant was replaced by three aggressive figures.

Each figure was huge and appeared intent on using their weapons. One figure held a war hammer, one a long slender sword, and the center figure a spear. The figure with the war hammer reminded him of the seated Olaff. *How weird is this?* he wondered.

Traveler's mind snapped back to the present as he saw the giant's shoulders were hunched and his fingers bulged with a powerful grip, Olaff was restraining a massive strike.

"Hold that blow, sir," said Traveler as he looked Olaff directly in the face. "We are no friend of the mage. In truth, we found your retreat here as a safe haven while we avoid him."

Glenda nodded her agreement then offered her sweetest look at Olaff. Once again beauty was able to soothe a savage beast, or in this case a perplexed giant.

Olaff's hand relaxed its grip while still holding the shaft. He could still easily sweep across the table removing any person or group across from him. "Tell me more. Why are you here in the fortress and hiding? What is your cause and concern with the mage?"

Glenda accepted the question with another smile that said, "Trust me". "The answers come with a long tale, one we are pleased to share with you. The short version is that we were sent here by our own mage to either kill or contain this mage. Our mage is a true god called Theo, and is the essence of fairness and good power.

"In fact, what you see and call a mage is not that at all. This mage was truly once a man but is now a vessel for an evil being. We call the being a 'jinn' or sometimes a 'fire creature'. When you look into the mage's eyes you will sometimes see that a fire appears to flicker in his eyes. This shows the presence of the creature lurking inside."

Both Glenda and Traveler saw that Olaff was now visibly relaxed. His right hand moved from the shaft of the war hammer to the large jug in the center of the table. "I listen best with a mug of ale so indulge me before starting."

He proceeded to fill his own enormous mug and then set much smaller mugs in front of his newly accepted guests. The ale poured out as a dark liquid with a thick foam forming on top. Glenda gave Traveler a sidewise glance that said, "We're in big trouble."

Quaffing a deep drink, the seated giant nodded for their tale to begin. Using the story as an excuse to avoid the threatening ale, Glenda started with a sly grin, "Traveler, feel free to drink up while I do the telling. Don't leave our host feeling he is drinking alone or his ale is not to your liking."

Annoyed with her unwanted suggestion, but trying to act casual, Traveler raised his mug. He saluted both companions and took a tentative sip. The liquid flowed down smoothly and reminded him of a thick root beer back in Charlottesville. *I can easily handle this, and I like it*, he thought. A second deeper sip followed.

Glenda watched Traveler take his second sip and decided to follow suit. *Whatever big boy can do, I can match*, she thought. The ale hit her stomach and was welcomed. *This is definitely a Norwegian ale and the stuff of battle lore.* Her second intake was almost a gulp and she realized it had a bit of a mind-kick to it.

Olaff was pleased as he saw his guests accept his hospitality and ale with genuine enthusiasm. Of course, he never knew the two were first timers at the bar as they quaffed with confidence. *Veteran battle warriors*, he incorrectly thought.

Neither "would be" warrior knew their true battle would come in an hour or so when the friendly dark ale showed its ambush side.

Glenda took the lead in starting their saga against the jinn. "Our story begins in a museum where we first met the fire creatures, which we later called jinn. An ancient stone portal had just been assembled as a major display piece. I read the glyph symbols and felt the portal bringing a low vibration into the room. I knew this portal represented a great danger. I left at a fast run to bring help while Traveler stayed alone as our watchman. It was darkening when I left and knew it would be scary in there all alone."

She gave effusive praise on Traveler's stand-alone bravery as she described the next actions. "Once the room was totally dark a number of the creatures emerged from the portal. Traveler was prepared to fight the creatures by himself, probably to his death. When our own god-being, Theo, arrived, the jinn creatures instantly scattered, he was their own great threat. One of them escaped and appears here and now as the mage."

Olaff was now appraising Traveler as one prepared to stand his ground in a death match. Olaff concluded that the young man would be a formidable opponent against virtually any foe. However these fire creatures, or jinn, were a different threat. Olaff had seen how easily the mage has taken control of the fortress and the duke. He had wisely chosen to avoid contesting the mage.

Glenda saw Olaff's assessment happening and nodded toward Traveler, "Yes, he is truly courageous even when the odds are totally against him. Some may question his judgement to face the creatures alone but none his courage." Traveler swelled up inside and took another long sip of ale. He put on his best, "A guy's gotta do what a guy's gotta do" modest face. Naturally he was beaming.

What a great story, she thought, then noticed her throat seemed awfully dry from the storytelling. She lifted her mug and enjoyed a long sip quickly followed by a second deeper one.

"Excuse my poor manners as your host. I was so into the tale I was a bit slow to refill your mugs, however, I did my best to catch up once I noticed."

"You did us justice, sir," said Traveler. "I never noticed if my mug got empty. It was like a cornucopia that always provided a sip when I needed it." Olaff beamed at the recognition of his being a good host.

While Traveler and Glenda were again lifting their mugs, Olaff frowned and asked, "Why are you two here rather than this Theo? Surely if he scattered numerous jinn creatures, handling one should be easy for him but dangerous for the two of you. Does he not care about you?"

"I'll answer that, princess, you sit back and enjoy your ale."

Glenda quickly accepted Traveler's offer. He was not upstaging her, just permitting her some time to relax with her mug. *Storytelling requires a lot of effort and he's being the gentleman.*

She also noticed there now seemed to be two gentlemen Travelers beside her. One second there was just a single Traveler then a moment later a second Traveler would arrive. *Ale magic,* she giggled to herself.

Traveler cleared his throat to start and found for a moment he had lost his tongue. This was not the "frog in the throat" case as happened on occasion with Glenda but a lost tongue. His tongue was hiding somewhere in his mouth.

Finding his tongue, he started, "Theo is our guardian but..." The "but" hung in the air. For a moment he felt his chair was moving to possibly go toward the ceiling and he thought, *This is not the time to levitate.* With an effort he pushed his feet hard against the floor.

"As I was saying, Theo is our guardian but also our trainer. He expects us to constantly advance our skills. To advance we need to be severely challenged. Confronting the fire creature together is necessary for us to continue our development as Theo's allies. The two of us are a team and Theo expects us to work together to defeat this jinn."

Olaff was captivated by their tale. He looked into the fire as he reflected on all he had just heard. These two could become his own significant allies, or he theirs.

Glancing over at them he suppressed a chuckle. He rose up in time to catch each of them as they were falling off their chairs. *These two certainly have special skills but drinking my ale is not one of them. Of course, my body makes five of the lad's, so I'll cut them slack. Time enough for drinking later, as allies I need them clearheaded.*

Tucking one under each arm he easily carried them back to the bed and placed them down gently. *Plenty of room here for normal little people. I'll keep them far enough apart so if they can't make it to the bathroom, they won't splatter on one another. Between the two the girl is the one to be most embarrassed. If she is indeed a princess, she has a family reputation to maintain.*

I think when they wake they will pray for deliverance from Bacchus, the Roman god of wine and good times. It's a shame that the early good times always get followed later by bad times. I guess that's the price you pay when you drink with the god of merriment.

Returning to the dining room, Olaff sat down and permitted his mind to explore options against this jinn. He felt his mood swinging away from hopeless despair to upward-swinging victory. *These two young people bring skills that may offset the mage's powers. Strength in numbers,* he thought.

With the fire casting a cheery glow he placed his massive head on massive forearms and fell into the first untroubled sleep he had enjoyed since the mage had appeared.

Chapter 88

Camped by the Throne

Traveler was the first awake, being conscious was perhaps the better description. His stomach was contesting with his head over which could punish him the most. The stomach won and he bolted toward the throne room.

His stomach demanded he stop and capitulate to the upward pressure of an internal volcano. His mind denied the stomach's urges long enough so that he made it to the dumping ground for unwanted ale. He fell down in front of the high bowl. The mind acquiesced and the volcano stomach began a series of jerking eruptions.

The jerks made Traveler felt like he was riding a rollercoaster through a series of sharp twists and turns, ups and downs. Dizziness was a constant companion as he clung to the side of the throne and tried to survive his stomach's revolt.

Finally the stomach took a timeout, either from exhaustion or being totally empty. *Actually I was far beyond normal empty.* Traveler tried to rise, cautiously checking out his balance and his energy. Both resisted his effort and he decided to crawl. He barely made it to a stack of the heavy woolen towels. *I'll just rest here for a moment*, he thought.

A sympathetic Morpheus appeared, patted him on the head and sent him into a sweet slumber. A grinning Bacchus watched, saying to his sleep-god friend, "As Shakespeare will write in a future time, 'Sleep that knits up the raveled sleave of care,' and there is quite a raveled sleave lying here. These mortals need to bless your name, Morpheus. I'm the bringer of excess joys and you're the after-cure. May I offer you a cup of my finest while he slumbers?"

Traveler was in a deep dream state when he felt the air vibrating from volcanic eruptions. A sea of russet, reddish hair framed the throne. White fingers clung desperately to the sides. Mournful sounds came from deep in the bowl. The head and hair muffled the sound, but it still brought Traveler to a semi-awake state.

Misery loves company, he thought. Lying on his side he finally saw the creature from the bowl raise its head. The volcano seemed to have taken a break. Gripping several of the heavy towels he gave them a weak toss to land beside the pale, disoriented Glenda. "Trust me, make a pillow and stay put. I'm off to slumber land again."

Glenda waited for a humorous follow-up but received none. Traveler was already making soft sleeping noises. For a moment she tried to get to her feet, but realized a fall was in her immediate future. *I'll rest here for a moment, then go back to bed.* She barely bunched the towels into a pillow before Morpheus provided the same balm given to Traveler.

Bacchus looked down critically at the youths, "These two would never have survived my Greek and Roman festivities. Maybe modern humans are a tad smarter but certainly no match for those early party animals."

Morpheus simply nodded in agreement. He had a god's long lifetime watching humans first discover the virtues of alcohol and the subsequent price paid for their excess enjoyments.

Chapter 89

Olaff Meets the Mage

Olaff awoke from a pleasant dream, the mage had been bested and the duke was back in control of himself and the fortress. More importantly he had embraced Olaff as his longtime friend and companion, a true brother.

Chuckling to himself he thought, *Time to look into the condition of the sleeping imbibers. They should start to feel semi-human now and ready to test their balance against gravity. I'll help them rejoin the living by feeding their sore stomachs. He took a large tray and placed fruit, bread, chunks of chicken, slices of a sweet cheese, and mugs of sweet milk and water on it.*

Olaff knew exactly where to find them. Walking into the throne room he saw that they were each lying on their sides, awake but trying to gather their wits while ignoring each other. Embarrassment hung in the air like a thick fog.

"Time to pull yourselves together. The drinking party starts again in half an hour and your ale is waiting for you. In Rome this is just the second stage of the party." Then the giant laughed.

At the mention of ale both Traveler and Glenda turned an even whiter shade of white. Olaff smiled condescendingly. "We've all been there. The best cure now after a long sleep is food. I'll leave this, feel free to join me when you're ready."

Glenda was now sitting up and leaning against the throne. Reaching onto the tray she took a piece of the bread and a small piece of cheese. She nibbled at first, then her stomach demanded its share and she realized she was famished. Glancing over she saw Traveler was already holding chicken in one hand and bread in the other. He was not quite gorging, but close.

"Don't bite your hand, big boy."

"Unbelievable. I thought I had died and now I'm alive and so hungry. I know I should slow down but my stomach seems in control of everything."

"Me too. I think the stomach knows that we burned up a lot of energy and is doing its job to refill the calorie bin." She took a deep drink of the water, then switched to milk.

The two continued to eat but at a slower pace before Glenda said, "I am so thirsty. It's funny that after drinking all that ale I'm thirsty, but I sure am."

"Yeah, go figure. After watching a lot of people get drunk on TV, now I understand the aftermath. I think Olaff's ale was far stronger than what normal people drink. Only two steins and it did this."

Glenda started to laugh. "Two! Hate to tell you, but you lost count. I know since I lost count after two. But then who really wants to count when they're having fun?"

Traveler acknowledged his poor arithmetic with a sad head nod. "OK, I'm sure you're right. Let's go have a sit-down with the really big guy. Sit-down is the operative word for me."

Once in the dining area they found the short walk had helped them reenter the world of the living. Olaff looked at them, shrugged his shoulders, and said "Can we discuss how best to proceed?"

Glenda gave him a weak head nod, "You start first. Tell us how you ended up down here, we heard that you and the duke were like brothers."

"Fair question with a sad answer. It started with a scout arriving on a lathered horse. Clearly both scout and mount had been traveling for many days and both were exhausted. I was with the duke when the scout gave his report.

"He said that there was an unstoppable invading horde of mounted warriors from the east. They were coming through the long passes that connect the frontier and our fortress. They traveled fast without slow-moving siege equipment. He estimated they would arrive within ten days.

"The scout said that he had approached their camp to observe their numbers and armament. Apparently their armament was primarily their bows, but he said these bows had a range and striking power well beyond our own bows. He claimed he watched mounted warriors practice their archery while racing on their mounts. He said their accuracy was stunning and far beyond anything he had ever seen.

"Finally he estimated their numbers as being in excess of 40,000. He cautioned it could be much greater since their line of mounted warriors stretched far out of sight in the mountain pass.

"Dall and I accepted this threat as being accurate. Our scout was experienced and fearless. He was proven to be an accurate observer even in the face of overwhelming odds. And he was an accomplished archer himself."

"Sorry to interrupt, but who is Dall?" asked Traveler.

Olaff chuckled, "That's the duke's non-titled name. I guess I'm the only one who calls him that, and only in private. To all others he is Duke or Sire. Of course, we were traveling companions and fighting companions before we arrived at this fortress and assumed command. To me he is simply my friend, ally, and brother.

"When we arrived, he assumed the role of protector of the fortress and never went far away. I took on the role of a traveling peacekeeper. The roles suited each of us. Funny though, neither of us can remember exactly when or how we ended up here. Maybe my ale has something to do with our lost memories. One of life's many mysteries, I guess."

"How did you fall out of Dall's grace either as a friend or a fighting ally?" asked Traveler.

"It happened after the scout was dismissed. Dall opened a map of the region through which the Huns were reportedly coming. We identified the best bottlenecks for an ambush. Mounted riders lose much of their advantage when they cannot spread out. We knew these mountain roads and decided on the place to defend against a much larger enemy.

"We discussed over many hours the best means of moving our own army with its necessary armament. We have found there is a great advantage in placing Roman catapults behind our troops. With narrow openings out of the pass, the catapults can wreak havoc on horsemen bunched together.

"Once we had our battle plan in place, Dall asked me to remain behind. While this was the opposite of our normal roles, he said that in the event he failed to stop the Hun I was the greater warrior. He thought I could better hold the fortress until our neighboring lords came to our support."

"OK, that sounds like a solid plan," said Traveler. "So, what happened? Clearly Dall came back as a victor."

"He returned a victor, but not the friend that I knew. To welcome him I had our castle guard outside the fortress gates in a parade formation. Trumpets and drums sounded across the approach field and victory flags streamed in a brisk breeze.

"The first thing I noticed with his approach was that the old mage rode beside him. This is a position reserved for a hero on the battlefield. It may be a captain or a simple warrior but only extraordinary merit in combat earns this place. I could not see how the old mage could have earned this honor.

"I also noted that the returning army seemed intact without the expected losses. But even without losses it was a somber army returning. As they marched past me into the fortress, I raised my war hammer in salute and a few raised their swords and spears but without the expected vigor of winners.

"Dall came right past me but never gave me eye contact. Only the mage stared at me as he passed. I thought he was ill since there was a red gleam in his eyes."

"We know that look," said Glenda. "That was not the mage that you knew."

Olaff nodded in agreement, "I learned that sad fact over the victory banquet that evening. As I walked to my usual position on the podium the mage was sitting in my place beside

Dall's right hand. I was more than annoyed. I was angry at his presumption of his importance.

"My seat is recognized by all as my co-chair with the duke. This mage knew better than to test me and I had no tolerance for his hubris. For a moment I considered teaching him his place by picking him up and putting him down on the floor below to sit with the common soldiers. He reminded me of a dog who was trying to sit where it knew it did not belong.

"As I turned to remove him, I heard a soft voice coming from Dall, more of a whisper. I looked down to see a single finger motioning me to bend down to his face. For a moment I was confused and angry. He knew how I would react to the mage's insult, but then his eyes stopped me.

"The eyes told me my friend was in trouble and it was trouble he could not manage. I immediately bent down and heard him whisper, 'Avoid the mage, he is a demon. Avoid me. Go now, hide and survive.'

"As I was about to ask my friend further questions, I became aware of the mage staring at me as he rose to approach me. His stare sent a shock through me, and very little shocks me. Scrambling I said, 'The duke asked me for his special wine. He seems to have a very sore throat and cannot call out to a page. May I secure a mug for you also?'

"The mage gave me a nod of dismissal followed by an insulting command to, 'Hurry and fetch the wine.' For a moment I thought of lifting him off his feet and sending him flying, then I wisely gave him a slight bow. He accepted my bow as due him with his ascendant role in the fortress. Without hesitation I left the podium.

"Rather than going for the wine myself I sent a page. I knew I should not draw further attention to myself. I proceeded to the kitchen and packed several heavy bags of food and a keg of my own brewed ale. I knew I was in for a siege and provisions are critical for survival. The cooks know me well and I had the best choices. I carried my stores in both arms and on my back and hurried toward my safe retreat where we now sit.

"The hidden access to this safe place was created by Dall and me when we first took control of the fortress. The entrance was designed to blend into the wall, and was only known to the two of us. Of course it's known to you also. I doubt whether Dall has a memory of this place, I saw he struggled to give me his simple message. Now a question for you, how did you two discover this place?"

Traveler gave a short version of following the water route to the iron gates, diving down under them, and then surfacing in the interior lake. Olaff listened and then said, "Dall and I created the guarding gates of the strongest iron. We took the gates down to the floor of the river. For you to work your way under them is remarkable. You must have lungs like balloons to hold that much air."

Traveler noticed Glenda was blushing her deepest red. He wisely chose not to mention how he had transferred air to her while she descended.

Chapter 90

First, Study Your Enemy

"We have found our common bond," said Olaff, "and it is a common foe. We must overcome this jinn creature masquerading as the mage."

"That is exactly our goal," answered Glenda. "How we do that is the question."

Olaff frowned in thought, then answered. "Like any enemy to be engaged, first we need to learn more about him. We need to observe his common patterns of movement and critically who his allies may be. With this demon I expect he is alone and has no need for allies. Strong scouting may offer us an insight about how to master him."

Traveler nodded in agreement. "Glenda and I will be the stealth scouts." Looking at Glenda he added, "Let's separate. This place is huge and we can cover more apart."

Glenda nodded, "I'll follow the duke since the mage is always close to him."

"Good idea, I'll scout the rest of the fortress. I have an idea that I want to think through. Olaff, for right now you should stay hidden. I think when we need you it will be at full strength."

Olaff smiled back. "I accept your offer to play the rear-guard role, much as I did for Dall. Besides, I'm tired from trying to sleep sitting in a chair, I'll create a suitable bed here by the fire."

With their roles determined Glenda and Traveler went to a moored boat and crossed the lake. Traveler did the rowing honors and Glenda leaped to the pier when they were close. With the boat secure they proceeded up the stone staircase with caution. As they ascended, they now understood the rise in the steps was designed for Olaff and Dall. Once they had reached the fortress main hallway they separated.

Glenda stood quietly as she planned her first spying effort. After some thought she decided the kitchen was a good starting place. *Everybody, including the mage, needs to eat so I'll follow the food trail.*

She pulled her hair up into a tight bun and then wrapped a piece of wool cloth around it to form a servant's cap. Smiling to herself she thought, *A woman's job is never over, for sure not in a place this big. Give me a broom to carry and I'll be invisible even without my stealth skill.* To anyone noticing she was just another servant girl hustling through the halls.

Once she reached the kitchen she paused just inside and watched the cooks, assistant cooks, scullery maids, and various serving staff at work. Cooking was a fulltime operation given the number of the people that lived in the fortress. It was now approaching the early midday meal and baskets were being prepared to take out to workers at their sites.

Glenda noticed that one young servant was preparing a silver tray. The cooks were personally placing the best choices on this tray. Each added piece was carefully inspected before it was deemed worthy. Hot soups and meats were covered with hot iron lids to retain heat. *This tray must be going to the duke and mage.*

Glenda watched the serving girl carefully lift the tray to avoid any spillage. The kitchen overseer, a large thickish woman, admonished the girl, "It's a heavy tray but you must keep it level. If the mage finds you've made a mess, it's a dark time for you. The mage also expects the food to be hot so I suggest you move quickly." The girl kept her head down to avoid looking at the overseer and only nodded as she headed to the passage door.

Glenda followed behind her at a distance that was sufficient not to bother the girl yet close enough to observe her every step. The girl was walking inside a long, wide tunnel. After less than five minutes Glenda heard the girl's breathing begin to labor. Glenda knew the girl's arms were weakening and spillage was fast approaching.

Glenda quickly stepped beside her saying, "If you stop for a moment, I can carry that for a while, it looks terribly heavy." The girl stopped as requested. The girl's face was pale from the stress of the weight as well as the anticipated punishment for delivering a messy tray.

As Glenda took the tray the girl whimpered, "Thank you so much! My arms are aching and we still have the stairs to climb. I know I could not have made it. The overseer is angry at me and this was her way of punishing me." Glenda noted the tears that were already filling the corners of both eyes.

Glenda held the tray perfectly level and walked forward with a confident stride. "I saw you leave and knew this was an impossible job for one person, so I decided to follow and help. I'm on my own lunch break so I have some extra time. We servant girls need to help each other."

With Glenda easily carrying the tray, the two could now fast-walk through the long connecting tunnel. At the tunnel's end was a thick oak door with iron bands across it, but it was open. Clearly the door was a defensive device that, when locked, would stop any attackers from ascending the staircase. Looking ahead Glenda thought, *I bet these stairs will lead to not only the duke's room but also the creature's sanctum.*

Ascending the stairs Glenda saw a wide landing at the top. Hanging above the landing was a heavy iron gate. The gate could be lowered to seal off the stairway's top access. Once lowered, iron rods slid into slots in the stone to secure the gate. Set ten paces back on the landing was a massive iron door. It was obviously the entrance to the duke's residence. The two gates and door would each require a battering ram to gain entry.

The landing continued around the side wall of the duke's sanctuary and opened into a corridor. At intervals along the corridor were alcoves cut into the solid stone. The alcoves appeared empty but were possibly storage areas for food or armaments during a siege.

Glenda walked forward, then stopped a short distance from the door. She motioned for the girl to take the tray, "I'll knock on the door but then I'll retreat into an alcove. You should receive all the credit for doing a remarkable job of carrying the tray. Even this mage should be pleased over your effort. Remember I am not here, you are alone and there is no need to share credit." The girl nodded her understanding as she took the tray.

Glenda knocked and then ran to the closest alcove and knelt down. She had a full view of the landing platform and a bit of the door. She slid into her stealth mode and calmed her breath as she calmed her mind, *Must not give the creature any awareness of my being here.*

A few moments passed and the great door slowly swung open. Standing to receive the tray was the duke. Glenda observed his persona was that of a subdued servant. His eyes simply stared forward. His mind seemed to be looking inward.

While accepting the tray he nodded at the girl to wait before leaving. As the door remained partially opened Glenda heard the mage call out, "Place the tray on the table and remove the covers. Let's see if a disciplinary action is required for the delivery girl."

There was a pause followed by a slurping sound and a sharp intake of breath. "This soup is the hottest we have received. This human body can barely accept it without harm. Tell the girl she is dismissed." There was no praise or thanks, only a door closing on the girl.

Glenda stood and waved at the girl to head back. Once the girl was out of sight and going down the stairs Glenda bounded down to catch her. "Well, we know you did a remarkable job even if there was no praise. The overseer will know how well you did since she is likely expecting you to return with cuff marks and bruises… or worse."

"All thanks to you my protector and, may I say, my lady."

Glenda liked the sound of "my lady" but accepted the compliment with a modest, "You deserved help and I am glad I could offer it. I do have a question, however."

"Anything. What would you like to know?"

"Is this the usual routine for their meals?"

"Yes. Unless there is a special feast, they take their meals together in the duke's quarters. The overseer takes her orders only from the mage, and the delivery instructions never change."

As an afterthought the girl added, "This overseer was appointed by the mage to replace the old overseer who we all liked. This overseer has a nasty streak to her, maybe that's why she was chosen. She assigns the delivery crew as one of her ways to maintain absolute control over the kitchen staff. She picks harshly on the younger staff, but even the grown men avoid irritating her, she has a sharp tongue and an unforgiving memory and she can bring in the mage if needed.

"Typically she sends two of the younger boys to carry the tray. The boys spell each other the same as you did for me. Nobody wants the chore due to the scrutiny of the mage over spillage and cold soup.

"Many boys have returned with deep red welts from leather straps. One lad returned like a different person. He was of no further use in the kitchen and was placed in the fields to plant and harvest. The one with him refused to tell what happened, he only trembled when asked."

As she listened to the girl, Glenda felt a plan forming in her mind. The predictability of the meal delivery offered the possibility of an ambush. She was excited to share this discovery with Traveler and Olaff.

Chapter 91

A Plan Emerges

Once she was back in Olaff's retreat she found Traveler and the giant Olaff in a heated conversation. "Nothing works!" pronounced a clearly frustrated Traveler. "We have thought of every possible way to either control or kill the creature but it's an impossible task, we just don't know enough. We need a stalking horse to learn more."

Olaff frowned, "What kind of horse is a stalking horse? I've never seen one."

Traveler snapped out of his funk, "The phrase originally described how hunters would walk beside their horses to hide their presence from game. The hunters used the horses as a form of camouflage to get closer."

Olaff understood the use of a decoy and now the stalking horse phrase. He then said, "Glenda, you were our stalking horse. What did you find out?"

Laughing she answered, "Thank you, Olaff for making me a horse." Laughing she added, "Stalker 'yes' but horse 'no'. Let me start by saying I feel great about stalking and surviving. Let me share what I've found out, but first my throat is dry. Permit me to prime the throat pump." Glenda settled down on the bench with a mug of watered cider, took a deep drink, then proceeded.

She described how she found a way to observe both the mage and the duke. "I actually used the stalking horse idea. I knew that the creature needed to feed the mage's body as well permit the duke to eat, so I followed the food.

"In the kitchen I spotted a girl that was taking a silver tray with choice foods and figured she was taking the tray to the mage and the duke. She literally became the horse to my stalking and I joined her to deliver the tray.

"I found out that the duke and the mage always eat meals together in the duke's quarters. And now we know where they are located. Their retreat is hidden at the end of a long stone tunnel. It's well-fortified with heavy gates and doors and it would take an army with a battering ram to gain entry.

"The good news is that the mage is overconfident. There are no guards and the sealing gates are always open. We can walk right up to the front door and knock on it. Even better, their location has a number of adjoining alcove areas that are perfect for a surprise attack. As powerful as he is, the jinn is vulnerable for a close-up ambush."

Both Olaff and Traveler began clapping. Olaff was the first to say, "Well done, Glenda! You are both clever and a first-class scout. Your information gives us the basis to plan an ambush strategy."

Traveler gave Glenda a big thumbs-up sign as he asked, "How did you avoid detection?"

"Turns out that was easy. The mage sends the duke out for the tray. All I had to do was stealth-hide inside an alcove and watch the exchange between the kitchen girl and the duke.

"I was close enough that I could hear the mage's voice ordering the duke about the tray's placement. My guess is the mage is continuing to exercise his control over the duke to ensure there is no resistance left in him. His commands to the duke sounded like puppy training."

Olaff's face developed a deep frown, his eyes appeared like an erupting volcano ready to spew out blue lava. The idea of his friend being reduced to the status of a puppy was anathema to him. There would be a reckoning day for the creature, and Olaff would relish that day.

Traveler took inventory of their findings and said, "Now we know where to attack. The problem remains how to launch a successful attack. We have seen how the creature can easily take control of any man, even the duke. We need a way to neutralize his power, any ideas?"

Glenda was in a thoughtful place as she said, "Let's start with some group brainstorming. Nobody should hold back because they are afraid of suggesting an idea that may embarrass them. No ego concerns are permitted."

Olaff frowned again with the strange word "ego" but decided he could understand it from the context, *It likely just means pride in this case.*

Traveler started the brainstorming, "Let me review the ideas that Olaff and I kicked around while you were gone."

Glenda gave an encouraging nod, "That's the spirit! Fire your ideas at me. If I have an idea while you're talking, I'll throw it out. Of course, both of you should do the same. Sometimes hearing an idea a second time leads to a new thought."

Traveler began a slow, thoughtful recounting of the previously discussed options. Olaff added his comments as each action step was presented. As Traveler described each idea, he took his time and invited criticisms. Everyone reflected on an action's merits and risks. There were a number of constructive comments from Glenda who was hearing this for the first time.

Following the intensive review Glenda asked the obvious question, "What are we missing? Why does every action end in disaster?"

Olaff was sitting quietly in apparent deep thought, then he offered, "Is there an ally, not necessarily human, that we've missed? Is there any anything the creature avoids?"

"Well, he sure avoids Theo," replied Traveler. "Sadly we cannot use Theo, we're on our own."

"Another possibility is water," said Glenda. "I sense the jinn has no use for it, I think it avoids it. Somehow water may present some impediment to its powers."

Traveler was intrigued and said, "That's an interesting possibility. I remember M's story of hiding from the jinn on the island and they never crossed the river. While water won't kill them, maybe it deters them in some way. The question is, how can we use that to our advantage?"

Traveler leaned back in his chair, shook his head and said, "My brain hurts. Overthinking without getting an answer is bad on my pride as well as my problem-solving skills. Let's take a break and revisit all this tomorrow, right now I need a rest."

Glenda and Olaff nodded in agreement. Glenda added, "Keep using your problem-solving skills, Traveler. Maybe an answer will come while you sleep. I have faith in you."

With Glenda's praise Traveler felt his spirits and pride lifting. He found to his surprise that he was fully awake and sitting straight in the chair.

Olaff stretched his arms, rolled his neck around, then stood up. "All this talking and thinking has made me sleepy." He disappeared and shortly reappeared carrying a mountain of heavy woolen blankets.

On the top were thick canvas-like horse blankets. Glenda and Traveler watched as he first made a thick floor cover using the horse blankets beside the fire. Next he layered the heavy wool sleeping blankets. Once this blanket platform was finished, he inspected it with a critical look. The bed was over nearly a foot high.

"That should do the job. Even sleeping on a side my shoulders should still be cushioned from the floor." With that he sat down, pulled off his boots, pulled a remaining sleeping blanket across his body and head, gave a deep sigh, and disappeared into giant's slumber land.

"Sweet dreams, friend," murmured Glenda. Looking down at Olaff's boots she grinned and whispered, "We could ride in one of those across to the landing, who needs a boat?" Traveler barely smiled back. His mind was far away twisting his mental Rubik's Cube for a possible solution.

He's still thinking, maybe something will pop up, best to leave him alone. As for me, I'm not inspired except to go crash. With that she stood up to head out. After a few feet she briefly turned back, "Speaking of big boots, please don't drop yours on the floor when you take them off. They sound like explosions in the sleeping cave." Traveler nodded back. Later his brain delivered her request, *Of course I will take them off. I'm a gentleman.*

Sitting beside the pile of blankets that was the sleeping giant Traveler stared into the dying fire. He watched small flames move up through openings in the dying embers. The flames were clearly hungry and called out to be fed. Rising up he placed several more logs across the hot bed of coals. Flames rejoiced as they grew in size. Their thanks were expressed by an increase in their radiating heat.

Pleased, Traveler sat back to watch the flames twisting through the log pile. He found his own mind was fully alert. He began again to consider their conundrum in confronting the jinn.

Since he had gotten a second mental wind, he decided to stay by the fire and give Glenda plenty of time to relax and fall asleep. He and Olaff needed her at the top of her game. Traveler knew she had great problem-solving abilities when rested and right now she needed to recharge her brain battery.

Traveler found his own mind was fully engaged in how to contain the creature. He had no confidence they could kill the jinn but maybe containment was possible.

Relaxed while watching the fire, he had an epiphany. Rather than relying on his brain's normal "go-to logic" for a solution, he would turn the free spirit of his creative mind loose. *Creativity may succeed where logic fails,* he thought. *Let me try a totally unstructured approach.*

As he let go of the stress of logical thinking, he found he had drifted into a semi-dream state while watching the shifting flames. The flames did not logically study log placement for greater oxygen, they followed their instincts. They became creative in finding their breathing paths.

Just as the flames found their paths so did Traveler. A solution arrived without conscious effort. His creative mind had accepted all the previously discussed facts and possible options with their bad outcomes. Discarding these past thoughts, the creative mind moved on.

When the solution arrived, Traveler realized it had been kept buried under too much prior data and structured analysis. Creativity had cleared the fog of distraction away. *You were hiding in plain sight*, he thought.

The solution had arrived like an unexpected dream, it was not invited it simply arrived. Like any dream, Traveler knew that dreams are quickly forgotten. He went to the nearby table and picked up a writing stylus and parchment. He first made a drawing of the model the dream had presented. He quickly followed the drawing by writing down the action steps in their necessary order.

Once fully recorded he stood up, walked out to the landing, and took deep breaths. He came back in, sat, and reviewed his notes. Satisfied, he felt an inner glow. *I think this can work! Thank you, Glenda, for encouraging me to stay with finding a solution.*

Leaning back and studying his solution he knew he had been inspired by some creative part of his mind. That part had refused to be bogged down with mind-numbing details. He recalled how Alexander the Great had faced and solved a similar problem.

Alexander had defeated the mighty Persian empire ruled by King Darius in 333 BC. Following this great victory, he led his army into modern Turkey.

According to the legend he entered the capital city of Gordium and encountered the famous Gordian Knot which was tied onto a yoke. Legend said that whoever unraveled the knot was destined to be the ruler of Asia.

Alexander loved the challenge of difficult puzzles and was fascinated by the complexity of the knot. He immediately worked to untie it. After repeated attempts, all of which failed, he had an inspiration.

Realizing the only requirement was to separate the knot from the yoke he drew his sword. In a single stroke he cut through the knot. His solution was recognized by the citizens of Gordium as an indication of his problem-solving genius. True to the knot's prophesy, he continued onward to conquer large parts of Asia.

Traveler's ego was not so large that he placed himself on a par with Alexander, however he saw the similarity in their situations, the creature was his unsolvable knot. His solution required mental concentration combined with a single powerful stroke.

With the possible solution in hand he was suddenly exhausted both physically and mentally. *It's amazing how just thinking can tire us out*, he reflected.

He followed the hallway to the sleeping chamber. He noted Glenda's deep breathing and carefully removed his boots. He lay down, turned on his side facing the dimly lit doorway and found Morpheus greeting him with a congratulatory smile.

Chapter 92

Setting Up the Plan

Traveler felt like a waking bear inside the dark quiet room. He was refreshed and famished. He noted that the princess was gone and wondered when she had left the sleeping cave. Pulling his boots on he stretched, took deep breaths and walked to the dining area. He felt the warmth of the fire before turning the corner to enter the dining space.

"I thought you were going to hibernate for the whole day. I know bears are ravenous when they wake so there is a nice lunch here, not up to M's standards, but plenty good for bears. Try the tea, it really is up to M's standard." She proceeded to hand Traveler a large mug with an aroma of cinnamon and nutmeg coming off the steaming top.

Traveler accepted the mug, took a deep sip and smiled. "Thank you, it's delicious! You sweetened it with honey and that's exactly what this bear needs to stop growling."

Glenda smiled, "Yes, it is delicious! We need to tell M the ingredients, assuming we ever get back."

Traveler heard an opening to present his plan and jumped on it. "We are getting back, Glenda! I followed your advice and think we have a winning plan."

Glenda immediately perked up, "Really? I'm all ears and eyes, tell it to me."

"Should we wait for Olaff? Where is he anyway?"

"He was gone when I got up, no idea where he is. Give me the plan while you eat. We can decide whether to present it when he's back. Let's not get his hopes up until we're both excited about it. Believe me I want to be excited. I'm already excited and I haven't even heard it yet. Tell me the way we win at this jinn game." Grinning she added, "Gin game pun definitely intended."

"I'll present the plan first, then I'll eat. Right now I'm too excited to eat." Traveler walked over to his notes and waved them in the air. To bolster his confidence he called out, "It's showtime!"

Then with a nervous look he added, "Maybe my brilliant idea will fade in the light of an objective critic. He slapped a fast cadence with his fingers on the table and said, "Anyway here goes, drum roll, please!"

Traveler started by first verbally highlighting his plan. His enthusiasm and nerves combined to have him talking a little too fast. He saw that Glenda was concentrating on his message and several times it looked like she was going to raise a question or make an observation. Each time she stopped herself to permit him to continue. "OK, so far?" he hesitantly asked, and received a controlled head nod back.

"Rather than keep talking I'll show you the written designs for the heart of the plan." As he presented his detailed sketches, he found he could now calmly explain each part in detail. He then showed how the separate constructs came together as a whole.

"Well that's it. That's the best solution I could find." Traveler hesitated to say more since Glenda was sitting with a strange look on her face. "Did I bomb out and you're trying to let me down gently?"

To answer Glenda rose up, came around to his side of the table and gave him a giant hug. Traveler found his face was covered in a mass of reddish hair while his cheeks were deepening to match the hair. "It's brilliant, Traveler! Really brilliant! M and Theo would absolutely agree. I'm sure Olaff will sign up. Traveler, I think you have found the solution. I'm ready to shout out 'It's Jinn time!' Let fate deal the cards."

Traveler found his heart was beating fast and his face was warm. The throat frog started to croak, then a simple "Glad you like it," came out. "I wasn't sure about it and really needed your opinion. You know there are still big risks with the execution."

Glenda was sitting back across from him and beaming, "Of course I see the execution risks, but Olaff is our ace in the hole that will make your plan work. You and I alone couldn't pull it off. By including Olaff's unique talents in your strategy, it can and will work! That's what teamwork is all about! Let me repeat, I am really impressed, Traveler."

Traveler found his internal dog's tail was wagging like crazy. He had gotten far more praise than a simple "good boy".

At that moment a hulk filled the entry door from the landing. Olaff entered carrying a large sack in each hand. "Knew you two were exhausted so I made a stealth-like trip to the kitchen and picked up fresh food and breads. Let's eat while it's still warm."

Placing a wide assortment of fruits, breads, and omelets on the table, Olaff handed plates out and sat down at the head of the table. Smiling the giant said, "Don't wait for me, eat before I make all this disappear."

The three began a serious attack on the food. Eyeing the choices, Traveler selected a large pink and orange melon. He cut it open, took a tentative bite then proceeded to devour the sweet firm meat. "Delicious."

As he was finishing the melon slice an early childhood memory arrived. He was six years old eating breakfast at the kitchen table before school started. His mother was strongly encouraging him to eat the fruit before heading off. "You should eat fruit first thing in the morning. It wakes your body up and is very healthy. Besides it's delicious!"

With the mom memory fresh in his mind he thought, *No matter where you are or what you're doing, Mom's long arm reaches you. It's Mom magic.* A wave of nostalgia followed the memory,

Traveler realized how much he missed his mom and dad. *It's easy to take parents for granted; you think your parents will always be around, but not necessarily.*

"I'm heading to see Mom the minute we get back. I need to visit Dad also. He's in New York on business and the Big Apple is loads of fun over the Christmas season." Looking at a forlorn Glenda he added, "Of course you're invited." He was pleased to see the big smile that passed over her face.

Conversation took a needed timeout. The only sound was three sets of mouths chewing and swallowing. Hands repeatedly tore into the offerings. Finally, as if on cue, all three sat back in their chairs.

"Olaff, we have a plan," said Glenda. "Actually, it's Traveler's plan and he walked me through it while you were foraging for food. He's surprisingly modest on this, so let me say that he was inspired. He has nailed how to attack and control the creature. Traveler, may I present your plan to Olaff?"

Traveler went to his notes, came back and handed them to Glenda. Then he sat across from the giant to read his reaction. Glenda began with the same explanation Traveler had given her but she delivered it in a much more theatrical style. She was engaging the giant not just with logic but with enthusiasm.

Olaff sat in his chair and listened intently. Every school teacher wants that same focus from their students. As Glenda continued, Traveler noted slight nods coming from Olaff. He was absorbing the plan in its entirety before commenting.

When Glenda finished both she and Traveler looked at Olaff for a reaction. The giant stood, came around to Traveler, and effortlessly lifted him out of his chair. "The princess is right. You have indeed created a brilliant plan. I see where it can fail, but the weak points seem to revolve around me doing my role properly. Believe me, I will execute with great enthusiasm."

Chapter 93

Hidden Passages

"Can you find the construction material we need?" Traveler asked.

Olaff gave an affirmative nod, "I know where we keep those supplies. Where do you want me to bring them?"

Traveler answered, "Given the weight of the larger sheets I think we need to do the construction close to the duke's living area. One big problem is how we get the materials there without being caught on the staircase coming up. I know that is one of the high risks with my plan. We are dead meat if the creature catches us in transit on the staircase."

Olaff gave a sly smile, "This fortress has many hidden passages that even the all-knowing mage is unaware of. Dall and I explored every part of the fortress when we took it over. We received much of the knowledge from an old stonemason who had learned the passage secrets from his master.

"Our access is better seen than described. You'll see where we have a secure place to work. Shall we head out now?"

Both Glenda and Traveler gave quick nods to proceed. Of course they had already explored many of the passageways but they decided to keep this to themselves right now. Olaff was a man, or rather a giant, on a mission. Why take away from his excitement?

When they got out on their landing pier, they saw they needed to cross the lake in separate boats. As soon as Olaff stepped into a boat the water immediately approached the top of the gunnels. "What does he weigh?" Traveler mused.

"More than a lot," was Glenda's response.

Once across, Olaff led them up the long stone staircase to the landing. Traveler noticed how easily the giant went up. *That's a lot of weight to take up stairs and he makes it looks easy.* At the top both Traveler and Glenda took a moment to catch their breaths while Olaff moved to open the heavy door and make sure their exit was clear.

Turning to them Olaff gave a hand motion and the three were quickly out, down the quiet hallway, then into the door leading into the armory. Once inside the armory they went to the back and moved the torch holder. The stone wall opened and they entered the stone passageway. As the door was closing Olaff quickly lit the torch, "Follow me."

Glenda and Traveler were back on the interior passage they knew well. Traveler broke the tension with, "It's OK to talk, nobody can hear us through these stone walls. How far do we go?"

Olaff was aware that his two companions had previously found this passage as he said, "You know where this passage ends with a solid wall and where you could enter the great room from above?" Both Glenda and Traveler nodded together, and Glenda said, "Sure we do. This is a dead-end passage."

Olaff smiled, he knew more than them. "Not as dead as you think."

In a short time they were standing by the wall facing the great room. Traveler looked down and said, "This is where you can move this lower panel, then you can crawl out onto a wide crossbeam."

"We've been here already and done the cat walk on the beam. That beam leads to a crow's nest and gives a big view of the great room, however this passageway is a dead-end. Are you sure this is the passage you remember?"

Standing in front of the dead-end wall Olaff ignored the question. He reached up to his full height, put powerful fingers into a hidden groove carved into the top stone on the facing wall. He twisted the groove and a portion of the wall began to rotate into the tunnel. An opening of three feet appeared.

Glenda and Traveler stood with stunned looks. They could never have found the entrance.

"The old saying of 'Open Sesame' doesn't work in this case," said a satisfied Olaff. "What's required is great height and strength, fortunately I am blessed with both." Looking down at Glenda he added, "Princesses first."

Glenda peered cautiously into the darkness. Olaff leaned past her and lit another wall torch. "I like your caution. Looking before committing always makes sense."

With the passageway illuminated Glenda took the torch and motioned Olaff to lead ahead. "This is your fortress, so lead on."

The passageway was wide enough for Glenda and Traveler to walk together but Olaff's bulk narrowed it to a single file path. After a few minutes they came to another solid wall. Again Olaff stretched up, put his hand on another groove and slowly twisted. A ray of light now emerged from the other side. Olaff pressed his face against the opening and peered out. "See anything familiar?" he asked as he stepped to the side.

Glenda pressed her face against the narrow opening and gave a satisfied, "Yes I do! We are close to the alcove furthest from the duke's quarters. If we went straight out, we'd pass the three alcoves. Continue straight ahead, then a right-hand turn around a corner and we'd be at the duke's door."

Glenda stepped aside and Traveler peered out. "Olaff, you have just solved one of the biggest problems I had with my plan. I didn't see how we could construct our model without being caught, now I do.

"We can build the model on this side of the wall, and when we're ready we can move it out. I'd say our odds of winning just went from five percent to fifty percent. Ambushing the creature is still a big challenge, but we've definitely reduced the chance of an early discovery."

Chapter 94

Building the Model

Glenda turned back from the now closed doorway. "OK, I'm tired of looking at stone walls. Let's get this show on the road. How do we find the materials to set up shop here?"

"That's all on me," said Olaff. "I know where to find exactly what we need. I will need some help getting it all here." Smiling at the two he added, "Know any strong, young people who need a fierce workout?"

The three allies backtracked to the hidden entrance of the armory. They entered the armory then proceeded to the main hallway. Once in the main hallway Olaff made a right turn. "We go this way, it's less traveled and leads directly to our supply center." Glenda and Traveler tucked in behind him and followed like ducklings trailing the mother duck.

When they arrived, they were in front of a thick door. They saw it was solid iron. "Why iron?" Traveler asked.

"This storage room is a vulnerable spot in our defenses. Once a person is inside and locks this door, they are safe. The door will stop just about anybody from getting in." Olaff proceeded to raise the solid iron locking bars, grasp the heavy iron handle, and pulled on the door.

Traveler saw the muscles swell on the giant's forearms. He noticed arm glyphs seemed to briefly move as though providing increased power to the arms. *I never had a chance matching his hand power, he was simply testing me.*

Olaff entered through the doorway and gave a short bow to Glenda. "My lady," he said as she stepped in to join him. Once Traveler joined them Olaff closed and locked the door.

Traveler stood in amazement taking in the room. It was cavernous with multiple aisles curving and winding to various supply bins. The bins were filled with building supplies of every need and description. The roof reminded Glenda of huge European cathedrals whose vaulted domes soared up to great heights.

Thick beams crisscrossed to anchor themselves in large columns and into the sides of walls. The beams supported the massive ceiling weight resting on the walls. The walls were thick stone and could withstand catapults and battering rams.

"This feels like an oversized Home Depot," laughed Traveler.

"Much bigger," said Glenda, "and much nicer. Just look at the mosaics on the walls and parts of the floor."

What's a home depot? Olaff thought as he proceeded to walk down aisles. Periodically he would pause for a moment, study where he was, then continue. After a series of final turns, he stopped in front of an enclosed brick storage bin with a double door. "If memory serves me, this should be the compartment we want. The Romans built this storage bin and we have had little use for its contents."

The doors were held shut by a single crossbar which Olaff easily removed. He then swung both doors open. Next, he lit a large torch that was resting in a holding stanchion inside the entrance. Once lit, a bright flame lit up the room. Using the lit torch, Olaff lit two others. The combined illumination filled the storage room. "Nothing burns in here so we can use multiple torches and save our eyesight."

Glenda and Traveler stepped in together and their eyes quickly adjusted to the torch lighting. They were staring at sheets of thick metal stacked against each other. The sheets were organized based on their various sizes. Some of the sheets had holes drilled through them.

Finally, there were bins containing metal rods of varying diameters and lengths. These rods were intended as holding rods that could join the heavy sheets together.

Traveler carefully studied the available materials. He made dimension estimates using his own height, arm length and hand spread. "We have found the mother lode," he said grinning. "Everything we need is here and it's cut to meet our needs. Our model may be a bit larger than necessary but that's just fine."

Glenda placed her hands on one of the upright solid poles, "Wow, I'm strong but this is really heavy. I can carry a few part of the way, but I see a lot of starting and stopping along the way."

Traveler chose not to try a similar pole, no reason to get her started in a strength contest. He lifted a single plate. He strained as he lifted the plate off the floor, grunted, and added, "When you're right, you're right. This stuff is beyond what a single man can carry. Of course Glenda and I are a lot stronger than the normal man, but still everything is darn heavy. We can whine a little about the weight but heavy is what the model requires."

Olaff watched them with a slight smile on the corner of his mouth; *No reason to show off right now, that will come soon enough without even trying.* "Should we make a trip back right now with our first load? Are you up for this effort or do you need to think about it?"

Traveler knew this was not a serious challenge but was a teasing encouragement to get started. Nothing would be easy, so why not step up right now? "Yeah, I guess we might as well start, my muscles are getting tired just looking at this stuff. What do you think, princess?"

Rather than answer Glenda carefully stacked three of the longer poles across her right shoulder and balanced them with her left hand. She then braced her neck and back, and headed out the door. "Try to keep up, big boy, I can't slow down with this load." Traveler ignored the parting shot as he studied how to move the heavy plates.

"The plates are awkward to carry, use this back harness," Olaff suggested as he helped Traveler put his arms through harness straps. Next he lifted a plate and secured it to the harness's carry sack. Traveler was standing up straight when the full weight descended. He was suddenly falling backwards when powerful arms helped him right himself. "Best to lean forward, you'll find the right carrying angle as you adjust to the weight." Olaff added a second plate, "You OK?"

Traveler nodded, "Thanks for keeping me from becoming a turtle lying on its back." Without trying to talk further he followed Glenda, determined to catch her. *I know she's faster but I'm stronger, and that should matter in this situation.* Heading out of the vast storage depot he thought he remembered the directional turns to reach the main hallway.

As he proceeded through the maze of aisles, he sadly discovered he was off-track. *This pack mule needed a guide. Should have gone left back there, what a bummer. Bet she remembered the turns. No way I'll admit that.*

Annoyed with himself he accepted his own mistake and had to backtrack. Naturally the load reminded him of his mistake and he leaned forward a bit more and grunted. Two correct turns later he found the exit door into the main hallway.

He proceeded down the hallway and saw there was no Glenda in sight. Finally he reached the armory door. It was slightly open and he used his foot to open it enough to carry his load through. Sitting in a chair was a smiling Glenda. "Didn't forget the turns and have to backtrack, did you? Or did you need to stop and rest?"

Traveler took the weight off his shoulders by resting the bottom of the plates on a tall stool. Still strapped in, he frowned preparing a caustic comeback regarding who carried the heavier weight. Then unexpectedly he started to laugh, "This is sad on so many levels. You know me too well, what can I say. Right turns should have been left turns and I paid the price. I'm not the smartest mule in the herd."

Glenda grinned back, "Truth be told, I wanted to stop many times but didn't want to hear your comments coming from behind. I barely made it inside before putting those poles down; and yes, your plates are much heavier, I know that."

A moment later Olaff filled the doorway. Strapped across his back were plates of various sizes. Leather bags hung from both hips and his arms carried poles of various lengths that were bound together by thick ropes. Glenda and Travel stared at the weight in amazement. Neither said a word, what they thought was, *That's not possible.*

"It would be easier for me to keep going, if that's alright with you two. You can rest a bit then follow me into the passageway. Take your time, no reason to hurt yourselves.

"I would appreciate your opening the passage, though. You should also secure the armory's hallway door before joining me in the passageway. No need to worry guards about an open door, would not want them bringing anything to the creature's attention."

As the giant was moving toward the entry wall for the passageway Glenda stood, "My load is resting, Olaff, and thank goodness for that. Let me open the passage door for you." She twisted the wall sconce and the hidden passage door slowly opened. Traveler and Glenda both watched Olaff step into the passageway and light a torch. Watching the giant move Glenda remarked, "He's not even breathing hard, truly unbelievable. Boy, I sure like having him on our side."

Traveler had stood up when Glenda did and was following Olaff through the open door. Turning to Glenda he said, "Could you shut the hallway door while your poles are resting? Once you're in the passage, go past me and I'll shut this entrance."

"Sure," was all Glenda could say. After she locked the armory door, she hoisted the poles onto her left shoulder this time. *Need to balance the shoulders,* she thought.

As her body attempted a left tilt, she thought, *A girl needs to keep her posture straight and I'm tilting too much.* She relieved some of the weight using her right hand then followed Olaff down the passageway. Behind her she heard a grunting Traveler mule bringing up the rear of their wagon train.

When Traveler reached the now open dead-end wall, he entered to find Olaff had placed his materials and Glenda's into organized groupings. Plates, poles, and rivet nails were organized by their priority use in the construction phase.

"Let me help you with those plates, they're heavy ones," said the giant. "Well carried each of you!"

As the plates were removed and placed on their appropriate piles all Traveler could say was, "Thanks, I'm really glad to lay that burden down." He reflected, *He's praising us for doing something he could do without an effort. He's a really good guy, or a good giant, or a good whatever he is.*

Looking at Glenda as she was working to straighten her shoulders and back Traveler quipped, "Bet you're happy to lay that burden down."

Glenda gave him her best smile, "Pack mules know each other's burden, big boy. By the way be aware that you're still tilting a tad backwards." Traveler laughed but straightened himself.

Olaff reflected, *One minute they are jousting with each other and the next are in a serious discussion. They instinctively know which is appropriate and that's good. This plan requires split-second coordination among all three of us.*

Grinning back Traveler said, "I guess this pack mule is ready to haul another burden. Not eager, but resigned," said Traveler.

Glenda gave a tired nod of agreement, "It's not going to get any easier, so let's do it."

Olaff simply said, "Check out what we already have. If my count is correct it should all be here."

Traveler stood beside the pile of materials, noted the dimensions and quantities then began to construct the model in his head. He did the mental math twice then stood with a big grin. "You're amazing, Mr Olaff, you nailed it! You brought exactly what my diagram called for. If there's a mess-up, it's on me."

Glenda had been silently constructing the model in her own head and agreed, "Bravo, Olaff! You would be an A+ student in geometry class."

Looking at the supplies and then the two young people, Olaff shrugged his massive shoulders. "If we're all rested, I suggest we start the assembly. Occasionally even the best drawing comes up short when put to the test. Does assembling it right now work for both of you?"

Traveler thought, *How can we quit now when he's done the really heavy lifting?* They nodded in agreement.

Smiling at Traveler, Glenda suggested, "Traveler this is your design, so why don't you guide us. You tell us what to do and consider us your dutiful servants."

I like the sound of that, thought Traveler. He put a serious look on his face saying, "I'll get us started but I'll work also, 'Lead by example' is my motto.

"First we need to place the largest diameter pipes down and use them to roll the device forward when it's assembled. If we forgot to do that, then we'd need to take it all apart." Traveler walked to the pipe pile, bent to pick one up, and found it was heavier than expected. He noticed Glenda watching him with a smile. "Yes, princess, it is quite heavy."

They easily fell together as a team. Each seemed to know what the next step was, but they still deferred to Traveler for confirmation. The first stage went quickly as they positioned the rolling poles to carry the weight.

Once the rolling poles were in place, they prepared to place the largest plate on top of the poles. Olaff took one end of the plate while Traveler and Glenda took the other end. "On the count of three, lift!" said Traveler. The heavy plate was now resting in the center of the roller poles. Traveler put his foot on the back end of the plate and tested how it rolled forward.

"It's really easy to roll forward. These poles are totally uniform in their diameters. The load is carried evenly on each pole. Those Romans sure were precise engineers."

Walking back to the material piles, he selected four tall poles. We need to insert these into each corner. "Glenda please keep the bottom plate in place while Olaff and I place the vertical poles."

"Easy peasy. I like your leadership style right now, big boy."

The construction continued with the slowest part being the carrying of the heavy materials. Glenda assumed a permanent role of the master steadier, "You two strong gentlemen keep up the good carrying work, and I'll make sure the assembly stays intact. My job will be the quality control manager."

Traveler, who now had small streams of sweat running down his body, glanced up, "There is always room on the carry crew if you're get bored being the QC manager."

"Never bored, just in awe of your strength and endurance. You are an inspiration! Keep up the good work."

Traveler was too tired and winded to even start a comeback. He simply grunted, "Sure," at her.

The construction went in stages and each stage became easier as they advanced. After the first stage was completed, Glenda did join the carry and construct crew. The structure of the model made a three-person crew more efficient than the two-man crew, and the weights were also getting lighter. *I joined at the right time*, Glenda thought.

After some time as a carry mule, she found streams of sweat were now cascading down her body. *Boy, is this going to be a bad hair day.*

Finally the construction was complete. The three stood there relaxing and admiring their creation, then Traveler said, "Sorry team, but we need to seal everything tight now to finish the job.

"Let's go back to the storage building for the sealant and the carrying jars. We'll need to make a lot of trips since the jars can only be partially filled. We don't want to leave a trail down the hallway for a curious guard to follow."

The three again backtracked through the passageway to the armory. Moving through the armory they opened the door enough to check whether the hall was clear. If they were spotted Traveler and Glenda's presence could be explained as two servants going somewhere as part of their job. Olaff would be another matter and they needed to avoid any discovery of his presence. They moved fast.

Once inside, Traveler headed to the sealant bin that he had spotted on their first visit. Glenda and Olaff were securing large jars and placing them beside an internal well. "Good news," Glenda called out. "We found caps that will secure the tops and prevent spillage. We can fill these jars right to the top. Of course that makes them heavier to carry, but we're a strong group, right?"

Yeah, I'm feeling strong right now… not, Traveler thought, then answered, "I'll take two of those caps for my sealant jars."

Traveler used a large wooden spoon to fill the jars. He did his best to avoid the sticky substance but still some found his hands. Naturally his nose itched and he instinctively rubbed it without a thought. Looking up from her filled jars Glenda just had to say, "Circus is coming to town, I see the clowns but where are the elephants?" Olaff glanced over, looked at Traveler, and began to chuckle.

Traveler rolled with the joke, "I guess I'm the clown. I'd honk my nose at you but I think I already did that."

"While you're both in good moods, let me strap on your shoulder-carries."

Olaff proceeded to place wooden carrying staves across each of their shoulders. He placed a sealant jar on one side and a second jar on the other and then helped Traveler rise up. Traveler felt himself listing to the left-hand sealant jar side. "Can you move this one a little closer to my center, just a smidge will do it."

Olaff nodded and moved the fastening rope to a closer notch on the carry stave. Traveler stood again, nodded and said "Much better balance. This mule or clown had better get going, I feel the weight of the world on my shoulders."

Olaff then equipped Glenda with her balanced load and she quickly followed Traveler. Walking behind him she called out in a low but commanding voice, "Hyah, mule! Hyah!" Traveler's response was a series of muffled, mule-like snorts.

When they were inside the armory and opening the hidden door, they heard Olaff. "Please step aside so I can enter the passage sideways. Also shut the armory door if you would."

Looking at Olaff they saw his stave was made from iron with a padded cushion for his neck. Hanging from his stave were six jars on each side. The jars were touching each other and appeared stable with the contact.

Traveler pressed the latch to open the door and watched Olaff make a smooth ninety-degree turn, pass through the doorway, then rotate back. His load filled the passageway on both sides with just inches to spare from stone walls. His stride was smooth and the hanging jars never swayed on either side. *He's a master mule, well more like ten mules*, thought Traveler.

Glenda entered and followed Olaff. Traveler put his load down inside, went back to secure the armory door, then moved inside quickly as the passageway door closed. Bending over he placed the stave across his shoulders, rose up with a grunt and followed. *I guess the clowns are bringing up the rear of this circus.*

The only sound in the long passageway was controlled heavy breathing from Traveler and Glenda. Initially Traveler wanted to catch Glenda from behind and make a mule snort sound, but his burden quashed that idea. *Slow and steady is this boy's course. Time for humor later... assuming there is a later.*

Just when Glenda and Traveler thought their shoulders were ready to collapse, they heard, "You can put your burdens down. Let me help, I'll take the loads off and set them down." He came behind Glenda first and lifted her stave, "Ladies first, of course. We'll take the materials inside as we need them."

After Olaff removed Traveler's stave Traveler gave a deep sigh, "Check my height please, I think I'm a foot shorter. I swear the bottoms of the jars were almost touching the floor at the end."

Glenda was nodding in agreement. "I've seen women in movies and TV carrying large containers on their heads up a mountain trail. They must be Amazons, I see it but don't believe it."

Giving another deep sigh Traveler said, "Since I am the unofficial leader today, may I submit a suggestion to the crew? Let's call it a day. I need a relaxing shower, food, and sleep in that order."

"Now that's leadership, big boy. You've got my vote. I call dibs on the shower since it's ladies first."

"I agree with the lad. It's been a demanding day. You two head back now and I'll catch up."

For a moment Traveler was going to ask Olaff why he was staying behind, then he thought better of it. *He'll get back when he gets back. Plus, I'm really too tired for a conversation.*

Chapter 95

Preparing for War

When they were back in the safe confines of the hidden retreat Glenda said, "I need water, lots of water. First, cold water to drink, then really hot water to shower." With that she filled two mugs from the water cask. Handing one to Traveler she said, "Drink up, leader. This is the stuff our bodies really need right now."

Traveler was sitting on a large chair by the fireplace and immediately began chugging down his mug. "Slow down, big boy, you sound like you're drowning." Traveler lifted his head with a full mouth of water and gargled a response. Glenda shook her head, "I'll take my dibs on the shower while you perfect your act." Disappearing around the corner she heard a second louder gargle following her.

Once showered, Glenda returned to the table to find a sleeping Traveler. His head was resting on his elbows on the table. For a moment she was going to wake him and tell him a skunk had wandered into the room, then she took pity. *Let him sleep, we need him at full strength for tomorrow. Yeah, I think tomorrow will be the day, no reason to put it off.*

As Glenda was quietly settling into a chair by the fire a voice boomed into the room. "Fresh goods from the kitchen!" Traveler awoke with a start, his eyes swept the room and then settled on the smiling giant.

"Good morning, big boy. You slept through the night. Do feel ready for today's battle?"

"Very funny. I waited so long for you I dozed off. What I am ready for is a shower. Did you use up the whole supply of hot water?"

"Not quite. I highly recommend you double-time it to the shower. We'll wait for you. You are our team captain." Pausing a moment she added in a teasing voice, "Unless we don't. What do you think, Olaff, should we start to eat right now? I'm famished."

Not a serious question. Methinks she enjoys prodding him. I also think he enjoys it. "We'll wait for the lad. He has earned first picks with his plan. I'll have a nice mug of my ale while waiting." With the mention of Olaff's ale unpleasant memories rushed back, both winced and shook their heads.

Traveler hit the shower, increased the hot water flow, rubbed himself with soap, then embraced a washing sponge and proceeded to attack the results of the day's labor. The sponge did its best, but multiple cleansings were needed. Finally, Traveler stopped the hot water completely. He had reduced the temperature to that of the incoming icy mountain stream. *Only a polar bear would enjoy this*, he thought. He did not play the polar bear part for more than a few seconds. Shivering, he was now wide awake.

Dressed, he joined his companions. "Did I hear I get first claims?"

"Indeed. To the brilliant planner goes the spoils!" said Glenda.

Conversation was limited. Eating became a serious undertaking. All bodies demanded their fuel supplies be replenished following the day's intense labor. When the hunger urgency was met, Olaff lifted his mug, took a deep sip and said, "Good news. I naturally visited the kitchen ostensibly for food but really for information. There is a new head cook and she seems an unpleasant sort.

"I told her I had a trainee working with me and tomorrow the trainee would take the breakfast meal to the mage and the duke. The silly woman began to lecture me about work schedules and who was in charge of setting them.

"She seemed to be under the impression she had absolute authority over all the staff. I have the ability to change attitudes pretty quickly and I changed hers. I noticed the nearby staff was silently applauding me behind her back."

"I know the 'why' of their applause," said a grinning Glenda. "She is a mean-spirited kitchen tyrant. She deserves to be demoted to a scullery maid and a washer of pots."

"Scullery maid. Sounds about right. Anyway, we are now set for tomorrow. Agreed?" Glenda and Traveler nodded in agreement while looking at the pensive expression on the giant's face. While his face rarely showed strong emotions, it now had deep lines of concern wrinkling his brow.

"I accept that tomorrow is a reckoning day," said an animated Traveler. "Let's make it a reckoning for the jinn he'll never forget! I feel great about our plan and even better about my companions executing it. We are forever bonded as allies." His confidence brought strong reaffirming nods back.

Go us! Go Team! flashed through Glenda mind.

The lad is a warrior and a leader, thought Olaff.

Glenda suddenly felt her energy level hit the lowest point on her body's energy gauge, "Gentlemen, I'm calling it a day. It feels more like two days, so I'll see you both in the morning. Olaff give me a shout if I'm sleeping, I know we need to be up early tomorrow."

Traveler had mixed reactions as Glenda headed off to sleep. He knew his body and mind were both exhausted but he was still wired from the day. Olaff looked at him and gave a giant's fatherly advice. "I suggest, lad, you get some sleep now. Even if you can't go under, your body needs the rest."

"You're right," Traveler agreed. He kicked off his boots and headed to the sleeping quarters. *In case the princess is struggling to sleep I'll try not to make noise.* Once he touched the side of the bed he rolled in, faced the doorway, and was greeted by Morpheus within seconds.

Chapter 96

A Day of Reckoning

Long hours of sleep passed in minutes. A deep-voiced chanticleer crowed from the bedroom entrance, "Rise and move. Although it's still dark you need to get your bodies ready for the battle. Food is waiting but I suggest a visit to the personal room first. A second visit before the confrontation has proven to be a sound battle tactic."

"I'll go first," Traveler said. Glenda gave a bare grunt of agreement. Once his throne room duties were completed Traveler joined Olaff. The fire had been resupplied and was now roaring. Giant flames were devouring the logs as they made their escape up the chimney. The aroma of burning logs added to the sweet scent of bacon and freshly baked bread.

Traveler discovered he was ravenous. As he heaped his plate Olaff offered more battle advice. "The trick is to eat enough to have your power but not so much that you lose your speed." Traveler gave a sheepish smile and cut his portion in half. He knew from school sports how to eat before a game. Use intake discipline before the game, then pig-out after.

Glenda arrived with a spring in her step just as he was descending into his pile of ripe berries, "Save any good stuff for me?" she asked.

"More than enough, your highness, but remember you will need your best speed. I suggest you go easy on the bread and bacon, I'll eat for both of us."

Early morning banter. How many battles have I been in when warriors start the day with friendly pokes? That's an excellent sign. Relieves the tension and gets the mind focused, reflected Olaff.

The light joking quickly disappeared. Gallows humor had a very short half-life. Looking at their faces Olaff decided it was time to move out, *Must not let them spend too much time reflecting on what's coming. A stationary soldier is called a target*, he thought.

"Glenda, I suggest you and I leave now. Best we get to the kitchen and confirm all is in order. I want to make sure the cook does not forget my directions from yesterday. She's indeed nasty and could send a couple of servants up early just to get even with me. Of course that would be a big mistake on her part, but it would alter our plan.

"Assuming all is well, you will remain in the kitchen area until it's time to carry the tray up." Glenda nodded in agreement. She also had a bad feeling about the overseer woman, so better to get there early.

"Traveler, after Glenda's kitchen plan is in order I'll come back and meet you in the armory. The two of us will proceed to the alcoves."

Giving them a final encouraging look Olaff added, "Since we are now approaching battle time, I suggest you both retire to the personal room." Without embarrassment they followed Olaff's advice.

Olaff was on the landing waiting when the two companions returned. He stood near his own large boat confirming it was riding high in the water and ready to accept the weight of his giant body.

"You OK?" Traveler asked Glenda in a quiet voice.

"I am if you are," she whispered back. Neither spoke again.

Both were doing their best to keep a positive mindset. Both focused on the plan and the execution steps. With a shared glance of encouragement at each other they entered their boat. Olaff led the way across. Landing first, he secured his boat and waited to help them out of their boat.

With boats secured they ascended the stone staircase with Olaff leading the climb, followed by Glenda and lastly Traveler. Olaff set a fast pace for his ascension and the two companions instinctively tried to keep up.

When Glenda and Traveler reached the top they paused, they had to give their racing hearts time to slow down. Their elevated heart rates were a result of stress combined with the climb. As their rates recovered they agreed the rapid climb had helped them regain control over their nerves and spinning minds. It was a good thing.

Olaff opened the door and confirmed it was clear. All three quickly entered the hallway. Traveler turned toward the armory while Olaff and Glenda turned toward the kitchen. Traveler gave Glenda his most encouraging smile, "See you upstairs, Glenda. Now don't spill anything, you know how annoyed the mage gets." Pausing, he grinned, "Let's give him an annoyance he'll never forget."

Glenda's mood lifted with Traveler's sendoff message. He was recognizing the difficult task facing her. While each of them had their own challenging tasks, hers came first. She was the point of the spear they would attempt to drive into the jinn.

Traveler entered the armory and shut the door behind him. His legs immediately called out for relief. *Leg nerves*, he chuckled, then promptly sat down on a large keg. Alone, he felt the weight of the stillness descend on him. His mind flashed back to being alone in the museum before the fire creatures emerged from the portal. This had the same unsettling feel.

This is different, he reassured himself. *This time I have allies and we're prepared. I trust my companions. Let the isolated creature know fear, not us.* This self-assurance buoyed his spirits, he found the room's weight lifting from his body and his mind.

Time passed without notice for a resting Traveler until a soft knock alerted him. Olaff promptly entered and gave Traveler a look that said, "Time to go." Mache schnell was understood.

Locking the door behind him, Olaff opened the passageway door and stepped in. Traveler followed, closed the door, and fell in beside the giant. The two walked together in silence. When they reached the final wall to enter the last passageway Traveler asked, "I assume all went well in the kitchen and Glenda is on her way?"

"Turned out all right, but good thing we were there early. That silly woman was indeed trying a sneaky move. She had already prepared the breakfast tray and was ready to send it up when we surprised her. She froze as I walked up and peered down at her from my great height. All I said was, 'Why annoy me?'

"She thinks pretty fast. When she found her tongue she claimed it was such a busy morning she had forgotten my request. My look told her I thought otherwise. Even in the hot kitchen her face paled.

"I might add that the little exchange helped bolster Glenda's spirits. She was very quiet the whole way there and I knew she was really nervous. Well, I'm nervous also, and I have been in more battles than I can remember. This little skirmish broke her somber mood. She actually grinned as I took the arrogant woman to task."

Smiling at Olaff, Traveler said, "Let's think of this kitchen victory as a harbinger of what's coming next, and 'next' is right now. We sure can't keep the princess waiting with the tray."

Olaff nodded with a look that said, "Of course".

Once inside the final passage they doubled-timed their walk. Olaff's fast walk was Traveler's fast jog. Reaching the last wall Olaff quickly twisted the overhead latches and swung the wall away. When the wall opened they found Glenda already standing there with a warm smile.

"Welcome gentlemen, you're expected and right on time! I came early so I can help roll our model into place. The tray is stowed in the alcove closest to the door." Looking at Traveler she said, "I'm here, tell me what to do."

"Well done on the timing, Glenda! More hands are welcome, for sure," said Traveler. "Olaff, you're in charge of moving our device, so please take over."

Olaff nodded, "I'll do the pushing. You two remove the back roller poles as they are freed up and place them in front.

Once we're out on the landing, start angling the poles so that our device can be placed inside the alcove. We've got to keep it hidden until the last moment.

"Everyone clear?" Two heads nodded back. "OK let's roll over 'em now." Pausing he added with a hint of a smile, "'Roll over 'em now', that's an old battle joke."

Who knew he had a sense of humor? Glenda and Traveler thought at the same time.

The heavy construct advanced easily on the roller poles. They quickly moved it straight ahead from the assembly area until they reached the exit point. Turning to Glenda Traveler said, "You're up! Take the lead determining the roller path into the alcove. You place a roller then point me. We do need to move fast."

Glenda beamed. Traveler, the math guy, had deferred to her geometry skills. Her mind immediately created a mental pathway to the alcove. She could picture where each pole needed to be placed. "I see our path. I'll place the first pole then point."

"Lead on," Traveler said. Olaff observed this exchange and the quickly defined leadership role for Glenda. *They are easily on the same page. Good for the lad to defer to her judgement, that bolsters both of their spirits for what's coming.*

While the two were agreeing on the division of roller-path labor, Olaff returned quickly to the assembly site and brought the remaining materials out and placed them out of sight inside the alcove.

While Traveler and Glenda were moving the construct, Olaff triggered a hidden release on a back wall sconce, then rotated the sconce. The wall slowly closed back and was again a solid stone face.

Glenda led the pole placements toward the alcove at a quick pace. She could visualize each pole's placement and Traveler immediately followed her pointing directions. Glenda's mental geometry was spot on. With the last pole placed, the construct was now totally hidden inside the alcove.

Next they took one of Traveler's two sealant jars, opened it and applied its contents according to the plan. The other jar remained sealed. Finally they emptied the contents of all the large jars into the open construct.

The three looked at the product of Traveler's plan with satisfaction. This was exactly what he had envisioned, and here it was, ready and waiting.

As Glenda started to walk toward the furthest alcove to retrieve the breakfast tray, she paused then said, "I'm a little early for the delivery, but that adds a little unknown for the creature to deal with."

Traveler gave her a reassuring grin, "Yeah, and Mr Jinn won't know the breakfast is no longer hot, but that will be the least of its worries."

Carrying the silver tray Glenda headed to the duke's entry door. She forced deep controlled breaths and cleared her mind. Her next few moves would determine their shared fate. *Don't think about outcomes, only focus on the action steps.* Now she was in front of the door thinking, *It's showtime!*

She gave the usual soft, tentative knock. Her voice did not need to be forced to offer a nervous greeting, "I have breakfast."

As usual the duke was at the door with the mage standing at a distance behind him. The mage gave his normal response in a commanding voice, "We assume there is no spillage and all is at an acceptable temperature."

Looking at the mage Glenda did two things at once. She stuck out her tongue and replied, "Screw you!" At the same time, she permitted her mind's guard over her vibrational field to drop slightly. The mage instantly responded to the vibration. "I know you from the museum. Seize her!"

Fortunately the duke's reflexes were slower than Glenda's. As he tried to grab an arm, he felt a sleeve pass through his fingers and the girl escaped. Turning to run, Glenda dropped the tray, spun out of the doorway, rounded the corner and disappeared.

The mage called again, "Follow and seize her. Do not let her escape or you will feel pain beyond your understanding."

Once she turned the corner and disappeared from sight, the duke's limited focus failed to notice the slippery mess on the floor. As he hurried forward his large feet suddenly took separate paths as they tried to schuss down a steep ski slope. Out of control he landed first on the breakfast then the floor.

The mage was quickly beside him shouting commands, "Stand up, dolt! After her! The fool has gone into an area without an exit. She cannot escape you." The duke was already on his feet before the mage's admonishments reached his ears.

The duke was battling a mix of confusing thoughts. The mage seemed overly concerned with a simple peasant girl. This servant girl offered no possible threat to the mage's power, yet he reacted with an emotion the duke had never seen.

The bigger thought was the mage's threat of pain. The duke had previously experienced pain so severe that it immobilized him. That single experience had instantly conditioned him into accepting unchallenging obedience to the mage. The duke's sole focus now was capturing the girl.

Entering the landing area, the duke saw the red-haired girl had retreated to the far end of the landing. Her back was pressed against the solid stone wall. She was contained in a dead-end alley. There was no way out.

For a moment the duke considered the distance she had covered in virtually no time. Even with a dulled mind he momentarily wondered how she had gotten there that fast. However, thinking was not in his mission statement and he refocused on the helpless girl.

Advancing behind the duke was the mage. The jinn recalled meeting this girl in a museum before it had to flee from the dark god. She had powers beyond those common for the human species. Possibly the god had given her some enhanced capabilities. The jinn also knew her powers, enhanced or not, were no match for its own.

For the first time the jinn was close to absorbing a superior member of this human species. The jinn was eager to close the trap and absorb this human. The girl's knowledge of the dark god could result in the host achieving a final conquest of the elusive god.

The duke was closing cautiously on the girl. He knew she was fast, very fast. His advance had to be planned to ensure she could not dart past him. The duke extended his long left arm to reach the left side wall while his right arm extended to reduce escape on his right. The duke relaxed slightly as he saw the mage was now on his right side, sealing that exit route off.

The girl made no attempt to try and rush past the duke. Any forward move would lead her into the arms of either the duke or the mage. She stared at them with an apparent acceptance of her fate. She was a trapped prey facing vastly superior hunters. She knew the outcome.

The mage was now less than eight feet away. The jinn prepared the mage's body for a final fast-close. It paused for a moment to study the girl's body posture and feet to detect any tension that could lead to a last-minute attempt to escape.

The woman's body displayed nothing beyond acceptance. The jinn was ready. The creature knew that it would momentarily lose control over the duke as it focused on absorbing the girl. It was confident that the duke would predictably stay in place.

Closing to five feet, the mage heard a deep voice behind him in the dark alcove call out, "Stun the creature now!"

The jinn saw the boy from the museum leap out from the dark alcove to join the girl. The creature immediately thought, *I will absorb both. Even together they are no threat.* That thought lingered as the mage's body suddenly froze.

Glenda and Traveler had prepared for this moment in their previous mind-control encounters. They focused their minds on the mage's brain stem and took instant control. With control of the nervous system they stopped all muscle movement.

The jinn had so embedded itself in the mage's brain and body that it was a momentary prisoner. It could not instantly leave the mage's body. It never considered that it would have to.

Before the jinn could start to respond, it was lifted off the ground by the giant. The giant placed the immobilized body into a coffin-shaped container filled with enveloping water. The body was immediately pressed against the bottom.

The mage's flickering red eyes stared up through the clear water in anger, then in helplessness as a heavy lid came down on top of its body. The lead lid totally covered the mage's body holding it flat against the bottom. Neither mage nor jinn could move. They were wedded and immobilized together.

Next a second lid came down on top of an enclosing larger coffin. This coffin was also filled with water.

The creature had no awareness of the third and final lid that sealed the largest coffin shut. The final lid was rendered airtight and watertight by a thick sealant. The sealant thickly coated all internal edges of each container coffin.

A final, external coat of the thick sealant was applied from the last jug Traveler had brought. The outside edges of the coffin and its lid were doubly-sealed. This final sealing was unnecessary Olaff had said, but "Better we overkill the containment when an actual kill of the creature cannot be accomplished."

The trapped jinn was now resting inside tightly sealed, water filled, lead coffins that resembled a Russian Matryoshka doll. The creature was trapped inside as the smallest doll. Of course the jinn was no cute painted doll. It was a monster.

"Time to put this bad boy away," said Traveler. With that Olaff bent down and pushed the coffin forward into a recessed opening in the solid stone back wall of the alcove. He then turned a lever that caused the opening to be sealed by five feet of sliding solid stone.

Pleased with the final enclosure, Olaff added, "Dall and I added a few hidden improvements to the fortress once we were the masters of the fortress. You never know when secret storage places may be needed."

The emotional letdown suddenly demanded a physical sit-down. They each retired to the floor to provide relief to trembling legs. Sitting there they all stared at the solid wall that hid the buried coffin. After a few minutes Traveler looked at Glenda, "I don't sense a vibration of any sort, do you?"

Glenda shook her head. "None. I think the creature is insulated from us, and more importantly from its own kind. It's trapped inside the mage's dead body. I believe if these creatures can go crazy, then this one will. It has never existed for long in total isolation from its own kind."

All three jerked their heads up as a massive man descended to sit beside them. "It deserves worse. Much worse," replied the smiling duke. "My mind became my own again as I watched the creature get sealed up. To be back is a gift from each of you. I am in your debts forever."

Sitting beside Olaff he placed a heavy arm across Olaff's shoulder. Olaff's first comment was, "Welcome back, brother. If we were standing I would give you a giant bear hug. One giant bear to another."

The duke smiled back, "I believe bears can hug sitting." And with that the two giants gripped each other.

The duke's attention then shifted from Olaff and began studying the two young people. He saw the respect Olaff clearly had for the two and understood they were close companions of his friend. He knew they had played a significant part in his own liberation. He accepted that he owed them a great deal, possibly his life.

"I want to hear all that has happened. I have been existing in a fog that rarely lifted. Occasionally I saw something and tried to speak or act but the fog quickly returned. I don't know how that was done to me but I do know the body you just hid was at the center of my helplessness. May that being stay there and suffer through eternity."

Suddenly a bright smile flashed across the duke's face. "Would it sound strange to say I am beyond ravenous? I believe I was kept on a diet of some sort."

Olaff returned the smile, "We are definitely with you on that, our breakfast was battle-ready small." Laughing he added, "Your own breakfast is back on the floor. We should go to the kitchen and truly feast there."

"Agreed," replied the duke.

As they walked Olaff said, "While we are there, I suggest a change in roles for the kitchen overseer." The duke had a puzzled look at this comment but decided to wait and see why Olaff had brought it up.

Olaff continued, "There is a lot of storytelling to catch you up with, but first we feast then start the tales. But the best tale is about our two heroes here. Without them you and I would not be ourselves, possibly we would not even be here.

"They are very special, and I am more than proud to call them my friends. Our young lady here, you may call her Glenda, could pass for a Valkyrie. Our young warrior, name of Traveler, has a grip that would crush our best warriors."

The duke looked at Olaff, then Traveler and Glenda, smiled and said, "A feast with great hero tales. My life is good again."

When they entered the large kitchen, they saw the staff bustling with the morning fare. The four stood back in a quiet place and watched the overseer as she bossed and criticized the workers.

The duke quietly watched as long-time staff were beaten down by her tirades. He knew many of the staff since their childhood and considered them friends as well as hard-working professionals at their demanding trade.

Enough of this, I understand my brother's comment. He strode up to the woman and placed his giant hand on her shoulder. She jumped at the strong contact, turned with an angry expression, then froze. She quickly made a deep bow. "Lords, how may we serve you this morning?"

Staring into her eyes the duke said, "To start with, a friendlier countenance for your fellow staff. Leaders do not abuse their comrades. Where is Andre who has held this position for years?"

The woman fought back a grimace as she answered, "The mage found him less than adequate and replaced him with me." She paused then quietly said, "I placed him with the stable boys."

"Well, things will return to normal starting now." Motioning to one of the young staff, he said, "I am back and in charge of all. Bring Andre here and inform him he is again the overseer."

Turning to the rapidly deflating woman he said, "I have sent the mage on a journey that better suits his talents. None of us will see him again. Andre will find a job for you that suits your own talents." The duke then dismissed her with a short flick of his hand.

"And that's how justice should work, fast, direct, and fair," Traveler said under his breath to Glenda.

They moved to the group dining room, selected a bench and were quickly served an impromptu feast. Leading the caravan of servers was Andre. He knelt down by the duke as he handed up a large flagon of ale. "I believe this is your preference. I hid a full barrel from her."

The duke smiled down, "Rise up, Andre, and share a mug with me." The duke poured out a stein and handed it to a trembling Andre. Andre politely sipped then backed away. "I must return to my duties, my lord, there is much that needs to be corrected here."

As Andre turned with a bow, he added in a quiet voice to the duke, "This is a day my family will remember that a lost treasure was found. You, of course, are the treasure."

The duke laughed, "Don't believe I've been called a 'treasure' before, but it does have a suitable ring. Right brother?"

"I believe the treasure I would like right now would be a mug of that ale," Olaff answered.

As the four started on the first of many courses, they focused on their hunger. Stomachs demanded their undivided attention. Finally, Olaff lifted his eyes to Traveler and Glenda and said, "Permit me to do the honors of starting the tale that led to today. I want the duke to hear it without false modesty from either of you. He'll enjoy me being the bard at the table."

"Tell us your tale, bard, I know it will mystify as well as entertain," encouraged the duke with a broad smile.

"Strange you used the word 'mystify' because that is very appropriate. Now prepare, brother, to hear our tale. It is a true saga and needs no exaggeration to be stunning." Olaff began the tale with his discovery of Glenda and Traveler in his hidden lair. He recounted their strange abilities, their courage, and their own tales about how they came to the fortress seeking the creature known as the mage.

As Olaff talked the duke was drawn into the story. He accepted it without interruption. From time to time he would focus on either Traveler or Glenda.

Finally Olaff said, "And that, my old friend, my brother, brings you to this time and this table. I've told it as I personally experienced it, and I have no reason to question their tales as told to me."

The duke shook his head in wonder but with an undercurrent of soft skepticism. He would never call his brother an exaggerator, but still the story was hard to fully accept.

Looking at Traveler with a smile he said, "After a solid meal and drink, my warriors enjoy a table game of 'hands down'. Since we are all the best of friends here, I would like to test your famous grip. So, Traveler my friend, would you like to join me?"

"As you wish. I know this game and played it with Throbb a while ago."

The duke rose and sat on the bench directly across from Traveler. "I recognize I have a rather large height and weight advantage, so I will not use close to my full power. I certainly don't want to damage your hand or arm. This is all just good fun, and a little table exercise will help rid us of today's stress."

Neither Olaff nor Traveler seemed bothered by the duke's friendly challenge. Traveler simply rested his elbow on the table, smiled up at the duke and said, "Take your time, I'm ready when you are."

The duke positioned his elbow beside Traveler, then he slumped down as far as possible on the bench. "I'll add a handicap to myself by getting down to your level, don't want you trying to lift this big body anywhere. Olaff, give us a short count to begin."

Olaff responded with, "Gentlemen, are you both ready?" Two heads nodded an affirmative. "Three, two, one, commence!"

Olaff and Glenda watched as two arms pressed against each other. The duke had a slight smile as he gripped Traveler's hand and pressed both arms together. He intended to first apply a strong squeeze to alert Traveler what was coming, he knew the lad was a good friend to Olaff as well as a good friend to himself. He had no intention of harming him. Curiosity and a little skepticism required a simple testing of this famous grip and arm.

Traveler remained a stoic as he looked into his challenger's face. He gave the same look to the duke as he had Throbb. He noted the duke's slight smile on his face and in his eyes. Traveler understood why the challenge was made, *He's another "trust but verify" guy. Can't blame him, ours is a hard story to believe.*

As the squeeze increased Traveler felt the downward pressure begin. He divorced his mind from all sensory input and focused on the grip as the center of the force. He judged each increase in the opposing force and determined his response.

Interestingly, he felt he had added strength since the Throbb and then the Olaff contests. Maybe their recent victory over the jinn was already increasing his book-developed strength. He increased his own grip and downward arm force. The duke's face now had a serious look. His eyes seem perplexed.

Even with the recently gained increase in strength, Traveler's effort was approaching its limit. He felt himself close to being overwhelmed as his focus began to slip away. Then Traveler felt a second force joining him.

Olaff had wrapped his hand around Traveler's and looked the duke in the face. "Brother, I think the lad has satisfied your skepticism regarding his ability. This is where you, as the champion, declare the contest a tie. Of course if you feel the need to continue, I can accommodate you."

The duke's concentration broke and he gave a great sigh of relief. Then he laughed and his huge body shook. Gently clasping Traveler's hand in both of his giant palms he said, "You are indeed a champion among champions, my young friend. Never has a man held against me as you have, with the exception of my big brother here. It is my honor to say that the story Olaff told is one I fully accept."

Looking at Glenda he gave her a large smile, "I also accept the young lady would equally meet any challenge I might offer, so I bow to her both as a friend and an ally."

Rising up from the table, the duke said, "I suggest we retire to my quarters. There are many questions yet to be asked. I want to get to know my two new friends here much better."

As they rose from the table Glenda whispered to Traveler, "Our mission here is over. I think we should return to Chicago and report to M and Theo."

"I agree. They must be anxious to know whether we succeeded or became part of the jinn."

Turning to the duke and Olaff, Traveler said, "My sister and I need a little private time and I think both of you do as well."

The duke nodded in agreement. "Olaff and I have much to discuss that would bore two young people." He laughed and continued, "You certainly know where to find me." Then jokingly he added, "Watch out for the floor mess when you enter, it's quite slippery! On second thought, I think that cleaning up that mess will be the first task for our former kitchen tyrant.

"Now come up as it works for you. I am hosting a great feast this evening to make it clear to all that the mage is gone and I am back. Naturally both you are invited as guests of honor to join Olaff and myself at the head table."

With that the duke and Olaff turned and began walking away. Glenda and Traveler remained at the table watching the two giants greet servants and warriors as they left. Suddenly Olaff turned, spoke to the duke, and came back alone.

"Why do I think you two may be leaving now? I trust my ale was not so bad as to chase you away."

Glenda found she was suddenly misty-eyed. She rose up on her toes and gave the giant the biggest hug she could. "We will meet again, I'm sure. You are a true and amazing friend."

Traveler kept a quiet smile on his face. When Glenda disengaged, he reached out to shake the giant's hand and found himself enveloped in a bear hug. "Warrior brothers hug after a victory. Our tale of victory over the demon jinn will be told for many generations to come."

Olaff now had what some close observers would claim was dampness in his eyes as he said, "I believe the shortest partings are the best while shared memories last forever."

With that the giant turned and walked back to join the duke.

"I know exactly where to go now, follow me," said Glenda.

She entered the stables and began walking down the long aisle to the rear. The stable workers were eating their midday meal and only the horses watched the two as they walked to the ladder. A few alert horses slowed their eating to observe how the two ignored the ladder and leaped up to the loft, then disappeared among the haystacks.

Grinning, Traveler said, "Right again, princess, this is the best launching pad to return. I think we had better do our slow dance before you start sneezing and scare the horses." He naturally received a fake sneeze back.

Stepping forward they had a moment's hesitation before clasping each other tightly. Red hair again obscured Traveler's vision and he found it quite acceptable. Then they pressed their bracelets together. Shutting their eyes, and holding their breaths, they felt the world shrink around them.

They squeezed their eyes even harder while an unknown pressure forced them even closer. The dice were again being shaken in the space-time container.

Just as they were both ready to gasp for air their eyelids registered light. They slowly opened their eyes to find themselves back in their Chicago sanctuary.

Chapter 97

Hail the Conquering Heroes

As their eyes slowly opened, their ears registered vigorous clapping from a beaming M. Theo was beside him and his long tail was swaying rapidly in approval while he emitted strong purring vibrations.

"Welcome home! I salute my most amazing students, and more importantly, my amazing friends! Welcome home, Glenda! Welcome home, Traveler!

"The celebration feast is ready and Theo and I are anxious to hear all of your adventures. Your books are equally eager to experience your challenges and victories!"

Glenda was the first to hug M and then she gave him a second even bigger hug before moving to wrap her arms around Theo. Traveler remembered Olaff's adage and gave M a warrior's hug, then joined Glenda in hugging the tiger-sized Theo. The room echoed with the most pleasant of vibrations.

Glenda paused then said, "I am beyond excited to be back and tell about everything. But please hold the feast until this girl returns to her room for all the necessities, starting with a proper shower and a suitable dress."

Traveler was already heading to his room while saying, "I'm all over that."

M smiled, "That was expected. To quote an old saying, 'Hail the conquering heroes!'" With a laugh he added, "Now go shower. Please!"

Once in her room Glenda quickly shrugged out of her peasant clothes. Before dropping them in her hamper she paused and suddenly embraced them, "You served me so well. Better than any designer dress could have. We may meet up again."

As she stepped into the shower she thought, *Home is where family and friends are, but importantly, also where the shower is.* She permitted the falling water to almost drown her. She luxuriated in the heat and pressure across her body from the cascading flow. Her mind relaxed and all thoughts of mages and evil jinn creatures receded far away.

Traveler rolled his clothes into a tight ball, threw it across the room and watched it disappear into the hamper. "He comes off the bench and scores the winning basket!" Then he was a salmon swimming upstream against a hot flowing waterfall. He took the soapy sponge and began to seriously scrub. Multiple scrubs followed until the water bouncing off his hair and body seemed to sparkle.

Dried off and standing by the bed he said, "What do we have here?" The bed had skipped his usual jeans and instead provided him a formal look. A black tux and a formal, starched, white shirt with gold cufflinks greeted him. Rather than a bowtie there was a red cravat. He tightened the cummerbund, checked himself in the mirror, and nodded in approval. He added a mental, *Looking good, big guy,* and proceeded to the dining area.

Traveler was the first to arrive and assumed his usual chair. *No funny stealth tonight,* he thought, *that routine is getting a little old anyway.* Resting beside his plate was a mug emitting a sweet steam. He took a slow sip, nodded his head and thought, *A special recipe made by M to celebrate.*

His relaxed mood took a jolt when Glenda came striding toward the table. Her russet hair threw off sparks of gold and red from the overhead lanterns. An emerald green tiara held the hair more or less in place. Her dress was a blend of a prom dress and the classic little black evening dress.

When Glenda had put the dress on, she thought, *Traveler's mom would definitely approve. She would love to wear it to one of her business dinners, but only if nobody else had it on. Of course nobody else could have it. It's one of a kind.* Laughing to herself she added, *But so am I.*

Traveler rose to pull out her chair, then remembered her normal reaction and began to sit down. Glenda observed his being halfway up and halfway down. She threw him a sweet smile, "This lady would certainly appreciate the gentleman's help."

Traveler was struggling to adjust from casual Glenda, the burlap peasant who needed a bath, to this runway model. He started to say something witty starting with "I recall…" then the frog announced its presence and his voice stuck in his throat.

M smiled to himself. He understood Traveler's sudden loss of words and came to the rescue, "Glenda, Traveler. Would you like to start with the soup or the egg rolls? Of course you may sample both, they are equally excellent."

Glenda gave M an understanding smile as she said, "While Traveler ponders his choices, I'll start with the egg roll." Traveler nodded quickly in agreement. M knew they were both avoiding the risk of soup splatter. To himself he thought, *I'll enjoy the soup and let the aroma taunt them.*

Once the dining choices were presented, the food and conversation flowed. Glenda and Traveler took turns describing the events from first landing in the thick, old-growth forest to the final arm-wrestling between Traveler and the duke.

M was captivated as they recounted each challenge. Theo was a vibrating tiger who would press his head against each storyteller to encourage them to tell the tale in its fullest detail.

Finally the tale ended as did the dessert. Satiated from food and talking, Glenda said, "That's our story. We never knew how it would or could end until the end actually arrived."

Traveler added, "The two super-sized men, call them giants for lack of a better description, would make the best of allies. I sense they have an amazing history, but we'll probably never know it."

M reflected, "I agree, they sound like supernatural forces of nature. They are early men of the icy north and far from their place of origin. Who knows if their story will ever be revealed.

"You not only succeeded in your mission to contain the fire creature, you also lived during a critical part of European history. High school students usually learn about the Mongol hordes of Genghis Khan and their vast empire, yet little importance seems to be placed on Attila. He was the real deal as an invader of Europe and you know more about him than most historians."

Rising up, M gave them a smile, a bow, and a departing comment, "Enjoy a long sleep tonight. Your books are looking forward to your adventures and successes. I suspect they will be generous and rewarding with your next stage of studies." With that he retired.

Glenda watched M disappear into his kitchen then said, "It's Theo time." She proceeded to the giant cat now resting beside the fireplace. Sitting down she nestled against him. Traveler was a step behind.

As they pressed into Theo he expanded in size and his fur grew thicker and warmer. His approval of their accomplishments was clear as he continued to send out strong vibrations of respect and congratulations.

Then the vibrations shifted and took on a deeper, and far more significant meaning. It was a message of his love for each of them.

FINIS

Epilogue

Attila Reflects while Rome Quivers

Attila stood high in his saddle looking down at the vast city. This was Rome, the capital of the world for six centuries. The glory of Rome was reflected off marble pillars and monuments with a blinding glare. Water glistened as it flowed into hundreds of fountains ensuring that no Roman would go thirsty.

The wealth of this city cannot be measured, thought the Hun. *One Roman conqueror, Julius Caesar, had brought back the entire wealth of Gaul. It is ironic, that at the height of his benevolence and power, a handful of men had killed him in the street. Fear is the way to govern men, not charity and mercy.*

Attila was in a somber mood. The Hun army had fought an epic battle at the Catalaunian Plains in Gaul and had suffered high casualties. It was not a total defeat but neither was it a victory. Now his warriors were expecting to lick their wounds by the sack of Rome.

Earlier he had studied the Roman army placed to defend the city. This army would offer no threat to his forces. The jewel below was there waiting to be seized.

Attila was not a religious or superstitious man, however he accepted there were forces stronger than his own. Many years before he had seen a great power unleashed. He had agreed to a parley and an aged man came into his tent. The old man had to be a god in disguise as he released a red demon. The demon passed through and killed all his attending guards.

Now, years later, another parley was requested and Attila felt a warning pass through him. The parley would again be with an older man described as the religious leader of Rome. The man's title was "pope", meaning "father". Attila considered that his own name meant "little father" or simply "father". Reflecting, he thought, *Tomorrow we meet and decide who is the greater father.*

The next day arrived and with it the man called Pope Leo. Attila observed he was a man dressed in the silk robes of a priest. Once again Attila was alone with an older priest who showed no fear.

Looking into Attila's eyes the Pope smiled then began to talk to him in Latin. As Attila listened, he felt a power flowing out of the man. The man said he represented the one true god. He cautioned Attila that Rome could not be attacked without incurring the fury of the one god. Attila remembered a time long ago a similar man telling him to turn his army away. That man had proven to be a god.

With quiet confidence Pope Leo advised Attila to lead his army back to the east. The Pope told Attila he would create an empire that would be named after his people. Its name would be Hungary.

Attila suddenly found himself kneeling before this Pope. The man lifted him to his feet and embraced him. Attila left the tent with a feeling of great joy for his people and himself. He would turn back east and create Hungary, the empire for his people.

As for the savior of Rome, Leo became known as Leo the Great.

About the Author

Dave lives with his wife Nancy in rural Virginia. They are surrounded by large oak trees having many growth rings. Dave likens his personal growth experiences to that of the tree rings. Important early rings include being an Eagle Scout and class president.

Following graduate business school he became an actuary and a consulting mathematician. As he developed over the working years, his career led to CEO and COO responsibilities with a national consulting firm.

Following an early retirement he taught pre-algebra and algebra to middle schoolers. It was a great experience for him and he continues to enjoy connecting with today's youth.

His current growth rings are developing as a story teller and writer.